DAWN
OF
COBALT
SHADOWS

A BURNING EMPIRE NOVEL

EMMA HAMM

Every once in a while, you meet someone who lets your soul run free with theirs.

I hope, someday, you meet this person who knows you're going to render their soul to ashes.

But who also knows a dragon cannot burn.

the
CRIMSON
PALACE

Glasslyn

Misthall

Falldell

Bymere

SIGRID

DAPPLED SUNLIGHT PLAYED ACROSS SIGRID'S FACE. THE WARMTH OF the sun stroked her cheeks and left lingering heat in spots on her bare arms. Birds sang bright and clear, their songs lifting up to the clouds, twirling in the wind that toyed with her loose golden curls.

How long had she felt trapped here? How long had she lingered in the shadows of this land hoping that someone would leave her alone long enough so that she could feel this one more time?

"Sigrid?" a voice called out.

And there went her peace.

She rolled onto her side. The skirts of her simple overdress twisted through her legs with her movement. A white undershirt kept her arms warm. The chill of autumn had arrived. Thankfully, the afternoons were still filled with the sun, if she could find a private spot to linger in solitude.

"Camilla," Sigrid called out. "You're supposed to be at the

feast."

Her dearest friend, the only person she would truly call her sister, pushed aside a branch and ducked into the small clearing where Sigrid waited. Camilla, as always, was dressed like a wild thing. She'd taken to wearing furs now that it was colder out. A hide skirt revealed the long expanse of her bare, dark legs. A leather corset paired it, and she'd placed a sheepskin over her shoulders for a little extra heat.

One of the other Beastkin had braided her hair into rows at the top of her head. When had Camilla's hair gotten that long? The ends hit her hips as she walked and whirled like whips when she turned too quickly. The look suited her, although it made her perhaps a little less approachable.

Sigrid and Camilla had always liked being intimidating, however. Perhaps this was her friend's way of continuing to push people away.

Her onyx skin gleamed in the sunlight like the sheen of her warhorse after battle. Camilla's face split into a grin, and she shook her head. "The feast? You mean the one which can't start without you?"

"They know very well I don't care for those kinds of revelries."

"And they're still waiting for you." Camilla crunched through the fallen leaves, then landed hard on the ground next to Sigrid. "They'd rather have their *leader* eating amongst them."

Sigrid hated it. She'd somehow managed to gather herself an entire kingdom of people who wanted her to be something she wasn't. They wanted her to be lethal, a dangerous creature who thirsted for blood and wanted to burn all the kingdoms to the ground.

She might be a dragon, but she wasn't a monster.

"Well, even leaders need to get away from everything sometimes." She rolled onto her back and stared up through the red leaves rattling above them. "Maybe I should disappear in the night and not return for a few days. Would they starve themselves, you think? Or would they somehow manage to survive?"

Camilla smacked her shoulder with a laugh. "Get up, you. They're going to start gnawing on each other's arms if we don't get back soon."

Good. Maybe they would relax once the blood started flowing.

Shaking her head, and knowing it was a bad idea to stay, Sigrid sat up and rubbed a hand on the back of her neck. "Help me with my hair then?"

"They don't care what your hair looks like, Sigrid."

But that was the difference between her and Camilla. Her owlish friend could walk among them and no Beastkin would ever question why she was there. They would look at her and laugh, no matter what clothing or style she chose. If she wanted to walk through the camp naked with her face painted, she could.

Everything Sigrid did was a sign to them. If she changed her clothing style, then suddenly everyone in the camp was wearing the same kind of dress. If she wore her hair down, they wondered if she was sick. If she wore it up in a different way, they wondered if something was changing.

Each detail of her life had suddenly become an omen. She had to watch what she said or did.

This was worse than Bymere. At least there, the people had looked at her as if she was some kind of nightmarish creature. They'd wanted nothing to do with her and, because of that, they'd freed her from the cage she'd always lived in.

It seemed that she'd traded her freedom for yet another cage.

Camilla must have seen all the emotions playing across Sigrid's face, because she sighed and twirled a finger in the air. "Turn around then, you fool. If that's how it's got to be, then I'll make sure the braids look normal this time. Do you remember what happened when we tried a different style?"

Sigrid snorted. "I don't want to see that many people running around looking like we were going to be attacked from every direction. Did you know that you'd given me a traditional battle hairstyle?"

"Of course I did. That's why I gave it to you. I thought it made you look fierce."

She didn't need anything else to make her look fierce. Sigrid was a perpetually terrifying creature with eyes like steel and a second form that could raze kingdoms to the ground. Of course, her friend didn't see her that way. Camilla only saw her as the little girl who used to play with her through the corridors of the castle, finding all the secrets hidden within the walls.

And Sigrid loved her endlessly for it.

The soothing touch of her friend lulled her into a false sense of security. The forests here were lush, untouched by man and barely touched by beast. When they'd first arrived, the leaves had been so green they looked like emeralds hanging off of each branch.

She enjoyed seeing the seasons change. From the bright

colors of spring, the warm tones of summer, and now to the burning, fire-like qualities of autumn. But she wasn't looking forward to winter, when all her people would be cold and would have to hunt for meat that would inevitably become harder to find.

Camilla stroked a hand down her hair which was now half up and braided in random strands. "There. I suppose you look a little more like yourself."

Together, they stood. Sigrid immediately placed a hand on her hip, only to find that her mask was no longer there.

The item had become a symbol of slavery. A symbol of all the things the Beastkin had suffered and all the mistreatment at the hands of both Earthen folk and Bymerian.

She still missed it.

Camilla's keen eyes stared at Sigrid's hand on her hip. "You still look for it?"

"Every day."

"Why?" Camilla had always had a hard time understanding it. "Those things were on our faces, hiding who we were, for centuries. Not just us, but all the Beastkin who had come to the Earthen folk's halls for safety."

"I don't know how to explain it." Sigrid shook her head and started back toward the keep. "The mask was more than just something to hide my face. It gave me a sense of... safety, although I'm sure that's the wrong word. I wasn't a woman when I wore that mask."

"You aren't a woman now. You're a *Beastkin*, and a dragon at that. You are so much more than any other woman."

If she heard that one more time, she was going to scream.

Sigrid forced her face into a mask, changing her features to remain still and cold. Even to her best friend. "Then we should get back to the feast as soon as possible. They'll want me to be among them."

Their trip back to the keep was silent. Camilla clearly knew she had said something wrong. Sigrid felt her gaze on her face throughout the short trip, but she didn't say a word.

Camilla didn't understand why she wouldn't just accept the fame and enjoy it. There were many people here who were so happy she existed. Finally, it wasn't just the small number of Beastkin living in the capital who knew they had a much more powerful ally than each other. They had something that was more powerful than all Beastkin combined.

She had never felt so isolated in her life. Sigrid didn't want this kind of fame, and she certainly didn't want to use the dragon to fight. She'd done that once already, and the guilt burned in her chest far hotter than any dragon fire.

Nightmares plagued her every night. She still heard the screams of Bymerians as she rained fire down upon their castle. The Red Castle, the place where she'd learned so much about the people she'd always thought were monsters.

The Bymerians were supposed to be terrible people. All of them. They were supposed to be monsters who didn't care for their children, who threw Beastkin into pits of flames, who hated anyone different that crossed into their kingdom.

Instead, they had been... not open-minded, but at least interested in what she had to say. The people on the streets had at first been the monsters. But she had seen a different side of them that confused her. A side which was soft and kind, thoughtful and accepting.

And then Nadir had turned into a dragon, fought with her

14

midair, and she didn't know what to think about it.

She had been certain they were going to slaughter him at his weakest moment. That they would have destroyed him where he lay just for being the kind of creature that she was. But then Raheem had told her he was still alive and she had to see him.

He was *hiding Beastkin*. And delivering them to her side just to save them.

Sigrid's mind was in such a constant state of shock she didn't know which way was up most of the time. She couldn't even tell her dearest friend, because she knew what Camilla would say.

Stop talking to the Sultan of Bymere and remember who your people are.

Her lungs seized and suddenly, she felt as though she couldn't breathe. Sigrid burst through the edge of the forest, her feet striking the cobblestone path. She scanned the scene in front of her with a mixture of disdain and pure disappointment.

Living with animals sometimes had its benefits. They were never hungry, because most of the Beastkin could live entirely on meat. Those who couldn't, could smell out food that was safe to eat. They hadn't even needed to start a farm this year, because there was plenty to go around.

But then sometimes, living with animals meant that they lived in filth. All her eyes could see was the destruction of the keep around her. They'd started the feast without her, or at least, the drinking part of the feast.

In a daze, Sigrid walked past a tent that had been shredded by claws. The bedroll inside hadn't fared much better, and she knew the inhabitant would be getting to stay inside the keep tonight. Shards of pottery littered the ground, likely the last of the precious few she had brought back from Greenmire Castle the last time she'd spoken with the Earthen King.

Sigrid stooped down and ran her finger through what looked like a river of red. She touched the finger to her tongue, relieved it was wine and angered that they were wasting so much.

A Beastkin man stumbled by her. One of the Bymerians who clearly wasn't used to the strength of Earthen alcohol. He weaved down the street with a hollowed out gourd in his hand. Liquid sloshed, spilling over the edges and falling onto the stone path.

"Dragoness," he said, slurring his words. "You were supposed to be here a while ago."

"And drink wasn't supposed to be opened until this evening," she replied, catching ahold of his arm when his knees buckled. "Which tent is yours, brother?"

"I don't rightly know where I am, to be honest." He leered up at her, his eyes crossing for a moment before he righted himself. "You've got beautiful eyes, love."

Camilla ducked between them before Sigrid lost her temper entirely. "I'll take him back to his tent. I know which one is his."

The anger within her burned so hot, she almost punished him for the words regardless of her friend stepping in. But that wasn't her. That was the ridiculous creature inside her who was making itself more known as of late.

Sigrid stepped back and nodded. "See that you do."

The hissing whisper of her friend filled the air as she dragged the man away. "What are you trying to do, get yourself killed?"

Even her own people worried that she would lose her mind and burn them all to the ground. Comforting thought when she lay in her bed alone at night.

Sigrid curled her fingers into fists, squeezing so hard she nearly drew blood. The pain helped her focus, so she wouldn't think dark thoughts. That after all this bloodshed, after starting a war between two countries, that she could ever regret freeing the Beastkin.

She turned and made her way to the castle. It loomed in the distance, ominous and bold as ever.

They'd yet to name it. Mostly because neither group could decide on what to call the place. Castle, palace, or keep felt wrong to say even though those were technically the words they should be using. They felt too cold to make this place a home, and there were no kings or queens here.

Sigrid was the unofficial matriarch, but the panel of people who made decisions for the Beastkin came from each of the houses that were forming. Predators, prey, avians, all the creatures seemed to have someone who wanted to rise to the forefront. But everyone listened to Sigrid and Jabbar.

She set her shoulder against the double doors leading into the great hall and shoved hard. Think of the devil and he shall appear.

Jabbar sat reclining on top of a large table at the far end of the hall. He lifted a fist full of what she could only assume was cow meat, rivulets of dark blood dripping down his hands. The Thunderbird preferred to have his meat either raw or barely cooked.

Even Sigrid wasn't so savage.

The interior of the keep hadn't fared any better than the outside. Food splattered the wall, decorating each and every surface with a mess she couldn't overlook. There was a splatter of blood coating one side. Hopefully not from one of the Beastkin but from a poor animal they'd feasted upon. Clothing hung from the rafters, and a table was overturned in the corner.

Laughter filled the air along with the sounds of animals grunting and groaning. These, she was certain, were actually Beastkin.

Jabbar's voice boomed throughout the hall. "Ah yes, the illustrious fighter returns from her solitude!" He lifted the hand full of carrion in her direction. "Welcome home, dragoness."

It had been Jabbar who'd started calling her that, and the others had fallen quickly into place as well. They had little interest in declaring themselves nicknames that linked them to their creatures. But for her? They wanted her to know that she was different.

Sigrid knew it didn't come from a dark place. They wanted to honor her with the name, as if she was some kind of mythical creature who had appeared out of nowhere to save them.

To her, it felt like just another declaration that she wasn't the same as them. That she was some kind of creature who had to be held apart from all the others.

With a sigh, she held her head high and made her way to Jabbar's side.

He watched her with a calculating gaze. Everything she did was weighed and measured by this man. He didn't care if their people prospered, not really. Now that they all had a warm place to sleep at night and food in abundance, his mind had turned to darker thoughts.

"Have you finally come to your senses?" he asked as she reached him.

"No," she answered bluntly. "There is no reason to create a warband. There is no reason to attack the Earthen folk."

"They held your people captive. 1 think that's enough reason right there."

"With the understanding of our own Beastkin. The captivity was an agreement on both sides. It is no longer an agreement we wish to stand behind, and so we left. They have not followed us, nor have they put up any kind of fight when we tried to free our sisters." She put heat behind her glare. "Leave it be."

"We cannot attack anyone without your agreement, Sigrid."

"And my answer will always be no."

He shook his head, but his eyes were watching her as if he could see right through her thin control. "You'll change your mind eventually, dragoness. I'm trying to save you an outright war. Even your own sisters agree with me. Attack the Earthen folk. End this before you regret your decisions."

She wouldn't. Sigrid was confident in that regard, but perhaps she was the only one who was. The Earthen folk were not going to attack the Beastkin. Why would they be so foolish? They had seen firsthand what Sigrid was capable of. Rumors and myths traveled fast in these places. No one would take such a risk when there was a dragon willing to burn their cities to the ground.

Her stomach twisted as guilt ate at her gut. The screams of Bymerian women and children filled her ears until she had to blurt out words just so her own voice would overpower them.

19

"Why does the great hall resemble a barn?" she asked, her tone icy and her voice hard.

"I don't think your people would like you comparing them to farm animals."

"Then perhaps they should start acting like humans."

He raised an eyebrow, then sucked his tongue over his teeth. The sound cracked into the ceiling. "Careful, dragoness. You don't want your people thinking ill of you. They are, after all, the ones who made you so powerful in the first place."

It wasn't the Beastkin who had made her powerful. It was her mother. The woman who had passed down the ability to shift into the great, serpentine beast she was.

But this wasn't what Jabbar was referencing. His words were a whispered threat that even a dragon could be taken down by Beastkin if they wished. There were enough creatures here that they could have their own uprising if she didn't do exactly what they wanted, whenever they wanted.

More and more, she resented setting them free. They wanted her to do everything. They expected the world to be handed to them.

The Wildewyn Beastkin were like this, because they *had* been waited on hand and foot within their old lives. The Earthen folk hadn't wanted to anger them. They were too powerful to make angry, but they'd also treated them like pets. She knew of only a few who could even clean up after themselves.

The Bymerian Beastkin hadn't ever had anything as nice as this place to live. They treated it as they would have any of the ruins they had lived in. This was just another thing to destroy until they found another, more suitable, home.

Sigrid nudged a larger chunk of meat, clearly inedible at this point, with her foot and pointedly stared at it. "Even you can't want to live like this."

"I see no problem with living the way we were meant to. We're animals, Sigrid." He gestured at her with the hunk of meat. "Perhaps you should try it sometime. You're holding onto the old ways, and it's making the others nervous."

A surge of anger made her cheeks hot. "Is it?"

"Indeed. There aren't any good memories from their old lives, but here you are waving it in their faces. Memories of things they don't like are bound to stir up trouble."

"I grow weary of your thinly veiled threats," she growled.

"What threats?" Jabbar licked a drop of blood from his arm. "I'm merely telling you how your people are feeling. If that information makes you uncomfortable, dragoness, perhaps it's because you know I am correct."

She might have flown at him if the doors hadn't slammed open. She spun on the intruder, her skirts whirling around her like petals opening around a flower. Although the movement might have been graceful, it was filled with deadly intent.

She remained stiff and poised for battle even as Camilla raced toward her. Her friend's eyes were wide, her jaw ticking. That could only mean one thing.

Trouble.

"What is it now?" Sigrid hissed.

Out of breath and clearly disturbed, Camilla snapped, "Greenmire calls for you."

"Greenmire?" she repeated. "The Earthen folk haven't called for me since we took our people back. There's no reason why they should need to speak with me."

"And yet, there is a courier standing in front of the castle. I think…" Camilla's eyes darted toward Jabbar, then she lowered her voice. "You should probably get out there. The others aren't happy that a human is here."

"Children," she hissed. "They should greet any guest with kindness."

"I don't think they see it that way."

Jabbar began to chuckle, the dark sound filling the great hall with a promise of more bloodshed to come. "They don't want humans around here. Beastkin lands should remain in Beastkin hands."

"Is that what you've taught them to chant?" Sigrid asked, already stalking away from him. "You should remember that prejudice has a way of coming back on you."

"They're weaker. Soon, they won't be around anymore."

"Not if I have anything to say about it." She waited until Camilla was at her side, then slammed the doors behind them.

Let the foolish man rot alone in his keep, thinking that he's far more powerful than he actually was. She didn't care what he wanted to do with his free time. Their people needed someone with a softer heart than that. Someone with a more open mind who would guide them into a future where they could live in harmony with the other race who inhabited their lands.

"Was that wise to say?" Camilla asked. She spoke quietly and low, making certain any other Beastkin wouldn't overhear them.

"No," Sigrid replied honestly. "But eventually, this will come to blows between the two of us. He wants to destroy all that I hold dear, and I won't let him."

"What is there to destroy? This place has never existed before."

Sigrid gestured around them and began the quick walk down to the front of the keep. "All of this. This place, these people. They are seeds we have planted into the ground. If we don't water them with kindness, let the sun kiss their face with honor, shelter them from storms which would rip out their roots and history, then they will blister, die off, and eventually become something twisted and wrong. This, I believe. Pouring poison into the soil like Jabbar wants us to do... that will only end in madness."

If she could have plastered the words over every surface of the keep, she would have. It seemed as though the Beastkin refused to see reason. They'd already had their battle. They'd seen dragons fighting in midair and the fall of both creatures of old.

Why were they not pleased with what they had already wrought?

Sigrid shouldered aside a Beastkin man with a beard so long it touched his ribs, then pushed against the shoulder of a lion who stood at the entrance to the keep. There was already a growing crowd, those who wanted to protect their home against any intruder, and those who hated humans so much it made their chests ache.

She didn't want the courier to have to suffer this injustice. Hallmar, the king of all Earthen folk and Wildewyn, would expect more from her.

The courier stood alone beside his horse. The animal was white as snow, and its hide rippled with fear as more and more animals arrived. She was shocked the beast remained where it was, but it was obviously well trained.

In contrast, the man standing next to the beast was little more than a child. *His* beard had barely grown in and suffered from a patchiness of young men not yet grown. His clothing was simple and plain. Perhaps to allow him to travel to this place easier and without people wondering why the king was sending a message to the Beastkin. Or, perhaps because he wasn't really a courier at all. Just a farm boy Hallmar had commandeered away from his family.

She'd seen worse things during her stay in the castle, but always in the name of the kingdom. If she could say anything about her renounced king, it was that he was just and fair.

Sigrid strode toward the boy with purpose, her gaze cold and her temper held in check. "I apologize for the unusual welcome. You'll have to excuse my brethren. We are unused to guests."

She hoped he heard the words underneath those she spoke. The ones that said she was embarrassed, to hold his tongue when he returned to the king. That she would make it up to him with gold and food if he made certain her secret was safe.

The courier bowed awkwardly. "Milady dragon. I've heard tales of you in the capital."

"I'm sure you have," she murmured softly. "They are likely true and untrue. What news do you bring from our king?"

"Our king?" he repeated.

Her blood froze in her veins. No answering murmur rose from the crowd behind her, so it was unlikely any Beastkin had overheard her words. They weren't so discerning a folk that they would listen to her speaking to the courier. To them, every word was something only royals knew. They let her do the talking and then report back when they wished to know what had happened.

But she would have to be more careful. She needed to remember that Hallmar *wasn't* her king anymore. No matter how much she respected the man, no matter how much she regretted her choices, she was not to refer to him as her own king.

Sigrid cleared her throat and looked the boy in the eye. He flinched back, perhaps not used to someone directing their words so painfully toward him. "He used to be my king as well. I honor him, as I understand he would do for me."

The boy nodded. "He respects you a great deal, milady."

As he should, she was the only barrier between him and outright war.

Sigrid glanced back at the swarm of Beastkin still within the castle walls. They stared back at her with fear in their eyes, and rage. A rage so powerful it swelled around them in a powerful crest that threatened to break over their own heads.

How could she teach them rage like that could only end in bloodshed and sadness? How many more people had to pay with their lives until they saw the world as she did?

"I'll go now," she said. "I suspect he's summoning me for a reason and hasn't sent you with just a message?"

"No, milady." The boy cleared this throat. "He'd like you at Greenmire as soon as possible, but also requested I tell you he understands you are a busy woman and—"

"I said I'll leave now," she interrupted. "Camilla?"

Her dark friend stepped forward, owl eyes watching the courier with curiosity. "We're leaving, I take it?"

She wouldn't take anyone else. Camilla was the only

person she trusted, save one Bymerian man who had taken to wandering Wildewyn rather than staying within the keep.

"Are you flying or riding?" she asked.

"If there's an option of riding, I'd rather not tire my poor little arms," Camilla replied, dryly.

Sigrid felt the change flex through her. Elation at becoming a dragon once again made her head spin and her nerve endings spark with joy. Together, they would fly to the King of Wildewyn's home.

She just hoped he wasn't about to tell her about another impending war.

NADIR

"SULTAN? PERHAPS YOU WISH TO GIVE YOUR VERDICT ON THIS CASE?"

The words came out of nowhere, although they were likely words he should have been listening to. Nadir sat on his throne in the massive hall where he met with his people, and where they voiced their complaints.

Great swaths of red fabric streamed from the ceiling to coil in snake-like tendrils on the gold, marble floor. Pools lined either side of the room and, if he'd looked within, fish swam in the shallow depths. For all intents and purposes, this was a beautiful place filled with so much splendor that it should have made his eyes water.

It didn't. But then again, it never had before.

Nadir straightened on his gold throne. When had he leaned his chin on his fist? And had his eyes just been closed?

The advisors all stared at him with varying expressions of disappointment. The expressions weren't any different than what he'd been getting for months now.

In a way, he didn't blame them. No one wanted to lose their power suddenly, and they certainly didn't like that their words weren't heard anymore. But Nadir simply didn't care what they had to say.

Poison had flooded his city for too long, and they'd suffered with a sultan who did not know what he wanted. Or even how to find out what he wanted.

Those times were long past. The city had begun to rebuild itself under his watchful eye. It was a struggle. Every step of the way was faced with people who didn't want to work with a dragon, or those who didn't like change. But he'd fought each battle as Sigrid had taught him.

Quietly. With poise and a calm demeanor that won people over before they even realized they'd let him do what he wanted.

He just hadn't realized it would make him so *tired*.

Clearing his throat, he pressed his spine against the back of the throne and nodded. "Say it one more time. I want to make sure I understand the issue fully before I give my verdict."

The man in front of him wasn't the man he remembered before. This was just a farmer, and wasn't he supposed to be a tailor? Or had his eyes closed before the other man had even left?

The farmer gave him an odd look, but clasped his hands in front of him once more. "My cows have a sickness, Sultan. I'm inquiring if I may go outside of the city to buy new ones from Misthall?"

Oh, that was all? Nadir waved his hand in the air. "Please do. Take a few other farmers with you. Perhaps they too wish for new bloodlines in their stock."

Why were these questions even directed at a sultan? They were simple answers. His people didn't need to confirm whether they could go out and do something that would make the kingdom better.

Sighing, he gestured the man away and placed a hand to his forehead. A throbbing headache pounded beneath his skull. Every sound echoed in his head with an answering thump.

One of his advisors stood, and it took every bit of Nadir's strength not to stiffen.

Abdul was a good man. Nadir still believed that, but his actions of late were certainly suspect. The older man liked to voice his opinion a little too loudly and in the company of those who were far too susceptible to his prejudices.

He wore his white hair pulled back in a leather thong. His beard was carefully trimmed into a point, and his clothing finely pressed. In theory, he carried himself like a man who knew what he was doing. But Nadir saw through the mirage. Abdul was, as always, a man clawing at the social ladder hoping for more and more power.

"That will be the last of them for today. The council would like to have a word with you in private, Sultan."

"In case you didn't notice, Abdul, it might be best if I retire for the afternoon," Nadir replied dryly. He could hardly keep his eyes open or his head up. What did the other man expect from him?

"You'll wake right up when you see what we have to say." Abdul held out a hand for Nadir to take. "Come, Sultan. There's much for us to talk about."

So it seemed he wouldn't be able to rest today. He nearly groaned as he stood. Sometimes, he wanted to go back to the way things were. When the advisors had taken care of all the difficult things he now was responsible for. When he'd been able to laze the day away and do next to nothing.

Nadir didn't take Abdul's hand, but stood on his own. Albeit slowly, but he didn't need to lean on his advisor. He had to hide the tired groan that threatened to escape his mouth, however.

He followed the train of advisors to a more private meeting room. He'd always hated this room with its floor to ceiling gold. Every ornate piece was beautifully hand carved, the attention to detail more than impressive. But it felt less like a room in the palace, and more like a museum where he couldn't touch a single thing without worrying he might break something. Pottery of the highest quality stood on stands in many of the corners. Tapestries hung from the walls. And stained glass windows cast colored shadows on the floor around them. A table sat in the center, precious mahogany wood underneath a thick slab of quartz.

The advisors gathered in a flock together at the end, each whispering among each other while Nadir situated himself on a seat at the head of the large table.

He took his time deliberately. They needed to remember they couldn't summon him whenever they wished. He was a busy man now.

At the thought, his chest swelled with pride. Finally, he could say that he was truly busy. His brother would have been proud.

Abdul cleared his throat. "Sultan?"

"A moment." Nadir ran his hand down his red silk tunic and billowing pants. He tucked the fabric more comfortably around him, a waste of time certainly, but a reminder to the others not to toy with *his* time. "Proceed."

The frustrated huff of breath from his advisor was more than a little pleasing. "We, as a council, have been considering the integration of Beastkin into our society, as you have requested."

"Ah, yes. I did request that you work with me on assisting in easing public discomfort in the presence of Beastkin." Nadir nodded sagely, but narrowed his eyes on the advisor. "However, I did not ask your opinion in whether or not we should do it. We're moving forward with the idea. I didn't ask if you thought it wise."

"Nevertheless, it is our job to consider the health of the kingdom—"

"That is not your role on this council any longer," Nadir interrupted. "Your role is to advise me on your thoughts, nothing more, nothing less. I've heard enough about Beastkin from all of you. I know your thoughts. I have listened. Now, I am sultan of this kingdom, and I choose to move forward in reintegrating them to Bymere. Your job is to assist me in that. Nothing more. Nothing less."

Abdul's jaw fell open and for the first time in his life, Nadir had successfully shocked the man.

If the iron in his voice hadn't convinced them he was serious, then he didn't know what would. Nadir planned on moving forward regardless of their opinions. He was married to a Beastkin. What else did they want from him? If anything, it was their mistake in the first place.

They were the ones who had requested he marry Sigrid. They were the ones who thought such an alliance would stop the war, although he now knew they had other intentions the entire time.

Now, they could live with the consequences.

Gathering his dignity close, Abdul straightened his shoulders and loudly sniffed. "We're well aware of your opinions, and while we do not agree with them, we thought perhaps there is a way for all of us to get what we want."

Nadir leaned back in his chair, noting the dark expression on Abdul's face. What had his advisor planned out? "I hardly think that possible, advisor, but perhaps you can teach me something new after all."

Abdul lifted a hand and snapped his fingers. One of the other advisors, a person who should have thought of themselves at the same station, rushed to the doors behind Nadir and opened them.

He would not shift. He would not move to look behind him until they brought whatever it was before him. A sultan did not have to move unless he wanted to.

The clanking of chains reached his ears. He didn't know of any prisoners. Not yet, at least.

Nadir gritted his teeth so hard he could hear them, but stilled his body in anticipation. He could not show them any kind of response, because that was what they wanted. This entire council enjoyed playing games. It didn't matter that it was another person's life. A game was still a game.

His gaze locked with Abdul's, then Nadir parted his lips in a sneer. "What have you done, advisor?"

"Only what you would have done, Sultan."

Before he could ask what that meant, a woman walked in front of him, trailed by the other advisor who had let her into the room. There were two armored guards behind her, their helms gleaming and reflecting rainbows of light as they passed by the windows.

His attention didn't stay on the guards, however, but the woman who walked in front of them. She must have been a beauty in her day. Her dark hair gleamed even through the matted tangles, and her skin was caramel smooth. Unfortunately, it was also dotted with hundreds of scars.

They'd dressed her in little more than a sack. It hung from her figure limp and loose, but the closer Nadir looked, the more he realized it wasn't because she was thin or malnourished. Instead, the clothing was simply too big. Muscles bulged from her arms, impressive in size and strength.

This was no weak woman.

She glanced up at him, as if she felt his gaze, and her eyes seared him to the bone. There was so much hatred locked in her eyes, along with a desire to live that resonated within her soul.

Manacles encircled her wrists, connected with a chain that looped through a metal collar at her neck. The clanking sounds echoed in the room, but he didn't care so much about the bindings. He'd seen many more people in chains than most would in their entire lives.

What he did care about was the way her eyes flashed from human to animal. Back and forth, almost uncontrollably as if they had done something to her.

A growl rumbled in his chest. "Who is this?"

Abdul swept the long train of his tunic to the side and strode toward the captive woman. "You wanted a way to encourage the people to trust. This is, perhaps, the most dangerous Beastkin woman we've ever encountered. To show them that this one can change would go a long way in convincing them that your intentions are to protect Bymerians."

"And how am I supposed to convince them of that?"

His advisor ignored Nadir for a moment, moving in front of the captive woman and tucking a finger underneath her chin. To her credit, she stared at Abdul with just as much hatred and anger as before. He hadn't managed to intimidate her.

A smile spread across Abdul's face, but it wasn't a nice one. "There are ways to break a mind. We'll work with her, tame this creature, and you can show the rest of Bymere that Beastkin can change. We can train them to be more than just animals."

Fire burned in Nadir's chest. It seared his bones and sizzled in his veins until he was little more than rage. Forcing his words to remain steady, Nadir replied, "We are not animals, advisor. Or perhaps, you have forgotten that a Beastkin sits upon the throne."

"By choice of the people." Abdul looked over his shoulder, finger digging into the woman's neck. "And that choice can change just as easily as it was made."

Nadir didn't want to admit that he was correct. It was hard enough to have his secret out in the world. People still flinched away from him in fear when he walked the streets. As they should. He was a dragon, after all, and could easily destroy the entire city if he wanted to.

But he didn't want to. The fact was an important one that he needed his people to understand fully and completely. Unfortunately, he couldn't convince his people of that without the support of the council.

His fingers curled around the arms of the chair he sat in, squeezing so hard he was surprised the fragile wood didn't shatter under the force of his rage. Pushing himself to standing, he flicked his fingers at Abdul.

"Move."

Abdul stepped back just enough so that it appeared he respected Nadir's authority. But not so far that he couldn't overhear everything Nadir would say to the Beastkin woman. Let him. Nadir didn't care if his advisors heard the words he was about to let slip off his tongue. They no longer ruled here, although they liked to think they had him pinned down.

He let the thoughts fall away from him and stood in front of the Beastkin woman. Not a single clue marked her body to hint at what she might be. Her eyes, though changing back and forth from human, could have been anything in their golden hues.

She stared up at him just as defiantly as all the others. Perhaps she hadn't heard their sultan was a Beastkin man as well. Or perhaps, like so many others, she simply didn't care.

"What is your name?" he asked.

"Tahira."

"What do you turn into, Tahira?"

She glared at him and remained silent.

Nadir noted the thick metal around her throat had rubbed the tender skin nearly raw. Red tendrils spread out from it, and he wondered if that might mean it was infected. "You are safe here," he tried to reassure her.

"Safe?" she spat at him, anger simmering until her eyes were nearly red. "I've never been safe in Bymere. Neither has any of my people."

"You are now." He hoped. Nadir realized he couldn't quite promise that, and in fact, it was likely still a lie. He was the only

Beastkin they tolerated, and that was because he was useful. Blowing out a slow breath, he shook his head. "Or will be. So why don't you tell me what you turn into?"

"You'll find out someday, boy king."

He likely deserved that, but it wasn't particularly an answer that helped him. Glancing over at Abdul, he nodded at the woman. "She's not an easy one."

"There are ways to break a person."

"And none of them you will use on her." Nadir looked back at her in time to catch her expression of surprise before it shifted back to anger. "We've done enough to this poor woman."

Her cracked lips spread into a smile. "You have no idea what goes on behind closed doors, little sultan. You think you're a man? You haven't seen a single thing of what your advisors do when your eyes are closed or your back is turned."

He'd suspected as much. There were a hundred things he'd uncovered and he'd likely find another thousand more. But here was a chance for him to start making amends. In an exaggerated sweep, Nadir bowed low to her and quietly murmured, "I know, huntress."

The honorable word was only given to women who had proven themselves to their sultan and to their country. He only knew of a handful, and they all lived in Falldell where the greatest assassins were trained.

Glancing up, he saw her face turn white. In horror or shock, he didn't know. Neither mattered.

Nadir nodded at one of her guards. "Have her placed in the other Beastkin woman's quarters for now. Tell the concubines to wash her and dress her."

"Sultan?" Even the guard was surprised he'd place her with the women who were considered the nation's flowers.

"They've dealt with two Beastkin women before," he replied, amused. "They'll know how to deal with her as well."

Truth be told, he wasn't so confident his concubines knew what they were doing. But he'd give them the benefit of the doubt and hoped they knew how to do something with the woman. Unlike Sigrid and her people, they enjoyed making other women look like delicate little flowers. They were good at that, and their skills were far beyond his own.

His advisors thought they were going to catch him with this. They thought he wouldn't spend the time to encourage the Beastkin woman to be more human than animal. That he wouldn't work with her or put forth the effort.

He was curious what she turned into. That would help him perhaps understand her mind. As far as he knew, the Beastkin were different personalities depending on the creature they had inside them. He'd observed that with Sigrid and her friend, Camilla.

Gods, he hoped he was right.

Waving his hand, he gestured for the guard to take the woman away.

She glared at him. Tahira, the woman who had no fear in her eyes. He'd have to remember her as something like this. She might be a little more frightened in the coming days.

"Where are you taking me?" she asked the guard. "Another prison?"

"Something like that." The guard's voice was amused, and Nadir's lips twitched in a small smile.

At least there were a few Bymerians who were more curious about the Beastkin than the others. This guard in particular seemed to see the women as something more than just an animal. Men? It was a little harder to look another soldier in the eye and think them stronger. But women pulled at the heartstrings. They were bringers of life. They deserved respect no matter what they were.

Nadir turned back to the table and again took his time reseating himself. The advisors hadn't moved from their places around the table, so he assumed there was more that they wanted to tell him. As if he had time for this foolishness.

Sighing, he dragged a hand through his hair and yanked it from the tie. The strands pulled too tightly at his scalp when he already had a blistering headache. "What is it?" he spat.

"There's more, Sultan," Abdul replied. He pitched his voice low as if what he was about to say would anger Nadir.

It likely would. Everything did these days when there wasn't an icy woman next to him soothing the anger in his soul.

"Out with it then."

"The King of Wildewyn has requested another audience. He would like to end the war before it begins."

"What war?"

"The one we started when the Beastkin attacked us. Wildewyn is standing by their... animals." Abdul carefully chose the one word that would get under Nadir's skin. "He wishes to speak with you directly and come to an understanding, apparently. The messenger he sent wasn't particularly forthcoming with his king's plans.

He was too tired to deal with this. Nadir squeezed the

bridge of his nose. "I am also uninterested in continuing a war that will only hurt both of the kingdoms. Return the messenger to the king and tell him so. We will not be launching any other attacks upon his kingdom unless they attack us first."

The advisors stilled. One whose name he couldn't even remember cleared her throat. "Tis a little too late for that, Sultan. The people are calling for blood once again."

"Our last battle ended with nearly the entire kingdom being burned to the ground. Or do I need to remind them that dragons fought above their heads only a few moons ago?" He lifted his hands and slammed them down on the table. "It is our duty to ensure this doesn't happen again."

Abdul shook his head. "The only way to ensure that is to make sure there isn't another dragon to attack us out there. Until then, there will always be the threat that she will return."

"Must I remind you that she is my *wife*?" Nadir's words cracked through the room and slammed back down on him in an echo he couldn't get out of his mind.

His wife. Sigrid. The woman who had awoken his soul, and then betrayed it with a simple action that made him want to both wring her neck and drag her back to his side so she wouldn't be subjected to war again.

He shook his head and continued, hissing the words at his advisors in hopes they would understand he refused to budge on this. "I will not speak of this again. If there is a war to be had, then we will talk of it then. But until the moment Wildewyn is on our doorstep, I will not entertain the idea."

Abdul leaned back in his chair with a sadistic smile that Nadir knew all too well. It was the expression the old man wore when there was a fight to be had, and one he knew he would win. "That's just the case, Sultan."

"What?"

"The Wildewyn King's messenger also stated there wasn't any choice in the matter. That the king himself will be coming to Bymere, and that he asked the Red Palace be ready to accept him. Whether we are willing to host him, or not."

Gods. This was the king he'd met who seemed so cool headed? Nadir had only met Hallmar once, but the man had seemed to have a good head on his shoulders. He'd admired the king's grasp on politics and how easily he twisted words into something that could be conveyed as kindness but were really an insult.

How could such an intelligent man be so foolish as to think he could waltz into another kingdom without repercussions? Especially a kingdom that desired a war with his.

Nadir leaned his forearms against the table and stared down at the smooth marble. "Why would he do that? Someone, *explain*."

Abdul drummed his fingers against the table. "It is our impression that he wants to show Wildewyn is capable of handling a war. Such an act can only be viewed as a threat."

Anger simmered beneath the surface of his skin like a living creature, writhing and coiling until he could barely think. "That would be a foolish thought, and I don't think Hallmar is a fool."

"Why is that?"

Nadir didn't know if Abdul was asking why he thought Hallmar wasn't a fool, or why it would be a foolish thought. Either way, the answer was the same.

He looked up from the table, sensing his eyes heat. He knew they had shifted from man to dragon. The yellow gaze sweeping across all his advisors and membrane flicking down over the color to wet the slitted orbs.

"Because we have a dragon. And no one threatens a kingdom with a dragon to protect it."

SIGRID

WIND STROKED HER SCALES WITH THE LIGHTEST OF TOUCHES. THIS WAS when she was most comfortable, when she was most confident. Nothing but the clouds and the air. No one to distract her or who needed her attention.

Sigrid drifted on a current of air, wings stretched open wide and eyes scanning the valley so far below her. The clouds obscured the visions of emerald green waves every now and then, but that was all right. She enjoyed looking at the puffy white clouds as well. In a way, they were soothing. Although they were sometimes disorienting, it also meant that very few people could find her up here.

Camilla's legs tightened at the base of her neck. There wasn't much but spines for her friend to hang onto. Just a few flimsy handholds, and that meant it was a little too easy to fall.

Not that Camilla couldn't just change into an owl. The time it would take to change would save her from a plummet to her death. But still, it was frightening to not be in control.

Sigrid craned her neck to glance back at her sister. A smile twisted her snake-like lips when she saw Camilla had her arms outstretched and her head tilted back. The wind twisted in Camilla's braided locks and made her shirt billow out around her like a cape.

It was a beautiful sight. And one she needed before they began to land in Greenmire Castle. This was why she was doing all the work. Every small bit of responsibility was worth it when she could see her sister happy like this.

They were finally, finally free.

She focused on landing them safely on the cobblestones in the castles center courtyard.

The white marble spires of the castle stretched up around them with delicately carved arches lifting up to mimic the tall peaks. Trees tangled through the carvings, giving the entire castle an otherworldly look. Both castle and nature were linked together in a way that no one else could mimic. It was beautiful, and it made her homesick for a time when Camilla and she would run through the halls of this place as children.

They hadn't been free then, although it had felt a little bit like they were. The Earthen folk had tolerated the Beastkin children with wry smiles and empty threats when they misbehaved too much. But they hadn't ever struck the girls as they might have their own children.

Now, Sigrid saw that it was still a life of captivity. They were looked at with a fondness in the same way someone might look at a pet.

The insult still stung. She had seen these people as an extended family who had appreciated her. Who had wanted to take care of her, and make her happy.

But the older she had gotten, the more she realized her childish fantasies were far from the truth. Letting go of that illusion was far more difficult than she could have ever imagined.

Landing hard on the rocks, she huffed out a breath and lowered her head so Camilla could dismount. They'd have to figure out a better way for them to travel together. Sigrid actually liked having someone who wasn't an animal with her.

It helped ground her.

Shifting where she was, Sigrid reminded herself not to look up at the startled faces of the Earthen folk. At her hip was the golden mask they were used to, the one that so many Beastkin viewed as something terrible and bad.

It was a symbol of her responsibilities. A symbol of who she was, and what she had become. For the Beastkin, she shouldn't wear it. But for the people here, the ones who had raised her, she would.

Sigrid affixed the golden mask to her face and sighed. It shouldn't feel like a shield she'd put in place that no one could break through, but it did. Even now, after all she had fought for, and all she had won, she wanted to wear the mask just so that she could hide a little bit longer.

The Earthen folk were staring at her, but not because they could see her face. They likely hadn't seen a Beastkin change before. That didn't mean she needed to indulge in answering their questions or explain how it was possible.

They didn't get to ask questions like that. They didn't get to try and touch or tame her.

Footsteps rattled through the courtyard as armored boots raced down the stairs toward her.

"Ah, yes," she muttered under her breath and straightened. "Hallmar's personal guard still thinks I'm here to burn the whole place down."

"Some things don't change," Camilla replied. A grin split her face with a bright happiness that Sigrid didn't understand. How was it possible for her friend to feel so at ease here when so many ghosts roamed around them?

Hallmar strode behind his guards, impeccably dressed as always. He was a handsome man in his youth, and that had carried over as he aged like a fine wine. The stern look on his face was both intimidating and reassuring.

The emerald green of his velvet tunic was accented by golden threads embroidered in swirling patterns across the entirety of the jacket. A plain white shirt was open at the throat, revealing an amulet of blue quartz that eerily looked like ice. That was new. Or perhaps, he only wore it when he was welcoming important guests.

She wouldn't know.

He lifted his arms in greeting and smiled at the two of them. "Ladies! Welcome home."

And damned if she hadn't been waiting for those words. Sigrid wanted to run into his arms as she would have as a child, feel the strength in them as they closed around her shoulders and pulled her against his broad chest.

He'd always made her feel so safe when he hugged her like that. As if he could take the weight of the world from her, all her worries and fears, and place them somewhere else as long as she was in his arms.

But Sigrid wasn't a child anymore. She was a queen of her own kingdom, a rival kingdom at that, and she couldn't break that vow to her people by welcoming him as an old friend.

She swallowed hard, touched a finger to the edge of her mask to make sure it was still in place and nodded. "Thank you for the welcome. I wasn't expecting a messenger from you any time soon."

"And I wasn't expecting to have a war on my doorstep." He let his arms drop to his sides, one hand at his hip. She remembered he used to hide a wicked, curved blade in his pant leg. Had he brought a weapon to speak with her? As if she would ever attack him? "But this is still your home, Sigrid. If you ever have need of it."

Camilla cocked her hip out to the side, raised a hand, and said, "I'm standing right here."

His booming laugh filled the courtyard like sunlight after a storm. "I have missed your humor, Camilla. You are always welcome as well."

"I know." She flicked the ends of her braids over one shoulder and winked at him. "I just wanted to hear you say it one more time."

This was how it had been, before the king thought it would be better for Sigrid to be married. Before an arrow had silenced a good man forever. Before the world had changed and a dragon had awoken in her soul.

She was grateful for the mask, because Sigrid couldn't have hidden her crestfallen expression if she tried. "Shall we?" she asked.

"Ah, yes," Hallmar replied, sweeping his arm out for them to follow him into the castle. "A little privacy after such a long trip would be greatly appreciated, I'm sure. Come with me, ladies."

Sigrid didn't correct him that they were to be given more respectful names now. She didn't know what the Beastkin wanted to be called. Matriarch would have been correct long ago, but now there was a council of Beastkin making decisions, and they tried to throw their weight around no matter what she wanted to do.

Sometimes, it felt as though her council fought with her just *because* she had voiced an opinion. Anything she wanted to do, they wanted to do the exact opposite. It was like dealing with children at times. And she hadn't signed up to be a mother.

She followed Hallmar into the castle and breathed out a sigh. Relaxation flooded through her veins at finally being in a place that was more familiar to her than the back of her hand. She knew every hidden corridor, every guard's favorite napping place, and every leaf that would fall through the windows from old trees that peaked in to see what the humans were doing.

This place had been her childhood.

Ducking her head as they walked past a servant, she tried to tell herself that this was different now. She wouldn't be able to act as she had before. Certainly, she'd always been the leader of the Beastkin. But there hadn't been any power in the name.

Matriarch's came and went. They advised the king on what their people wanted, but they didn't have a choice in what the kingdom did. Their role was to take care of their people, which hadn't changed. But now she had a castle, a war, an army...

Her mind was whirling. What did he want from them? What would he ask for that she wasn't going to be able to give?

How did she say no to the man who had helped raise her?

A hand slipped into hers, strong fingers squeezing in

encouragement. Sigrid glanced over at Camilla, freely without her mask, easy-going and so confident it made Sigrid's heart clench.

Her sister smiled. "Everything will be fine."

"I just want to get this over with."

"I don't think he wants to wait." Camilla nodded ahead of them. "He's taking us to his private quarters. That means no one else is involved but us. Sounds like he's going to ask a favor."

"One I won't be able to give."

"We don't know that yet."

Sigrid snorted. "The Beastkin are many things, but forgiving they are not. Even our own sisters want to see this place torn down stone by stone. They aren't going to help the Earthen folk."

"I think you judge them too harshly. They're angry right now, and they have a right to be. But they haven't suddenly become heartless."

It was the reminder Sigrid needed. Her people, although animalistic by nature, still saw the good in people. She should trust them to do the right thing when the opportunity arose.

Blowing out a breath, she nodded and squeezed Camilla's hand in return. "Thank you. You always seem to have the answer I'm looking for."

"Your head is so far in the sky; I can't even imagine what you see up there. I'm happy to give you perspective from the ground level." Camilla winked. "Or remind you when your head is getting too large, *Matriarch*."

Laughing together, they entered Hallmar's private chambers. The room was exactly as she remembered it. Warm, cozy, and filled with earth-tones that immediately set her at ease.

A large fireplace was inlaid in the wall. Cracking logs burned low. Embers scattered around them. Furs covered the four seats around a small table where someone had set tea and scones, while a thick tapestry hid the four poster bed from their sight.

Sigrid couldn't remember Hallmar ever having someone who stayed in the room with him. He'd always been a king who ruled without a queen. Never entertained those who would have spent a night with him, as far as Sigrid knew.

The man in question strode to one of the chairs with antlers for a back, and poured himself a cup of tea. "Would you like one? I'm afraid I don't remember how you take your tea."

Camilla opened her mouth to direct him, but Sigrid couldn't stand the sight.

She let out a frustrated sound, then took the teapot from Hallmar's grasp.

"That's hot—" he began, then shook his head with a laugh. "I forget so easily."

Sigrid cupped the base of the teapot with her bare hand. It was likely hot and filled with boiling water, but that wasn't something which could stop her. Her lips twisted into a wry grin, one he couldn't see, and then she began to pour them all tea.

"It's been a while since we've been here, and I'm certain there are more important things for you to do than think about the days when we roamed your halls."

"But I have been thinking about it a great deal," he replied. "This castle is far too quiet without your people. I regret to say that I miss them, even though I know you're creating a life for yourself."

Camilla dropped into one of the chairs, legs sweeping up over the arm as she dramatically hung off the other. "Why did you let us go so easily, anyway? The Beastkin have always been something of a security for you. And you just... let us go?"

"When a full-grown dragon lands in your castle yard demanding something of you, there isn't much choice." But his voice was filled with humor. He blew on his teacup and tried a sip before responding. "The Beastkin have always been a temporary addition to the castle. I knew this from the first moment I became king."

Sigrid poured herself a cup and sank down gently next to him. "You were the first king to think that then."

"Perhaps. My father always thought that a war would come from Bymere, and that we would need to use your people to protect ourselves. I thought it too cruel for a king to order people to fight for him when those people weren't part of our kingdom at all."

"Perhaps," Sigrid mimicked his response. "But our kind was forced to fight before, and no one felt any regret."

"No, I suppose they didn't." He lifted the tea to his lips and fell into a comfortable silence.

She'd missed this. Hallmar had been the one to first teach her about proper etiquette. He advised on how to hold her teacup, how to pour the tea in a way that wouldn't insult anyone, even how to sit so that she was still viewed as demure but also powerful.

He hadn't ever made her feel as though she were a pet. Perhaps that's why she managed to capture so much time with him as a child. He'd always taken the time to make her feel like a person. To respect her as so few others did.

She sighed and put her teacup on its saucer. "I'm afraid we don't have a lot of time for niceties, Your Majesty."

"Please. You've long past earned the right to call me by name." His eyes twinkled with mirth. "Hallmar will suit just fine."

"You've always called me Sigrid, so I cannot return the favor."

"You could take off your mask." He watched her with an intense stare that made her sweat. "I haven't seen your face in a very long time, dragon. So long ago you likely don't remember me even seeing it."

"I don't."

"All the other Beastkin I've seen no longer wear their masks. The Bymerians never did in the first place. Why do you?"

She didn't have a good answer for that. She didn't want to wear it, not really. It still felt stifling, and it was physically uncomfortable to place on her skin. But she also didn't want to lose the armor that covered her face. For some reason, she was far more nervous to have people see that than anything else.

With a sigh, Sigrid reached up and unhooked the pieces in her hair that held the mask in place. Gently, she tugged it away and set it on her lap. Looking back at Hallmar, she steeled herself for what he would think.

His gaze softened, his lips curved into a smile, and his shoulders relaxed. "You look like your mother."

"You saw her without her mask?"

"There are still a great many things you don't know, Sigrid.

Some things I will tell you. Others, you need to find out for yourself." He shook his head. "But you could be her if I didn't know she was put in the ground long ago. From your forehead to your chin, there's not an ounce of you that doesn't look like her."

The words heated in her chest with pride. "Why did you call us here, Hallmar?"

The relaxed expression wiped off his face immediately. "There's going to be a war, which you know already. I'm going to Bymere myself to see if I can stop it, but I don't have high hopes for that."

"You're going to Bymere?" she repeated. "They'll kill you on sight."

"Maybe. But that is a risk I have to take for this kingdom. Wildewyn cannot fight without the Beastkin, and the Beastkin are no longer part of my kingdom."

"Then we will fight." Sigrid ignored the breath Camilla sucked in.

"I won't ask that of your people. Not after everything they've fought for. This Earthen King will give your people a chance to start." He waved a hand in the air. "Besides, that piece of land has been rotting for ages. If you can make it into something better, then perhaps someday we'll find a way to trade."

She eyed him, thoughts whirling in her mind. Was there any reason for him not to command them to fight? Not that she could think of. Hallmar was well within his right to be asking favors, and yet, he wasn't.

"Why aren't you asking us to fight?" she finally voiced the most pressing question. "Honestly, please. I don't care about the politics nor do I wish to read between your words. Tell me plainly, Hallmar."

He sighed, leaned forward, and braced his forearms on his knees. "If you haven't figured out why yet, Sigrid, then I won't explain it yet. Go back to your people. Tell them that a war is coming, and if they wish to fight, I will not stop them. But I will not ask, nor will I dictate what you or your people do. I asked you here to warn you that there will be Bymerians coming to our doorstep if I don't try and stop them."

"Then I should go with you."

At that, Camilla's feet fell off the arm of her chair and thumped hard on the ground. "No, you won't."

"The Beastkin have many more leaders than just me."

"But you are the symbol of their freedom, not to mention the dragon that just attacked Bymere. You think they'll kill him on sight?" She pointed at Hallmar. "They'd hang you in the square and set your body on fire, Sigrid."

"A dragon cannot burn."

"It can if it's dead." Camilla reached for Sigrid's hand, squeezing it tightly between her own. "I share your worry for him, but we are not just Beastkin anymore. We have a kingdom, people, and a responsibility to keep them safe. That is why he is risking his life, and that is why I cannot let *you* do the same."

Sigrid stared into Camilla's dark eyes and wished for a different life so violently it made her flinch. She didn't want to be the queen of the Beastkin. She didn't want to be anyone but Sigrid for once in her life.

Still, her sister was right.

Nodding, Sigrid looked back to Hallmar. "Fine. Go, and let us know when you return. I'd like a full report on Bymere. It's best to know our enemies well before we are attacked."

He shrugged. "I think you have more information in that regard than I do. Living amongst them will help, but having Bymerians under your care... You and your people are significantly more prepared than we are."

And the Beastkin wouldn't even assist in protecting those who had protected them for so long. The truth stung, but Sigrid knew she wasn't wrong.

"I will try," she whispered. "But I cannot promise we will help."

"That is all I can ask of you."

Their conversation complete, Sigrid hesitated for a brief moment. She almost wanted to stay for a little while longer. The promise of warmth and civilized conversation was more tempting than returning to the madness of the Beastkin home.

And yet, she knew she couldn't stay. This was a gilded cage for her people; no matter how much the king had enjoyed their company. She must leave and do something more than revert back to the old ways that, although broken, had been comfortable to her.

She stood and nodded gracefully. "Until I see you again."

"I hope we do, dragoness."

It felt too final, this meeting of theirs. She didn't want it to be the last they had together, but had a feeling he thought it was. That was why he brought her here.

Of all times, she didn't want to lose him just yet.

Blowing out a breath, Sigrid nodded and left his private quarters. Camilla's footsteps trailed behind her, but she barely registered that her friend was following her.

Mind whirling, she raced through the halls of her

childhood. Her pace was quick, but still respectable if anyone was to see her as she walked by them. They would say she looked like a woman on a mission. That the determination showed in the set of her shoulders and the cold gaze of her mask.

They wouldn't see her expression of heartbreak and sadness. They wouldn't understand her fingers were curled in fists, because she was barely holding herself together. Not that she was an honorable leader who was carefully keeping herself in check.

People scattered as she entered the courtyard. A woman grabbed her son's arm and pointed at Sigrid while saying, "Watch, my love."

They were making her a spectacle.

Again.

Camilla touched a hand to Sigrid's shoulder and muttered, "Are you all right?"

No. She felt as though something in her soul had broken, and she didn't know how to deal with these emotions. She wanted to scream and shout, to break something like a child in a temper tantrum. And then she wanted to run back into the castle and throw herself into Hallmar's arms.

She wasn't a little girl anymore. The only man who had been a father figure to her was about to risk his life with the man she loved.

One of them would likely end up dead. And her mind didn't know which one she wanted to see come out of the bloodbath.

"We leave now," she growled and changed so violently that Camilla was thrown to the ground.

Her sister scrambled back to her feet, reached out for the spines along Sigrid's back, and threw herself onto the dragon right before she suddenly lifted into the air. Gusts from her wings made people run screaming, but she didn't care if they were afraid of her. They should be. Wasn't that what they wanted?

A monster who they could tell their children to be afraid of. A figurehead for how bad all the Beastkin were. A shield for her own people to hide behind.

She was overwhelmed. Wildly tossed against the rocks of her own mind until all she could think was that she wanted a few moments to herself. A few moments when her mind wasn't screaming and she could finally *think*.

The journey home was quick and silent. Camilla left her to herself, though she knew Sigrid could hear her words. They landed in the middle of the keep which was falling apart already, and Sigrid felt her blood begin to boil again.

Too many of her people lay about doing nothing, while there was a war to plan.

Before Camilla had even slipped from her neck, Sigrid had changed. She pressed her fist into the ground, crouched before the inhabitants of the unnamed keep, and stilled her tongue.

Say nothing, she told herself. There would be a time to speak, a time to yell and scold, but not when she wanted to fly at them in a rage.

The crack of clapping struck her ears. She told herself not to flinch, but couldn't stop the violent curling of her fingers into the mud.

"A mask again?" Jabbar asked, his voice slithering through the keep. "I thought we'd gotten rid of those a long time ago."

"I visited the Earthen King," she replied. "They expect certain levels of decorum we no longer acknowledge here."

"Then shouldn't they be using our customs? Are we not the superior race?"

She gritted her teeth. "I will not have this argument with you now, Jabbar. Call the council members. There is much for us to talk about."

"Oh, I'm sure your meeting was very enlightening." He stooped down in front of her, one knee on the ground. "I don't think he'd have anything interesting enough to tell us honestly. Feel free to call the council, but I don't want to hear any more of his poisonous words."

"Hallmar, Earthen King, is a good man."

"How can you say that when he kept your people in cages?"

Don't, a voice whispered in her head. *Don't encourage him.* But she couldn't stop the words that fell from her lips. "They kept us in castles, with our own quarters and a respect for the old ways. Yes, we were not normal citizens, but we were not mistreated."

"Many of your fellow sisters would disagree with you."

"Their minds are clouded by anger instigated by *you.*"

She looked up at him then, feeling her eyes heat until she was certain it was a dragon staring back at him. To his credit, he didn't flinch. But Jabbar had never been afraid of her. A thunderbird at heart, he was one of the few who could likely put up a fight with her.

He met her anger with heat of his own, grinning as he stared back at her. "Why, little dragoness, do you want to fight me?"

"I am not an animal."

"On the contrary. You're as much an animal as the rest of us, and the sooner you accept that, the better."

"I am not."

He reached forward, pressed a single finger against her shoulder, and held it there. "You are worse than any of the others. A dragon should be free. Instead, you dishonor us all by denying who you are."

"I have never denied my lineage."

"Perhaps not your lineage, but you have denied the creature inside you. You still hold yourself separate, as if you are somehow better than the rest of us who are both man and animal. Now, let me tell you, Sigrid. You're not better. Your Earthen King is weak, and that is why you still cling to him like a child." His eyes shifted, yellowing and cracking with electricity. "Because *you* are weak."

The finger on her shoulder flexed, and then he shoved her just enough to rock her back a step.

It was as if he'd lit a fuse to something inside her that was just waiting to explode. Without thought, without control, she shifted into the dragon.

Leathery scales scraped over the ground as she lifted herself onto her legs, spread her wings wide, and roared up into the sky where the sun had begun to set. Fire burned in her chest, casting a glow over the courtyard and over Jabbar who stepped back a few paces and laughed.

"You see?" he called out. "You are just the same as the rest of us! When you want a fight, dragoness, you should indulge in your animal's needs."

She would show him a fight, if that was what he wished.

Faintly, she heard Camilla shout at Jabbar to stop. That he didn't know what he was doing.

But that didn't matter anymore. Sigrid hardly remembered that she'd even had a friend at all. Sisters weren't something dragons cared about, and the human part of her mind was dangerously close to being swallowed whole by a monster that had always lurked underneath her skin.

Jabbar's human skin melted into a bird larger than most houses. His beak stretched open and a painful cry made her ears ache.

Sigrid shook her head, swaying back and forth. She opened her own mouth and hissed, falling back to the ground, pressing her wings against the earth and the muck. Opal scales reflected the dying sun back in her eyes, but she knew where he was. She couldn't miss him.

He shot up into the air as more electricity crackled along his feathers.

Camilla shouted, "Sigrid, no!"

She followed him with a ragged wingbeat. Flying still wasn't easy for her. She hadn't done it for such a long time that those who already knew how to fly could easily overtake her. But once she lifted herself from the ground, she could follow him anywhere.

Eyes narrowed, blood boiling with the hunt, she shot up through the clouds. Her tail whipped behind her, the thin spikes at the end already tingling, like they knew she was about to catch her prey.

Bursting through the tops of the clouds, she hovered in the air and waited for him to show himself. If she'd had a voice, she would have taunted him. Instead, a low growl erupted from her chest which glowed with more fire.

Soon, soon she would clamp her jaws around his neck. She would pierce his soft flesh with her claws and dig until his heart was within her grasp.

A bolt of lightning shot past her, slicing through the clouds and giving her a small opportunity to see him. He thought he could hide beneath the fluffy whiteness. Likely, he could have, if Sigrid had been completely in control of herself.

Instead of a woman, a dragon hunted him now.

She took a deep inhale and caught the scent of him on the wind. Cold and faintly tasting of metal on her tongue.

Her pulse jumped. She could find him anywhere now, no matter how much he tried to hide himself.

Another bolt of lightning launched past her, this time catching the edge of her wing. Shocks traveled up the appendage. For a moment, she couldn't use it correctly and dropped until her tail skimmed the edges of the clouds.

Enough. He'd had his fun. She'd indulged him far more than she wished to. And now, he needed to learn that taunting a dragon was a swift way to find himself dead.

Sigrid inhaled deeply again and turned toward the metallic scent. She beat her wings, found the perfect air current, and then shot toward him like a bolt of his own lightning. She heard the answering squawk of fear before she opened her mouth and closed strong jaws down where his wings met neck.

His talons clawed at her chest. Over and over again, he struggled to free himself while slapping her back with his wings. He only managed to injure himself on the plated armor of her body and the spikes at her back.

Blood coated her tongue. She couldn't think of anything

but that she'd caught her prey and that he tasted so sweet. Adjusting, she sank her jaws deeper and deeper, wings curling around him and mind forgetting they were in the air.

One of his talons finally pierced through the armored scales, dragging a long gouge through her chest. The pain didn't register at all. She didn't care if he tried to hurt her. Let him. He would soon find that there was little which could stop a dragon.

They plummeted through the air toward the ground. She opened her eyes just in time to see they were going to hit one of the towers of the keep, before she rolled them at the last second. They struck a hill near their home, both rolling down the large expanse.

She lost her hold on his neck in the process and gave a draconic groan of frustration until she struck multiple pine trees that halted her roll. The pain in her ribs and back exploded.

The dragon relinquished her hold, melting away into a woman crumpled at the base of a tree. Sigrid hugged her torso, feeling as though she was on fire everywhere and that everything ached with a pain that was her own doing.

She didn't look to see if Jabbar was still alive. She didn't care.

Twigs snapped and a veritable army of Beastkin raced through the trees.

"Sigrid?" Camilla shouted from where Jabbar had landed. "Where is Sigrid?"

She should have been able to call out, but her lungs still didn't want to drag in enough breath for words. Instead, she let out a guttural groan that she'd never heard her own body make before.

Camilla cursed and ran toward her, leaping over a fallen tree that had been uprooted in their fall. "There you are, foolish woman. What were you thinking?"

She hadn't been. And that was enough to make her worried.

Sigrid shook her head, trying to push herself up from the mossy ground, only to fall back to its soft embrace.

"Don't try to move just yet," Camilla whispered. She hovered her hand over Sigrid's shoulder, hesitating for a moment before she gently let it touch a ragged, bleeding wound. "You've nearly done yourself in this time."

"Not by choice," she replied.

"What?"

They shared a worried look before another group of Beastkin caught up with her. They were mostly Bymerian men, all laughing and jostling each other.

One, Jabbar's right hand-man if she remembered correctly, knelt before Sigrid. His dark eyes sparkled with merriment, and he shook his head. "You just made me a lot of money, Matriarch. Too many of our men were betting on Jabbar, but I think you bested him."

Camilla sighed and interrupted before Sigrid could speak. "Take her to my room, please."

"We'll take the matriarch to her own quarters."

"To *my* room." Camilla's tone left little room for argument.

The men lifted her to standing, threading her arms over her shoulders and helping her limp back toward the keep. She might have insisted that they let her walk on her own, if she hadn't seen that Jabbar was getting similar help.

Blood streamed off his shoulder in a small river of movement. It hadn't yet begun to close at all, and she'd be sad to see the flow of red become sluggish. Served him right for pushing her past all the boundaries she'd put up.

There was a reason why Sigrid locked things up tight within herself. Namely, because she knew things like this would happen. Her temper had to be buried beneath miles of ice or should would end up...

She shook her head, trying to clear the thoughts out of her mind. It wouldn't do to dwell on the things she'd done. Yes, they were far worse than she ever thought she'd do. She'd try to kill someone who was more than just an advisor, but a savior for most of the people here. What must they think of her? Attacking the man who had risked his life for years just to ensure the Bymerian Beastkin were alive?

The laughter in the keep was still boisterous and loud. Most shouted out words of encouragement, saying they'd wanted to see a fight between their two main leaders for a long time.

"Did you best him?" One of her sisters, a woman who changed into a falcon, asked. "I put money on you winning, and this fool thought I was wrong."

Sigrid flicked her gaze to the Bymerian man beside her sister, the man she knew turned into an elephant when he wished. "I did," she replied.

The man groaned. "Damn it. Now I owe her more than just a drink."

"You owe me an evening of your time."

The eyes they made at each other turned Sigrid's stomach. She didn't need children running around the keep, knowing full well they would only follow in the footsteps of their foolhardy parents.

She limped up the stairs into the tower where Camilla had claimed her room. It was a solitary place, but that wasn't all that surprising for an owl. The tallest peak only had a small room at the top. A circular bedroom with nothing but a bed, a desk, and a fireplace to keep her warm.

Camilla pointed at the bed. "Put her there. I'll take care of her for the evening."

"We've a healer, owl," the man holding Sigrid advised.

"And I've taken care of her before. Don't question me, Najib."

That's right. His name was Najib, and he turned into a leopard. She'd seen him fight before, in the battles that almost tore Bymere apart. He was a fierce fighter, capable of downing multiple men in battle, but he'd also seemed to keep a cool head.

How had she forgotten that?

He eased her down on the edge of the bed, keeping a hand on her shoulder to make sure she remained steady. Instead of leaving, as she had expected from a man who had sworn Jabbar his allegiance, Najib surprised her and knelt in front of her.

He touched a thumb to her chin and tilted her head to the side. "You'll have quite the bruise here from him."

"It's not the first bruise I've suffered."

"But it is the first he's given you." Najib shook his head and dark shadows played in his eyes. "He'll like it that he marked you. That's just the way he is, has something to do with his beast."

"He won't do it again." She knew it deep in her gut that the next time Jabbar pushed her too far, she would put the albino man in the ground. He had no right to question her, and he was the one who had put her in this position.

If he wanted someone to lead them, someone to use as a figurehead to guide them, then that meant he had to listen to her as well.

Najib sighed and stood. "If that was the way of things, then life would be a lot easier. Jabbar gets what he wants, Matriarch. Even you will be hard-pressed to stop him."

"I nearly did today, didn't I?"

"That was just testing your abilities. To kill him, you'd have to fight a lot better than that." Najib leaned over and pulled out a small roll of cloth from the bedside table. He placed it on the blanket next to Sigrid, then strode to the doorway. "Take good care of her, Camilla."

When she couldn't hear his footsteps walking down the stairs anymore, Sigrid pressed a hand to her ribs and raised a brow at Camilla. "He knew where the bandages were?"

"A lucky guess."

"How silly of me to even think he'd been here before," Sigrid replied, wryly. "You're allowed to have relations, you know."

"Relationships are another story." Camilla moved to stand in front of her and gestured with her hands. "Arms up. Let's get these clothes off you and see what damage he did."

"Not too much."

"There's blood leaking out of your sleeve. I think he did more to you than you know."

Sigrid lifted her arms and let her friend do whatever she wanted. She wouldn't be surprised if the pain simply wasn't registering. She'd gotten good at that even as a young child. Pain didn't make her brain spark the way others did. It simply *was*. The white hot edge could take control of her mind, or she could refuse to let it.

Camilla stripped every inch of clothing from her body then forced her to lie down. A small bottle of salve appeared in her hand, but Sigrid didn't know where Camilla had found it. Maybe she healed more people in this room often. Or maybe, she'd known this was going to happen.

While her friend worked, Sigrid stared up at the ceiling. Worn, wooden beams crisscrossed above her. Someone had poured years of work into this place, so much that it had managed to stay standing after the test of time.

And now, the Beastkin were going to be the ones to pull it to the ground piece by piece.

"What dark thoughts are going through your head?" Camilla asked. She wound a strip of cloth around Sigrid's arm. "I know that look all too well."

"I can't control them," she whispered. "I was supposed to bring them somewhere they could live. Where they could prosper and become a people that other kingdoms would admire. All I've done is given them free rein to be even more animalistic than before."

"That's not true. They have a warm bed, clothing, food aplenty. That's a lot better than the lives they had before."

"It's better than the *Bymerians* had," Sigrid corrected. "The Wildewyn Beastkin are used to living in castles. They're used to speaking with nobles and wearing gowns made of silk. How am I supposed to replicate that kind of life for them?"

"Has anyone asked for that?" Camilla gently cupped

Sigrid's cheek and forced her head to turn. "Even the Wildewyn Beastkin are happy here. I'd know if they weren't."

"This isn't what we were supposed to live like. We were supposed to create a kingdom, and all we're creating is ruins."

She thought for a second that Camilla might argue. A spark of anger, one she'd never seen before, made Camilla's jaw tick before her friend finally blew out a breath.

"I can't argue with that," Camilla replied, turning her attention back to the jagged wound across Sigrid's chest. "This isn't the place I thought it would be either. But the Beastkin don't want a queen. They don't want someone with a crown telling them what to do, because that's not how it works in the wild. They don't need a royal, they need a leader."

"And yet, they look to Jabbar for that." Sigrid winced when Camilla prodded the edge of her wound. Dirt and mud encrusted it, likely going to cause some kind of fever if Sigrid didn't shift again soon.

She didn't want to give the dragon another reason to take control over her body. It had already done enough in the past few hours.

Camilla smoothed a hand down Sigrid's arm and laced their fingers together. She tugged until Sigrid looked back at her. "The only time they listened to you was after the battle. When they saw what you would do for them. That you would sacrifice everything to keep them safe."

"Then they want a martyr, not a leader."

They both froze, stared at each other, and an idea formed in Sigrid's mind at the same time as it did Camilla's.

"No, Sigrid," she said. "You're not doing what you're thinking."

"If I want to give them a chance, this *kingdom* a chance, then they have to be respected among the others. We can't be animals. We have to look toward the future and not the now."

"Dash the thought from your mind, sister. It's not the right way."

But it was, and in that moment, Sigrid began to plan how she would gain control over the Beastkin once and for all.

NADIR

HE SAT ON HIS BLOOD-RED HORSE IN FRONT OF THE CASTLE, WAITING for the first sign of movement on the sand. A courier had ridden ahead of the Earthen King. He wanted them to know when he was arriving, to ensure that no one was startled, the courier said.

Nadir had a feeling it was more to make sure that they were ready to receive him. There was a certain level of decorum kings expected. Nadir didn't really care what people thought when he rode into the cities. But he did like to make a scene when he arrived, so he understood the king's decisions in a sense.

His horse shied to the side, hide rippling with agitation. The warhorse was more suited to battle than it was to waiting, but Abdul had insisted they at least meet the king with their own forces.

A cloud appeared on the horizon, but not one that was filled with rain. Nadir pointed toward it with his scimitar. "And finally, there they are."

Abdul snorted. "It'll take them a while still to get here."

"So we're to sit on our horses, with half the army, and stand still while they arrive?"

"Patience, my boy."

He didn't have any. Nadir had lost patience the moment Beastkin had attacked his kingdom and he'd watched the woman he loved breathe fire over his home.

Nadir let out a soft snort, then swung his leg over his horse. Sliding down the hide of the beast, he soothed its twitches with quiet sounds. He pressed a hand against its neck and stroked the strong muscle that shifted beneath his palm. His horse didn't want to wait for the Earthen folk any more than he did.

"Nadir," Abdul said, his voice pitched low but clearly scolding. "What do you think you're doing? You're meant to stand with the army."

"Why?"

"To show that you are here for us. That you are going to fight with them if they need you to."

Nadir shook his head, patted the horse's hide once more, then looked up at his advisor who sat straight and proud astride his own horse. "But we don't need an army for this anymore. We need nothing more than *me*."

The change rippled over him as easily as it was to change clothing. Nadir didn't know when it had grown this easy for him to change. There was no pain. No guilt. Nothing more than the overwhelming sense of freedom that rolled in his gut until he didn't know which way was up and which way was down.

Shaking his head, he shifted his neck to look back at the army of men who had all taken steps backwards. Those on horses tried to quiet their mounts which reared up in shock. But his own warhorse stood silent with legs locked.

A good, fearless horse. He hadn't expected that.

He nodded at his advisor, then stretched his wings wide. He took a few beats and lifted into the air. Opening his jaw, he let out a roar that echoed over the desert. Fire bubbled in his chest, and he didn't hesitate to let it free. Let the Earthen folk see for themselves the dragon their people had fought. Let them understand the fear which had caused their brethren to ultimately flee.

He looped around the Wildewyn army. Taking his time to peruse the amount of people the Earthen King had brought. There weren't as many soldiers as he expected. Actually, it was a relatively small number of people who had crossed the border.

Did the king think he wasn't in any danger from the Bymerians? He most certainly was. Nadir's army could destroy this small army with little more than a thought.

Fire built in his chest at the slightest hint of anger in his body. *He* could destroy this army with nothing more than a breath.

A few of the soldiers looked up and pointed at him. The sound of their distressed shouts reached his ears and made him want to roar once more. They needed to understand that no one would attack this land again when dealing with Nadir personally. And that a full-grown male dragon was something to fear.

Still, they had come here in peace. A soft voice whispered in his mind that Sigrid would expect something better from him. That she would expect him to be a gracious host who would try to understand what these foreigners wanted.

Even now, these were the words that made the fire die in his chest. These were the thoughts that stilled the animal which wanted to crawl out of his chest and rend flesh from bone. The dragon wanted to feast on the approaching armies simply because they were within his territories. The man understood that politics had to be observed.

A sultan was there for his people. A dragon was only there for war.

Circling one last time, making a point that he was a dangerous man who should not be toyed with, Nadir landed in front of the army. He opened his jaws and hissed at them, the sound blasting sand into their faces.

By the time the sand settled, he was a man once more, kneeling in the sand with his fist pressed against it.

A wind tugged at the baggy, silk pants. The yellow fabric covered his entire body, and perhaps hid him from view until he stood up, his dark hair brushing in front of his face.

The feral grin which spread across his face likely did nothing to soothe the soldier's nerves. A group of ten men raced forward, spears in their hands as they set themselves in front of a large, brown horse.

Nadir recognized the king. He was a man who easily stood out from the crowd with his broad shoulders, perfectly groomed beard, and eyes that could have sliced through ice. Blue as the sky, they found his gaze even through the line of shouting soldiers.

"Enough!" Hallmar bellowed, raising a hand curled in a fist. "Stand down."

"Highness, we will fight the dragon for you," one of the soldiers yelled in return.

At that, Hallmar swung off his horse and strode toward the man. He grabbed onto the edge of the soldier's metal armor, right near his throat, and hauled the man toward him. "What did I say, soldier?"

"Stand down, Highness."

Nadir could almost hear the man's gulp from where he stood.

"Correct," Hallmar said. He gave the man one more shake before tossing him aside. "Next time, follow orders immediately."

The disobedience forgotten, the king strode toward Nadir with his hand outstretched. "It's good to see you again, Sultan. I see you have some surprises to tell me."

Nadir furrowed his brows, but stepped forward to greet the king in the same manner. He allowed the other man to grasp his forearm and shake it before tilting his head to the side and asking, "That's it?"

"What's it?"

"You have nothing more to say than I have surprises to tell you? As if we're old friends?"

"Are we not?" Hallmar tugged him a step closer and dropped his voice. "I gave you my most precious possession in this world. I think we're friends at this point, Nadir. Although, if you didn't treat her as well as I think you did… well. Perhaps then we're not."

"We did start a war."

Hallmar lifted a pale brow. "That you did. But wars are started between lovers every day. The first battle is always a little bloody, but that doesn't mean the war is over. Now does it?"

73

The words had so many hidden meanings in them that Nadir's head started to spin. What did the king mean? A battle, a war, every lover doing the same?

This wasn't the same as any other relationship on the planet. His and Nadir's life were so dangerously intertwined in the worst way possible. They couldn't be together without more fighting starting, no matter what kingdom they were in. But they were both intrigued by the other, and tied together by a similar life which could not be untied even with a knife.

Nadir cleared his throat and stepped back. "I think we have a lot to talk about, Earthen King."

"I see that. You did arrive all by yourself to greet me. I must profess, I assumed I would be greeted with an army before I met with you."

"Well," Nadir glanced pointedly at the sky, "there is the small matter of the dragon."

"I suppose you don't need an army anymore, now do you?"

"An army can still take down a dragon. It's easy enough to shoot something like that out of the sky."

A deep growl rolled out of Hallmar's mouth. They both stood still for a second, staring at each other in surprise before Hallmar cleared his throat. "Yes, I have heard that you've created a way to shoot dragons out of the sky. Haven't you?"

Gods. Nadir didn't know how to reply to that. He *had* been part of creating a weapon that could kill both him and Sigrid. That wasn't a secret, obviously, but he'd thought that he and Sigrid had laid that to rest.

"I did," he finally replied. "To protect both of our kingdoms, I would happily share the blueprints with you."

"I don't need that, boy." Hallmar's words were harsh, but his expression had softened into a fatherly look of sadness and guilt. "If someone is going to kill a dragon, then it should only be one of their own kind. I learned that the hard way."

"The hard way?"

"There's much for us to talk about, and I have no interest in allowing prying ears to eavesdrop." Hallmar glanced at his soldiers who had somehow moved closer to them. "Shall we?"

"The Red Palace is ready to receive you, Earthen King."

"I suppose we should offer you a horse then? Since you didn't arrive with your own."

At that, Nadir's cheeks burned. "Thank you. That would be much appreciated, although I can fly above you."

"No need to tire yourself. For now, we are all among friends."

Nadir didn't want to point out that both their armies disagreed with that statement. They'd both arrived armed to the teeth, ready to protect their leaders to the death. The Bymerians might have an army, but he had a feeling the few men Hallmar had brought were just as deadly as Nadir's best soldiers.

They traveled in silence across the sands. Nadir listened to shifting saddles, the quiet hush of sand sliding over metal armor, and the occasional shake of a horse's head that made the reins slap against their necks.

His horse was a relatively quiet beast. It didn't shy away from him, a rarity that he appreciated, but also seemed content to simply follow Hallmar's horse anywhere it might want to go.

It dawned on him as they approached the army that Hallmar had placed him on a pack horse. Nadir sighed and allowed the sleight to fall to the wayside.

Perhaps, a year ago when he had still been young and brash, he would have insisted the king make amends for it. But now, he wasn't interested in an argument at the man's attempt to make him seem less important. He'd come from the sky in the form of a great red dragon, breathed fire over Hallmar's armies and made them quake in fear.

He didn't need to remind them who was the more dangerous ruler.

"Sultan!" Abdul called out, a hand on the hilt of his scimitar. "All is well?"

Nadir gave his advisor a confused look, playing an act that he knew Hallmar would appreciate. "I don't see why it wouldn't be? Hallmar, king, is certainly no fool. He will not attack a dragon if he has no reason to. We head to the Red Palace where I expect food and drink to be ready for his men. They've traveled a long way to speak to me." He emphasized the last word, knowing his advisor would hear the intent.

He didn't want any of his personal advisors to be there while he spoke with Hallmar. There was so much he wanted to ask, and their opinions would only cloud his judgment. This was a decision he would make on his own. No one else would sway his words.

The king glanced over at him with a small smile. "I see much has changed since the last time I saw you, Sultan of Bymere."

"Ah, but some things don't change. I'm still as arrogant a fool as you've been expecting." Nadir's weight shifted as the horse began the steep ascent toward the Red Palace where it glowed in the dying light.

The sunset always made his palace turn blood red. He looked up at the new buildings and felt a surge of pride at what they had been able to do. His people were far hardier than he'd ever given them credit for. Perhaps they really could rebuild something great even after something so disastrous as a dragon attack.

Nadir guided his horse to the side route that would lead to the castle gates. He didn't want to parade the King of Wildewyn in front of the Bymerian people. They already hated each other. The last thing he needed was some foolish peasant tossing refuse at the king.

He stopped his horse before the Red Palace, handed the reins to the boy waiting for him, and didn't stop to direct the king. He could follow Nadir if he wished, or be left to the crowd that was gathering to stare at them. His people hadn't seen someone from Wildewyn in a very long time, other than Sigrid who seemed an entirely different creature than the Earthen folk.

The clipped steps of the king and his soldiers followed him quickly through the halls. He strode past the billowing lengths of red curtains touched by a gentle wind. Past the pools of glistening water and the arched doorways leading to endless libraries filled with knowledge that Nadir couldn't even begin to comprehend.

Only once he reached his personal quarters did he stop and look over his shoulder. The king stood with his soldiers behind him, utterly out of place in this castle.

Where his people were worn by the wind, Hallmar and his men were strong and solid like trees growing deep in the ground. The Bymerians were used to the hardships of the sands. They blended into crowds easily, hid from prying eyes, sometimes even disappeared from view like the djinn.

These people wanted to be seen. And perhaps that was what had always bothered him about the Earthen folk. They were unashamed to be seen and heard. They stomped through life with little resistance.

Nadir wished he was like that. He wanted for so many years for someone to *see* him, the real him, and now thousands of people knew what he was. He'd take it all back if he could.

He looked over the soldiers with their hands forcefully gripping the hilts of their swords, ready for any attack, and then snorted. "You're not bringing your soldiers into my private chambers, Your Majesty."

"You can hardly expect me to go anywhere without protection."

Nadir arched a brow. "Yet, you want me to allow your men entrance with blades that can easily kill me? I think not. This conversation should be made king to king, and that is my final offer. You wished to speak, Hallmar. I'm offering you a conversation."

"I have no wish for prying ears to hear what I have to say."

"And there will be none." Nadir pointedly looked at the door to his room, a solid oak structure they'd pulled up from Wildewyn a long time ago. It was the only room thus far which had a door for a reason.

Hallmar's shoulders sagged and finally he nodded. "If that is what it takes."

A soldier stepped up. "Sire—"

"I'll have none of your arguments. If the sultan wishes to speak with me privately before we have an official attendance with his advisors, then this is what we shall do."

The king of Wildewyn walked toward him with a set to his shoulders that suggested he thought Nadir was going to attempt to kill him. Strange, really, because Nadir hadn't done anything thus far which would make the man think that.

Arriving in the form of a dragon certainly wouldn't have been seen as *that* much of a threat. He hadn't tried to kill anyone, and he certainly hadn't eaten any of the soldiers no matter how enticing it seemed.

Once inside his personal room, Nadir cast a glance around to make sure everything was in order. The crimson blankets covering his pillow strewn bed were as haphazard as always. The hand-carved desk was piled with vellum and parchment he hadn't looked at yet. The pools in the corners of the rooms shifted as the fish inside them struggled to catch the bugs he threw in every morning.

Silence rang true and loud as the door shut behind them. The shifting of metal armor behind it suggested Hallmar's men hadn't gone very far.

Nadir pointed at the noise. "Will they press their ear to the surface?"

"Are your doors not thick enough to discourage snooping?"

The king had a point. Nadir sighed, then stalked to his table and pulled out a drink. "One for you?" he asked.

Hallmar shook his head.

Did the king think Nadir was planning to poison him? There were far easier ways to kill someone, and much less messy than watching them foam at the mouth. Shrugging, he poured himself a glass of the carefully curated wine and drank deeply.

Wiping his mouth on the back of his hand, he finally let out a frustrated sound. The question which burned in his mind finally burst free from his lips. "How is she?"

Hallmar met his gaze with a bemused smile. "Who?"

"Don't play with me, Earthen King. You know of whom I speak."

"I have no idea why you'd be asking about the creature who tried to kill much of your people, unless you want to know whether we put her down."

The glass in Nadir's hand shattered. When had he grown so angry? The king was only saying the same thing that his own advisors had said. There was no reason for Nadir to still be attached to the girl. She'd done enough to prove that she didn't care for his kingdom.

Or him.

But he still dreamt of her at night. The way the firelight had played across her face the first time he'd seen her. The arch of her neck when she tilted her head just so, to see the smile in his eyes that he always had hoped she saw.

He blew out a breath, trying to dispel the ghost of her memory. "Just tell me."

"She's doing well," Hallmar finally relented. "The kingdom she has created flourishes, as far as I know. Although, she seemed tired the last time I saw her."

"Aren't we all?" Nadir replied with a scoff. "I don't remember the last time I got a full night's sleep."

"You'll get used to it." Hallmar strode to the chair in front of Nadir's desk and sank down into its plush pillows. "You seem to have taken much more control than I remember you having."

"Someone told me that a ruler chooses, but a slave waits for others to tell him what to do." Nadir tilted the glass in a mock toast. "I took that to heart."

"As much as I wish to take credit for this change, I have a feeling it has very little to do with me."

"You might be right about that."

Hallmar cleared his throat and leaned forward, bracing his forearms on his thighs. "You are a Beastkin as well?"

"I thought rumors of that would have reached your kingdom by now."

"Hearing it and seeing it are two very different things. Rumors always hold a fraction of truth, but I never guessed these tales were entirely truthful."

Nadir spread his arms wide and let the king look his fill. "Then see the Beastkin for yourself, Earthen King."

"That must have been difficult for you," Hallmar murmured. "Considering how adamant you were that there was no such thing as a dragon Beastkin."

"Can you not understand why? I hardly wanted to believe that I was even capable of this madness. Seeing another person who was the same as I was? Afflicted by the same plague which had always made me hide in the shadows? It's not something I ever wanted to face in my lifetime."

Hallmar leaned back forcefully in his chair, then hooked his ankle over his knee. "Is that what you believe? That being a Beastkin is something like a disease or an illness?"

Nadir watched the king's foot bounce and pondered his words. If he'd asked them years ago, then his response would have been a very swift and resounding *yes*. Of course he had believed the Beastkin were a problem. They were a pest which needed to be dealt with swiftly and eradicated so the rest of his kingdom could flourish in their absence.

Now, he wasn't so certain. He'd seen the way Sigrid had been an asset to his kingdom. She'd guided his people toward a softer future, one where they were significantly kinder to other people. Even to each other.

"I don't know," he replied honestly. "I don't know what to think of the Beastkin. On one hand, my entire training and life has been spent hating the creatures. The history of my kingdom is in direct opposition to them. But on the other, I've seen what they can do. I've seen the good in their hearts and how their children don't view us as anything other than a terrifying mass of people who want them dead. It's hard to reconcile what I know with what also is."

"Being a king isn't all that easy, is it?"

"A sultan," Nadir corrected. Then cautiously added, "but you are correct. I have to think from every angle. I will admit, it's difficult to view the world as some of my own people do. Namely, because of what I am."

"This is why I wanted your ear." Hallmar stared him down, blue eyes so full of emotion they almost glowed. "Our people don't need to fight. This is a century-old hate that comes from Beastkin and humans, not from kingdom and kingdom. What fight do we have together? There's no reason to hate each other's countries."

"It's widely known that Wildewyn steals water from Bymere, which is why our kingdom is arid and desert."

Hallmar waved a hand in the air, dismissing the words and wiping them away as if Nadir had never said them. "That's simply the way the world was formed. Wildewyn didn't do anything other than survive with your leftovers. Flourish, even. Our people want to live in peace, just as yours do."

The words made sense, but they didn't fit in with the world Nadir knew. He'd already seen that there was much he didn't know. So many things that Bymerians had gotten wrong, or perhaps just the royals had gotten wrong.

Stories and fables were one thing, but facts that he could see, touch, understand were far more important to him now. Nadir nodded slowly. "I see your point, Hallmar."

"Then you do not wish for this war either?"

"I didn't say that." Nadir rifled through some of the paperwork on his desk, then slid a single sheet of parchment toward Hallmar. "You also can't deny the truth in this."

The king's eyes scanned the document for a moment before glancing up. There was a haunted look in his eyes, one that Nadir recognized from staring in the mirror in the morning. The king had the same reaction to the truth in front of him. That was just how Nadir had felt when his advisors had brought it before him.

"Damning evidence," the king said quietly. "I'm not sure how or why you have this."

"Neither am I. This is one of the many documents of Beastkin hunting in Bymere." Nadir leaned back, exhaustion riding on his shoulders like a well-worn cloak. He'd felt this way so often lately that he didn't know what it meant to not be tired. "If this gets out—"

"Then we can't let it."

"How am I supposed to stop people from finding out the truth? Your people used to hunt ours for sport. That's how the Beastkin ended up in Bymere. That's why we hunted them in return, and that is why such hatred grew."

Hallmar leaned forward, his voice pitched low and his shoulders tense with emotion. "We cannot let this get out. This is something you and I can control. Let such foolish pain remain in the past and our people will forget the follies."

"If I had that much control over my advising council, do you really think I would have accepted your visit?" Nadir tilted his head to the side and felt the satisfying pop of his neck. Some of the tension drained out, but not enough. "I wish there was more I could do, Hallmar. They're blackmailing me just as much as I am blackmailing you."

"Then there's nothing you and I can settle on?" he asked. "Nothing at all that could save our kingdoms centuries more of fighting and death and bloodshed."

"If I could do more, I would. My people desire some kind of retribution for the attack from before, and all the history between our countries. I don't want to fight anymore." Nadir clenched his fists. "There's only so much control I've gained here, and much of it is superficial. I have to be careful about my decisions in the coming years. Once the kingdom rallies behind me, I can get rid of my council for good. These are words that stay between the two of us, yes?"

Hallmar nodded.

"Then listen to me, Earthen King. If you can survive a war for the next few years, then I will be able to do much more than just sign paperwork. I can stop our people from fighting. I can do more than a sultan can do now. But in this moment?" Nadir shook his head and tried to hide that his fingers were shaking by crossing his arms. "I cannot stop the growing beast of hatred within my kingdom. I've tried. And I failed."

"I had hoped my appearance here would somehow ease the fears of Bymerians. They could see that myself and my soldiers are nothing more than men. There are so few Beastkin in my kingdom."

But that was a lie, wasn't it? There were far more Beastkin in the king's homeland than here in Bymere.

Nadir shook his head. "That's not exactly true, now is it? You've not only harbored Beastkin for centuries, but now you've given them a kingdom. I have no more words to argue with. The Bymerians are convinced you support the animals who have attacked us for years."

"I do," Hallmar replied. "And so do you."

"In this case, my wishes are irrelevant." Nadir reached forward and took the parchment back from Hallmar.

He wished he didn't feel powerless now. When Abdul had brought the documentation to Nadir, he'd done everything he could to prove it wrong. Surely this was forged. There was no way that the Beastkin had been sent by a previous Earthen King. No one was that foolish.

But apparently, they were. There were problems across every kingdom on this godsforsaken rock, but this was something that couldn't go unnoticed. It didn't matter that it had happened centuries ago. It didn't matter that Nadir's line likely hadn't even risen to power yet.

It mattered that the Wildewyn people had hunted, murdered, and eaten many Bymerians in their days. Something like that couldn't slide by without a good sultan addressing it.

He'd tried to argue they could seek restitution in another way. That the Wildewyn king could pay them in food, grains, water—anything that would make the people prosper and grow without more bloodshed.

His advisor council had shot down each suggestion, growing more angry each time. They wanted bloodshed. They advised that a kingdom grew more during times of war. That he would be a fool to pass up an opportunity like this.

And then Abdul had said the crowning words which had forced Nadir to this moment in time.

Nadir would never forget the words that were now burned into his mind.

"You may love her, Sultan, but that doesn't mean we won't take the steps to give this kingdom what it deserves. If you aren't prepared to do this, then the council members will take it upon themselves to reveal the truth to our people. No matter what the cost."

At first, he'd thought it a bluff. The council wouldn't go behind his back. They wouldn't try to strong-arm their sultan into doing what they wanted.

Only after he pushed did he realize they were all very serious about the transgression. The copy they had given Nadir was nothing more than a copy. The original was locked away somewhere, far from Nadir's grasp. They would do whatever it took to make sure the Bymerian people knew that the Earthen folk were the monsters underneath their beds at night, the howl of the winds at their door, the drag of a sword across their throats.

A war was coming. Whether Nadir wanted it or not.

The tension in the back of his neck burst into an aggressive headache that made him wince. He touched a hand to the tender flesh at the back of his neck. "I wish there was more I could do, Hallmar. I really do. There's so much our people could build if we could but work together. I want you to know I see that. The future in my mind is not war or bloodshed."

"And yet, you will do nothing to stop this."

"I cannot."

"You are the Sultan of Bymere. The fact you still think there are chains around you shows that you haven't grown as much as I thought you had." The Earthen King stood abruptly. His eyes stared down at Nadir, disapproving and cold. "The way Sigrid spoke, it sounded as if you were well on your way to being a respectable ruler. I see now, she was wrong."

"There's only so much I can do."

"You are the royal blood. You are the Sultan, their leader, their god if you wish to be. Do not tell me there are limits to what you can do."

Hallmar stalked to the door without looking back. He slammed the door open, the precious wood hitting stone walls with a thud that echoed throughout the room.

Soldiers snapped to attention, the metal of their armor clanking as they tried to prepare themselves for the wrath of their king.

"We're leaving," Hallmar snapped. "This was a wasted effort. The entire kingdom is filled with fools."

"Careful what you say," Nadir called out, eyes still on the desk in front of him. "You are in my kingdom, Earthen King. Only so many insults will be ignored before I will have to take action and make sure you remember insulting the Sultan of Bymere is a dangerous thing to do."

Rage shook Hallmar's shoulders. His voice deepened in his reply, "You are nothing more than a boy."

An answering anger rose in Nadir's chest. Slowly, he stood

from his desk and straightened his broad shoulders. He waited until the Earthen King looked toward him, then Nadir lifted a dark brow.

"I may be a boy king," he replied, "but I have an army at my disposal and a dragon in my chest. Threaten me one more time, and I will pick your soldiers' meat from between my teeth with *your* bones."

The Earthen King and his soldiers stalked away, leaving Nadir with a pit in his stomach. What had he just begun?

SIGRID

SIGRID CROUCHED ON TOP OF THE HIGHEST PEAK OF THE KEEP, watching the Beastkin work in their daily toils. Her hand curled around a tall wooden spire. It crumbled beneath her solid grip, but she continued to slide her hand down to give herself balance.

If anyone looked up, they would see their matriarch precariously close to falling. Not that it mattered really. She would change before she hit the ground.

But that was the main problem, now wasn't it? The Beastkin were almost too powerful. They could change at will, tumble from the sky, fall off a cliff, and they would still come out unscathed. How was that fair to the humans who had looked to them as monsters in the night? They couldn't fight against animals. They couldn't battle creatures that looked one way and then changed in a moment's notice.

In some small way, Sigrid understood why the humans feared them so much. Why they would want to destroy every last one of them if only to sleep well at night.

Feathers touched down on stone beside her. Sigrid hadn't heard Camilla approach. The owl's wings were far more silent than any leathery appendage, or even that of a hawk or eagle.

Her sister planted her butt on the steep roof, crossed her arms over her knees, and stared down at the people as well. "You've receded back into your mind," she commented.

"It's the only safe place for me to truly say what I think."

"You could always talk to me."

"You're one of them," Sigrid replied, but her tone was soft and kind. "You always were more like them than I ever could be. I never understood it until all of us were together. You see the animals inside them, and you accept that for what it is. You can hear their voices in your head, and it doesn't sound like a garbled bang of animalistic sounds. Their language is yours."

Camilla shrugged. "It could be yours as well if you let go a little. But you've always had trouble with that. It's why I've always stuck around beside you. I help."

But could Camilla help her any more? Sigrid wanted desperately to learn what the other Beastkin were thinking. She wanted to let go of her human chains and become something *more*, like they had done.

She didn't think it was possible. Every fiber of her being wanted something more than to be just a dragon. Something more than just... Sigrid sighed and shook her head to clear the dark thoughts from her mind.

There was only so much she could dwell on before it all turned to shadows and darkness in her mind.

Camilla shifted again, staring straight at her with eyes that saw too much. "Sigrid, tell me what's going through your head."

"You were right," she whispered. "They don't need a queen or a leader. They need a martyr, a symbol that will make them realize the world isn't at their feet. Someone has to prove to them that the world out there can be more than just enemies."

"I don't like where your thoughts are going."

"Neither did I. But the more I thought about it, the more it made sense." Sigrid met her friend's gaze and tried to soak in every inch of Camilla. It could be a long time before she saw her sweet sister again. "And I need you to help me."

"What are you planning to do?"

She almost didn't want to tell her, but there was very little time to put it in place. Sigrid had spent the better portion of the night staring into the darkness, thinking about this moment. There were times when she wished she hadn't ever become a matriarch.

This was one of them.

Sighing, she released her hold on the spire and slid down beside Camilla. Taking her sister's hand in hers, Sigrid lifted it to her mouth and pressed a kiss to Camilla's knuckles.

"They need a martyr. And the only way to do that is for someone to die."

"You aren't killing yourself."

"I wasn't planning on it." Sigrid looked down at the dark hand in hers and wished they'd had more time together. Camilla was her dearest friend, but also part of her own soul. How could she say goodbye when there was so much that was going to be left unsaid? "Remember the stories you used to tell me? The ones your mother always told by the fire before the sickness took her?"

"Which ones?"

Sigrid lifted their joined hands and pointed toward a range of mountains almost entirely out of sight. "The ones about those hills. About the caverns and the people who lived in them."

Camilla nodded. "The ancient Beastkin who could not die, and who could not live among us. Sigrid, those were just stories. Little things to tell children so they believed in a history that wasn't just death and sadness. The ancients aren't real."

"But what if they are? What if those legends were passed down through generations because the ancients wanted us to find them?"

Sigrid hadn't put much thought into the stories either until she'd been dragged all the way to Bymere and realized there was so much more to this world.

Lying in the darkness of her bedroom, terrified that the path she'd led her people down was even more dangerous than their original one, she'd heard Camilla's mother's voice in the shadows. Like tendrils of a song, they reached for her and whispered the old tales.

In her mind, she saw Camilla's mother, the woman they'd both only known as "Mother," beckon them forward.

"Come here, little girls. Would you stop putting your fingers in the bread before its risen, Camilla? My goodness, the two of you are going to be the death of me. Sit by the fire, if you're so impatient, and I'll tell you a story."

They'd raced to the hearth immediately, tumbling on top of each other in a tangle of girlish limbs and giggles that lifted into the rafters. Mother had smiled, patted the both of them on the head, and then settled into her rocking chair she always kept by the flames.

Sigrid could still smell her scent, the warmth and happiness in her gaze when she and Camilla remembered the little things she'd taught them. Camilla's family had taken her in when her own mother had died. They'd given her a good life. One that made her more than just a dragonling, but a little girl.

"Have you ever heard of the ancients? No? Well, let me tell you then, my sweet. Long ago, before the Beastkin climbed down from the mountains and into the arms of men, we lived in a kingdom all of our own.

"There were many of us there, so many that the animals left the mountains alone, because even they knew that only magical creatures could live there.

"But even more than that, there were Beastkin who were immortal."

Both Sigrid and Camilla had gasped at that, their minds whirling with the possibilities. Immortal? Creatures who couldn't die, no matter who tried to kill them?

Mother had laughed at their questions.

"No, children. They could be killed. They were not impervious to the blade of a sword. But they would live forever if they wished and stayed out of trouble.

"Among them was the greatest of all Beastkin. Maja. Mother of all, and the eternal matriarch who was the first to give flight to the great phoenix of old.

"She was the one who first breathed life into the other Beastkin. It's said her tears could heal even mortal wounds, and that she watched over all her children with a shrewd eye. That's where the great river comes from, the one that runs from Bymere all the way through Wildewyn. Legends say when the first Beastkin climbed down from the mountains, Maja cried so much that the world overflowed with her *tears."*

Sigrid had shifted, looking up at their shared mother with large eyes. "Why did she cry? Isn't it a good thing that the Beastkin came down? We live in harmony with the humans now?"

Shadows darkened Mother's eyes. She'd shook her head, reached down for Sigrid's hands, and squeezed them tight. "You are far too kind for your own good, little Sigrid. Someday, that will be your undoing I worry.

"Maja cried because she had seen the future. She knew what the humans would do to her children, and there was nothing she could do to stop them. They would put them in gilded cages, only taken out to fight in defense of a people who did not truly love us. That is the greatest story of them all.

"For even though she didn't agree with the choices her children had made, she let them go. For the love in her heart was far greater than the worry in her stomach."

Sigrid squeezed Mother's hands back and looked at Camilla. "But, if she knew it would be bad, why wouldn't she just tell them?"

Mother had shrugged and released Sigrid back to Camilla's arms. "No one knows. Perhaps she didn't know it would be like this. Or perhaps, she knew there was a greater story coming and that she couldn't intervene. Someday, one of us will travel back into those mountains and find the ancients.

"It's said they know secrets that the Beastkin have long forgotten. Secrets that could change the world forever."

Mother's voice faded from her mind and melded with Camilla's on top of the keep. Her sister pulled her hands out of Sigrid's.

"What are you thinking? Sigrid, those are just stories!

There's no such thing as ancients. There's no secret power in this world that will make the Beastkin better. Don't you see? Mother used to tell us those stories just to get us to quiet down. We were unruly children. It was hard enough to keep us entertained without stories that would make us have nightmares."

"I don't think that's what it is." Sigrid shrugged. "In any sense, I can't stay here."

"Why not?"

"You've seen that I'm different from the rest of them. They don't look at me like a Beastkin. They already look at me like I'm some kind of paragon. The longer I'm here, the sooner they'll discover that's entirely false. Then where will they be? The dragon female who saved them is just a woman, and they're just Beastkin. And the world isn't what they think it is."

"Sigrid…" Camilla's voice trailed off, and she stared down at the Beastkin below them.

In some way, her sister had to realize Sigrid was right. She didn't belong here in this house filled with animals. The mere dirt offended her, more than it had when they were traveling. This place was supposed to be a home, and instead, it felt like a barn.

Finally, Camilla cursed and nodded. "What's the plan then? What are you thinking?"

"We're supposed to have a gathering in an hour or so. Jabbar wanted to address the crowd, something about his new plans for how we're going to engage any human who comes to our doors. He doesn't want the Earthen King sending any more messengers without us knowing."

"And?" Camilla asked when Sigrid paused.

"There's a rise over where we usually meet. Up on the mountain peak, where I can be visible and seen. I'll address the rest of them over Jabbar, let them know that humans are friends. That we cannot view them as an enemy or they will become one. Then, I want you to shoot me with an arrow."

The long pause between them stretched until she thought Camilla had stopped breathing. Her friend stared at her in shock before shaking her head.

"What?"

"Not fatally. Just through the shoulder but close enough so it'll look as though I had died. Something like that should do well enough to convince people that we were attacked, and that the matriarch was the target."

Camilla scoffed. "They'll think it was the humans. This will backfire tremendously."

"Not if you convince them that you saw a Beastkin with the arrow. We'll carve a mark on it, one that the Wildewyn beasts will recognize from Bymere. It's a simple thing to do, really. Cause a little bit of mistrust between the two groups so they all take a step back and look at their actions."

A chip of the stone roof loosened beneath her foot and skittered down the steep edge. Sigrid listened for its strike to the ground, the shattering sound similar to the pain she felt in her chest.

"I—" Camilla hesitated, then licked her lips. "Then what?"

"We'll tip the arrow in verdant poison. You remember the frogs we used to catch when we were little? Those will send someone into a deep sleep. It's like death, but they'll wake up after a time. Dangerous, perhaps, but I remember the amount that we'll need to use. You'll bury me with the rest of them, and then, when all is said and done, I'll dig myself back out."

"Are you going to tell Raheem?" Camilla asked. "You know he's not due back for a little while."

"I sent a message." The pigeon had been disgruntled at being used so early in the morning, but Sigrid was confident it would find Raheem in time. "If he gets back, then he'll help dig me out of the grave. If not, I think I can manage on my own."

"I don't like it." There was something hidden in Camilla's gaze, something that spoke of an age old heartbreak and a vast desire to fix something that would forever be broken. "I don't think you have to run from these people, Sigrid. I think you could stay and we could fix this. Together."

"We both know that's not true." She touched a finger to Camilla's chin. "I don't expect to be gone forever, just enough to find out where we came from. Who we are. If I don't find these things out soon I feel as though I'm going to burst."

"You can't be a real Beastkin until you know the answers to these questions, can you?" Camilla's voice was quiet, a whisper on the wind as silent as an owl's wings. "I'm afraid for you."

"You should be afraid for yourself," Sigrid said, her lips quirking in a smile. "I want you to take over for me. Let them know that you are my successor. That *you* are the only one I would choose to be Matriarch after me."

"Brynhild is bigger and stronger."

"But no one has a mind like yours. No one understands the Beastkin so thoroughly, with so much kindness and the ability to see what others do not. I want you to lead these people out of the darkness and into your own version of light." Sigrid tapped her chin for good measure. "That's final, Camilla. You'll do better than you think."

A ragged sound of frustration and sadness tore out of her friend's chest. "I don't want to do any of this without you, Sigrid."

"We don't often get what we want," Sigrid replied.

She stared down at the kingdom she'd created and marveled at how much could change so quickly. She wanted to help them, but in that desire came her own need for freedom. She'd traded cages for cages her entire life. Just once, she wanted to be selfish.

She wanted to be free.

THEY ALL GATHERED IN THE SQUARE OF THE KEEP. PERHAPS THEY WERE waiting for her, perhaps they weren't. Sigrid wasn't really sure if Jabbar would start his speech without her.

She thought he would. He'd never liked sharing the spotlight when it didn't suit his means, and he wanted them to disregard anything she had to say. Sigrid was a thorn in his side, because she didn't think the Beastkin could be so ready to break away from the humans. A shame he didn't see the world the way she did.

Sigrid spread her leathery wings wide and circled the courtyard one more time before making her way to the spot where she would, effectively die. She thought in this moment she would be a little uncomfortable. Who wouldn't be?

Instead, she had complete trust in Camilla's ability to do

everything exactly as she was supposed to. There wasn't a bone in her sister's body that would let her make a mistake in this moment.

Her only regret was that Raheem wasn't here. He'd gone off to investigate the rest of the kingdom for her, and now he was going to return only to hear about her death. The messenger pigeon had returned empty-handed, but that wasn't like Raheem. He would have sent her a message as well, one that would have yelled at her for making foolish decisions. That she was too much like Nadir.

It was too late to stop now.

She landed on the stone ledge where she'd made so many difficult choices. Settling down comfortably, she folded her wings at her sides and shook herself. The change shuddered through her being until she was a woman once again, plain gown hugging her curves with a golden mask in her hand.

This would be the last time she saw the metal apparel. It needed to stay here with her sisters, so they would have something to remember her by when the world felt as though it was falling down around their ears. It wouldn't be an easy loss for them. Sigrid had always been something like the glue that kept them all together. The others were so much more prone to arguing with each other, fighting, throwing tantrums....

She couldn't worry about them anymore. She'd already made this choice, and it was the right one. It had to be.

Jabbar's voice reached her at the cliff edge where he'd already begun without her. In some ways, she was correct. The man didn't want anything to do with her, because he thought she was going to mess with him.

Sadly, she was right about his speech as well.

"We cannot allow humans anywhere near our homelands!" he shouted, his voice carrying with it an air of crazed madness. "They want to take everything we have fought for. What reason have they to let us have these lands without a fight? They will make sure we regret every instance of our rebellion, and that all starts with the first human to take foot in our lands without permission! It is already starting, brothers and sisters! And it has only just begun."

His insanity ran deep inside his being. Why hadn't Sigrid seen that from the first moment she met him? Even in their home country of Bymere, he'd been a radical. There was a violent streak of hate in him that he couldn't see past, and that was going to drown him.

She cupped her hands around her mouth and let out a whooping call. It echoed through the air, striking down upon the Beastkin crowd like arrows hailing from the sky.

They all paused in their movements, then looked up at her where she stood on the cliff edge.

They wouldn't be able to see her face, so she would need to make things a little easier for them. Sigrid wasn't one to speak of her emotions often. It felt wrong to give them voice when she already hated them so much. But it was important now that they not misunderstand her. They needed to get every inch of her knowledge before she tore their world away from them.

"Brothers and sisters!" she called. "Do not listen to these poisonous words for that is all they are! Poison to turn your mind away from the future which we could have!"

A ripple spread through the crowd. Some of the Beastkin turned to see her, and she knew these were the ones who thought she was the better fit as a ruler. They were the ones whose opinions she could easily change. It was the ones who looked to Jabbar for his reaction that would be much more difficult for her to convince.

"The humans are not monsters," she said, letting the wind carry her voice to the Beastkin below her. "They want to leave us alone. This is what the Wildewyn King told me, and I believe him!"

Jabbar's laughter filled the air like a cloud had passed over the sun. "You believe him? The king of fools who kept your people in cages? I know you have a soft touch, Sigrid, but I thought you would be more inclined to condemn him for all the things he has done to you and your sisters."

"I don't claim what he did was right," she replied. "I don't claim that we should remain in cages. I acquired this kingdom for us in a political deal, not through bloodshed for violence. This is the direction we should turn our minds. How can we convince the people of Wildewyn that we deserve what we have taken? How can we assist them so that, in return, they assist us? This is the life that we have desired for so long. To be seen as *people*, not as animals."

For a second, she thought she might have them. The Beastkin below murmured among each other. Maybe Camilla was right. After all this time watching them, Sigrid might have been wrong. They might have wanted more than just animalistic natures that beckoned them into the forests where they would disappear forever.

Then, one of her own sisters raised her voice. "We don't want to be humans, Sigrid. That's something you could never understand, because you always favored them over us. But we don't want to be like them. We want to create a kingdom of our own, not mimic something humans have done for centuries. Look where's it's gotten them! Nothing but war and violence. We can stop that right now."

As quickly as she had gotten their attention, she lost it. They turned in on each other, voicing words of agreement that the humans had done so many wrong things. No Beastkin wanted to be like the humans.

Why would they? Humans had kept them in cages. Humans were the ones who had made them work or hunted them nearly to extinction.

She could almost feel the surge of triumph that made Jabbar's back straighten and his chest puff out. He could control the crowd of Beastkin with a single word, and he knew in that moment he had won.

Or, at least, he thought he had won.

Sigrid glanced toward the tower where Camilla was waiting. The sunlight glinted off the metal point of the arrow pointed directly at her.

It could have been no one else. She didn't trust even Raheem to shoot her from such a distance. But she had trained her entire life with Camilla by her side and knew how dangerous her sister was with a bow. If she wanted to shoot an apple off a mountain peak, Sigrid thought she might be able to do it.

Breathing out a slow breath, Sigrid nodded. "I ask you to trust me, Beastkin brothers and sisters. Did I not fight for you? Did I not destroy a city and rend another dragon from the sky? How else can I prove myself to you? That I seek only your best interest at heart?"

Jabbar pointed up to her. "You are nothing more than a

child. Never been married. Never had children. You haven't experienced enough of life to be able to guide us."

If she could have torn out his throat where he stood, she would have. The man had no right to judge her knowledge based on a limited number of years. She had experienced more in her time than most her age. That didn't change how much she knew, or what was right and what was wrong.

"I am begging you now, my people, my family, my friends. Do not turn your eyes away from the humans so easily, or we will all be lost." She tried to pour all her feelings and worries into the words, but knew they would be lost under the swelling wave of hatred pouring out of Jabbar.

For a moment, she thought she could almost see it. The burning ties of anger and rage that had festered inside him for so long. They stretched out toward her people and tangled around throats, wrists, ankles, anything they could find that would bind the users until they couldn't think, breathe, or hear anything but his twisted words.

"They won't listen to you on this, Sigrid," Jabbar called back. "They need to listen to me now, so they will remain safe."

"Safety isn't hiding away in caves or creating a dark space where you can remain until you rot," she replied. "Safety isn't a place; it's a state of mind."

The laughter which erupted from his mouth would echo in her mind until the end of time.

She looked back toward the window and gave the slightest of nods. Her people wouldn't have seen it. They weren't even looking at her anymore as Jabbar continued with his poisonous talk.

If one of them had noticed, they would have seen her eyes

locked on a figure in the distance, and that she poured so much love into the look that she could hardly breathe.

As the arrow whistled through the air, Sigrid let out a soft sigh. "It could only be you," she said quietly, hoping the words would fly on the winds to her dearest of sisters. "I could only trust you with this."

The arrow thudded into her torso with a blistering crack between her ribs. The pain didn't register at once. Instead, all she could feel was the cold spread of the poison they'd doused it in.

Almost immediately, she felt it weave into her blood. The drug made her body sleepy, but her mind all the sharper. It had been used many times in a king's interrogation. Let the mind see all that was done to the body but never have the option to stop what was happening.

She staggered, falling to a knee and pressing her hand to the wound.

A lone scream lifted into the air, a wail of shock and anger. At least her people were reacting. That was the plan, even if it made her heart hurt.

There was the pain. It started quietly at first, something so small that wouldn't make her entire body rebel until it realized something foreign was imbedded there.

Sigrid looked down at the arrow tip, the green fletching and rune like a sun inscribed on the side. Camilla had made the mark so well, she wondered if perhaps the Bymerian soldier had helped her. That would be a difficult thing for her to explain to anyone else who asked, but she wasn't about to look a gift in the mouth. Even the Bymerians would wonder if it was one of their own who tried to kill her.

Just in time, she heard Camilla's voice lifting from the crowd. "Matriarch? Matriarch!"

The Beastkin looked up as Sigrid held out a hand smeared with blood. It doused the front of her dress with crimson.

"*No!*" a shout echoed through the crowd.

Sigrid listed to the side as her body grew weak and numb. She was so cold. Cold as she'd never been in her life.

As she fell onto the ground, she sent a silent prayer to her ancestors. Let them have used the right amount of poison.

Or she would meet her maker this day.

CAMILLA

CAMILLA WATCHED THE FUNERAL PYRE REACH FOR THE NIGHT SKY.
and though she knew her sister wasn't dead, it still hurt to
watch Sigrid's body become engulfed in flames.

What if they hadn't measured the right amount of poison?
What if she never woke up?

It wasn't a future she could look into without tears building
in her eyes. Perhaps that was an even better addition to her act.
None of the other Beastkin would even look at her.

Her chin shook, and she took a deep breath to still herself.
There wasn't time for fake emotions like this. Sigrid would be
fine. Camilla would make sure of it, and then all would be well
in the world.

But it wouldn't. Her sister was going off on her own,
leaving Camilla here with the rabble to take care of something
that Sigrid didn't want to do.

Her heart had nearly broken in two when Sigrid had told
her the plan. She didn't want to almost kill her sister. She didn't

want to submit to this plan that would take Sigrid so far away from her. They were a pair. They went everywhere together, even when they were children.

What would she do without her sister?

"I'm sorry for your loss," Jabbar said. He appeared out of the shadows. How, Camilla could never understand.

The man's skin was white as the moon, silvery in the nighttime. He nearly glowed, and yet, could hide himself whenever he wished. Perhaps that was something to do with the thunderbird side of him. She didn't really care enough to know.

Camilla dashed a few tears from her eyes and nodded. "Thank you for that."

"Grieving is healthy, although it can be painful." He stood next to her and tucked his hands behind him. The fire reflected in his eyes. Dangerous eyes that saw far too much. "You will miss her?"

"How could I not? She was my sister."

"You're all sisters if I remember it right. There's more to those tears than just sadness at losing one of your own."

"You know nothing about my pain," Camilla spat. "We were raised together as children, spent every waking moment together. She was an extension of myself as I am an extension of her."

One of the Earthen Beastkin stepped forward and placed a bundle of lavender on the pyre. It immediately went up in flames with the rest of Sigrid's things placed beside her. The sudden burst of light reflected in Brynhild's eyes, who looked at Camilla.

"It should be her," Brynhild said, pointing at Camilla with

a shaking hand. "That's what Sigrid would have wanted."

So, it seemed she wouldn't have to plant the seed at all. Sigrid had thought the Earthen Beastkin would want someone stronger to be their leader. Camilla had agreed with her, and shock froze her next to Jabbar.

"Me?" she finally stammered. "Why me?"

"Because Sigrid trusted you as no other. She thought the world of you, Camilla, and that's something the rest of us should respect."

"We were sisters once," Camilla murmured. "I thought of you as my family in the days when we served the Earthen folk, but I left you to be with Sigrid. I journeyed across the lands, and I didn't stay by your side when you needed me most. Why would you give me any chance to make amends for that betrayal?"

"Because you see it as a betrayal." Brynhild fell to one knee and pressed a hand against her chest. "You deserve to take her place. You will honor her memory and continue her work to make us a better people."

Jabbar stepped forward at that. "There's no reason why we should add someone to the council who knows nothing of what we've spoken of. There are plenty of us who could step into —"

"No," Brynhild interrupted. A ripple of fur unfurled from the top of her head to her toes in a single wave that promised her beast — a bear — was very close to the surface. "You will not twist my words now, Jabbar of Bymere. It was one of your people who tried to kill her."

"Mine?" Jabbar laughed and opened his arms wide. "Prove it."

"The arrow. It was marked with the symbol of Bymere."

"And you think that was a Beastkin? It could easily have been a human who climbed down from the mountain, because he didn't want us to be here. There's no reason to think it was one of us, the people who have asked to be family and have been nothing but that."

The seeds of doubt were sown. How had Sigrid known things would fall into place so easily? Camilla didn't understand her sister's thinking sometimes. It was as if her human side was stronger than the dragon.

Shaking her head, Camilla stepped in before it went too far. A brawl would only end in more blood, and as much as she wanted to see Brynhild fight Jabbar, she knew it wouldn't end well.

This was Sigrid's plan. And she had to stick to it.

"Stop it," Camilla scolded. "This isn't what we're here for. You can fight each other in the morning if that's what you wish. But tonight is for her."

She pointed at Sigrid's burning body. The sight made her eyes tear up and her nose run.

Emotions making her voice warble and lip quake, she added, "That is my *sister*. And she is burning on a pyre because none of you could save her. You were all squabbling and listening to idle prattle. It doesn't matter if it was a Beastkin or a human who killed her. *Because she is still dead.*"

The last sentence was a shout that carried across the crowd and echoed into the night sky. An owl took up her call, hooting with a sadness that she couldn't express in this form. She shouldn't be mourning. Her sister wasn't dead, and yet...

Camilla turned back to the fire, filling her eyes with the sight of Sigrid's fake death and let the emotions swallow her whole.

She fell to her knees next to the fire. Slowly, she lifted her arms out at her side and lifted her face to the sky.

"Behold, ancient mothers of old. Before you lies a queen whose battle cry shook the heavens with her anger and her rage. She holds her people's love in her still hands. Her people cry for her."

It felt wrong to invoke the rights of death for a woman she knew was alive, but this was only the first of many lies she would spread. And she would do so gladly if it meant their people would take a better path.

Camilla kept her eyes closed until she heard the sound of earth shifting next to her. Opening one eye, she glanced over at Brynhild who had settled onto her knees.

Perhaps it was a cruel thing to do. There were some among the Bymerians who would mourn for Sigrid's death as well. However, the Earthen Beastkin needed to be separated from the men, at least for a time. Their minds needed to clear from lust and awe.

The Bymerians wouldn't know this ritual. They wouldn't know the words, the song, the movements that her sisters knew since birth. Instead, the men would be forced into the shadows as the sisters of Wildewyn mourned the loss of their own.

Brynhild's voice was deep and chilling in the cold night air. "Behold, ancient mothers of old. Here lies a woman who sacrificed blood, life, and freedom for her people. Her people sing—" her voice cracked, "—their queen is dead."

She reached out and wove her fingers together with Camilla. Their arms remained raised, linked together through pain and loss.

Another Beastkin woman, a lioness if Camilla remembered correctly, fell to her knees on Camilla's left.

"Behold, ancient mothers of old. Here lies a woman whose body shall turn to ash and dust, but whose spirit will search for you in the beyond. Her people sing so that her soul may be guided into the afterlife."

Over and over, Beastkin women fell to their knees and reached for each other's hands. They all stayed linked, whispering words of encouragement for the ancients to take one of their own beloved sisters.

Camilla stared hard at Sigrid's body, and saw a single tear slide from her sister's eyes and sizzle on the wood beneath her. The others might think it was her soul leaking out, thankful for their help, but she knew what it was.

This wouldn't be easy for either of them.

Camilla sniffed hard, tears streaming down her cheeks freely now. With a great surge of self-control, she let a hum roll in her chest and throat. A quiet sound, a soft whisper in the night that would hopefully encourage the ancients to see her sister. To come and reach out for one of their own.

Neither she nor Sigrid had ever really believed in the old ways. They didn't believe there was an ancient Beastkin mother who would come and collect their souls. But in the moment, Camilla felt the chilling bite of the wind and hoped they weren't wrong.

This wasn't what she had wanted to do. And yet, this was the only way their people would be safe.

The Beastkin women remained on their knees, humming until they lost their voices. Only when the sun rose on the horizon did they slowly stand, knees aching, and release their hold on each other.

Brynhild pressed a hand to Camilla's shoulder. "I will take her to the resting place."

"No," Camilla shook her head forcefully. "It should be me."

"No one should have to bury their blood."

She shook her head again, pressed a shaking fist to her mouth, then stepped toward the pyre. "It will be me."

Sigrid remained untouched by the flames. A dragon could not burn, even in death. Camilla touched a finger to her sister's warm face and breathed out a soft sigh of relief.

The Beastkin women gathered behind her. "Would you like us to walk with you?" Brynhild asked.

"No. I will take her to the final resting place."

"Make sure you sit her up." When Camilla sharply glanced back, Brynhild shrugged. "Don't curl her up like the others in the tree roots. She wouldn't want to be in a position so delicate."

"It will offend the gods."

"She always did anyways." A smile softened Brynhild's usually fierce expression. "Let her continue doing so in death."

With that, Camilla swung Sigrid's body up into her arms with a grunt. She would carry her friend as far as she needed to go. Then, she'd wait until her sister awoke.

THE MOON FLED THE SKY IN THE WAKE OF THE SUN. CAMILLA WATCHED it trace the silvery lights away and bleed into the horizon with streaks of red and gold. Soon, she would awaken her sister.

Some of the other Beastkin women had come to say their last goodbyes. Camilla had been forced to place Sigrid in the ceremonial seated position of the dead. Her heart had nearly pounded out of her chest when she folded Sigrid's hands in her lap and tilted her head back so that her unseeing eyes could see the sun.

This was wrong. This was a sacred rite, and they shouldn't use it so lightly. Not when so many of their sisters *had* died in such a way, and they needed that respect far more than a ploy to get Sigrid out of the keep.

Now, she sat next to what seemed like a dead body and watched the sun rise in the horizon. The streaks of color reminded her that there was more to this world than what she could understand. The gods didn't seem angry when the world was so beautiful. They hadn't greeted her actions with a storm or hail. Instead, they showed her the most stunning sunrise she'd ever seen in her life.

Perhaps all would be well.

One of Sigrid's fingers twitched. Just the slightest of movements, but still enough that Camilla knew the poison was wearing off.

"Sigrid?" she asked, crawling toward her sister and tilting Sigrid's head so she could stare into her vacant eyes. "Wake up, sister. It's long past time for you to leave."

A low sigh erupted from Sigrid's lips. It was more than she'd breathed in what felt like a lifetime.

"Thank the gods," Camilla whispered. She began stroking Sigrid's fingers, pushing the blood where it needed to go and hurrying up the process of her waking. "Come on, you can do it. The poison is wearing off but you need to be going a lot faster than this. The others are going to come soon, and I have to tell them that I left you here exactly where you were. The Bymerians need to take the blame for moving your body, and not the humans, I know that was the plan."

Sigrid blinked her eyes.

Grinning, Camilla shook her head. "You were always too stubborn for even poison to kill you. Just a little bit more now, fight through it."

Together, they battled the poison out of her body until Sigrid could lean forward and scrub her hands over her face. She looked tired. Dark circles around her eyes, puffy face, even her hands were shaking when she reached out to grab Camilla's shoulder.

"Thank you," Sigrid whispered. "It was a beautiful ceremony."

"All true, you know. That's one way to see whether or not people still like you. Fake your own death and the masses will come." Camilla hesitated then added, "It didn't feel right though. Like we were doing something wrong."

"We were."

Leave it to Sigrid to not pull punches. Camilla watched as her sister rolled onto hands and knees, took a deep breath, then shoved herself up onto her haunches and slowly stood.

It was a process. Everything would be a process until the poison finally ran its course. She'd have to figure out how to walk in a way that would push the poison into certain parts of her body.

Camilla remembered this particular technique for torture. Her own mother was the one who had remembered the plant from the old legends and brought it to the Earthen folk. But her mother had always loved the Wildewyn people far more than the other Beastkin. She saw use in the humans that others could not.

Sometimes, Camilla still heard her voice on the wind. Telling her to be kinder, be softer when the humans were pushing her a little too far.

"They are weak, Camilla," her mother used to say. "They need someone to look after them. Every inch of their flesh is soft, and they do not have claws to fight back with. We have to take care of them. Someone has to."

Maybe that was why she'd always found something in Sigrid that she loved. The stoic woman reminded her very much of her mother.

Sigrid stumbled toward a nearby tree where Camilla had left the pack. She bent down, pulled at the strap, and opened it up while holding onto the small of her back. "Everything is here?"

"As requested. I put a little extra water in there, because I'm quite certain you're underestimating how far you're going to have to travel." Camilla pushed her braids out of her face. "Straight on toward the mountains, yes?"

"I remember." Sigrid hesitated for a second and looked into Camilla's eyes as if there was something more to say.

And there was. Camilla wanted something like "I'll miss you." Or "you've been a sister to me like no one else has ever been," something that would have been sentimental or perhaps warmed her heart in the dead of night when she was wondering whether or not Sigrid was dead.

But that wasn't her icy sister's personality at all. Sigrid

instead just nodded at her, swung the pack onto her shoulder, and blew out another ragged breath.

"I'll head straight for the mountains and find the ancients if they're still there. Otherwise, I'll find whatever proof I can so as to make up some kind of story when I return."

"That should do," Camilla replied, her voice quiet and sad. "Are you so certain you'll be able to return?"

"I don't know." Her sister no longer looked at her, but toward the mountains that hid a world of secrets. "But I plan to find out."

And with that, Sigrid turned and walked away.

Camilla watched her and tried to still the tears from falling once again. She didn't need to worry about Sigrid. Her sister had proven that time and time again. She was stronger than the rest of them. Far more capable of handling the cruelty of the wilds.

Still, she worried that this might be the last time she saw Sigrid, and her soul wept.

NADIR

WHY WAS IT THAT EVERY TIME HE TURNED HIS BACK, SOMETHING BAD happened? Nadir cracked his neck and slumped in the chair beside his desk.

Yet another backstabbing moment from his advisors who had already said they sent an "experimental troop" of assassins to follow the Earthen King home.

Oh, they wouldn't attack the king. He was assured of that. The advisors weren't so foolish to endanger the kingdom like that. But they wanted the know the route the Earthen folk had traveled. They wanted the know the easiest way to get back to the castle where the Earthen King lived.

He'd already told them how foolish that was. Hallmar wasn't an idiot. He wasn't going to take the easiest path back to his home, and he certainly would realize they likely had someone following him. It was wasted effort on soldiers who should be home with their families these last few days before the war broke out. No man wanted to say goodbye to his family, but his advisors had already brought the kingdom to that point.

Sighing, he scrubbed a hand over his face and felt the prickling of a beard growing. Since when had he any facial hair? Was that new or had he not noticed that his body was aging?

The next thing he knew, he'd be finding gray hair at his temples, and he wouldn't be surprised in the slightest. They were going to drive him to an early grave with all this stress.

A few hours of sleep might help, if he could manage to lay his head down to rest. He didn't know what kind of dreams would plague him. Still, he was willing to face the guilt of his life if only that meant he could close his eyes for a few moments.

Nadir stood, cracked his back which was suddenly tight, and strode toward the comfortable haven of his bed. The silken sheets would slide over his body in a cool caress. The pillows would hug him as no one had in gods knew how long.

He was so excited to *sleep* that he almost missed the curtains of his balcony shifting. A smarter person would have tried to make the movement look as though it were the wind. Someone who didn't want to be found anyway.

Nadir's shoulders curved forward in defeat. He didn't want to fight anyone, not tonight when his bed was *right there*.

Gesturing with his hand, he beckoned the person forward. "I know you're there. Come out. If it's an assassination attempt you're trying, then you could at least be quick about it. I'd like to try and sleep tonight."

"You're rather cocky," a voice wove from the shadows of the balcony. "You might not be sleeping at all, but might find a permanent kind of darkness."

"Then so be it. I'm not afraid of death and would welcome it at this point in my life. The kingdom might be better for it anyways." He rubbed the back of his neck, pondering whether or not he should try and tackle the person. It would be so easy to force them to the ground and shout for his guards.

But not nearly as fun.

The curtains shifted again and a woman stepped out of the shadows. Her dark hair had been cleaned since the last time he'd seen her. Smooth and grease-free, the torches reflected off the dark mass until he thought perhaps it swallowed light.

She stared at him with a ferocity he hadn't seen in a while. Nadir was surprised to see that her eyes weren't as dark as he remembered. Instead, they were caramel colored. Warm toffee poured over a treat like he hadn't had since he was just a little boy.

Clearing his throat, he pointed toward the desk. "There's food and water in the bottom drawer if you need any."

"Your concubines have already fed me." Somehow, she made the words feel like an accusation.

"I see they've cleaned you as well, and given you clothing that actually fits." Although, it wasn't the clothing his concubines would have chosen for her. She was dressed in men's clothing. White, billowing shirt and wide pants that wouldn't hinder her movements too much.

What was she doing here? He'd made it very clear that he would deal with her once he wrapped his mind around how to address her situation. The advisors were likely keeping even more of the Beastkin in the dungeons, hidden away from him.

That, in itself, posed a problem. He was supposed to be sending these Beastkin to Sigrid. Regrettably, he hadn't the time for as many as he liked. When he knew they were going to be burned or killed, he stepped in to save them at the last second.

Never on his own orders of course. There were plenty of people who were sympathetic and who were happy to hide the fact that the sultan was helping them. Some didn't even know it was he who was the benefactor to their operations.

But this woman... her dark eyes saw much more than most. She stared at him with a mixture of hatred and apprehension, something no other Beastkin had done in the recent months. She looked at him almost as though she were waiting for something.

For him to recognize her? That couldn't be what it was. He'd never seen her in his life. Nadir would have recognized those dark eyes, the curves that stretched across her form. Wouldn't he?

He shook his head and then a chuckle slipped from his lips. "You're escaping, aren't you?"

"Did you really think your guards could hold me for long?"

"I've never had too many complaints about them." Nadir strode toward his bed and fell into the pillows. He let his body relax for the briefest moment, his muscles easing as his mind relaxed. Looking up from his nest, he jerked his chin toward the balcony. "Go on with it then. I'm not going to stop you."

"You aren't?"

If she was surprised, he didn't really care. Of course he was going to let her go. Nadir had no use for her. Too many eyes were watching him right now for him to get her in contact with someone who would get her across the border. The woman would have to fend for herself.

She seemed perfectly capable of doing just that.

"No," he replied. "I have no fight with the Beastkin. That's entirely the advisors who have me by the throat with all their lies and scheming. If you disappear then I have the unique opportunity of blaming one of them, having them beheaded, and replacing them with someone I trust. So please. Go."

She didn't reply immediately. Nadir hoped the silence meant she had taken him at his word and slipped out the balcony. It would be better for them both if she disappeared quickly.

Something tapped the wood of his desk. A glass? Gods, the woman was pouring herself a glass of brandy, wasn't she?

He leaned up and grunted when he saw she was doing exactly that. "That's expensive."

"I would hope so. You are the Sultan of Bymere after all." She tossed the drink back and sighed. "Just as good as I remember."

"As you remember?" he repeated.

The slave in front of him seemed to change. Her shoulders straightened, her eyes gleamed with a deadly intent, but it was mostly the way her sudden demeanor shifted without a single hesitation that made him realize she wasn't who she pretended to be.

Nadir took a step toward her, his eyes narrowed and his jaw tight. "Who are you really?"

"I don't know what you're talking about."

"I think you do." He gestured up and down her body. "This is all clearly an act, and I need more information than just a lie. You aren't some Beastkin woman they picked up out of the desert and threw into my dungeon. I'd hazard a guess you wanted to be there, though perhaps not for as long as you actually were."

"You're asking for a closely guarded secret, little sultan." She sucked her tongue over her teeth. "But perhaps it's time for you to know who we are."

A shiver of distrust and fear ran down his spine. "*We* is rather ominous. Please don't tell me there's another group within Bymere who wants to see me dead. I'm not sure I could survive it."

"It sounds as if you don't really want to."

If she'd said the same thing a year ago, he would have agreed with her. Back then, it seemed easier that he slipped away from life. His kingdom would have flourished under a sultan who cared about them. His lands would have overflown with goods aplenty that he couldn't seem to acquire for his people.

But now? He understood what to do, and how his ideas could benefit those who had less. He didn't want to give up his chance to make this kingdom better than what it had been before him. He wanted to leave his mark on Bymere so that all would say his name long after his passing.

Old habits die hard, however, and a part of him still whispered that his people and all that he loved would be much better off if he… simply wasn't there at all.

Shaking his head, Nadir replied, "I say the words, but they don't have the same meaning as before."

"Ah," the Beastkin replied. "Then I should first say my name is Tahira."

"I remember," he whispered. The name had been branded into his mind as another to add to a long list of people he should have saved. The guilt burned in his chest, aching every night when he tried to sleep. "You may call me Nadir, if you're going to tell me some secret I do not know."

"I'm telling you more than a secret, little sultan. I'm giving you a chance to change the world as you know it."

How many people had said that to him recently? The world was already changing. He'd taken the first step the moment he took power back from his advisors and stepped into the role his brother should have had. Did she not see the way the city had rebuilt itself? Did she not see the droves of people who were now flocking to the Red Palace in hopes to see their king?

He tilted his head to the side and asked, "How can I change it more than it already has been changed? The Beastkin might not see the effects of what I'm doing, not yet, but I need a little more time to fix what has been broken."

"That's not what I'm talking about." She started toward the balcony, then glanced over her shoulder. "Come to Falldell and see where you were wrought."

"Excuse me?"

"You've always thought your mother was dead, because she died when you were just a boy along with all the people you loved. But there was your real mother who still lived. The one who gifted you the treasure that you are now. She summons you to her side."

A flash of heat traveled from the top of his head to the bottom of his toes. His mother? He didn't have a mother, not anymore. She had died from a fever that blistered through her body when he was just a boy. There wasn't another woman in his life other than the creature who had gifted him a curse, not a treasure.

How dare she suggest there was another? It was an insult to his *real* mother's memory. He opened his mouth to give her a scathing reply but was interrupted by her laughter.

"Easy, Sultan. There is more to this life than you know. A mother who loves you is one thing. A mother who is useful and ancient is another entirely. Come to Falldell, let us teach you where you came from, and show you *who you really are*."

"I know who I am."

"Do you?" She lifted a dark brow. Tahira grasped the curtains on his balcony and twitched them open. The starlight beyond framed her dark hair and gave her an otherworldly look, as if she were a djinn who had stepped out of the sands. But this wasn't a wish he would have made.

He didn't want this.

Nadir's lips twisted into a snarl. "You can tell that woman I have no interest in anything she can teach me."

"We're going to send someone to take the throne in your place. You'll need to harm yourself somehow in a way that will force you to hide your face while it heals. Not exactly the best way to hide, but effective in its simplicity."

"I'm not going to do that."

"You will." Tahira stepped beyond the curtain and melted into the darkness. Her voice was all he could hear, but the words were like a lightning bolt to his soul. "The Alqatala of Falldell call upon you, Sultan, to greet them as one of your subjects. Whether you want to see your mother or not, you cannot deny us when *we* summon you."

"What?" he stammered, his voice shaking. "The Alqatala of Falldell are a children's tale. There are no more assassins that can call upon the king, or legendary warriors who protect Bymere."

No one replied to his shouted question. The Beastkin

woman—assassin—was gone.

It wasn't possible that the Alqatala were real. They were only characters in children's stories who came out in the middle of the night to right the wrongs of the kingdom. As sultan, he would know if they were real. Someone would have suggested he use them at some point, that he call upon the powers that were far stronger than any army.

Try as he might, he couldn't really remember the stories. Only that they were terrifying men and women who moved impossibly fast. People used to say they were actually djinn. His brother had tried to capture one by buying a ridiculously expensive lamp from a street vendor who said he'd seized one of the Alqatala within its fluted neck.

Obviously, the man hadn't done so. They had rubbed the lamp for hours, lit the oil within it, to no avail. Disappointing for boys as they were, but probably for the best. They wouldn't have known what to do with a legendary warrior such as that.

And his mother?

Nadir purposefully stayed away from the thought. He didn't want to know there were even more dragons out in the world. The last thing he needed was yet another threat in the kingdom for him to worry about. It wasn't possible that the woman was alive.

Besides, his father would have taken care of such a threat a long time ago. The woman who had birthed Nadir would have a claim on some portion of the throne if she wished it, although his father had done everything in his power to make sure Nadir would never take the throne. Hakim had been the perfect son, the picture of health, until someone from Wildewyn had killed him.

Shaking his head, Nadir turned toward his bed. In the morning, it would seem like a dream. And if the Alqatala did send someone to take his throne while he traveled, he would turn the man away. That was the smart thing to do. There was no reason for him to do anything else.

He huffed out a breath. "Go to sleep, Nadir," he told himself. "This will all disappear in the morning with the tail ends of whatever nightmare holds you awake."

With that, he flopped down on the pillows, shoved his head under a particularly thick carpet, and folded his hands over his chest. The bed was so comfortable it nearly made him weep. He wanted to sleep so badly that his body actually hurt from it.

And yet, he couldn't fall asleep no matter how much he wanted to. There were too many thoughts dancing in his head.

Was the woman telling the truth? That was his primary concern. If she were lying, then he could dismiss it all. But if she were telling the truth… then he had to do something about it.

He couldn't go to Falldell. Not when there were so many things he needed to watch over here. He didn't trust any of his advisors taking the throne, and he certainly didn't trust some man he didn't know. This could all be some elaborate ruse to take the throne from him, and what an end that would be.

If she were telling the truth, however, that was almost a bigger problem than he wanted to think about. A mother? Gods, he didn't know what to do with a woman who wanted to see him only have twenty years of existence.

And then there was the issue of the Alqatala. They could kill him in his sleep if he didn't do what they wanted, and no one would question their actions.

He sat up and scrubbed a hand down his face.

"Fine," he muttered. "Sleep evades once again."

Nadir stood from the bed and left his bedroom without a goal in mind. He needed something that would help him sleep. The healers would have something. Perhaps a draught that would knock him out for a few dreamless hours.

However, he couldn't go to them. He'd already asked them a few times to help him sleep and they would eventually get suspicious why he was asking so much. No one could think him weak. He was the Sultan of Bymere. There wasn't a reason for him to have sleepless nights when the kingdom was beginning to prosper once again.

It had only taken three seasons. A remarkable comeback after a war, his advisors said. Even the people whom he spoke with on a weekly basis expressed their appreciation for his abilities. They were happier now than they had been before the war, they promised. That had to account for something.

Something in his gut twisted at the thought. It all seemed too good to be possible, but he didn't know how to find out whether everyone was telling the truth.

It seemed as though he didn't know what truth sounded like anymore. He'd lived for nearly his entire life so wrapped up in lies that the world seemed a darker place. It was hard to see in the shadows when everyone around you had them hanging off their shoulders like tendrils of night.

"Sultan?" the librarian's voice broke through his thoughts. "It's rather late at night, Your Highness. I hadn't thought to see you."

Where was he? Nadir looked around, only to realize he'd somehow ended up at the library. Why was he here?

Looking at the old stacks brought memories of his brother back to the forefront. Hakim had always harped on Nadir, saying that a good king knew the history of his kingdom so that he didn't repeat the mistakes of sultans past. Nadir hadn't been that interested in reading books. To tell the truth, he hadn't been all that good at reading. The words sometimes switched on him while he was attempting to read them. Letters shifting and jumping until they created similar words that weren't quite right.

He rubbed the back of his neck and met the gaze of the librarian before them. The man was older than he remembered, but he did remember him. No one could forget the round spectacles on the man's nose, or the rather large mole right next to the wire.

"Ah," he replied, "I hadn't thought to find myself here either, but thusly I have arrived."

"Is there something I can help you find?" the librarian asked, looking over the top of his spectacles which unfortunately shifted the mole directly onto the rims. "It's a rather large library."

"I think I remember my way around."

"Take the gloves please."

The gloves? Nadir looked down at the velvet pieces in the man's hands as he thrust them out. Why in the world would he wear gloves?

The librarian grunted. "The books are too fragile to be touched. The oils on your hands will ruin them, Sultan. Royal or no, I won't have you destroying books because you got it in your head to visit after ten years of silence."

"I could have you beheaded for such insolence," he replied

while taking the gloves.

"And then who would run the library? Better to let me do what I know, and you do what you know." The man looked down at the book in his hands, sat back down at a desk Nadir hadn't noticed was there, and ignored the sultan entirely.

He couldn't really argue with the old man. The librarian was correct. Nadir had always valued people who knew what they were doing, and did their job well. This librarian had been around since before they'd lost his brother, and that said something sincerely important.

The library stretched before him. Shelves more than five men tall stretched up into the ceiling with ladders interspersed, so librarians could reach up to the highest peaks. Those were the less popular books, but from what he'd heard, those were the ones that contained the most secrets.

How did these stacks work again? He should remember simply because his brother had dragged him here so many times, but he couldn't for the life of him think what system they used. The stacks seemed to loom over him with judgmental weight that made his chest tight.

What was he doing here?

Still, his feet managed to move without him telling them to. They remembered the path he'd taken with his brother. They remembered how to move through the library quietly.

His hands knew the gloves like they were old friends. He slid the kid leather over his hands, catching on calluses he didn't remember having. And when he reached the very last stack abutting the wall of his palace, his hands reached for the ladder and pulled it into place.

Nadir didn't know what he was looking for. Somehow, his

body had a mind of its own in this moment. It knew where to take him, what his mind needed to calm down.

At the very highest peak of the stack in the library of Bymere, an ancient book rested. It appeared as if no one had picked it up for centuries. Dust had settled in a fine layer over the red leather, so thick he left fingerprints in it when he lifted up the tome.

Brushing his fingers over it, he touched the golden clasp that held it shut.

"The knowledge of the Alqatala," he murmured, reading the words that had been inlaid with gold leaf.

Lifting the book, he blew the dust off its cover, and then slowly made his way back down the ladder. Perhaps there was something in here that would tell him what to do next. Something that would explain why he was given this task by legendary assassin who shouldn't even be alive.

And yet, it seemed as though they were.

Nadir took the book to a small seating area in the back corner where no one would find him. There was a candle and a box of matches on the table next to the chair, although neither had been used before. He placed the book carefully on the small table, struck the match on the side of the matchbox, and lit the candle.

The wax heated, and for a moment he saw figures in the candle flame. Dancing figures who lifted their arms above their heads and swayed to music he could almost hear. Drum Beats, ancient and powerful, flowed through his veins like water.

What was happening to him? This wasn't something he'd ever seen before. Nothing he'd experienced, and yet, there it was.

Shaking his head, Nadir settled onto the chair and resolved to spend the rest of the evening in the library. He was going to discover what this Qatal wanted from him, this assassin woman who had broken into his palace with the sole intent to speak with him.

He'd deal with thoughts of his mother later, but for now, he needed to know what the assassins wanted from him.

SIGRID

WHAT HAD POSSESSED HER TO THINK UP A MISSION LIKE THIS? SIGRID shaded her eyes and stared up at the sky, glowering at the snow which fell in heaps around her. She couldn't even see where the sun was, or if the sun was still on the horizon. Instead, a blanket of snow covered everything the eye could see.

Even the sky.

Shaking her head, she shifted the straps on her shoulders and continued trudging through the frigid snow.

She didn't know how long she'd traveled. It was easy to lose track of time in this place. She knew it had been at least a week of walking through the forests of Wildewyn. She didn't know what region she was in anymore, or if it were some unnamed region that no one had seen in centuries.

The moment she'd seen the mountains close enough to touch, she'd known she was close to the ancients. The ground seemed to hum with power here. Perhaps not that of the earth, but something far more than just earthen people who tilled the land. There was a call inside her chest that beckoned her forward.

"Come to us," the words whispered on the wind. "Find us, little child. We were looking for you, too."

It was the promise to know who she was. To know who her sisters were, where they came from. All the secrets which had been kept from her since the moment of her birth. The longer she traveled, the more Sigrid *needed* to know the answer to these questions.

Her entire life, she'd been given a designation by other people. She was the daughter of the last dragon. She was the adopted child of an owl but never the same as the rest. She was matriarch, sultana, warrior, all the things that she had been told to be.

No more. She wanted to know who she really was, and that need was something stronger than the desire for water or food.

Thus, she'd climbed the mountain. The first few days had been a struggle. The rocks shifted under her feet and moved when she clambered over them. A few times, she'd been concerned she would fall to her death down the sheer cliff edges. But she'd managed, and eventually she crested the top.

That first moment of elation in knowing that she'd conquered the mountain quickly fell apart when she realized that the mountain wasn't one peak.

It was many.

The range stretched farther than she could see, disappearing into the horizon and fading away. She would have to make it across all these mountains before she found any secrets. She was almost certain of that.

Even that didn't deter her. A mountain was still a

mountain. She'd already climbed one, and she would climb many more if that gave her answers.

Then, it started to snow. The blistering cold winds wiggled beneath her clothing, forcing her to wear more and more layers until she ran out. Even that wasn't enough.

Now, her fingers felt as though they were about to fall off. She couldn't feel the tips, and they'd turned a frightening shade of blue. She wasn't entirely confident that everything was all right with her body. Even the dragon inside her had quieted into a lethargic grumble.

More snow blasted down from a mountain peak higher up, and Sigrid forgot how to breathe as the cold stole air from her lungs and sent a shiver through her body so forcefully that it nearly knocked her to her knees.

She needed to get warm. Had to find some place to rest, even for a few moments. A winter storm like this couldn't stay for too long.

A shadow appeared in the distance, looking like a person waving their arm. Sigrid frowned. It wasn't possible that someone was out here with her. No one would be so foolish as to brave such a storm without good reason.

But there the person was. Standing in the middle of the snow, waving their arm like they thought she couldn't see them.

For a second, she hallucinated that it was Nadir. Her heart beat faster and her breathing turned ragged. Had he come for her? Had he really come for her?

Of course it wasn't her husband. He was still in Bymere, with the rest of his people. The ones he'd chosen over her.

Sigrid stumbled, falling to one knee. Icy particles of snow, perhaps freezing rain, rained down on her face. The prickles of pain woke her up a little bit, although her body wanted to stay on the ground. There was something warmer about lying in the snow. She didn't know how that was possible considering when she placed a bare hand in the stuff it made her fingers ache. And yet, lying down still felt so comfortable…

No. There was a person on the horizon and perhaps they could help her. Maybe there were still people who lived up here. Maybe they had a house, a warm fire, something that would keep her alive for one more night.

She could wait out the storm in their home and then continue on her journey. Surely anyone who lived in this forgotten place would be kind. They'd have to be. The only travelers who came here were sorry souls like Sigrid.

With the promise of somewhere warm to lay her head, Sigrid forced herself back onto her feet. Snow sucked at her boots as she struggled toward the waving figure. Ice jabbed her face and forced her back a few steps every time the wind decided it wanted to push her even farther down the mountain.

Sigrid was persistent, however, and she was not a woman to fall prey to the whims of the earth. She was a dragon, and dragons did not fail.

Step by step, she made it closer to the figure in the distance. Would they be kind? She sincerely hoped they were. She needed someone to take care of her just for a little while. A blanket, a cot, she didn't even care if it were just lying on the ground in front of their hearth. She wasn't someone who needed a castle to keep her happy.

The dragon inside her lifted its head, sniffing the air and trying to figure out what kind of person waved to them. But the cold shards of the air stifled any scent. It was as if there were no one else on the planet but Sigrid and the snow that surrounded her.

"Just a few more steps," she muttered through chattering teeth. "A few more and then you'll be there. They'll give you food, water, maybe a fire. It doesn't matter, just anything that's warm and comfortable for a few moments."

Her toes ached with every step. She couldn't even feel her fingers anymore, and then there was the way her face felt tight in the frigid air. Would she lose some of her fingers? She'd heard of people losing them before in such cold weather.

Finally, she was close enough that the figure should be able to see her. Lifting her voice, Sigrid called out, "I'm here!"

The figure didn't react. Instead, they kept waving as if she wasn't right in front of them.

"Hello?" she asked tentatively.

Again, no reaction changed as the figure continued to wave.

"Oh, no." Sigrid's teeth chattered harder and she made the final few steps to the "figure" in the distance who was supposed to be her savior.

She reached out and patted a hand to the part of the short, squat tree with only a single branch to its name. "Just you, old friend. Is that it? No one else?"

Sigrid sniffed loudly, swallowing her emotions and the distinct need to cry. The tears would freeze on her cheeks, and then where would she be? She wouldn't be able to think, breathe, or even dash away the tears, because they would then freeze on her blackened fingertips that she was already certain she was going to lose.

Looking up into the sky, she tried to slow her ragged breaths. "There's nothing you can do now," she told herself. "Just keep moving. One more step."

Her body didn't want to move anymore. She couldn't force herself to take one more step without resting for a little while. Sigrid slumped against the tree trunk and slid down it until her butt touched the ground.

There, that felt a lot better. She could think a little more clearly now that her lungs weren't working overdrive to feed her pounding heart. She could stay here for a few more minutes and warm herself up.

Body heat had to count for something. She pulled her arms out of the jacket sleeves, tucking them against her heart where there was still a little heat left. If only there was a place out of the wind, then she was certain she could figure out a way to heat herself.

The tree branches rattled above her head. The wind whipped across the mountaintop. She couldn't see if there was grass underneath all the snow, or if this was merely a barren wasteland of rocks and jagged stones.

Perhaps this was a pretty place once. She could believe that Earthen folk might have climbed to the heights just to see the view. Beyond the curtain of white, all of Wildewyn would be laid bare to her eyes.

She imagined the sight that the snow hid. It would be a glorious unveiling of emerald green and hundreds of rivers that snaked through the forests. Perhaps birds would burst into flight by a hunter who was making his way through the forest in search of something to feed his family.

Maybe even Beastkin could be hidden in that land. She

might be able to see the home of the ancients, tucked away far from prying eyes.

What would they look like? She didn't even know what to think. The legends said they were Beastkin just like her, but somehow, she thought they might not be. They were mythical creatures, stronger than any Beastkin alive. They couldn't be just regular people who found themselves with a good bloodline.

They might be taller than everyone else. Or maybe, they were so beautiful they would make her eyes burn.

Would they have golden eyes? Eyes that made her heart ache with memories she'd tried so hard to forget?

A gust of wind blew snow in her eyes, making them water in tune with her thoughts. If they were so beautiful, she hoped they might give her a break and not make her cry any more than she already had.

"You have to get up," she whispered to herself. "You can't sit here and wait for death to claim you. Stand *up*, Sigrid."

With laboring movements, Sigrid rolled onto her hands and knees.

"You've survived more than this. You can stand up. That's all you have to do."

The words were a lie. She couldn't think of a time when she'd been so close to death, and so very alone. A sob wracked her lungs, but she refused to entertain the thoughts that beckoned her to lie down and accept her fate. It would be okay to die in a place like this, the thoughts whispered. No one would find her, and the tree was already here for the ceremonial rights. And hadn't she already had them?

Perhaps this was the gods telling her that she should have

died on that funeral pyre. Maybe this was their punishment for desecrating the old religion.

"No," she grunted. "I will not die like this, today or any day."

She heaved herself into a crouch, then forced herself to stand. A fire burned inside her from an ancient past that refused to die. She would not lie down and let death claim her, not when there was still fight inside her.

"Now, find a place to stay for the night. Dig a hole in the ground if you must. Dragons are resourceful. Beastkin know the land, Sigrid. Find something more than just self-pity."

Had someone said the words to her before? She couldn't remember. They seemed to ring with a memory, but she couldn't place it with any particular moment in her life. Had her mother said the words?

She didn't remember her mother very much. They were alike, everyone told her. The dragon mother was in the set of Sigrid's shoulders. The way she squeezed her jaw when she was angry and the fire that burned deep in her eyes when someone said something wrong.

Even Hallmar had remarked upon it more times than she thought necessary.

"You are your mother's daughter," he used to say with a chuckle. "Dangerous and cruel at times, but always for the greater good."

There was no greater good if she was dead, so Sigrid needed to keep moving. She had to help her people. If that meant finding out who she was so she could lead them better, then so be it.

"Find something," she told herself again. "Lift your foot,

damn it."

Her foot lifted, then set down in the snow. Every step was an internal battle, and she waged war within her mind for every inch she moved forward. But she moved.

Shading her eyes, Sigrid searched the area for something, anything that would keep her alive. She could figure out how to start a fire. There was enough brush, even if it was hidden by the snow. It would light with dragon breath as long as she could wake up the beast inside her.

"There," she whispered and pointed out a dark smudge in the distance to herself. "That'll do."

The snow tried to keep her where she was. The white powder whispered that she could still lie down. There was still enough time for her to rest, just for a few moments.

She refused.

Sigrid fought her way to the small cave in the side of the mountain and forced herself through the lip. A bear might live within it, and she wouldn't be much of an opponent for anything at the time. Her greatest hope was that nothing would be so foolish as to live up here.

The snow had blown into the mouth of the cave. She crunched through the icy remains deeper into the mountain where the snow hadn't touched yet. It wasn't much of a cave really, shallow with only one turn.

She blew out a breath and reminded herself that beggars couldn't be choosers. This cave was a message from the gods, so there had to be something more to it. If it got her through the night, then it was enough.

With a groan, she dropped the pack from her shoulders and rubbed her aching muscles.

"Fire first," she told herself. "Then you can rest. But first, you have to get warm."

That was the most important thing right now, and the only thought she could have in her mind. It didn't matter that she was exhausted and wanted nothing more than to sleep. She had to stay awake for a few more minutes so she could get a fire started.

The cave was so dark; she couldn't see anything at all. Sigrid took a few steps deeper into it, then stumbled on a pile of something on the ground.

"Don't be bones," she muttered. Not that she was afraid of seeing human remains. She'd seen them many times in her life. She didn't want them to be there because it meant there *was* something living in the cave. She'd have to deal with whatever it was when it returned to its home to see her taking residence.

Dropping to her hands and knees, she felt around on the ground to touch whatever it was. Bones were usually smooth unless they were chewed upon. Even then, they had a texture she'd never forget. Her fingers bumped a small thing that rattled when she shifted it.

"Damn it." Her stomach turned into a pit of acid and worries. She didn't have the energy for this.

She grabbed the object and turned it in her hands. Was it… wood? Lifting it to her nose, she breathed in the scent of earth and dirt. Definitely wood.

"Why is there wood in here?" she muttered.

Sigrid blindly felt around in the darkness. There was a lot more of it, more than enough for a fire to keep her through the night, in fact. They were small, but she should be able to keep the heat centralized… Why was it set up as if someone had intended to build a fire?

Brows furrowed in concern, she reached deep inside herself and woke the dragon. Though cold and tired, it still lifted its head.

"Just a breath," she whispered. "Like the old times when we wanted to impress people who were visiting Hallmar. It's a trick of the mind, not a full shift. We'll get ourselves warm yet."

Opening her mouth, Sigrid felt the thrum of power deep in her chest. It wasn't like magic, although there were people in Wildewyn who would disagree with her. It was more like something else living inside her that poked its head out for just a brief moment.

Fire boiled in her lungs then expelled in one single breath. The fire jumped from her lips to the pile of wood which immediately burst into flames.

Gods, but the heat felt so good.

Sigrid stretched her hands forward, letting the fire nearly touch her fingertips. It wasn't enough, but it would have to be. Could it possibly ever be enough for a dragon who felt as though the world was coming down around her ears? She added a few more sticks just in case, but reserved the rest for later.

Rubbing her fingers together, she wracked her brain for the next step. Beastkin had trained for situations like this. She knew how to keep herself and others alive. It had been a long time since she'd had lessons with Hallmar and his soldiers, but she remembered their words. She had to.

"Survey the surroundings," she repeated as if Hallmar were standing next to her. "There must be something in the cave that is of use. If there are rocks to build in front of the mouth to stop the wind, then that is fine. However, there was a bundle of sticks already prepared. That means someone else has been here, and perhaps they've left something I can use."

She staggered back to her feet, trying not to groan at the pain in her back. Sticks were something. Maybe the person was deeper in the cave, dead or simply gone. They might have left a bedroll, or a blanket. Something that would help her keep warm while she dried out the clothing she was currently wearing. That would be a good next step.

Her chest warmed for a moment. Hallmar's approval or the dragon's, she didn't know. Both felt as though she'd done something right.

Sigrid looked around her, only barely keeping her jaw open. Another larger pile of wood was braced against the wall of the cave. Heavy pieces were big enough for her to build a fire that would certainly burn throughout the night. She wouldn't have to worry about heat at all.

Was someone looking out for her?

She shook her head, dashing the thought as soon as it appeared. There wasn't anyone else out here with her. No one would care that she'd come this far, and she wasn't that close to the ancients... At least, she didn't think she was.

Taking one of the smaller pieces of wood next to her, she lit it on the fire that crackled. With torch in hand, she made her way toward the back of the cave.

It appeared that the cave was naturally made. A great chunk of the earth had been taken out of the side of the mountain. Twisting slightly to the left, it was tall enough for her to stand comfortably and not worry about hitting her head. Stalactites hung from the ceiling, dripping onto the floor where their twins grew straight up.

She'd never seen anything like this in her life. Caves were abundant in Wildewyn, certainly, but never something this high up with no reason for it to exist.

A large boulder took up most of the path after she turned down the twist in the cave. Sigrid huffed out a breath. There wasn't much farther she could go. It felt almost like a disappointment. The cave should have held treasures, but her body wanted to rest and her mind wasn't certain it could hold up to any more surprises.

She turned to go back to the fire, but then felt a gust of hot air against her back.

"What?" she muttered, turning back toward the boulder and holding out her hand. There *was* heat coming out from a small crevice the boulder had created. Was there a hot spring back there? She was far too high up for something to be possible and yet... How else could there be heat?

Curiosity had always been her greatest flaw. If someone else had traveled with her, Sigrid never would have risked investigating.

"There better not be another dragon waiting for me," she angrily said under her breath.

She could light the torch again if it went out, so she placed it on the floor. The fire burned just enough for her to see that the crevice curved a bit at the end, but she should be able to fit through it if she pulled herself along.

"I hate cramped spaces."

Sigrid moved headfirst into the tight crawl space beneath the boulder. She didn't want to touch it too much, worried that it might fall onto her head if she moved the wrong way. What a way to go. Searching for the ancients only to end up frozen in a cave where a boulder had crushed her head. The last thing she needed was that.

Slithering through the cold rocks, she reached forward to grasp a small handhold on the ground. She tested it a bit, making sure it wasn't connected to the large boulder overhead before she used it to leverage herself forward.

Each wiggle made rocks shower down on her head. Tiny gravel stuck to her hair and cheeks as she pulled herself through. Her heart hammered..

Breathing started to be difficult as the air filtered away from the space. Or maybe that was the fear in her chest that was making her palms sweaty. Just a bit more, she could see the end.

The curved part came all too soon, and she couldn't reach the torch anymore. She should have thought this through better and not just tossed herself into the tiniest crawl space large enough only for a child.

"Stupid," she muttered, chest suddenly heaving with nerves. The curve was so steep she was almost sitting up once she managed to get herself in position. Rocks pressed against her back and front. If she moved in the wrong way, she'd be stuck.

Gods, she might die here.

Sigrid reached above her head and grabbed the top of the boulder that had fallen. It was the only handhold left, and she had to pray it was wedged in enough that it wouldn't move if she shifted it. Sigrid wasn't all that certain it was.

"If anyone is actually looking out for me, please don't let this boulder move. It's my own damn fault, and I have no idea how I'm getting out of this cavern now."

The way back was going to be infinitely more difficult. She couldn't go headfirst back, but how could she have known the curve was this steep?

How did she always get herself in situations like this when Camilla wasn't there to take care of her?

One big pull and she slid out of the tiny crawl space like a child being born. Breathing hard, gasping in air like she was a dying woman, Sigrid remained on the cold stone ground for a few moments. Just to get her bearings, even though that wasn't really why.

She told herself she was brave and strong, but she wasn't. That was the problem in every aspect of her life. She wasn't as strong as she wanted to be, and no matter what, she always managed to disappoint herself.

This should have been simple. She should've known she couldn't fit through it and should've left. It would only be more cave beyond it, so why should she go through all this trouble?

Because something in her chest whispered there was more to this place. No one would have set up a camp like this without having a reason to. No one was as insane as she was, struggling through the mountaintop only to set up a fire in the middle of a forgotten cave.

Someone had to either still be here, or have found something so important they caved the whole place in. Right?

She hoped she was correct in her musings, or this was all for nothing.

Sigrid pushed herself up, lifting her chest from the ground and searching the darkness for something she could light.

"Dragon?" she asked the shadows. "Any chance you can see in the dark better than my human eyes?"

Although the creature was thoroughly exhausted and needed to warm up, it still woke for her. Sigrid felt the heat behind her eyes, the strange feeling whenever the dragon took over a part of her body. Her pupils shifted, splitting down the center, and the cave around her burst into grey shadows.

"There." Just beyond her reach was another stick, this one wrapped with some kind of fabric.

Someone *had* been here before her. That meant there was something more to this place than just a cave. Why would someone have left a torch? An honest to gods' *torch*.

Sigrid scrambled on hands and knees to the item and lit it on fire without having to ask the dragon. She could force the flames out of her own lungs if she was desperate enough, and in this moment, she was.

The orange light burst to life and cast the small cavern into a warm glow. The dragon inside her reached for the fire. Sigrid wanted warmth too, so she held the flames in the palm of her hand and let it burn through her flesh.

She wouldn't have any blisters from the heat. As always, dragons could not burn.

Her eyes feasted on the wall in front of her.

"I knew it," she gasped.

Paintings stretched from floor to ceiling, old and crumbling but still there. They depicted so many things her eyes couldn't detect every single detail. Countless images of stories, each painstakingly left for someone like her to find.

Lifting the torch, she stepped forward and gently touched a single figure on the wall. It was a dragon, or something that looked like one. Golden as the sun, it didn't look anything like her own dragon or that of Nadir's. This creature was more than just a dragon.

It was a god.

Rays of sunlight burst out of it and showered down upon the green rolling hills. Beastkin were painted there as well. Some in human form, others as animals, some mid-shift and looking more like a monster than a person. But they were *there*.

Someone had come into this cavern and painted a story unlike anything she'd ever seen before. How could she have? This was made by her people so long ago they'd forgotten the story.

She traced the lines with her gaze, shocked to see that there was so much here. The ancients were *real*. They had to be. Who else would have painted this? She refused to believe for a second that it was some wandering Beastkin who had seen an opportunity to paint.

This had to mean something.

Sigrid stepped a few paces back then sank onto a larger boulder, staring up at the paintings. In some strange way, a story began to form in her mind from the paintings. She whispered the words to herself.

"The great dragon goddess created the world with her breath. A single exhale, and her fires scorched the earth, bringing about a new beginning. From the ashes rose a phoenix, a horse with mane of flame, and a swimming creature with a long neck that immediately made its way toward the sea.

"She ruled with her families. One made of water, who gifted the oceans with Beastkin whose powerful legs and gills let them breathe in their kingdoms. One for the air, who flew through the skies on feathered wings. One on the land, who made creatures that trampled the earth. And herself, a creature of fire and brimstone living deep in the mouth of a volcano with her people.

"Together, they ruled the lands until something else appeared.

"*Man*.

"The humans seemed good at first. They talked with the Beastkin, had a conference that…" This part had been scratched off the wall until she couldn't tell what it had originally been. Strange, every other piece of the mural was intact but this one.

"After that, things changed. Some of the Beastkin wanted to help the humans. Others wanted to ignore that they existed. The Beastkin of the water wanted the destroy the threat, saying that humans would eventually take over the world with their greed, their arrogance, and their weapons that plunged through Beastkin hide.

"The sun goddess waited to hear everyone's opinion before she said each tribe must make its own choices."

Sigrid's voice choked up as she saw the mural where the Beastkin descended from the mountain and made their way toward the human villages.

Unable to give voice to the painting, she stood once more and made her way to it. She traced her fingers over the cage bars where her people were imprisoned. She touched the chains around the neck of an elephant, the spears in the heart of a lion. So much war, and pain, and violence. All because they had given the humans a chance.

Even seeing this, she couldn't give up on mankind. Not yet. They were prone to violence and war, yes. She'd seen what they could do to a kingdom when someone disagreed with them, but she wouldn't allow history to cloud her vision.

They could be good if they were given the chance. If they were taught that Beastkin weren't terrifying and if people took centuries of work to make sure everyone was on the same page. She had to believe this.

Otherwise, her entire life was a lie.

The skittering of rocks drew her attention. Sigrid narrowed her eyes and looked toward a darkened corner of the room which appeared to have a corridor leading away from the mural.

"Hello?" she called out.

No one responded, but she had the distinct feeling she was being watched.

She didn't want to leave this cavern with the vivid paintings on the wall. It felt far safer than any other place she'd been on this journey. Sigrid was close to the memories of her ancestors here. She could almost feel their souls helping her, guiding her on a journey that would change everything.

And yet, she couldn't stay here when she knew something was watching her.

Blowing out a breath, she walked away from the beautiful paintings, the first hint that she was doing something right, and made her way down the corridor.

The firelight never cast its rays on something that lived in the cave system. She was guided by the sound of stones, but never saw who made the sounds.

"Am I going mad?" she whispered.

A gust of cold air was her answer. She rounded a corner and found herself in a very similar mouth of a different cave. It had to be a separate cave, there was no way she had somehow made her way back to the exact same one. There hadn't been any other exits other than the one with the boulder, and the one that led out into the storm.

She eyed her pack sitting on the ground next to a fire that was almost as big as the one she had left. Cautiously, she approached the pile of her things and nudged the leather bag open.

Nothing appeared to be disturbed. But something had definitely moved it.

Sigrid's legs suddenly turned rubbery, and she sank down onto the ground next to the fire. "Thank you, whoever you are."

Her words echoed in the chamber and nothing responded. Her body took over then, incapable of staying awake any longer.

Sigrid drifted to sleep knowing something watched her.

RAHEEM

LEAVES CRUNCHED UNDER HIS FEET, THE SOUNDS OF THE FOREST decorating the air around him like visible pings of light. He'd never thought the sound of birds calling could ever be so beautiful that he'd think of poetry. Here, the land spoke to him like nothing he'd ever experienced.

Everything was so *green*. The colors flooded his eyes until he was nearly overwhelmed. How did the people here live without standing still simply to gaze upon the beauty? The Earthen folk wandered around without a care in the world. Possibly, they took the greenery for granted, but he never would.

Raheem breathed in the scent of moss and dirt. He'd thought it would smell… well, dirty. Instead, the loam smelled like the growth of land and the great reach of trees who had been in the soil for centuries.

Hefting the pack on his shoulder, he stepped over a fallen log and continued toward the keep where the other Beastkin awaited. The welcome he'd receive likely wouldn't be all that good. His goodbye hadn't been much more than a good riddance.

It made sense they didn't want to trust him. He was a human, for one, and a Bymerian man for the other. They'd persecuted the Beastkin people for centuries.

Telling stories about his wife had helped. A few of the Earthen Beastkin had blushed when he'd described her dark eyes. How they'd sparkled even in the starlight, because she'd always worn her love so it was visible to everyone who looked.

Gods, he missed her every day.

Raheem reached up and patted the trunk of a tree as he rounded it. Four men wouldn't have been able to reach around the width, it had to be centuries old. But then, everything here was. Dripping in emeralds, so vivid it burned the eyes, and so ancient that stories seemed to radiate from everything by the moment.

The keep loomed in the distance. He straightened his shoulders and kept his eye peeled for any unnatural movement. The Beastkin were hard to spot, especially in animal form.

The gates were new, he mused as he stood in front of the keep. Where had they gotten those? The last time he'd been here, supplies were hard to come by.

He touched a finger to the wrought iron, surprised to find it was sturdy and well-made. Had they picked up a blacksmith somewhere? That was the only person he knew who could do something this intricate.

Opening it, he ignored the creaking sound and strode through the gates toward the keep.

A few Beastkin loitered outside, but far fewer than he

remembered. Raheem narrowed his eyes. The hairs on his arms lifted. Something was off, but he didn't know what.

One of the Earthen Beastkin, a woman with pale skin and yellow eyes, paused in front of him. Her gaze shifting. "Raheem?"

"Quite a welcome home," he replied, chuckling even though he felt as though a terrible change had occurred. "Where is everyone?"

The Beastkin woman twisted her hands. "In mourning."

"For who?" His gut already knew. There was only one person who could turn the entire Beastkin population inside out with her death. When the Beastkin woman didn't reply, he ground out a quick, "Enough."

Raheem didn't see much of the rest as he stalked toward the keep. His mind couldn't focus on the details of the world around him when something so precious had been lost.

Sigrid.

She was unlike any woman he'd met other than his beloved wife. She'd fought the world head on, unafraid of what it would think or do. He'd come to think of her as a close friend. There was no question in his mind she would listen to any trouble he had and act accordingly. Now she was gone?

He couldn't believe it. It felt wrong to imagine a woman so full of purpose and determination having fled from this life.

An old feeling of regret and pain bloomed in his chest. He'd lost a woman like her before; he wasn't certain he'd survive it again.

The doors to the keep slammed open, barely registering that *he* was the one who had burst through. His despair and rage took over his body until he was nothing more than an angered beast trying to find someone he could blame.

Long tables lined the great hall. Another thing he didn't recognize. He didn't really care what they did with the decor when they had been incapable of protecting the one person who mattered.

At least to him.

There were two people at the end of the hall, both hunched together and talking quietly. Raheem barreled toward them. Whatever conversation they were having could wait. Nothing was more important in this moment.

One of the people lifted their head. Dark eyes widened, her face like shadows, and Raheem immediately focused on her, as she was the only one who would likely give him a straight answer.

"Camilla!" he thundered.

She flinched. "Raheem, you're back early."

"No earlier than expected. And I return to hear the news that *our queen is dead?*" Rage heated his cheeks, his heart pounding in his chest.

How dare they? How could they let someone like her die? They had spent so much time getting her to this point where they were. She was the one who had managed to bond them together. She was the one who had created a kingdom with her words alone.

What had they done?

He lifted a hand and viciously jabbed a finger at Camilla. "This is your fault."

"Raheem—"

"No, don't speak. Not right now. There's something I have to say, and I'm going to get it out without you interrupting."

"You're going to regret any words you say in anger, so I have to ask you to stop." She hesitated for a moment, then stepped up to him and lifted her own hand. Carefully, she closed his fingers into a fist and held it within her own. "We're all angry right now, Raheem. I understand how you're feeling."

His breath caught in his chest. Even though she'd lost someone important, she still stood strong. How was that possible?

Looking at her, he saw the strength of all women wrapped up inside her being. She was handling the loss of her sister, her best friend, just like any minor grief. Her eyes reflected a deep sadness that made him want to weep, and yet she stood in front of him strong and capable.

Would he ever understand how women were capable of that? He only knew that she was something out of the storybooks already. She handled herself with such grace and poise she might have been a goddess if he looked hard enough.

Anger crumbling along with his resolve, Raheem's shoulders curved forward. "You're right in that. I shouldn't speak in anger."

The person standing beside Camilla cleared his throat. Immediately, Raheem stiffened again. He hadn't realized it was Jabbar who stood with them, and that made him all the more uncomfortable.

He didn't trust the albino Beastkin with even a second of his time. Let alone the feelings Raheem usually hid from all the people that he possibly could. Something about the Beastkin made him nervous, and it wasn't his looks or the fact that he could change into a thunderbird at will.

There was something deep inside Jabbar that was wrong.

A broken piece that wanted to see people and creatures bleeding on the ground before him. Raheem had seen such emotions in soldiers before, but only after a long war. Men had a way of becoming addicted to violence and pain.

Raheem had never seen it in a Beastkin before. Usually, they were a kind folk who simply wanted to live on their own without humans making decisions for them.

But Jabbar? This man wanted to feel human bones crunching under his feet.

Jabbar cleared his throat again. "Raheem. We weren't expecting you back any time soon."

"My travels took me far." He narrowed his gaze. "Too far, it seems."

"There was nothing you could have done to save her. She was far from all our sights, and a rogue assassin from Bymere killed her with an arrow."

The scene flashed in front of Raheem's eyes and he clenched his jaw. An arrow? That was a hard way to go, and one that he wouldn't wish on his worst enemy. Hesitantly, he asked Camilla quietly, "Was it quick?"

"Almost instant," she replied.

He blew out a breath. "Then at least she didn't suffer."

If he had been a different man, he might not have noticed the way her eyes darted to the side when he said the words. Raheem had spent much of his life on the battlefield and in conferences among nobles. He knew the ways people tried to hide secrets when they thought no one could see into their minds.

There were tricks to reading a person. Watch their eyes for the truth, their hands for lies, and Camilla was easier to read than a book.

Weren't all the Beastkin though? They wore their emotions on their sleeves other than Sigrid. She was impossible to even guess at what was going on behind those icy eyes.

Raheem schooled his features into a smooth lake of nothingness. "Jabbar, I would like to mourn my friend with those who appreciated her being here."

"You don't want to investigate who killed her?" The other man asked, his voice incredulous. "I find that hard to believe, Protector of the Sultana."

The title was as ancient as the Beastkin themselves. It had come from a history long forgotten in the Bymerian lines, although he wasn't surprised the Beastkin man knew about it. Once, the Sultana always had a single guard who was with her from the moment she became a royal. He protected her against all odds, tasted her food before she ate, stood at her side in front of a crowd who might grow angry. The Protector would give his life before any weapon would ever touch her skin.

It was a dig at him, and one that was effective. Raheem sucked in a sharp breath so he didn't flinch back in horror.

A Protector never failed to keep his charge alive. Those that didn't were brutally killed in front of their own people. Drawn and quartered was a favorite of the crowd, and he'd heard of one who was flayed alive. Prolonged by alcohol which dulled the wounds and smelling salts that continually awakened the man.

"Enough," Camilla scolded. "I don't know what history you two have, or even what Protector means, but you're upsetting him, Jabbar. I won't have you doing that any more than necessary."

"He knows what it means. And he knows that if he wanted to take that position on, then he failed her. He failed us all."

Raheem watched Jabbar leave the great hall with a sinking feeling in his gut. The Beastkin was up to something, and he didn't have it in him to figure out what. All Raheem wanted to do was find out what really happened to Sigrid, and then figure out where her grave was.

There were lilies in the forest he'd come across that she would have liked. Crystal lilies, the locals had told him. So pale a blue they were almost transparent. They looked very much like something she would enjoy.

"Raheem?" Camilla asked. "Come with me."

She didn't have to tell him twice. He would follow her to the end of the earth if it meant he found out what had really happened.

Together, they left the great hall and began the meandering walk up to Camilla's private quarters. He'd never been there before, though he'd seen the Beastkin woman leave dinners and make her way up the stairs.

The woman must have legs of steel if she'd made it all the way up here on her own every night. He counted nearly four hundred steps before they made it to the landing. She poked her head through the door, inhaled deeply, then gestured him through.

"Did you just *smell* your room?" he asked.

"I wanted to make sure we're entirely alone. Thankfully, we are."

"Why would someone be in your room?" He could already guess. Without Sigrid, the Beastkin factions were likely to fall apart once again. They needed one, unifying person to continually make sure they were all getting along. Sigrid had been a symbol of home for them. The loss of her must have taken a great toll.

"One can never be too careful. I have to tell you something, but you can't tell anyone else."

What a start to the truth she was about to tell him. The sickly pain of hope made him clench his fists tight. "Please tell me this is all some elaborate ruse."

She hesitated, licked her lips, then slowly nodded. "In a way."

Raheem reached out for the bedpost next to him, slowly sagging against it. "Thank the gods. She's alive?"

"Well, don't say it so loud, you dolt!" Camilla glanced around them like someone was going to peel out of the wall. "No one can know except us. I thought you got her letter?"

"What letter?"

As he watched her eyes widen in surprise, and perhaps a little horror, Raheem realized something had gone very, very wrong.

"What was the original plan?" he asked. "Tell me everything, in detail."

Camilla, gods bless her soul, didn't hesitate. She spat out the words faster than most people could have understood. Every detail was stripped clean, and she only paused when he interrupted her to ask a clarifying question. There was so much more that he wanted to know. Why had she left when there wasn't any real reason to? Why hadn't Camilla tried to convince her that the Beastkin just needed a little time? They had to learn how to be both human and animal. There were bound to be hiccups in this journey.

Camilla heaved a sigh when she completed her story. They'd ended up clasping each other's hands, she on her own bed, he in a chair he'd dragged closer to her.

"That was a very brave thing for you to do," he said, squeezing her fingers in his. "It mustn't have been easy."

"It shouldn't have been so hard. But I felt as though I were going against the gods will, for a sister who might not—" she choked up and stopped talking.

"You've been remarkably capable, my dear. Now, you can rest easy knowing someone else carries the burden with you. I'm sorry you've been alone all this time."

"Thank you." The words were almost explosive coming out of her mouth. They rocked her entire body forward as she curled in on herself, pulling his hands closer to her heart. "I didn't think anyone would understand. I've been so tired, so very tired and scared."

He'd never been able to stand a woman's heart breaking in front of him. Raheem stood, gathered Camilla against his chest, and leaned back against one of the bedposts.

He rocked her while she cried and marveled at how young some of these people were. Even Sigrid with her stalwart attitude and icy eyes was still just a child in the grand scheme of things. None of them had loved as he had. None of them had *lost* as he had.

His greatest fear was that they would all lose someone very dear to them, very soon. War had a way of doing that to families and friends, and this was only the beginning.

Camilla leaned back slightly, sniffing. "Did you find what you were looking for in Wildewyn?"

More than he wanted really. Raheem hadn't expected to

fall in love with the place while he searched for the locals' opinions on Beastkin. The land here was beautiful, the people kind, and he couldn't for the life of him understand why there was a war between the two kingdoms.

"I did," he said. "The people are not afraid of you. Most don't even know you exist."

Raheem had been surprised by the realization that most of the Earthen folk were completely oblivious to what their royals were doing. They stayed in their little villages on the edges of society, living lives that were... well, quaint.

The first person he'd come upon didn't care at all that Raheem looked different from them. The man had laughed at his accent, commented that it was difficult to understand him, and blushed because he felt it rude that he couldn't understand what Raheem was saying.

The man had then taken Raheem back to meet his wife and daughter, speaking in another language. His daughter had known more of the common tongue, her voice sparkling with laughter as she explained her father hadn't ever left the farm before. It was his father's, and his father's before that, so long a lineage on the same land that no one had ever felt the need to leave it.

This was mostly the same reaction he'd had throughout all of his travels. The Earthen folk who weren't really connected to the kingdom, but only to the land itself, were the ones who were much kinder than their leaders

War was something that had never touched them before. They couldn't remember the last time someone had gotten into a fight, other than the butcher's boy. But that child was always picking fights with whomever he could.

In time, Raheem realized there was a severe disconnect between the leaders of this country and their people. It was almost as if two castes lived in this kingdom. The people with money and royal blood, and those that didn't.

He explained all this to Camilla quickly, hoping it would distract her from the dark thoughts that likely still plagued her.

When he was finished, Camilla nodded. "That's how it's always been, but I'm glad to know they still don't think we're real. That will make things easier in the long run."

"How so?"

"If they don't know we exist, then they won't ever have to see us. We're content to be alone here."

The mere idea made Raheem's head hurt. "But that's not creating a kingdom? Don't you see that? The whole point of unifying the two kingdoms of Beastkin was to create a third kingdom where those who were different could be accepted. Interacting with other kingdoms is crucial to that goal."

She moved away from him then, wrapping an arm around her belly and looking decidedly disturbed. "That's not what Jabbar thinks. If we're isolated, then no one can hurt us."

"And since when has Jabbar been right?" Raheem reached out for her hand and tugged on it, forcing her to look at him again. "The Earthen King relinquished his hold on this land *only* because he thought you would make a kingdom out of it. If you don't become a prosperous neighbor, I would bet my firstborn that he'll take this gift back. There's no other option."

Her gaze became haunted with a weight she hadn't yet explained. Camilla slowly stood from the bed, moving a hand to her back like an old woman, and then walked to the window overlooking the keep. "Sigrid left me in charge, and I'm not sure she knew what she was doing."

"Why's that?"

"I don't feel strong enough to control them without her. Sigrid was..." she paused. "Larger than life."

"Don't say it like she's gone. You said yourself, she's still alive out there somewhere."

The sun outlined Camilla until she was nothing more than a dark silhouette standing before the window. A beautiful, strong woman, although she might not see it herself. He had half a mind to shake her for the loss of that vision. He believed in her. Hell, most of the other Beastkin believed in her. But she had to believe in herself for this to work.

Raheem stood as well, stepping beside her and clutching his hands behind his back. "She put you in charge, because she knew you could do it," he said. "I know you can as well. I have no question at all that you will bring this kingdom into a prosperity that no one else could have dreamed to be possible."

"Not without her."

"I think you'll do better without her. You aren't afraid to be alone, you know. You're afraid of your own potential. Limitless and vast, the world you could create now overwhelms you." Raheem cleared his throat, horribly uncomfortable that he was the one saying this. It should have been Sigrid, but she'd never been particularly good at the emotional aspects of life. "Once you figure out your vision, I think you'll be much less afraid."

She didn't reply. Instead, she stared down at the Beastkin brothers and sisters who had given her so much in this life. He understood her connection to them. It was very much the same connection he had with Nadir.

Raheem cleared his throat again, unhooked his fingers, and placed his hands on his hips. "I should be going."

"Where are you going now?"

He strode from her side and back toward the blasted stairs that would hurt his knees. "To find her, of course."

"You can't do that."

"Why not?" He paused to look back at her.

"Sigrid needs to do this alone. If the ancients want her to find them, then she's already within their grasp. You wouldn't have a chance to even find her. They'll leave you out on the mountain peaks as a warning to all others who seek their hidden homes without permission."

"I thought you said the ancients weren't real?" he muttered, a cold chill dancing down his spine.

"I always thought they were myths, just stories that my mother told us to calm us down." The haunted look returned to her eyes. "But now, I'm not so sure. I think you should go back to Bymere, as quickly as possible. Change is coming, and Nadir is going to need your guidance more than ever."

"Why do you say that?"

She shook her head. "Something's coming, Raheem. We can all feel it in our bones. It's not the humans in us who are afraid. The beasts are restless."

He felt the blood drain from his face, nodded once, and then made his way down the long stairs. He'd return to Bymere before madness descended upon the ranks of the Beastkin.

NADIR

SLUMPED ON THE THRONE, HE STARED AT THE LONG LINE OF PEOPLE waiting to be heard by the sultan. How many times had he done this in the recent months? This wasn't what he thought a sultan should do.

In answer to that, how many times had he told his advisors that he didn't want to do this anymore? A hundred? A thousand? This was one thing they refused to budge on, saying it was the most important part of building trust around him.

The people were still timid around their new dragon king. The man in front of him was gritting his teeth so hard Nadir was certain he'd hear a crack soon. His wife was quaking as she stood next to him.

"What is your complaint?" Nadir asked.

"My wife, sir. The child she birthed is clearly not mine." He nudged his wife hard, shoving at her shoulder until she opened her arms and revealed a small, dark child in her grip. It clearly wasn't the man's child. He was fairer than most of the

Bymerians, but what did that matter?

Abdul leaned down and whispered in his ear, "A punishment for such transgressions is normal, Sultan. The woman clearly strayed from her marriage bonds."

"Is it really all that important?" Nadir looked up at his advisor, fire burning in his gaze. "How much does that matter to a sultan running his lands?"

Without waiting for his advisor's thoughts, he looked back at the couple. "I cannot help you with your personal lives. This is something you and your wife need to discuss." He almost stopped speaking there, but something burned in his chest still. "That child was born into your arms. *Father* falls from its lips in reference to you and you alone. That is not something you should take so lightly. As your Sultan, I urge you to take the baby as your own and ignore the transgression. The child is innocent, your wife..." He looked at the woman. "Why did you stray?"

She shivered again, holding the baby to her chest with a gentle hold Nadir admired. "Not willingly, Sultan."

Rage burned so hot that he knew his eyes would change. The man stared at him, jaw agape. A dragon looked back at him, his anger heating the air. "Tell my personal guards who attacked you, dear one. Every detail you can remember. No one should touch a woman without her consent."

The woman nodded, seemingly dazed as one of his own guards stepped down from the podium and reached out for her elbow. She drifted from the hall, leaving her husband alone and defiantly staring at his sultan.

"It doesn't change anything," the man grunted. "She still strayed. That child isn't mine, and I have enough mouths to feed."

"Then you shall not have one more." It took everything Nadir had not to eat the man. The desire to feel his bones crunching beneath his teeth was so strong that he had to grip the arms of the throne not to launch forward. He glared toward his concubines and nodded at one. "See that the woman and child have a place to rest."

He didn't have to say it again. The beautiful flowers of his concubines immediately stood, and raced in the direction the woman had fled.

Again, he felt the ghost of Sigrid. She would have smiled at his actions here. Perhaps even squeezed his fingers to let him know she had approved. No one else would have known she had liked his choice, of course. She wouldn't have let anyone realize that.

Yet, he would have known. He had always felt her happiness like a touch upon his body.

The man before him spluttered, shouting curses at the sultan and immediately removed from the hall by guards who had stepped forward. The man would never see his wife again. In Nadir's opinion, it wasn't a great loss for the woman who had suffered so much. She'd be happy here. He'd make her a concubine, in name only, and ensure that her life was comfortable and her child well taken care of.

Such things meant more than a husband.

Abdul leaned down and hissed, "She likely has more children with the man, you fool. What will those children suffer now?"

He couldn't stand to listen to the poison in Abdul's voice. Instead, Nadir flagged down one of his guards to lean down.

As soon as the man was close enough, he said, "Find the rest of the children. Ask around and see if this man is as violent with his offspring as he is with his wife. If the neighbors are suspicious, take the children back here with you."

The guard straightened and immediately left with two other men.

A scoff echoed beside him. "Do you think this will win you the love of your people? You said it yourself, interfering with their personal lives is not your priority."

"No, I don't think it's going to win me that man's support. I think those children will be safer and happier here. It is worth the sacrifice of one person's opinion."

He needed to get out of this room. He could hardly breathe while Abdul stared him down, the rest of the advisors murmured among themselves, even the other peasants were talking. His actions were just, he knew that. Their approval was unnecessary when his gut told him it was the right thing to do.

Then why couldn't he breathe anymore?

They were staring at him with judgement in their eyes, he knew it. How could they not? Their sultan had been a selfish, vain man with nothing more than a few years of experience and a lot of people pulling his strings like a puppet. Having him change so much was bound to confuse them.

Everything made him uncomfortable these days. His palms grew sweaty just meeting the eyes of his people, even one person. His heart beat faster at the thought of their opinions. A mere hint of someone else's opinions gave him cold chills over his body.

Was there something wrong with him? He'd always wondered it, but hadn't realized how bad the state of his mind was until he had taken the reins of his own life. Nadir didn't know how to live. How to love. How to do anything other than look to another person to make decisions for him.

He stilled his bouncing leg, forcing his body not to get up and run. He couldn't leave without a reason, even though he was sultan of these lands. Damned lungs wouldn't inhale properly, leaving him almost gasping like a fish out of water.

Still your mind, he told himself. Imagining relaxation rising from his toes to his head, a wave of calm washed over him, and he wished it would help him through a few more hours of this hell.

Even that didn't work.

Eyes wild, he stared out at the crowd of people and tried to find someone to look at that wasn't judging him. Someone who was a kind soul, where the emotion radiated out of them and could ground him.

He paused, spine stiffening, when his gaze met another man's who looked remarkably like him.

Dark eyes, dark hair, caramel skin and a hawkish nose that was almost too sharp for his face. There was a roundness to the other man's features, perhaps puffier cheeks, that wasn't from Nadir's lineage. Yet, there was something familiar about the man.

The man looked toward a side door that lead into the throne room, one that was only used by servants as far as Nadir knew. Then, breaking eye contact, the man stepped away and disappeared through the door.

Did he want Nadir to follow him? That would be foolish. Far too many people wanted to see Nadir dead, and that included his first wife. This man could be an assassin for all he knew.

The thought made him pause. Assassin. Of course he was. This was the person whom Tahira had spoken of, the man the Alqatara sent.

He glanced at his advisors, still murmuring amongst each other, and decided in that moment it was worth the risk. Whether this man was an assassin sent to kill him, or an assassin sent to take his place, was a detail he couldn't risk losing because he brought a few guards.

Gesturing to one of the few personal guards left around him, he said, "I'll be back in a few moments. I need some water."

"I can get that for you, Your Highness."

"I'd rather stretch my legs. It's been a long day." He grinned. "And it's only going to get longer, wouldn't you agree?"

The guard seemed surprised for a moment, then nodded and hesitantly smiled back. Nadir missed Raheem. He would have jested back, treated Nadir like an equal, not like someone who was going to lash out and have him beheaded.

He stood, ignored the questioning call from Abdul, and made his way to the side door. The crowd of people watched as he moved. Nadir kept to the edges, making certain not to touch anyone or stare at them for too long. They'd expect something from the sultan if he gave them any attention. And right now, he wasn't the Sultan of Bymere.

He was just a young man, panicking at the power which he held.

Slipping through the side door, darkness immediately blinded him. To go from such stunning sunlight filtered through his throne room into complete and utter darkness was disorienting to say the least. Worst of all, he knew there was someone in here who looked remarkably like him.

A match struck in the darkness, flaring briefly to illuminate the face of the man. Harsh shadows appeared, narrowing the wider cheeks.

He looked like Hakim, Nadir realized. So much like Hakim that it made his chest seize with the specter of his brother standing before him so clearly.

"Follow me," the man said.

"Who are you?"

The man did not respond. Instead, he touched the match to a torch and strode down the long, narrow hallway.

Should Nadir follow him? His people would notice if the sultan was gone too long, and there wasn't much time for him to chat with this stranger.

He plunged into the shadows after the man, following the dim light of the torch.

"Where are you taking me?"

"Somewhere they can't hear us."

Nadir looked around them, certain no one would follow him into these corridors. It appeared even servants hadn't used it in ages. "I don't think anyone can hear."

"You've lived in this castle your entire life, and haven't realized the palace has ears everywhere?" The man turned. The look in his eye was so similar to Hakim it made Nadir's heart hurt. "I thought better of you, Sultan."

"Do we know each other?"

The man shook his head, "Not yet."

They paused next to a door, leading somewhere Nadir

didn't recognize. He hadn't been in this part of the palace since he was a child. Even then, his brother hadn't liked to take him into the servants' quarters. It wasn't proper for a sultan to be seen here among the folk that worked for them.

The man ducked his head as he entered, scanned the room, then dragged Nadir through by the arm.

When was the last time someone had touched him without asking? Sigrid certainly, his advisors only rarely, but Nadir was always asked to make sure he was comfortable. Did the man not understand he could have him killed immediately? All he had to do was yell and the guards would arrive.

Apparently, this visitor wasn't worried about that in the slightest. He pulled so hard Nadir stumbled into the store room which was filled to the brim with what smelled like potatoes.

"What are you doing?" he snapped, pulling his clothes down where the man had wrinkled them.

"You'll be fine."

"I haven't been handled like that—"

"Yes, I know. Likely never. I need you to stop talking now, Sultan of Bymere, and listen to me very carefully. The leader of the Alqatara has called you to her side. I don't care if she's your maternal mother. She didn't raise you, and you aren't the man she would have wanted you to become. With that aside, I am here to take your place."

Nadir looked the man up and down. How dare he? The audacity of the man! "Explain why I should trust you in the slightest. I have no idea who you are."

The man's smile seemed a little too sarcastic for Nadir's liking. "You'll find out soon enough. For now, I'm the man who looks enough like you to take your place on the throne. Now, I need you to go back and allow me to cut your face, like Tahira said. It's not exactly the best situation, but it'll have to do. "

Nadir lifted a hand. "Stop talking. Explain who you are, why you are qualified to take on the role of sultan, and what makes you think I'd go along with this plan so willing. I have no idea who you are."

"My name is Solomon. I have dedicated my life to the Alqatara, and thusly, am a trained assassin. I could kill you with just one hand. Likely the rest of your guards as well. And you should trust me, because the leader of the Alqatara does."

"Trust isn't laid at your feet like roses because you exist. Give me a reason to trust my kingdom in your hands."

The man, Soloman, scoffed. "Like you've cared about the kingdom so much during your reign? I won't change much, if that's what you're asking. My role is to stay as silent as possible, stop your advisors from doing foolish things, and give you the time you need."

"How long is that exactly?"

"Depends on you," Solomon replied, shrugging. "There's much you have to learn. I wouldn't expect you to be able to do it faster than a year."

"I don't like challenges."

"Why? Because you rise to them or because you don't appreciate being challenged?"

Nadir found he didn't like this man's face. No matter how much he looked like Hakim, the arrogance in his features was decidedly wrong. This man wouldn't make a good sultan. He wouldn't make a good leader or anything else that needed someone with a level head and a kind heart.

He wouldn't replace Nadir well at all. The man wouldn't

be able to keep his mouth shut long enough for Nadir to walk five steps away.

Two heartbeats passed and suddenly Nadir was an inch from Solomon's face. He didn't remember moving. The dragon in his chest heated so powerfully that he was no longer in control of his body.

Smoke curled out of his nose, obscuring his vision for a second. "You walk a dangerous path, wanderer."

"I do what a true warrior bids me to do. I feel no fear." Solomon's nostrils flared. "Do you, Sultan? Do you recognize fear in your chest? I wonder if that's why you're reacting so poorly. You really should control your dragon better."

"I bet you'd like that, wouldn't you?"

"We don't have time to argue like this. Your guards are going to wonder where you are, and I very much would like to kill them. It wouldn't end well for either of us, but I could paint your walls red and remind you why the Alqatara are feared throughout both kingdoms."

Nadir stayed as long as he dared. The man obviously meant the words he said, even though they were cruel and unusual. Stepping back a few feet, he clenched his fists and forced the raging dragon back beneath his skin. "Are you able to impersonate someone you don't know?"

"I've been watching you for months now, actually. You didn't see me. No one did. I know how you act, how you speak."

"Prove it."

Solomon's entire posture changed immediately. His shoulders were a little straighter, his face more relaxed, his eyes softening. He'd sucked in his cheeks, perhaps, and all of a

175

sudden it felt very nearly like Nadir was looking in a mirror.

He circled the other man, looking up and down while nodding. "It's not bad. But how's your speech?"

"Better than yours." Solomon's accent even changed in the slightest, so he sounded more like a royal Bymerian who was comfortable both in their language and the common tongue. "I have trained extensively for this moment in time."

"You make it seem as though the Alqatara have always planned this."

Solomon fell silent, his dark eyes finding Nadir's before he reverted back to himself. "Fine. I wasn't supposed to tell you, but we *have* planned for this. The goal was always to take you back home to your mother."

"Why?"

"That's a question you'll have to ask her, not me."

Nadir wanted to push. The moment he opened his mouth, however, he saw this man wasn't going to budge. This was a warrior who had dedicated his life to a single person. Secrets would never flow from his lips like a waterfall. Not to Nadir, at least.

Was this the right choice for the kingdom? The man had already said he didn't plan on changing things. The Alqatara didn't want to replace the royals with their own people. And from what he'd read of their association, that was true to who they were.

They were assassins who served the Sultan in times of great war and strife. They didn't try to overthrow the kingdom. They worked for it.

But he hadn't been a good Sultan in the past few years. Or... well, really ever. He wouldn't blame them for thinking it was something in the blood that made him such a poor ruler. Perhaps it was more than just his mind, but the way he was raised, and the bloodline that had ruled this kingdom for centuries.

Looking at the man in front of him, Nadir was quite certain that wasn't their intent. They wanted to meet with him. No one would tell him why.

He narrowed his eyes. "If I let you do this, why do you need me to wound my face?"

"Didn't Tahira already explain this? If someone looks at me, they'll know it isn't you. Anyone close enough to see you every day would know. We can't have that. I will need some excuse to cover that pretty face of yours. A little knife injury is quick enough to heal, but if you take time then I can explain it's the scar that makes me uncomfortable."

"You've really thought of everything, haven't you?"

Solomon inclined his head, "We do that."

"Yes, so I've heard. I spent hours in the library a few nights ago trying to find any information I can on you. There's not much."

"I'm glad that hasn't changed."

"Since when?" Nadir focused on the words that rang with some kind of truth he couldn't understand. Had this man been in the palace before? He looked so very much like Nadir. Not a single fiber of his being wanted to acknowledge this man might be some kind of relation. A cousin, perhaps? Certainly not someone he would have come across before.

"We're wasting time. If you want to do this, then we need to do it now. There's much to prepare for," Solomon urged.

"You're throwing a knife at my face. I don't think there's a lot to plan for."

"Then you agree?"

If the man pushed one more time… but there really wasn't anything else for him to think about. Nadir already knew he was going to do this. No matter whether it put the kingdom in danger, he had to know who he was. Where he came from.

Who his mother truly was.

He lifted a finger and pointed at the other man. "You don't touch my concubines."

"I wasn't planning on it."

"You change nothing about this kingdom. I've spent enough time trying to put it back together. There are a lot of good people in good places working to change the way this kingdom is run. If you throw a pebble into the wheel, everything will fall out of place. I won't pick up any pieces you destroy."

Solomon smirked. "I hadn't intended upon that, Sultan of Bymere."

"Don't forget that. This is my kingdom, my people. I will return and shred you. Assassin or no, you won't be able to fight a dragon in close quarters."

"Thank you for the warning." Solomon bowed low and deep. "Now go back to your pretty, golden throne. I have a blade waiting to taste your blood."

Nadir turned and left the room. He didn't need the torch, his eyes adjusted in the dark hallway easily enough. Regardless, he wasn't interested in letting anyone know where he was.

His footsteps thundered in tune to his heartbeat. Was he really going through with this? Was he going to let someone else sit in his rightful place, the place he'd earned through blood only?

The door to the throne room creaked when he opened it, and eyes from beyond stared at him with interest. They wanted to know what the Sultan was doing sulking in the hallways. Another rumor would fly from the mouths of nobles throughout the kingdoms saying they had never thought him normal.

He wanted to walk away and have no one recognize him. Just for a few moments in his life.

Heart pounding a rhythm in his chest, Nadir made his way back to the throne and sat down upon it.

Abdul leaned over and hissed, "Where have you been? People were talking."

"Let them talk."

"Everyone here is waiting for you to pass judgement. When you waste their time, you waste the time of the kingdom. Or have you forgotten all that I taught you?"

"I haven't forgotten, advisor," he snapped. Waving an imperious hand, he gestured to the guard holding back a teeming line of people who were already trying to push forward. "Let them through. Who would like to hear the sultan's words?"

A man stepped forward, but he couldn't focus on what his subject said. His palms were sweaty. Waiting for pain was almost as bad as the moment when he would feel it.

They hadn't talked about where this wound would fall. His pride couldn't have something that would scar him for the rest of his life. And yet, it had to be convincing enough for him to cover his face for a prolonged period.

Nadir realized in that moment he'd been a fool. No matter

what, he was about to change his own features forever. The wound must be believable. Which meant, it had to be bad.

A whistling sound was the only precursor to the blinding pain that sliced across his face. Nadir couldn't guess what the Qatal assassin had done to him. All he could focus on was the white hot ache that spread from his forehead, slashed diagonally down his right eye, and onto his cheek.

Gods, what had he agreed to?

Everyone burst into motion. Abdul shouted for the guards to find the person who had attacked the sultan, that they needed to have the person beheaded immediately. Four of his personal guards raced forward to circle him, their swords raised toward the crowd as if the peasants were the ones who had done this.

The screams of his concubines rang in the halls like the shouts of precious birds. They were ushered out of the room by the rest of his advisors, and someone grabbed his arm.

"Sultan, we need to move."

He let the guard lift him by the elbow and forced his legs to move. He pressed his other hand against his face.

Nadir drew his hand away when they left the throne room and stared down in horror at the amount of blood coating his fingers and running down his wrist. Was there supposed to be that much blood?

He could only see out of one eye. There was too much blood dripping into it. Or maybe the damned assassin had taken the eye entirely.

"In here, Sultan," the guard at his elbow said. He was steered into another room, set roughly down onto a cushioned seat, and then pushed down onto his elbow. "There's water in front of you. Splash your face so I can see the damage."

"There's koi fish in the ponds. I'll get an infection."

"Just do it."

Who dared—? Ah. The thought sparked in his mind. How in the hell had the assassin managed so quickly to not only find a guard's uniform and armor, but also be the one to get him out of the room? Were his soldiers so poorly trained?

"You?" Nadir grunted, leaning down and cupping the crystal clear water with one hand. "How did you manage that?"

"You're really underestimating the Alqatara. Splash, now. I want to make sure I didn't do too much damage."

"Where are the other guards?"

"Probably still marching down the halls and scaring people. They won't notice you've left for a few moments more. Which means we need to switch clothes immediately."

Nadir watched blood stream into the clear water and wondered what he'd done. He'd put the keys to the kingdom in the hands of a very capable man, but also didn't know where to even start with trusting him. He'd stolen *armor* and then managed to hide Nadir from the entire palace.

Who was this man?

Solomon reached out, grasped his chin, and jerked Nadir to face him. Surveying the damage, the Qatal grunted. "It's not as bad as I thought."

"For an assassin, you've terrible aim."

"I did exactly what I wanted. You turned at the last second. If someone is aiming for your face with a blade, don't move next time."

"I didn't know when you were going to throw the blade. Was I supposed to stand like a statue and not move? That wouldn't have made everyone suspicious."

Solomon grunted, then pulled him to his feet. "Take off your clothes, Sultan."

"I bet you've waited your entire life to say those words."

"Don't make me put a knife in your gut as well just to make things more convincing."

Glaring at each other, they both removed their outer layers as quickly as possible and swapped clothing.

Nadir smoothed his hand down the worn leather armor and the metal plates that covered the most vulnerable parts of the body. He knew this armor like a second skin. He'd spent years preparing to lead the armies, to fight and grow comfortable with weight on his body. As a child, he'd been a wiry scamp who had wrestled with the other boys just to prove a point. He was stronger. He was better.

He would become the personal guard of the sultan and right hand to the man who ruled the empire. When blood needed to flow, he would have been the one to open the dam. And now, look at him. Wasting away on a throne, because someone had told him that his brother was poisoned. Because someone thought it was a good idea to try and wipe out the line.

"It fits you just fine," Solomon grunted, pulling out the knife and handing it to Nadir. "I know you can't see what your own looks like, but anything close enough will do. The blood covered up most of it. You're a spurter, you know."

"Don't move," Nadir snarled as he moved forward to cut Solomon as well. "I'm going to enjoy this a little too much."

Solomon caught his hand as he moved forward. "There's a pack hidden behind the largest boulder next to the back gate of the castle. It has extra food, water, clothing, and a salve which will stop the bleeding of that wound. Travel south, as far as you can possibly go. The Alqatara will find you."

"I'll fly, thank you."

"Don't. Someone is bound to see you, and that'll get back to the castle. You cannot shift until you're as far from the city as possible. Do you hear me?"

The man wasn't wrong. Someone was definitely going to see him if he flew, and then what would he do? Even Nadir couldn't fly fast enough to stop his advisors from beheading Solomon and then the Alqatara were likely to start a civil war. All the work he'd done in the kingdom would be destroyed that easily.

So, Nadir nodded. "Understood. It would be wise not to."

"Good, I'm glad we see eye to eye on that." Solomon's fingers squeezed tight on Nadir's wrist. "Be careful, Sultan of Bymere. The path you walk will bring you to things you never thought could exist. To people you never even dreamed were real. The Alqatara are not like the legends, they are much more."

"And you be careful as well, Qatal. It's not called the Red Palace because of the stones it was built out of. Many people have found their death here, and many more will. Keep your mouth shut."

And with that, Nadir drew the blade down the other man's face, turned on his heel, and ran from the room toward an unknown future.

SIGRID

THE HIGH-PITCHED WHISTLE OF WIND THREADED THROUGH THE cavern like the sound of a flute. It rivaled the greatest musician in Hallmar's castle. The one he'd brought from a far off land, because he loved the sound of her music so dearly. Of course, Sigrid had always thought it helped that the woman was a willowy creature who looked like one of the mythical women made of mist who lured men into swamps. Never to return.

She sat cross-legged in the center of the cave, hands on her knees, breath even and deep. Her eyes had drifted shut long ago. Sigrid could hear better if her eyes didn't give away the source of the sound. She could feel the wind on her skin and the movement of things around her far more reliably if she didn't know where they were coming from.

A deep gurgle rocked through the earth as ice shifted all around her. It was the bass grunt of a troll, hidden far in the forests and away from prying human eyes.

Her wet clothing hung from a branch she'd crisscrossed

over the mouth of the cave. Wind brushed through them, the leather flapping like the wings of a great bird.

Fire crackled around her, but the soft pops were far more comforting to her than any other sound. She knew the way fire moved. She knew it's taste, its sound, the way it touched her skin in a caress none had ever been able to mimic.

She'd built the fire as high as it could possibly go, then taken off her clothes, spread them out to dry, and sat down in the center of the bonfire. The dragon in her spread its wings and let the heat sink into every part of its body. Sigrid herself finally felt warm for the first time in what felt like months.

This was where she was supposed to be. Deep within the arms of an ancient thing, impossible to ever understand. The elements were far beyond the minds of humans. Beyond the minds of Beastkin. None knew where the gods had gotten such things, but none should question such gifts.

It was an honor to have them. She would never forget that.

One of the embers near her right knee snapped. It popped off the log and fell tumbling to the stone floor, rolling and rolling until it came to a hard stop.

That wasn't right. Sigrid tilted her head to the side but kept her eyes closed. The ember should have continued to roll. There was a steep incline in the cave that brought it out to the mouth. She should have heard the continued movement, then the soft crunch of snow, the sizzle of water as it met a burning creation of the gods.

What else could she hear? The wind hadn't changed or shifted around a form that stood in the mouth of the cave. She hadn't heard the fabric of her clothing *hush* as someone pushed them aside.

It was possible someone had come through the other end of the cave. She hadn't closed the mouth of the previous place. If someone was daring enough to squeeze through the same route she had, then they were brave enough to face her in battle.

Sigrid's fingers inched to the side just slightly, still on her thighs, but ready to lunge for her sword if she needed it.

"Who are you?" she said, her voice a whispering thread that snaked through the cave.

The wind touched upon something. It rattled against the gentle movement, two or three items clinking softly against each other.

When no one responded, Sigrid tried again. "I can hear you."

"Your eyes aren't open." The voice was the rustling of reeds in a stream bed. Deep for a woman, but still softened by the years. Not quite dangerous, certainly not accusing, but still strong enough to give Sigrid pause.

"I don't need my eyes to see you, visitor."

"You are the visitor here, Beastkin. Open your eyes and see who has come to greet you."

Slowly, she blinked her eyes open and stared at the mouth of the cave.

A woman stood there, appearing unlike any female Sigrid had ever seen before. She wore furred boots, dark and nearly black. A loincloth split open down the sides of her legs, revealing pale thighs painted with dark blue stripes. Her torso was surprisingly uncovered. Nothing but long, black hair parted to cover her breasts.

Skulls dangled from a rope around her waist. Small creatures mostly, what looked like rats and perhaps a few felines. One delicate hand rested on the top skull, her fingernails overly long and jagged at the ends.

But it was nothing the woman wore which captivated Sigrid's attention. It was the large mask which covered the woman's face.

One large horn created an arch over the woman's head. Two more hung from the arch, seemingly held in place by silver hooks, dangling beside her ears like the finest of jewelry. The wooden mask over the top half of her face had no features. Only red paint that made it appear garishly created.

The bottom half of her mouth was revealed, and the lips curved into a smile. "Have you looked your fill, Beastkin?"

"There are no eye holes in your mask," she murmured. "How did you know my eyes were closed?"

"I do not need eyes to see either."

Sigrid unfolded her legs, stretching her toes out, then stood. "Who are you?"

"I think you already know."

She didn't have the faintest idea. There weren't supposed to be locals living this far out, and she couldn't imagine any person would willingly live in this forsaken place. That left only one answer, and it was one she didn't want to entertain.

Had Camilla been right? Sigrid had searched for the ancients what felt like forever. She'd traveled through this damned snow, nearly died on a mountain peak, only to find the ancients were... this?

The other woman tilted her head to the side, mimicking Sigrid's movement before, and then smiled. The firelight sparkled on something in the woman's teeth. Upon closer inspection, Sigrid could see that the woman had bored holes through all her front teeth. Tiny stones were inlaid in the holes.

"You know who I am," the mysterious creature whispered. "Why won't you admit it to yourself?"

"You can't be one of the creatures I've searched for."

"Why not?"

Sigrid had no answer. A part of her wanted to shout that it was because this odd, strange creature looked so unlike Sigrid. She wouldn't be caught dead in clothing like that, or wearing body paint, or having strange animal skulls clinking at her waist.

Perhaps the woman was a mind reader as well. She reached down to the skull at the top, a large rat skull, and brought it to her ear. "What's that Grim? You think she's frightened of us?"

"I am frightened of nothing."

"Then you are frightened of everything. True warriors know there is much to fear in this world. They let the emotion wash through them, like waves through sea kelp. They do not let fear rule their minds because they live alongside it. To not accept your own fears is to let them run rampant in your mind."

Sigrid hesitated. She didn't know what to say to this strange creature. What could one ask? This couldn't be the ancient of old, and yet, it seemed as though she might be.

Knowing the woman couldn't see her, she gestured back at the paintings far beyond the twisting cave. "Did you paint those?"

"No."

"Who did?"

"No one knows. Some old Beastkin who found their way to see us long ago. Perhaps one who had already met us and was trying to return home. I'm certain his bones linger here, along with the spirit who walks beside you."

A cold chill sent gooseflesh all down Sigrid's arms. "Spirit?"

"There are many who walk beside you, but one appears to be newer than all the others." The woman muttered something else Sigrid couldn't catch under her breath, then strode toward her.

She forced herself to remain still as the strange creature snatched at the air over her shoulders. More mutterings revealed the woman was speaking in a tongue Sigrid did not know. Over and over again the woman tugged at a world Sigrid couldn't see. And strangely enough, she felt herself growing lighter.

Eventually, the woman muttered in the common tongue, "Let go, you old fools. She's made her way to us at last, we'll take care of her from here. Off with you."

"Who are you talking to?" she asked.

"The souls who guided you here. Spirit guides, seekers of truth if you will. They wanted you to come here just as they wanted me to find you. They were the ones who told me you were in this cave, after all. But they're foolish things who speak too loudly. One can't think when they're all muttering over each other." She dashed away the last one, then lifted the skull to Sigrid's eyes. "Look into Grim, and see your future."

"I'd rather not."

"Some don't want to see the future, because they're afraid of it. Others, because they already know the path they walk will be a difficult one. Which one are you, Sigrid of Wildewyn? Daughter of Freydis the White?"

It was the first time in many years she'd heard her mother's name. Earthen folk didn't like to say the name of their relatives who no longer walked the earth. They thought it would bring their souls back in times when they should be resting.

"Freydis," she repeated, the word white and effervescent on her tongue. "You know my mother's name."

"And you had nearly forgotten it. Grim gave it back to you, not me."

Sigrid's eyes flicked down to the rat's skull and recoiled when she saw the black smoke deep in the creature's eye sockets. "What is that?"

"Old magic. Ancient magic that you should not touch. I told him that, but he wanted to meet you more than anything else."

"Why?" Sigrid stared at the swirling mass inside the skull and wondered if she was still asleep. This wasn't possible. People could turn into animals, their clothing remaining intact, certainly. But that didn't mean *all* magic was possible... did it?

"You'll have to ask him."

"I don't want to talk to your rat."

"He's not a *rat*," the woman replied, cupping the skull close to her bare chest. "Don't worry, love. I'll explain it all to her in due time. But first, we have to get her out of the cave."

"Why?" Sigrid asked again. "This is as good a place as any for you to answer my questions."

"It isn't. Simply won't do, because we aren't supposed to remain here and we're already late. I didn't want to rush you after your long journey. Sometimes, other people aren't as patient as I am." She tucked the skull back into its holder, wrapping the string tightly through the eye sockets. "Are you ready to go?"

"Not in the slightest."

"Well, hurry then, child. We've a long way to go yet."

Sigrid watched in astonishment as the woman reached out and pulled her clothes off the branch. They were thrust at her with no care toward the fire. Sigrid fumbled with the leather, rushing out of the flames and pulled them onto her body.

"You never told me your name," Sigrid said as she hurriedly got her things together. "And who is calling for me?"

"The matriarch. And my name is Eivor," the creature swept into a kind of bow, then tossed another layer at Sigrid. "Are you ready yet?"

"Eivor?" Sigrid repeated, pulling the shirt over her head. "I've never heard such a name."

"That's because it came from a time before you were born. A time before the Beastkin forgot where they came from, and what their true names were."

"My name is Sigrid; my mother's was Freydis. I know these names are true and ours." It felt important to say that, as nothing else she'd ever said before.

Sigrid finished pulling the shirt over her head, the last layer before her jacket, and froze when she saw the woman had lunged forward. Impossibly close, she could feel Eivor's breath on her face as she breathed.

The strange creature tilted her head, bones shifting at her sides and scraping down her shoulders. "You say it strangely, but your name *is* Sigrid. It's a name for victory. A name for wisdom. You will walk your path with strength, and it is the right one for you to take."

Apparently, all she needed was a woman who talked to dead animals to tell her that. Sigrid straightened her shoulders, and nodded. "I'm ready then."

"Good. We have but a short way to go."

Eivor moved away from her and Sigrid's jaw gaped open. "You mean, I've been near the ancients this whole time?"

"It's hard to find us when there's a storm on the horizon. You walked around us three times before you finally found the cave. The storm is over now, and I will take you to the matriarch without getting lost in the white beast. Come."

Sigrid snagged her pack on the way out, swung it over her shoulder, and plunged into the blinding whiteness of fresh snow.

Not a single thing had touched the blanket which now laid across the earth. Pristine and pure, she lifted a hand to shield her eyes against the blinding whiteness. There was at least a foot of snow which had fallen since last night.

She recognized the tree in the distance. It had appeared much taller in the dim light of the storm. Now, it looked more like a shrub.

Eivor moved across the snow as light as a feather. She barely even left footprints where she walked. "Come alone, dragon. There's no time to waste!"

If Sigrid could walk on top of the snow like her companion, that would have made things easier. Instead, she had to trudge through the wet, sticky substance. Every step felt as though it were sucking into the ground as the earth tried to hold her in place.

She was strong, she reminded herself. Endurance was the greatest gift of the dragon Beastkin. If this creature wanted her to walk through the snow, then she would. Over and over again until they reached their destination. She would not give up.

The sun lifted on the horizon above their heads and then dipped down onto the other side of the world. They'd traveled for half a day, and there she was thinking the woman had said they were close.

Huffing, face hot and back already aching, Sigrid called out, "How close are we?"

"Not far now!" Was the answering call that floated from somewhere up ahead.

"Of course," Sigrid muttered. She eyed the ground, trying to find the faint prints Eivor left in her wake. "It was 'not far' a few hours ago as well. Doesn't seem as though we're any closer, but what do I know?"

Snow crunched next to her as something plummeted from the sky and landed hard beside her. Sigrid lifted her fists, ready to strike out at whatever had dared startle her.

Eivor's mask met her gaze. "Not far, like I said."

"How did you —" Sigrid glanced up at the ledge above her. A great mountain peak lifted out of the ground, stretching toward the sky with small bits of stone arched over her head. "Ah."

"I have to make sure we're not being followed, Beastkin. Too many people are interested in your journey and not enough are willing to help."

"We're not being followed."

"There are creatures who can silently take flight. Those who burrow themselves into the earth and only awaken when footsteps disturb them. You know this, Sigrid, and yet you refuse to imagine there is more to this world than just humans and Beastkin?" Eivor clucked her tongue. "Someday, you'll learn to accept there are things you cannot understand."

"What are you, some kind of medicine woman?" she called out as Eivor darted past her on top of the snow.

"In part! I guide souls where they need to be, and collect them if they're wandering. Where did you think I got Grim?"

"In some black magic ritual where you sacrificed a rat?" Sigrid muttered under her breath, then called out, "Souls?"

"Everything has a soul. You, me, the trees, the animals. Everything leaves a little bit of themselves when they pass. It's a beautiful thing, and only some of us can see them. When the enclave finds out that you can see souls, we're all placed into a specialized training."

"Ah," Sigrid said. A large clump of snow fell from the cliff edge to land in front of her with a loud clap. She lifted her hand, shielding her face for a moment then continued. "So there are different positions within... the enclave, you called it?"

"The home of the ancient Beastkin, yes."

"So there's matriarch, medicine woman... what else?"

"Warrior, brood mother, there's a hundred different positions, each as important as the last. Why are you so curious?" Eivor paused and gestured with her hand for Sigrid to hurry up. "You'll find out soon enough."

"Will I?"

Sigrid huffed and puffed until she stood next to Eivor. The woman was exceedingly tall when she was standing on a foot of snow to prop her up. It wasn't fair. Sigrid had enjoyed looking slightly down at the woman. Now, she felt like a child begging an elder to tell the stories she'd missed.

Eivor smiled at her, lips curving underneath the lip of the mask. "Look your fill, dragon Beastkin. See where you came from and what you will become."

Sigrid followed the line of Eivor's hand and gasped. A large canyon spread out in front of them, made entirely of ice. Cold, clear blue like a precious stone, it sang an ancient, rumbling song.

Hung between the two giant cliffs of ice was the skeleton of a massive dragon. Its head rested on the top of the canyon, its bat-like wings spread wide between the expanse. Back legs hung over the abyss below. Shards of ice and snow dangled in great times from its toes and ribs.

"What is this?" she whispered.

"The very first dragon to ever walk this earth. This is your greatest grandmother to ever have lived. She was the sun dragon to her people, golden as the day is bright. A goddess among her people, and even more." Eivor's eyes filled with tears as she stared at the dead creature.

"You kept her? You didn't bury her or give her any kind of ceremony to guide her soul into the beyond?"

"Why would we do that? She never wanted to walk a path where she couldn't return from. She wanted to be with us until the end of time. Her soul is in everything around here, just as her body fed the ice and the creatures that live beneath it. The greatest of all matriarchs is still here with us. That is an honor, Beastkin. Not a slight against her soul."

Eivor strode down the steep path toward the canyon. Sigrid did not.

She stood, staring at the remains of the greatest creature to ever live, and met her own future head on. This would be her someday. She would be nothing more than bones hanging like this. Some great beast long forgotten.

Why had she come here? Why hadn't she stayed with her

family and friends, far away from this cold, desolate place?

"Come along! The matriarch has waited long enough."

Forcing her feet to move, Sigrid followed the medicine woman down into the canyon. She told herself not to listen to the haunting song of wind whistling through the giant rib cage above her, or the way the ice clinked together like the chimes of a bell. It wasn't the soul of a long forgotten creature trying to speak with her. It wasn't a sun goddess welcoming her home.

And yet... It felt as though it was.

The path down into the canyon was well-maintained. Unlike the rest of the mountain, this trail was mostly dirt and earth. Someone had recently spread soil across the expanse so her feet could find purchase rather than sliding wildly to her death.

Still, she saw no one. It seemed as though no one lived here other than the medicine woman and the souls of long passed things.

"This is where you live?" she asked quietly as they rounded a large boulder. "Alone?"

"Not alone. They're all within the enclave."

"Which is where?"

Eivor sighed, then pointed ahead of them. "Further on! We must pass through the ancient mother first, so we know she has blessed our journey. Stop asking so many questions, youngling. All will be revealed in time."

She didn't want to wait. Secrecy wasn't necessary in times like these, and she wanted to tell Eivor exactly what was going through her mind.

At the moment she opened her mouth, a rather large gust of wind pushed through the ancient skeleton above her. The echoing groan was a sound she'd never forget her in her life, nor the shifting of the tail that sent shards of ice raining down from above.

Perhaps the soul of the first matriarch wasn't all that much of a myth then. Sigrid glanced up at her ancestor and blew out a breath through her teeth. "Fine," she muttered. "I'll wait and see what is to be revealed."

The wind died down.

She followed Eivor for a while until they finally reached a small doorway carved in the great ice monolith. Symbols had been buried in the ice, refrozen so they would never move. Sigrid reached out to touch her finger to one which looked like a snake eating its tail.

"What is this symbol?"

"That of a house which lives within." Eivor pointed out others buried in the crystal clear ice. "So many of them used to live here. Some are long gone. Others are still here. We're a dying race. Still, we exist for those who need us. Like you."

The medicine woman ducked through the doorway, and then disappeared into the shimmering wall of the frozen waterfall.

Did she want to follow? This was her chance to leave. She could turn around immediately and go back to the keep where she would be warm and safe. It wasn't likely another snowstorm would pop up on her way back. If she were to believe the medicine woman, that was the ancestors guiding her anyways. She could forsake them and all this madness.

She reached out again and touched a golden medallion at the top of the doorway. A dragon had been etched into the soft metal, wings spread wide and mouth opened in a roar.

It felt as though she were meant to be here. Her entire life had drawn her to this point in time where she could finally figure out her story. The story of her ancestors, and where she'd come from.

After all this time... she wouldn't be alone.

Taking a deep breath, she plunged through the doorway and into the unknown beyond.

RAHEEM

THE DAMNED SAND HAD CLOGGED HIS NOSE SO DEEPLY, HE COULDN'T even breathe. Raheem pressed a finger against one nostril and exhaled as hard as he could. Still, it didn't dislodge the particles which had stuck so far up his nasal cavity that he feared they'd never get out.

And still, he'd missed this place.

He stared up at the Red Palace and felt something shift inside him. A small sliver of humanity that meant the world to him. This was his home. Not that emerald green place, so lush and overgrown that it overwhelmed him. This place with its golden colors and brightly decorated people.

The front gates to the palace stood open, guards on either side. They didn't give him a second glance when he carefully walked by. He'd wrapped his head in a scarf so no one would recognize him.

Were they laxer in their protection of the sultan? Not a single guard even asked where he hailed from or what his business was in the palace. Anger bubbled in his throat, pushing words against his tongue until they wanted to fly from his lips and shred the guards to pieces. They should be more prepared to protect their sultan at any cost.

Bymere looked better than he had expected. Though it had been over half a year since the war, he'd thought it would be far more damaged than it was. A dragon had destroyed the city, after all.

The buildings were still sheared off at the tops, but they weren't scorched anymore. Someone had painstakingly washed all the red rock and now built on top of the broken pieces. He could see the line where the damage had cleaved through the stone, and the new stone which mended the structures.

A gaggle of children raced past him, one of the larger boys striking his shoulder as they ran.

"Slow down!" Raheem shouted after them.

Their laughter trailed behind them like a beacon of brightly colored intent. They were probably going to steal something from one of the many vendors set out on the street. The moment he thought it, another man came charging down the main street, waving his hands above his head.

"And there's the shopkeeper," Raheem said out loud. A bemused smile spread across his lips. Oh, how he'd missed this place and all the people who had no problem expressing themselves. Earthen folk were cold compared to the loud, boisterous shouting of his homeland.

He strode through the streets confidently and without fear. No one would attack such a large man, but also because there was little violence within the shadow of the Red Palace. Up through the gardens of the palace he went, then slipped through a side door only the servants knew about.

Again, no guards tried to stop him. Why weren't there people at every entrance to the palace? Had Nadir lost his mind? Or had Abdul finally convinced him a god king no longer needed guards?

Raheem was going to give the boy a piece of his mind. He was foolishly endangering himself at every moment. Guards needed to be on their posts at all times. It didn't matter if they were tired. The man who fell asleep on watch was whipped publicly to remind everyone else what would happen if they endangered the sultan's life.

It wasn't that Raheem wanted to be cruel to those who protected the palace. He wanted them to take their jobs seriously, and only find reward in good behavior. Becoming a palace guard wasn't like a city guard. So many people, important people, lived within these walls.

He'd need his position back immediately. Whomever Nadir had hired to take on the role of Head of the Army was doing a terrible job.

Raheem walked briskly through the halls toward Nadir's private quarters. The boy would be there, as he always was. A few maids raced past him with sheets in their hands. Another one with a swath of brightly colored fabric.

Were the concubines being outfitted? The boy had seriously lost his mind.

Rage boiling beneath his skin, Raheem didn't knock on the sultan's door. Instead, he opened it immediately and strode into the room with words already dripping from his tongue.

"Have you lost your damn mind, boy? I walked into this

palace without a single question from any person!"

He'd expected Nadir to be relaxing on the bed, perhaps even at the desk overlooking some documents. But no one stood where the boy usually entertained himself. Even the sheets didn't look slept in.

Had he gone to spend more time with the concubines? After having a wife like Sigrid? Raheem wasn't going to just yell at the man he considered his dearest friend. He was going to punch him so hard in the mouth Nadir tasted blood.

The cold prick of a blade touched his throat. "And you are?"

"Raheem," he grunted, reaching up to yank the fabric away from his face. The blade held it in place at his throat, but at least the boy could see who he was. "I'd thought you'd know that, however."

"I'm afraid I don't. You've entered the private room of the sultan without permission. The punishment for that is death."

The voice wasn't... quite right. The tones were correct, the accent as well, but there was the faintest dip in the sentences that rang a bell in Raheem's mind. It wasn't wrong exactly, but it wasn't the boy he knew.

In fact, the lyrical voice was almost like one he'd heard long, long ago. And only in the Beastkin of Bymere.

Raheem slowly canted his head, glancing over at the man standing behind the doorway with a wicked looking blade. "You aren't the sultan."

A bandage wrapped around the man's head, crimson fabric hiding any blood which might have dotted the fabric. He was the right build for Nadir. Strong and broad, taller than most men and a wicked look in his yellow eyes.

Raheem was certain this wasn't the boy he'd helped raise.

The man narrowed his eyes. "Perhaps you've forgotten what I look like."

"Who am I to you?" he asked.

"Raheem, Captain of the Guard and wiped from all history for leaving with the Beastkin of Wildewyn and the dragon woman who destroyed the city."

"But who am I to *you*."

The man didn't have a response. His eyes remained narrowed, then he slowly removed the knife from his neck.

Raheem pressed a hand to his throat, making sure no blood dripped from a wound he couldn't feel, and nodded. "That's what I thought. Who are you?"

Staring down at the man was a little more difficult than he might have expected. There was something sinister about this one, unlike Nadir. It was the aggression in his shoulders, the way he tilted his head down and looked up rather than looking down his nose. He'd need to be a lot more careful than this if he wanted to be successful in impersonating the sultan.

"My name is Solomon," he gruffly replied. "I was sent by the Alqatara to take the sultan's place while he is trained amongst their ranks."

Raheem stiffened. "The Alqatara have awakened?"

"They have an interest in this sultan as no other. A Beastkin man ruling the kingdom is a good step toward a better future, but it must be the right Beastkin man."

"And you are?"

"The one who can take his place believably should something arise that keeps the sultan away longer."

Gods, Raheem thought he knew what that meant, but

didn't want to consider the idea. He knew the sultan's story wasn't as cut and dry as the others believed. Hakim had a different look about him than the boy. He leaned much more toward his mother's side of the family. Whereas Nadir had a faraway appearance that always made him different. And he hadn't looked like the sultana at all.

"What does that mean?" Raheem asked. "And be straight with me, I don't want any of the veiled truths the Alqatara are so talented at giving."

"I don't know if I can trust you."

"My entire life has been dedicated to keeping the sultan alive. Not Hakim. Not the bloodline. *Nadir*. He saved my life when I had nothing left, and I have vowed to make decisions that benefit that boy."

"Like leaving with the dragon who destroyed this place?"

Raheem wanted to punch the man. How dare he question motives that were pure? Motives that benefited Nadir? He straightened his shoulders and glowered at Solomon. "I followed her, because she is *everything* that is good in Nadir. She was the one who taught him to realize there was more to life than sitting in an opium den with women on his lap. She is more important to this story than others could ever imagine."

The pretender watched Raheem's words with rapt attention, then slowly nodded. "My mother is the leader of the Alqatara. She is the first woman to train the many armed assassins, the highest of our guild. She is also the woman who brought Nadir into this world, and then gave him to his father."

Raheem's mind reeled with the knowledge. Nadir wasn't truly the royal bloodline? A bastard on the throne was sure to be removed if anyone found out. "Why?"

"There is a prophecy. That a dragon shall arise to the throne and bring about a new age for all our kind. The time of the Beastkin has long since thought to be ended. We disagree."

"The Alqatara are Beastkin?"

"How do you think we were named the eight armed assassins?" Solomon reached up and removed the wrapping covering his face. "There is more to this world than you could possibly know. The Sultan needs to be prepared as no other."

"That doesn't include a war right now then. How are you going to stop this madness?"

"In whatever way it takes." Solomon finished pulling off the bindings and looked Raheem dead in the eye. "If you try and stop me, I will be forced to kill you. I am a Qatal. You will not stand in my way."

If Raheem could have spoken, he would have said the boy didn't frighten him. There were many who wished for his death, and none had survived it just yet. But he couldn't say a word to the haunting face before him.

Solomon looked like Hakim, a strange thing to realize when Hakim wasn't closer to the other two by blood. They were all half-brothers. Each a bastard in their own way. Hakim would never have lead the Beastkin, because he wasn't tied to them other than through his father. Nadir could never lead the Bymerians, because he wasn't truly royal. And this one, this boy, would never lead anything, because his mother was viewed as a monster.

What had happened to this family? What poison had spread through the line of the sultan that had cursed his offspring so?

Raheem blew out a ragged breath, turned on his heel, and

made his way toward the desk. A bottle of brandy awaited him in the bottom right drawer, as it always did. He planned to make good use of it.

Uncorking the bottle, he pulled out two glasses and gestured with one toward the cut on Solomon's face. "Was that your plan?"

"It worked, didn't it?" Solomon nodded in agreement to the drink, and put his blade back into its sheath at his hip.

"Just barely. They won't believe you forever, and as good an actor as you are... not everyone will believe you're the sultan." He handed the assassin a glass and toasted with him. "You'll need me if you want to convince them."

"How so?"

Sipping the brandy, Raheem lifted a brow. "You aren't so foolish as to immediately deny a need for assistance?"

"We are the Alqatara. When help is offered, we take it."

"A wise motto. Better than I expected." Raheem sank into the chair behind the desk and stared around the room where the boy had grown up. This place was as toxic as it was beautiful. Even the flowers here were poisonous. It was no wonder Nadir had become a rather vain, arrogant man when this place had groomed him so.

Perhaps the Alqatara would teach him to be even better. Sigrid had opened his mind to a different future, one he could already see the sultan had placed into his kingdom. Now, the Alqatara would change him even further. Would he recognize the man who returned?

Solomon sat in the other chair, crossed his legs, and sipped the brandy. "How can you help, Captain?"

"If I believe you are who you say you are, others will

follow. Of everything, I am the closest to the sultan."

"They are so easy to fool?"

"Oh, they won't be fooled. This place is full of those who are dangerous and poisonous, but look like flowers in a garden. Being a royal is a game that you must play the right way, or you'll lose your head. I can help guide you."

Solomon coughed. "You were banished from ever entering the kingdom again."

"And yet, I'm here without a single word from anyone." Raheem set his glass on the desk, then touched the ring mark from where Nadir always set his glass. "Let me be your shield between the viper's pit and the spitting cobras."

"Why would you do that?"

"For Nadir. For the boy I helped raise and the man I always knew he would become. I think you can help. Or perhaps, the Alqatara can help. If this is the plan, then we'll see it through to the end."

Solomon lifted his glass once more in a toast. "To changing the kingdom."

Mimicking the other man's movements, Raheem slowly lifted his own glass and stared at the amber liquid within. "To changing the world."

SIGRID

SHE STEPPED THROUGH THE ICE AND INTO A WORLD THAT DIDN'T SEEM possible. Man and beast living side by side inside a tomb made of cold air and frigid water. Homes were carved into the ice and into the mountainside beyond. Animals scurried past, some Beastkin, others not.

Her heart caught in her throat. These people, they were... perfect. Every inch of their bodies contained modifications she couldn't have imagined. Though they were all tribal, with furs and tattoos flashing as they moved, they were also intrinsically working together to survive.

Each of the houses had a kind of marker over them. Some were leaves and dried flowers bound together in a rope-like structure, hung over the opening of the doors. Others were carved directly into the ice or stone.

The Beastkin here were massive. They were all the same height as her. Some even larger. They walked by her with faces bared, unlike the medicine woman who had come to collect her.

Tattoos marked their skin, designating who or what they were.

A man strode past her with his arms full of logs. Scales had been tattooed from his chin to forehead, and a forked tongue stretched out of his mouth. His gaze locked onto hers, golden eyes turning to slits. And she swore he flicked out his tongue when she passed, tasting the air and her scent.

"Eivor?" she called out.

The medicine woman had disappeared in the flood of Beastkin making their way around their homes. A small dog ran by her with a startled yelping call. Children raced after it with sticks in their hands.

She'd never seen a life like this, where humans and animals were so... together. A woman walked by with a snake around her shoulders, another with squirrels that chattered on either ends of their perch. A man spoke quietly to the bear which lumbered beside him, and Sigrid thought she caught the tail end of their conversation which had something to do with getting more logs for the great fire.

The medicine woman popped out of the crowd in front of her and gestured with her hand. "Come, come. We're going to be late, Sigrid, and I don't want you to miss this."

"Miss what?"

The woman was already disappearing into the crowd again. Sigrid raced after her, apologizing to those who she shoved out of her way. One man tried to grab her, apparently recognizing that she wasn't from the enclave, but she pointed in the direction of Eivor and that seemed to change his mind.

Who was this strange woman to them? She didn't make sense to Sigrid at all. A medicine woman was, of course, important, but that didn't mean she should be feared or revered. The people reacted to her existence like a king or sultan had slapped them.

They flinched out of the medicine woman's way, soon leaving a clear path to her side. No one wanted to touch her. A few of the Beastkin even hissed when she got too close to them.

Sigrid slowed when Eivor did, then leaned over and whispered, "Why is everyone afraid of you?"

"The keeper of souls can take a soul if touched," Eivor replied. Her face didn't reveal any discomfort at the people's reactions. She seemed almost... used to the odd reactions.

"That's why you haven't touched me," Sigrid murmured. "You think you'll take my soul?"

"I know Grim wants it very much, but I don't want to hurt you."

"I don't think you can take my soul, Eivor. Thank you for being cautious but... if it pleases you, please touch me. I want you to be as comfortable as they are."

They walked through a sea of people parting in front of them like twin waves. Eivor looked over at her, mask blank and body moving as if she could really see. "You don't mean that, little dragon."

"I do mean it."

"Your soul is the most precious thing you have to offer the world. It's the only thing which remains when you leave, and offering it to me only means you'll remain when you do not wish to. I will use your soul as I see fit."

"Isn't that what my entire life has been?" Sigrid twisted her body, so she didn't bump into a horse which looked on with wide eyes. "I have given my life, my body, my time to all Beastkin. I don't mind if my soul stays to continue that work."

"You'd mind after death."

Enough with this kind of talk. She was tired of people telling her how she felt or why she should feel certain things. Sigrid reached out and grabbed onto Eivor's wrist.

The entirety of the Beastkin around them froze as one. They all stared at the contact as if she'd done something horribly wrong, including Eivor who tilted her head down. The bones beside her head swayed in the air.

"What have you done?"

"What someone else should have done a long time ago." Sigrid twisted her hand, twining her fingers through Eivor's, making certain she didn't cut herself on the long nails. "See? My soul is still intact, and is exactly where it was before. You cannot take a dragon's soul so easily, Eivor. And now I won't lose you in the crowd. You move much faster than I do."

The medicine woman's voice hitched when she replied. "The matriarch won't like it."

"The matriarch has not yet met *me*. She will like it, because I say it is fine, and that will be the end of the conversation."

Whether it was the right thing to say or not, Eivor continued through the crowd and it was easier to follow her. Connected by their hands, she was a much better guide. Over and over, Sigrid avoided the eyes of the crowd who stared in fascination.

Sometimes she heard them speaking in the common tongue.

"Who is this newcomer? What has she brought with her?"

"Why did the medicine woman go out into the storm? For this little creature? Certainly not."

"Is this the dragon?"

The rest was said in a language she didn't understand in the slightest. There was something odd about it, although lyrical. It sounded as if the Beastkin around her were actually singing the words they spoke.

Finally, Eivor untangled their hands and pointed toward a large door carved into the edge of the mountain. Vines and blooming flowers made out of stone guided the viewer into a cavern that seemed almost endless.

"The matriarch awaits," the medicine woman said, ducking her head and turning to leave.

"You aren't coming?"

Eivor paused, and Sigrid swore a smile crossed her face. "We'll meet again, little dragon. I promise."

The medicine woman, Soulkeeper, disappeared into the crowd of tattooed barbarians behind her. They parted like a wave, but soon even that was too far away for Sigrid to see. She was left with their questioning stares, their wandering gazes, and the lingering question that hovered in the air between them.

Who was she?

She turned down the corridor into the mountain depths. The vine carvings continued down the narrow path, trailing up and down in waves of movement that guided her toward the center of something great. Something new.

Sigrid reached up and touched her fingers to the meandering lines. The movement soothed her. The stone was smooth under her fingers and slightly flattened, as if touched by thousands of people before her. Deep in her bones, she knew this was where she'd come from. That long ago ancestors, a great-great-grandmother, had walked these halls in the same way.

The corridor opened up into a bright mouth where water fell freely. Lush and vibrant, the waterfall was so blue it nearly burned her eyes. The music it made as it tumbled down the rocks was like the low murmur of a hundred voices lifted in song.

There was nowhere else to go but forward. Sigrid glanced around for another passage, or some secret she hadn't grasped in her first cursory glance.

Beside her, a strange club leaned against the wall. Bulbous at the end, carved with swirling runes, there had to be a reason for it. She reached out, picked it up, and hefted it in her hand.

Not quite as heavy as she imagined, but it would do the trick. Sigrid held it over her head and dipped it into the curtain of water. It parted around the club. A narrow opening in the falls appeared, just enough for her to get through without drenching herself in the process. She slipped through, pausing at the last second to toss the club back to the wall in case others were following her and needed to use the item.

She turned and surveyed the cavern beyond the waterfall. She was on a precipice. A single, long stretch of stone that arched from one side of the cavern to the other. Each side dipped so far down she could barely see the end, and even then, all she could see was ragged stones that would rip and tear at a falling body. If they survived the fall.

The center of the long stretch of stone bulged out, nearly in a perfect circle. There, six stone pillars stood in equal distance and a large, flat altar in the center. Small stones had been placed in a path to them, swirls and intricate painted pieces making the entire path seem slightly magical. Reflective pieces bounced light spots onto the walls.

Long vines had grown down the walls, lush and green. They swayed with a wind she couldn't feel as she made her way toward the center.

The closer she got, the faster she realized there were *people* standing beside the stones. The humming sound, the song of the waterfall, was coming from them. Their mouths were open in a quiet song and their arms raised toward the sky.

A single woman stood at the flat altar, her head tilted back, dappled light reflecting on her face. In a way, the woman was familiar. Sigrid thought it was like looking at a reflection of herself.

The woman's skin was much darker than Sigrid's, burnished by the sun and worn down by years of work. Her face was heart-shaped, lovely bowed lips, with crow's feet wrinkles spreading out from the corners of her eyes.

Long, white hair fell straight as the waterfall behind them. The ends touched the back of her knees, swaying only slightly as she breathed. A strip of leather wrapped around her torso, covering her breasts, while two other matching pieces fell from her waist in a makeshift skirt.

The dismissal of decorum didn't bother Sigrid. This woman didn't look like a barbarian, or if she did, Sigrid couldn't see past the way her lips moved in time with an ancient chant that echoed in Sigrid's own heart.

She forced her eyes to move away from the woman, to look at the other people who stood at the pillars.

Her gasp should have startled them, or made them falter in some way, but it didn't. Their eyes remained closed and their shoulders squared.

Could they feel her eyes on them? Could they sense the way her gaze had sharpened and her mind had fractured?

These weren't people, but they weren't Beastkin either. Each of the women and men standing at a pillar were some kind of twisted version of the two. The woman nearest to her stood tall and strong on legs that bent the opposite direction, covered in a dusting of feathers. A man stood in the corner, lifting arms that ended in taloned hands like a vulture. Another's face had elongated into that of a canine, while the rest of his body remained like a man.

What were these people? They weren't Beastkin, not that she'd ever seen before. Beastkin were only beast or man. They weren't some strange amalgamation of the two that created the monsters in front of her.

The quiet hum of song died down, drifting like fallen leaves until they touched the ground and then there was nothing left at all.

Sigrid felt her own breath slowing with theirs until a cumulative gasp escaped them all at once. The woman at the altar lowered her arms, opened icy blue eyes, and captured Sigrid's gaze with her own.

She didn't know what to expect. Would the woman shout and throw her off the edge for interrupting what was clearly a sacred ceremony? Would she be angry that Sigrid was here, or would she welcome her with open arms?

They stared at each other for long moments before the woman raised an arm and beckoned her forward.

"Come, child. Let me look at you." Her voice was soft, like the first snow gently touching the earth.

She found herself moving toward the woman as if in a

215

trance. Her feet were careful to follow only the path, until she stood in front of the strange Beastkin woman who must be the matriarch of all clans.

"Sigrid," the woman said, pressing a hand against her own chest. "My name is Aslaug, matriarch of all clans."

"A pleasure." Sigrid dropped into a curtsey, even though she knew it would seem odd to them.

"You've traveled a long way to see us."

"I didn't really have a choice."

"I find that hard to believe." Aslaug smiled, and the wrinkles around her eyes grew deeper. "News of your deeds has reached even here. The woman who brought all clans of Beastkin together, after so many years apart. It is not a feat many could have achieved."

"And yet, I am here. Not with them." Sigrid glanced around at the others who remained at their pillars. One of the bird-like women smiled at her, while the man with the wolfen face gave her a nod. "I fear I am lost, Matriarch of all."

"Why is that?"

"I have brought them together, and yet, I cannot control them. They grow more and more volatile every day. They forsake what makes us human, embracing only the animal and slowly falling into chaos because of it."

"Hungry dogs will bite the hand which offers them food," Aslaug replied, her expression grim and her voice deep. "They see only their own anger, mistreatment, and madness. This is the way of the Beastkin since the ages of old."

Sigrid looked at the woman who had to know the truth, and saw the same world weariness that resonated in her own gaze. There was an exhaustion in leading people like this. A kind of sadness that echoed from deep within the belly.

A mixture of guilt, perhaps, and age old knowledge that no matter how hard they worked, there would always be something more to mend. It burned inside Sigrid like a poison shredding her body. She wanted to repair whatever was broken. She wanted to take them under her wing and nurture them into a people who would be respected and loved.

They discarded her at every chance. And then what had she done? She'd left them. Let them believe she was dead as a means to her own end. Was that cruelty? Or was it a kindness rather than let them know it was *they* who had driven her away?

Aslaug's knowing gaze watched the emotions flit across Sigrid's face as she struggled to find the words. The woman in front of her was more than just intimidating. She was a beast unlike any other. Kindness radiated from the very pit of her being, wrapping Sigrid in a warmth she hadn't felt in a very long time.

"Why are you here?" Aslaug asked, her voice carrying in the ancient cavern. "Perhaps we should start there."

Sigrid struggled to answer the question. There were a thousand answers in her mind, but none of them seemed right. Each one didn't have enough meaning behind the words. She was lonely, she wanted to know where she came from. She wanted to know her history, because if she knew there were ancestors out there somewhere then maybe, just maybe, she could... be someone.

Finally, she settled on, "I don't know."

The words felt fractured, and shame flushed heat to her cheeks. How could she not know why she was here? Why she had traveled across half their world just to greet these people.

There were so many better answers than she didn't know. So many more words that would have given them the respect they deserved.

And yet, Aslaug didn't laugh or jest. Instead, she smiled softly in that sad way, then held out her hand. "Let me show you, dragoness."

She couldn't think, could hardly breathe when she reached out and grasped Aslaug's hand. Together, they strode from the place of standing stones and down the other path. There wasn't a waterfall here. Instead, a wall of vines obscured the doorway Sigrid didn't see until they were upon it.

This one had a door. Had there been any actual doors in this place thus far? She couldn't remember any. Every archway had been marked, but there hadn't been a barrier preventing people from going where they pleased. Perhaps the other houses were marked in a similar manner. But somehow, she thought they likely weren't.

These people lived in harmony not only with the world around them, but with each other. That in itself was something that fascinated her.

Aslaug opened the door and brought her into a room lit only by torches. There was a small hole at the top where light filtered through and smoke filtered out. She couldn't tell if it was the outside, or merely dim light struggling through layers upon layers of ice.

The beam of light illuminated the center of the room in cold white. The rest of the room glowed with oranges, yellows, and reds as the torches flickered and brought the paintings to life.

Like in the cave where she'd spent the night, these were all hand-painted. Each more intricate than the last, they depicted battles of old, Beastkin from every kind of creature, and dragons flying in the sky.

Aslaug left her side, striding to the center of the room and allowing Sigrid to look her fill. Slowly, Sigrid lifted her hands and pressed them to her lips. She couldn't fathom a world like this. Where the Beastkin lived without fear or wonder what the others might do to them. She'd never seen anything like it, had never dreamed of a world where they could live so openly. So freely.

She turned to the matriarch and blew out a deep breath. "What is this place?"

"This is our history. The world unfolded. We call it the cave of memories, but perhaps you would have a better name for it."

"I have no words for a place like this."

Aslaug smiled and gestured with her hand. "Come, Sigrid. Let me show you the history of our people, and perhaps then you will understand why you are here."

She strode to the other woman's side, then allowed herself to be pulled toward the first wall. Aslaug pointed to a familiar set of standing stones. "In the beginning, there were only the first six Beastkin. The wolves of the Earth, the birds of the Sky, the dragons of the Flame, the whales of the Deep, and the twins of light and dark. Together, they created harmony on this barren rock. They fed each other, they dug claws into the land, and they made it something new."

Aslaug nodded to the dragon flying high in the sky. "She was the first of your kind. Her name was Amunet."

Sigrid frowned. "That's not a name I recognize."

"It's an old name, one not from here and perhaps more suited to Bymere than it is Wildewyn. Then, there were not two kingdoms. Only one that lived in harmony, because they worked to make it perfect. A world where Beastkin could flourish."

They walked down to the next part of a painting, where she recognized depictions of man.

"Then, the humans came to these lands. They arrived on boats at first, finding a safe haven on our shores. The Beastkin who were here, the children of the origin six and others who had flocked to this place, allowed them to stay.

"At first, we worked together with them. They were kind, and they were generous. They wanted our help, and we wanted to help them as well."

Aslaug nodded at a man with a spear in his hand.

"And then they weren't.The first war between Beastkin and man came shortly after their arrival. They had no need for us anymore, once they had settled onto the lands and wanted more for themselves. They didn't want powerful creatures who could easily kill them in their sleep around their children and their wives.

"We fought for years, and then things died down when we retreated to the mountains. Let the men have the lands we had built. We could do it again."

She pointed at a particular figure. A golden dragon flying above all the others.

"She was still alive then. Amunet, the first dragon and the mother of all. It was her choice to leave, her choice to take all the others and bring them here where the old ways could still remain. Some of the Beastkin stayed in the lands who did not want them. Most came with us. There was safety in numbers, and our numbers were growing smaller. The age of man had arrived. And sadly, that meant the age of the Beastkin was over."

Tears burned behind Sigrid's eyes. It was sad to think that all these people had fought for, the lives they had struggled to build, were all for nothing. They'd disappeared into the mountains, never to be heard from again by their family and their friends.

She cleared her throat, "If most went to the mountains, how did so many end up with the humans? Were those the ones who decided to stay?"

Aslaug shook her head and brought her farther down the great mural. "The Bymerians stayed. Those were the ones who didn't want to make the trek to the mountains, and I cannot blame them for that. It's understandable that times become rather difficult in these moments.

"The Beastkin in Wildewyn are a different sort. We struggled here, much like you are struggling with your people. Eventually, a group of holy men and women left the mountain and returned to the Earthen Folk who so hated them."

Sigrid could see it now. The many masked Beastkin who had made the long trek down the mountain. They were all painted in dark colors, their faces obscured by masks, like Eivor's.

"They were medicine men?" she asked. "Why do they wear masks?"

"They are like the one who brought you here. Soulkeepers and stealers of hearts. No one can look upon their face without losing their souls. It is the way of it."

"So the masks..." Sigrid's words trailed off, her heart thumping in her chest and anger making her eyes burn. "They came from you?"

"The masks were a way to show the highest of honors to the Beastkin men and women who wore them. Those who walk the path of the holy do not turn into one animal, but as many as the spirits they hold."

"Then how did my people end up the way they did?"

Aslaug pointed to the last painting on the wall. "The Beastkin dedicated themselves to helping the humans. Those who left were certain there was good in the people who had forsaken us for so long. They wanted to show the humans what we could do. That we could be something more than just the animals they thought we were.

"It didn't work. The longer they stayed in the human realm, the more they gave and gave. Eventually, they were nothing more than beasts of burden, too exhausted to remember the old ways and too tired to teach the younglings.

"They lost all that made them holy. Bit by bit, they began to change into only one animal, the one they were born with, the one passed down from their mother's mother."

Sigrid watched the paintings blur as tears gathered in her eyes. She refused to let them fall. She didn't want to seem weak in front of the matriarch but... this couldn't be right. It couldn't be possible that they were such a strong people, such powerful men and women, and that had been beaten down by the blunt tool that was human.

"Then what?" Sigrid asked, her voice thick with unexpressed emotion. "What happened after that?"

Aslaug pointed to the next piece of the painting. "Amunet cried. She cried so much that she used the air itself to express her sadness, draining all the water from Bymere and flooding

Wildewyn until there was nothing left of the kingdom. The Beastkin forgot who they were entirely, but they kept the masks in hopes that it would help them remember who they were.

"The masks have never been a trap as so many of your people think. They were never meant to hold you in a cage as they did. It was our gift to all of you, a way for you to come home to all of us who waited for those who were strong enough to endure." Aslaug turned and touched a hand to Sigrid's shoulder. "For *you* to come home to us."

Sigrid couldn't think with all this information going through her head. How did one even hear her own voice when a thousand others were screaming in her mind? This wasn't right. It couldn't be right.

She was so exhausted. She'd traveled across half the world to get here, only to be told that her entire history was built on the back of labor and mistreatment.

That she'd been wrong, and so many others of her kin had been right.

"Then," she whispered, licking her lips and trying to strengthen her voice, "everything I have done is for nothing? The humans do deserve the war which is brewing at their doorstep. They deserve the Beastkin to rise up, because they took everything from us so long ago?"

Aslaug's brows furrowed and she squeezed Sigrid's shoulder tight. "*No*, dragoness. That is not what you are meant to understand from this story. The humans were at fault, but we are a forgiving sort. Even Amunet allowed her people to leave, to learn their own path, and then gave her body so that she could continue to guide us even in death.

"This story is not meant to upset you. It's not meant to fan the fires of anger, hatred, and fear. Now you know where you came from, what history you need to overcome, but this is not your path. You were not meant to continue the mistakes of your ancestors."

"Then what was I meant to do?" A tear slid down her cheek. "I've been searching my entire life for meaning to my existence, and every corner I turn is just more and more confusing."

"You have a lot of growing still to do," Aslaug replied, then wiped the tear from her cheek. "You don't need to find the meaning to your existence, little one. It will come to you as the sun rises on the horizon each day. It will drift from the sky like a feather from a bird long gone. The meaning to your life is defined by you and you alone. It cannot be found, only received."

She felt herself tear at the seams. The mere thought that this woman couldn't tell her what to do, where to go, or how to be… Well, it made sense. Of course they weren't going to make every decision for her. But gods, how was she supposed to do it herself?

Sigrid was flying apart at every corner, and she didn't know where she was going to go after this. There were too many broken pieces in her soul, and she didn't know how to put them back together in the right way.

She'd started a war. She'd saved her people, but lost someone good in the action.

Nadir.

The name ghosted across her mind like a physical touch. She'd forced herself not to think of him, hoping that in the absence of thought that he wouldn't haunt her. But there he was. At every step she took, he followed closely behind, because he'd never really left her side. Not yet.

Wasn't she supposed to have forgotten him by now? The sultan who had stolen her away from her people, who had persecuted their own kind. The boy who had slowly turned into a man in front of her eyes.

She *missed* him. The laughter in his eyes, the surprise when he did something he finally felt was right. The way he'd squeeze her hand and the way he always thought she wasn't quite beautiful but strong, and that was all that mattered in this life.

A small sob choked her throat as she tried to speak, and she pressed the back of her hand against her mouth.

She wanted to say that all of this had been in vain. That every choice she'd made had only brought her farther and farther away from happiness and she didn't know how to grab onto that thread and drag herself out of this ever-sinking hole.

Aslaug reached out and pulled Sigrid's hand away from her mouth. Slowly, the matriarch drew her into her arms and touched their foreheads together. "Easy, child. You're here now, and you don't have to leave until you find yourself again."

"I just want to make the right choice," she whispered.

"For yourself, or for your people?"

To answer the first felt selfish. She'd carry that guilt with her for the rest of her life, knowing that she'd chosen to be herself while the rest of her people were in pain. But the second made her soul ache and her heart clench. She couldn't do that either. She couldn't choose them again while knowing it would only end in more heartache.

"Myself," she whispered, another sob shaking her entire

body within Aslaug's arms. "I want to choose myself for once."

The matriarch breathed out a sigh that feathered across Sigrid's eyes, chilling the tears there.

"Then we will teach you, dragoness. We will teach you how to choose yourself."

NADIR

WIND BLASTED THE SAND UP INTO HIS FACE, BURNING HIS SKIN AND stinging his eyes with the power of its rage. Nadir lifted an arm up to cover his face then swore under his breath. This journey was meant to be easier than just wandering through the desert, and yet, here he was.

His lips were cracked from lack of water. His skin was so dry and aching that he was certain it had split open in a few places under the layer of his clothing. He desperately need to drink and eat.

Hadn't Solomon said this would be an easier journey? He vaguely remembered the man saying that, or maybe the man who eerily looked like him had simply meant that it was a journey. He didn't know, and wasn't exactly thinking straight at this point.

The wind brushed by his cheek again, but this time it felt like the soft velvet of hair. He'd felt it before, so many times while he made this trek that he sometimes had a hard time figuring out whether it was real or not.

Sigrid. The damned woman was still here, whether he wanted her to be or not. She was in every step he took through the desert.

Sometimes he saw her standing on top of a dune, beckoning him in a direction he hadn't thought to go. And every time, he made sure he followed her. She'd never led him wrong before, and it didn't matter that this version of her was a mirage.

He hoped it was his mind telling him where to go. That his mind knew where this journey needed to lead him while his body slowly failed.

If he could change, this would be so much easier. The dragon still raged in his mind, slamming at the gates of its cage and desperately trying to save the two of them. He could fly up into the air, scout where he needed to go, and immediately change back if that was what Nadir wanted.

But it wasn't. He couldn't do that to the people, couldn't reveal that the sultan wasn't even in the palace where a man should be ruling them. Their sultan was wandering the deserts like a mad man, desperately trying to find Falldell when he knew damned well the kingdom had been lost for centuries.

No one knew how to get to the home of the assassins. Only the few people who had been brought there by one of the Alqatara themselves.

Stumbling, Nadir fell to his knees on top of a sand dune and tilted his head back. The wind was blistering and unforgiving. The sun burned through the haze of the sky, and his water had run out a day ago.

He didn't know how long he could go without water. He

wasn't like human men. He could likely go much longer, but that would only prolong his death.

Wasn't this what he deserved? Finally, after all his years searching for a way to end this curse of life, he was finally at the point when it would happen.

Again, the coil of hair slid across his face, trailing around his neck like a noose. He felt her lips against his ear, her voice so comforting he leaned into it.

"You don't really want to die," she whispered. "Not yet. Now get up, Nadir. There's so much more for us to conquer."

The dragon in him lifted its head, pleased at the sound of her voice, but even more at the images she conjured. They could take the world if they wanted. Spread their wings wide, breathe fire upon the kingdoms that didn't want them and take back everything they should have.

She pressed her lips against the whorls of his ear. "Get up, Nadir."

With her voice in his head, he slowly lifted himself onto his feet. There was more to do here, more than he could conquer and more he could learn. She was right.

Giving up wasn't an option.

His steps wavered, but he continued with shaky steps. There was a kingdom here, a city filled with people who knew how to kill with the smallest finger on their hand. He could find them. He was sultan of these lands, and damned if they would hide themselves from *him*.

Mere moments after the thought, or perhaps hours of nothing but quiet in his mind, he saw a figure appear on the horizon. This one was clearly more solid than the last, but it wasn't the woman his eyes caught upon.

A lion stood beside her, far larger than any creature he'd ever seen before. The woman was tall herself. Nadir had to look up to meet her gaze, but she barely reached the lion's shoulder. The beast was far too big for him to fathom, and yet there it was. Real and as solid as the sand beneath its feet.

He came to a stop at the bottom of the dune where they stood and looked up. Slowly, he peeled the fabric over his face away and called out, "Greetings."

The woman looked him up and down, clearly unimpressed. Her skin was as dark as the night sky, her eyes sparkling like stars captured within it. Vibrant blue fabric swirled around her figure, pieces of it whipping out like snakes snapping in his direction. "You are him I suppose?" she asked.

"I am the Sultan of Bymere, first of his name."

"You'll find there are no titles here, Sultan." She gave him a mocking bow, then stood up. Her hair was twisted into two buns on either side of her face, a rather unusual looking hairstyle but one that seemed to fit the laughter in her eyes.

"And you are?"

"A friend, for now." She nodded toward the lion. "He's here to make sure you actually make it to our leader."

"How so?" Nadir looked for a litter behind the lion, something the creature could drag along the sand so Nadir could rest for a few moments. There was nothing attached to the creature's hide. He furrowed his brows, glancing up to meet the creature's gaze that seemed to smile back at him.

The woman coughed. "You're going to ride him, Sultan. Or did you think we could make it all the way to Falldell on foot?"

"Am I not near it?"

This time, she tilted her head back and burst into laughter.

"No, Sultan, you aren't even close."

He watched the woman make her way to the lion's side, grasp a handful of his mane, and pull herself up onto his back. He didn't seem to react at the tugging of his hair, although Nadir was certain it must have hurt. She was no small woman, but strong and broad.

"Come on then," she said. "He'll manage you and your pack just fine."

Nadir didn't have to be told twice. He understood this was likely a one-time offer, and the lion was already pawing at the ground, ready to run. If they left him, then he was really going to die in this sands. Just another body lost to the desert like so many before him.

Sigrid's voice whispered in his mind again, and he refused to give up. Like she said, there was much left to do. He strode up to the lion, tossed his pack to the woman, and yanked himself up behind her.

Let her do all the work. He didn't know how to ride a lion like he did a horse. There was no saddle for him to hold onto. There was nothing but fur beneath his thighs. Gods, he was going to fall off as soon as this thing started to move, wasn't he?

The woman glanced behind her while leaning forward. "Hold on tight. This is going to be a quick ride, and if you fall off, we aren't stopping."

He didn't need to be told twice. Nadir reached out, hooked his hands in the belt at her waist, and held on for dear life as the lion lunged forward.

The beast flew across the sands in great, leaping movements that evened out and quickly became far smoother than a horse. The wide pads of the lion's feet blasted sand in every direction, but it didn't matter because they were long gone by the time the grains would ever even touch them.

Wind blew past him, and for the first time in what felt like forever, Nadir remembered what it felt like to be free. The wind rustled through the long length of his hair, the curls brushing against his face.

Freedom flowed through him in this moment with a powerful beast racing across the desert sands.

He didn't know how long it took them to reach their destination. Only that he enjoyed every moment of it. His thirst disappeared in the wake of awe and happiness.

Eventually, as the sun touched the horizon and the moon began to peek its face out, they reached a place where the lion began to slow. Its sides heaved, but he didn't think it was from exhaustion. If anything, the animal seemed ready to run even more. They must have been going for hours according to his tracking of the sun. And still, the beast was ready for more.

Was this a Beastkin? He couldn't imagine that it was. The legends always claimed some Beastkin in Bymere were far larger than what the action animals were like, but that was just a legend. He'd seen the Beastkin before. They were the same as the other animals, impossible to distinguish unless they had some kind of birthmark that crossed over when they changed. It wasn't like that; the change didn't make them *more* powerful.

Had he been wrong?

The woman in front of him patted a hand to the lion's sweaty side. "Not bad. I think you're losing your touch a bit though, old friend. That took us at least an hour longer than it should have."

The lion huffed out a breath.

"Don't argue with me. You know it would have been much easier if I took one of the younger ones."

Again, the lion let out a growling chuff.

"Fine. We were safer with you. I'll give you that. The older ones *do* know how to fight better." And with that, she slid off the lion's back and looked up at Nadir expectantly. "Well? Are you coming?"

Why was he following this strange woman's orders? He'd never taken well to people telling him what to do, but this woman appeared out of the desert and he did whatever she wanted. Still, he found himself sliding off the lion's back and looking at her expectantly.

Trying to take back a little bit of control, he squared his shoulders. "What now? Am I to meet your leader?"

"She called for you, didn't she?" The woman turned away from him, muttering just loud enough for him to hear, "Why, none of us will ever understand."

He didn't either. There wasn't much here for him. Of course, he should have visited a long time ago. Sultans were meant to know all the districts of their kingdoms without just assuming that one was running on its own. But that's how the Falldell had always been.

It wasn't really a part of his kingdom. It stood on its own with the understanding that should Bymere need to call upon it, that it would rise up and devour anything in its path.

Right now, he felt as though it were going to consume him.

He followed the strange woman, who had yet to give him her name, over the last dune and then gaped at the city he had never known was hidden in the sands.

A wall surrounded the entire place, writhing with carved

bodies of snakes, twining around each other. There seemed to be hundreds, perhaps thousands of snakes so large he couldn't fathom their size. The gate appeared to be the only place where one could enter the kingdom, and it was here where the snakes' heads began.

Twin faces stared at him, large rubies glimmering in their eyes. It seemed as though they could actually see him. Their expression so vivid, and their fangs so sharp.

The woman gestured with her arm for him to get a move on. "Come on then, Sultan of Bymere. The Alqatara will only wait for you so long before they decide to move on without you."

"And what exactly is moving on?" he asked as he rushed to her side. Sand kicked up at his feet like gold coins rolling through the desert. "What do the Alqatara want with me anyways?"

She shrugged. "I don't know everything the mistress wants. She says she wants to see the sultan. We make sure that she sees him. It's as simple as that."

"Have any other sultans been brought here?"

The woman didn't respond, but she didn't need to. There were journals kept by each sultan. Private thoughts and dreams that each one detailed while he was seated upon the throne. They were meant for other sultans, certainly, but there were no secrets among those of the same blood. He'd read many of them, and no one had ever been brought to the home of Falldell.

Nadir edged past one of the large snakes, watching it carefully to make sure it was actually a sculpture and not a Beastkin about to lunge at him. "When was the last time anyone saw one of the Alqatara?" he asked, already knowing the answer.

"Today," was her response.

He snorted. So she wasn't going to give him much of a response then. She'd earned that right. He could only assume that she was one of the Qatal as well, a deadly assassin who could easily kill him without a second thought.

That didn't make him want to poke at her any less. A voice deep inside his head whispered, "Just try her. See what she can do."

He'd done that with another woman recently, and he remembered how soundly Sigrid would have defeated him. He'd tired her out first with tens of warriors. A memory that still plagued him to this day.

Why had he been so afraid of her when he'd first seen her? Was it because he'd somehow understood there was a connection between them?

Nadir certainly hadn't believed she was really a dragon. He'd been raised his entire life to believe that there were no others like him. Beastkin weren't mythical creatures who could fly through the sky and breathe fire. They were regular animals, blending into the crowds of beasts until they were impossible to tell which was which.

It had been easier to believe she wasn't like him as well. He hadn't wanted to think that another shared his curse, the affliction that had made him different since he was a child. The affliction that he was certain would earn him death one day.

Now, things were different. He wanted to know what Sigrid was doing, because after all this time, he wasn't truly alone.

They passed through the twin snakes, which he swore

turned their heads to watch them, and continued down a path toward a city made of white stone.

The houses were a familiar style to the Bymerian peasants. Made of white mud and bricks, they were built from the ground up by careful hands. Each stretched out of the sand with a small opening on the top for smoke to leave if they were cooking, although most would cook outside.

This was the legendary Falldell? The small huts stretched as far as his eye could see, but there was no palace. No castle for any of their leaders to stay.

"Where is the leader of the Alqatara?" he asked. His spine straightened and his hands fisted. Surely, they wouldn't have played him like this? They wouldn't have brought him here only to force him to make yet another journey?

The woman glanced at him and raised a brow. "In the home ahead of us."

He looked for something more extravagant than all the others, but didn't find anything other than yet another white brick house. "Where?"

The hide curtain in front of the home's doorway shifted. A familiar woman stepped out of the home, striding toward them with confident steps.

Dark slashes of brows drew down the moment she saw him. Yet another person who immediately reacted with hatred when they cast their eyes on his face. Would he ever get tired of it? Yes, but there was still a thrill in his chest when he realized someone immediately didn't like him simply because he existed.

Nadir dropped into a mocking bow. "Tahira."

"Sultan." She faked a curtsey. "Welcome to the home of the

Alqatara."

"I'm afraid I don't believe you're the leader of these people, darling. But I have no time for such foolishness. My kingdom is in the hands of one of your own, and if you have double crossed me I will—"

She clapped her hands hard, forcing him to pause in the middle of his sentence in shock. Had she really just interrupted him?

"I'm not interested in a pissing contest with you. We're not hurting the kingdom. The matriarch would like to speak with you."

What else could he really say about that? They'd already gone around with this conversation, but he wanted them to know how important this was. Bymere was his *home,* and he'd only just realized that. He wasn't willing to give that up without a fight.

Following Tahira, he swept aside the leather covering and stepped into the small hut.

There wasn't much inside, but he didn't know why he expected more. The inside was painted a warm yellow, likely from the tiny water plants that grew next to any oasis in the desert. A fireplace in the dead center was cold. It was too hot for them to have a fire. A few paintings hung from the walls, but it was the cot in the corner that caught his attention.

A woman laid out on the small bed. Patch-work blankets laid across her lap, a thousand colors all tangled together in something so beautiful it hurt his eyes.

Not because the blanket was well made. It wasn't. There were stitches coming out of every corner, pieces of it falling apart, and one side wasn't even finished being sewn. But it had clearly been made with love.

It was an emotion he didn't quite know how to understand yet. Like a butterfly, it flitted at the corner of his eye. Always out of reach, but something he desperately wanted to know.

The woman under the blanket was so small he almost didn't notice her. The folds of her face were lined with hardship and a difficult life.

Tiny, so tiny it almost scared him, she shifted underneath the blanket made with love and smiled up at him. "My son, it's good to see you."

He bowed to the Matriarch of the Alqatara. "My lady, it is an honor as few sultans receive."

"I had hoped to see you before time took me away from this world. You are just as handsome as I thought you would be."

The words didn't quite sink in, even as he straightened and met her gaze. Then, all at once, it rushed down upon him like a waterfall of emotion. He saw the straight edge of her nose, the square shape of her jaw, the slight curl to her gray hair that was so rare in Bymere.

Above all else, he saw the tears in her eyes and suddenly understood what that meant.

Nadir didn't know how to process the thought. His knees went suddenly weak, and there was nothing for him to catch onto. Instead, he took a shambling step forward, halting before he could get too close to the bed. "What did you say?" he croaked.

"My son," the matriarch said again. "You may call me Nahla, if you wish. You were named after me, and the sands where you were born."

"Mother?" he asked. His mind raced to catch up with the conversation, but he couldn't think past the word. *Mother.*

He'd always had one in his life. The word meant a warm-hearted woman with hair that turned red in the sun and a smile that could light up the entire palace. The woman who would chase him and Hakim through the concubines' quarters with laughing bubbling up into the ceiling.

Until he realized she wasn't his mother at all. That she'd been the woman who had raised him, but not the woman who'd brought him into the world. The one who had been there for his first gasping breath.

He didn't want to feel like this. The memories of his own mother, the woman who had kissed his bruises and lifted him into her arms when he fell, burned in his memories. She was the one who had taken the time to teach him to be a good person.

And yet, this woman *looked like him.* He saw the shape of her eyes and saw his own emotions reflected in them. She looked up at him as if he was the one person left in this forsaken kingdom that mattered.

Maybe he was. In this moment, she wasn't the leader of the Alqatara. She was just a woman, seeing her child for the first time in a very long time.

He shuffled forward, dropped to one knee, and placed his hand on the bed beside hers. "Why?" he asked, his voice so quiet he almost couldn't hear it himself. "Explain that to me, please."

Nahla looked up at the other two women and nodded toward the door.

Tahira didn't move, crossing her arms firmly over her chest and glowering at Nadir. "I don't trust him, Matriarch. Excuse me if I insist upon staying."

"This is a conversation best left to me and my son. Leave us."

He thought for a moment that Tahira wouldn't listen to her matriarch. Such an action was expected from a woman so clearly upset that he was even there. He didn't know what he'd done to garner her hatred. Most people hated him already in the kingdom for all the things he hadn't done, but this felt a little more personal.

After a few heartbeats, she turned on her heel and left the home.

The moment the flap closed behind her, Nahla reached out and covered her hand with his own. Nadir marveled at the texture of her skin. Had he ever touched someone who was so old? Most elderly people were kept away from him. There was still a superstition in Bymere that they could pass on bad luck to those they touched.

She clearly didn't believe in these old religions. Instead, Nahla laced her fingers with his and let out a happy sigh. "It's been too long since I've held you in my arms, boy."

"Why did you let me go?" he asked again. "I heard the story from Abdul. That he came to take me away, that you seduced my father in hopes that one of your own lineage would take the throne."

"That's only part of the story."

"Then it's true?" he asked, searching her gaze for something more than a woman who had used a child to her advantage. He didn't want to be the son who was created for a purpose. Just once in his life he wanted to be... wanted.

She smiled at him, squeezed his fingers, then nodded.

"There's so much more I want to tell you. That's why I brought you here. Of course I wanted to have someone on the throne whom I could trust. Darkness brewed in the line of your father. I thought, perhaps, Beastkin blood could burn that away."

"Darkness?" Nadir couldn't imagine what she was talking about. His line had always been known as good kings. They took care of the kingdom, even through hardships, and made decisions others didn't want to make.

"The Beastkin have suffered under the rule of your father's line. They suffered before as well. I thought, perhaps, a child of both bloods might be able to bring them together." She coughed slightly, leaning to the side and catching her breath. "I was right. That's exactly what you've done."

He didn't want to agree. It somehow felt wrong, as though he was going against the memory of his family by saying he'd done all that this woman wanted, without having her guidance in his life.

Was it so wrong to agree though? She wanted the Beastkin to be part of the Bymerian empire. He couldn't disagree that it was a good idea. He wanted the same thing. So why was there a part of him that wanted to renounce the idea immediately because he'd followed in the footsteps she wanted him to traverse in?

He blew out a breath. "So this was your plan all along?"

"One cannot have a plan if the person involved doesn't know you exist." She pulled her hand from his and ghosted a velvet soft touch over his cheekbone. "You are more than I ever could have imagined. My handsome boy. Do you know what they call you on the streets now?"

"The boy king?"

"No," she said and shook her head. "They call you the God King. The boy who was, and the man who became a monster just to save them from the worst of the worst."

"I'm not a god."

"You could be, if you tried hard enough." Nahla struggled to sit up, lifting a hand and refusing his help when he leaned forward. "There is a difference between a man and a god. Do you know what it is?"

"Power."

Her gaze met his, and he was silenced by the sheer force of it. Suddenly, he understood why she was the leader of the Alqatara and no one else would suit. There was a spine of steel in this woman.

"No, my son. The difference between a man and a god is belief. Your people are already rumbling with the prayers to a god who is also a sultan. That is power you can wield, but only if they continue to believe it."

"Then how do I coax them to entertain the idea?"

"You give them a reason to believe it. Show them who you are and what you can do. In the moments after the battle, you sat with your people. Lowered yourself to their level and helped them understand that you were a man beneath all the scales. They needed that in that moment, so they would no longer be afraid. Now, there is no fear in their hearts about you. Only curiosity."

Nadir took a deep breath and held it. Slowly releasing the tension, he nodded. "I don't know how to make them continue to think in such a way. I don't know if I really want them to."

"You do." Nahla reached out, tucked a finger under his chin, and forced him to meet her gaze. "You want your people to look at you and see a god. They will not question the verdict of a God King. They will question the thoughts of a man."

"My advisors—"

"Are but pawns in this great game of chess," she interrupted. "You worry about their opinions far too much, my son. Soon, you will have no need of them. The country will look to the skies for the answers to their questions. They will pray to you and your wives in hopes that someone will hear their prayers. And you? You will answer them."

He'd never wanted to be a god. Not to his people, not to his family, and certainly not to the world. But the way she said it…. It did seem easier.

There would be no more advisors or people who tried to tell him what to do. There would be no one judging him for being just a man who made poor decisions. The world would have to agree that he was trying, or that they couldn't understand his methods, but that they must agree with them.

What would Sigrid say?

Nadir wracked his mind, but could only come up with a disapproving expression. She hadn't wanted him to be anything more than himself. She was the one who said his people needed to see a man before they saw a sultan.

And here he was, choosing to become a god.

His blood mother tapped her thumb on his jaw. "My son. I know this isn't the path you would have chosen for yourself. It's not the path I would have chosen for you either. But you must understand, Bymere is at a turning point. There will be a war. There will be so much violence neither of us can see through the blood. And the only thing that can stop that is a god who protects his people from certain death. Can't you understand that?"

He understood that people wanted to control him his entire life. Everyone he'd ever met wanted something from him, or him to *be* someone else.

This was his mother. The woman who had given him life. Who was he to deny her anything when she had gone through so much just to ensure he had breath in his lungs?

Or perhaps, he was merely weak. The small voice in his head which had been beaten back by the strength and determination within Sigrid awakened once more. It whispered he couldn't do this on his own. His decisions were always bad. He was nothing more than a child in a game that would devour him whole if he didn't listen to his betters.

He didn't know this woman, or why she wanted him to help her. But he did know she ruled the most important community of deadly assassin in the entire empire. She had to be trustworthy.

And so, the Sultan of Bymere lowered his head and placed it on her lap. "Teach me," he whispered.

"I will, my son. Before my soul joins the ancestors, I will teach you how to be a god."

CAMILLA

SHE KEPT HER EYES FOCUSED ON THE FOREST BEYOND THE KEEP, waiting for Jabbar and his men to return. They'd left early in the morning, saying they were going to hunt for the rest of their people. There was plenty of meat in their home. Camilla knew they were lying.

She just didn't have any idea what they were doing.

Now, the sun set on the horizon, and they still hadn't returned. A sinking feeling in her belly warned that something terrible was going to happen. Something she couldn't control.

Camilla had led these people well in the wake of her sister's disappearance. She refused to think of it as a death, although every day that Sigrid was gone stretched longer and longer. She couldn't believe her sister was dead. The mere thought sent her heart into a thundering beat that threatened to bury her under the sound.

Instead, she believed that Sigrid had found the legendary city. That she would return with new knowledge and purpose for their people. She had to believe. Otherwise, all she could think of was Sigrid's body on a mountain somewhere, and her soul wandering for all eternity because the ceremony hadn't been performed.

Warm arms slid around her waist, startling her out of her thoughts.

She glanced down at the honey-colored forearms, their strength easily visible as they flexed beneath her fingers. She'd seen these hands so many times, she knew them better than her own.

There was a scar on his palm if he turned it around. She'd asked about it once, and he'd claimed it was a right for young boys in Bymere to prove their bravery. Hold the bare blade of a sword as tightly as possible for long enough, and one was marked to be a warrior later on.

Najib had held the blade longer than any other boy in his camp.

"You're worried," he murmured, pressing his lips against the back of her neck and holding her close to his chest.

"I am."

"About what?"

Camilla felt a pang of guilt. She hadn't been able to tell him a single thing about her sister's crazed plan. As far as he knew, Sigrid was dead. She was the one leading her people, even though she knew she was only here by proxy.

Keeping secrets from him felt as though she were lying every day. She tried not to draw back from their new relationship. Something in his eyes had lured her to him from the first moment she'd seen him, emaciated in the Bymerian Beastkin camp.

He turned into a leopard at will. A great, beastly creature with scars all over its hide and eyes that nearly glowed with the hunger within them. That had died down now that he had her, she'd realized. He wasn't quite so angry all the time. Not quite so ready to destroy things that he didn't understand.

Instead, Najib watched her. He made certain she was comfortable, that she had everything she needed. In truth, he was the perfect mate.

But what cat wasn't?

She breathed out a sigh and turned in his arms. "A lot of things."

"Why don't you share?" He adjusted his grip, sliding his hands down her torso and into the dip of her waist. "I can take some of the burden."

She shook her head, then pressed her face against his shoulder. The problem was that she *couldn't* share anything with him. He didn't need to know that Sigrid was alive, and as much as she trusted him, it wasn't her secret to give away.

Sometimes, she wondered whether Sigrid had planned this all along. Had her sister somehow caught wind that she had finally, after all these years, found someone she could love? Had she wanted to tear her away from Najib's arms and force her to become something like Sigrid?

All her life, she'd loved her sister. That didn't mean she wasn't aware of Sigrid's flaws, and there were many. Her sister was cold. She avoided being around other people. She isolated herself, because she thought that was what she was supposed to do.

And Camilla understood being a dragon was different than being an owl. There were certain responsibilities with being matriarch. Personally, she'd never wanted them.

Camilla was the type to enjoy her freedom. She liked to leave whenever she wanted, drift through the winds and ripples in the air. Find her way to a tree and watch the world pass by. There was a quiet sort of peace in those moments.

Moments she didn't get now that she was Matriarch of the Beastkin.

"Hey," Najib murmured, pulling her back a little and staring down at her with a worried expression. "You can trust me."

"I know I can."

Just not with this. Not with something that wasn't hers to give away. Camilla pulled back and stepped toward the window, looking out at the forest for the torchlight that would mean Jabbar and his men were home. "Where are they?" she asked.

"I don't know. They didn't tell me where they were going this time. Apparently, they wanted to try and find new hunting grounds."

"There's more than enough food."

"And there are more people coming here every day. You cannot blame them for wanting to be prepared. Winter is coming faster. We can all feel it in the air. Bymerians aren't prepared to handle the cold like you Earthen folk."

Camilla made a face, eyes still trained on the forest. "That isn't the reason why he left, and you know it. Don't try to blow smoke in front of my eyes as he does with everyone else."

Again, Najib pulled her back against his chest. "Camilla, if I knew anything—"

She waited when his words trailed off for the lie he would

spin. Najib was a loyal man, and he'd been with Jabbar from the beginning. She'd never forget the rush of pride in her throat when she'd first heard the story of Jabbar saving Najib's life. It was the first, and only, time she would like Jabbar.

Finally, when he didn't say anything again, Camilla leaned her head back against his shoulder. "It's okay," she whispered. "I understand."

He remained silent for a long while, watching the forest with her. She wondered what was going through his head. Would he tell her the truth? Would he lie more for the man whom he owed his life?

In the end, Najib proved himself more loyal to her than he was to his master. "He wouldn't tell me where they were going, because they wanted to spy on some of the local human villages."

"They are not ours to spy upon."

"He thinks they might rise up and attack us."

"Raheem already scouted that route. He said they weren't interested in finding out anything of their new neighbors." She trusted Raheem more than she trusted most people here. He was a good, reliable man. Unlike man of the Bymerian Beastkin whose eyes were still clouded by judgement and hatred.

"That doesn't mean they won't change their mind." Najib bent at the knee, forcing her to look him in the eye. "Camilla? They want to make sure we're safe, no matter what happens."

"They're going to make the humans fight with us if they're skulking in the shadows."

"They've done this before. We know how to be careful. How else could we survive in Bymere for as long as we did?"

She wanted to say it was because the Bymerians weren't as

used to hunting and tracking as the Earthen folk. That the Bymerians lived in a desert world where most animals were dangerous no matter what, but the Earthen folk knew that monsters tracked them from the shadows every day of their lives. That they knew what the Beastkin looked like, what they were capable of, and knew how to capture them.

But the Bymerians had proven they didn't want to listen to her or her sisters. They thought they knew how to take care of everyone and didn't want to ask for help. That meant, no matter how badly she wanted to correct them, that she wouldn't do it. Couldn't.

They needed to learn these things on their own.

She blew out a breath and shook her head. "I don't want to argue tonight, Najib."

"Then we don't have to argue." He tugged her closer, his lips finding hers in a kiss that tasted like dark chocolate and coffee. "Come to bed with me, *habib albi*."

Gods, the words were almost her end. He'd called her that for weeks now, and she'd only recently gotten him to admit in the common tongue what they meant.

Love of my heart.

She didn't know how to tell him the same thing back. The Earthen folk were far more practical people. The Beastkin women were trained early on that they would be traded in a political alliance. She hadn't thought love would ever be in the stars for her, let alone a man who took her breath away just by existing.

Camilla reached between them and traced a finger over his lips. Those beloved, bowed lips that always curved in a cat-like smile the moment he knew she was under his spell. He wanted her to tumble into bed with him and forget everything for a little bit longer.

She didn't know how.

So many thoughts tangled in her mind, so many worries that made her want to scream. He didn't understand how important this was that she do well. The Beastkin women weren't just her people, they were her sisters. She'd grown up beside them, fighting with them, arguing with them until they were all blue in the face.

Disappointing them would be the greatest failure in her entire life. Worst of all, she didn't think she could disappoint Sigrid like that.

"I can't," she whispered. "I have too much to do."

"You always have something to do. Watching the forest for Jabbar and his people will only make you angrier. Let me take away all these thoughts for a little while."

She was thoroughly tempted. *He* was tempting just by existing, but she knew this wasn't the time or place. As much as she wanted to lose herself in him for a few hours, something was brewing in the air tonight. She didn't know what it was or what it meant. The hairs on her arms hadn't settled down in what felt like hours.

Something was coming. Something important, and she couldn't be tangled up with a man when it happened.

Just as the thought crossed her mind, a knock on her door made her flinch. Camilla gestured for Najib to hide. No one knew about them yet, a fact she wanted to keep to herself.

The Wildewyn and Bymerian Beastkin still weren't exactly friends. The loss of Sigrid had made that tension a little worse than it had been in a long time. They were all going to be walking on eggshells for a few more months before things settled down again.

She hoped Sigrid would return before that. But considering how many months she'd been gone…

Camilla didn't want to think about that.

She rushed toward the door the moment Najib was hidden in the wooden wardrobe. Opening it, she cleared her throat and met the gaze of one of her sisters. This one turned into a goldfinch whenever she wished, a rather pretty but small other side of her soul.

"Yes?" Camilla asked.

"Message for you, Matriarch."

The title was something she hadn't wanted, but the other woman insisted on calling her it. Taking a deep breath, she took the offered note in her sister's hand and nodded. "Thank you. Go back with the others."

"Matriarch—"

If Camilla had learned anything from Sigrid, it was that being harsh was sometimes the best option. She sharpened her tone and snapped, "Back with the others."

A swell of pride rose in the other woman's eyes. She curtseyed small, gave her a tight smile, and made her way back down the winding stairwell where the others waited.

She didn't want to appear cruel. Sometimes this felt a little more brutal than it should be. Sigrid's voice in her mind whispered they needed someone strong. Someone who could throw them all to the ground and teach them how to be better if it came to that.

Such was the only person a Beastkin would respect.

Najib opened the wardrobe door, a goofy grin on his face.

"Is it safe to come out yet? I wouldn't want anyone to know you've found a little bit of happiness."

"Enough."

"I'll let you know when it's enough." He jolted forward, racing toward her and lifting her high up in his arms. He squeezed her so hard she squeaked, then laughed deep in her belly at his antics.

"Stop it, Najib. I have a letter. I have to read it."

He let her drop back to the floor then dramatically fell back on her bed. "By all means. I wouldn't want to stand in the way of the great matriarch. I'm sure there's far more important things for you to be doing right now."

"Instead of you?"

He lifted a brow but didn't respond.

Camilla snorted and snapped the wax seal on the rolled up scroll in her hand. This was likely yet another close neighbor asking for their assistance. She hated saying no to all those leaders whom they had helped before.

Sigrid was right in that the humans needed help. Someone was going to have to break. Either they needed to learn how to take care of themselves, or the Beastkin would start doing things for them again.

They weren't beasts of burden like the Bymerians were. Perhaps that's what Jabbar's people worried about the most. The Earthen folk weren't going to send the Beastkin to work in the fields. They weren't interested in that kind of labor.

But the Beastkin women had played a large part in keeping the kingdom together. Carrier birds with important letters that could only be trusted with a Beastkin. Standing beside a local ruler as a reminder there were more dangerous things than a royal edict. Too many things for her to count.

The Beastkin were a way to remind people that danger lurked in the shadows. She thought, perhaps, that would be a good place to start once again. Having some kind of currency would only help their kingdom. No matter that Woodcrest was far away from everyone else. The world had a way of getting smaller with every breath.

Unrolling the parchment, she tried hard not to show any reaction the moment she recognized the looping script. Only Hallmar had worked on his letters for this long so that every word was like a piece of artwork.

She used to sneak into his room just to read his writing. It didn't matter what he had written about. Sometimes it was just the boring recounting of all the things he'd seen in the kingdom. Fields that needed tending, cattle that weren't doing well. She hadn't cared at all. Instead, Camilla had found peace in the way he flicked the ends of his f's and the intricate curl at the end of his h's.

My dear Camilla,

I hope this letter finds you well, although I've heard more than enough concerning details about the Beastkin community. I have only recently returned from Bymere, but thought I needed to see you.

I understand much has changed and that most of the Beastkin have no interest in seeing me.

And yet… I needed to hear it from you.

There is a light in the forest beyond your window. A light that only your owl eyes should be able to see. Please, find me.

Yours,

H.

Gods, she couldn't look at Najib now. He'd know

something was wrong. Tears boiled at the edges of her vision, too hot to think.

"Camilla?"

She burst free from her human form and allowed feathers to take over her body. The change was swift and painless. Immediately, she threw herself from the room, out the window, into the darkness beyond her tower.

Najib called out for her, but she refused to turn back. The man who had raised her was out there, somewhere, and another Beastkin could find him before her.

What would they do to the king if they found him here without any kind of protection? Hallmar was foolish to think they wouldn't drag him back to the keep and kill him. He was the reason why they felt as though they'd been imprisoned their entire lives. Him and all the other royals who had used them like objects or toys for children to take out when they wanted them.

It didn't make sense that she would be so protective of him. Camilla considered herself among those who hadn't liked her life in that gilded cage. She'd wanted to be seen as something more than just an animal. As a woman with thoughts and dreams of her own that didn't include staying inside yet another stuffy building.

Of course, now that she had her freedom, she was still trapped inside stone walls. Even her own people wanted to keep her trapped.

Now, she understood why Sigrid had fled so easily.

The wind whistled under her wings as she zipped through the darkness and searched for the small pinprick of light which would lead her to the king.

There. Far beyond the keep and beyond where many of the Beastkin would think to look. A light in the darkness between the trees, likely only by a simple torch held aloft by a foolish man who seemed to think he was invincible.

She flew to the torch, dropped from the sky, and landed on her hands and knees in front of him.

Hallmar flinched back, his hand dropping to the hilt of the blade at his waist. "Camilla, that better be you."

"Don't say my name so loudly, Earthen King." She slowly stood and wiped the dirt off her hands. The clothing on her body felt a little too tight, like she wanted to immediately turn back into an owl just with him looking at her.

And look he did. Hallmar's eyes searched her from head to toe, in a different way than Najib had just done. One Beastkin looked at her as if he wanted to devour her whole. The king looked at her as if he was expecting to see more scars, more bruises than what his eyes found.

Finally, he locked gazes with her, and Camilla almost had to look away. The sadness and grief in his eyes made her heart ache.

"Is it true?" he asked, his voice cracking. "I need to hear it from you."

She wanted to tell him that it wasn't. Sigrid wasn't so easily killed. She was something stronger than any of them could understand. A dragon didn't let something like an arrow end her life.

But that wasn't what Sigrid wanted. She had specifically said anyone, and Hallmar was included in that.

Words catching in her throat, Camilla nodded. "It's true."

She expected him to swear or break down like most men

would. Perhaps he would strike a tree with his fist.

Instead, Hallmar lunged forward and caught her against his chest. He pressed his free hand against the back of her head and held her as close as he possibly could. A great shudder ran through his body. "I'm so sorry, Camilla. This was never what I wanted for either of you."

Tears burned the backs of her eyes. She hadn't wanted this for them either. She'd wanted to stay free as the animals in the forest, with no one who could tell her what to do or where to be. But that wasn't a future any of them could ever have.

The world didn't want the Beastkin to be free. There would always be another cage. From the physical walls of the keep to the invisible chains of society. They would never be the animals in the forest, because *they weren't animals.*

How had Sigrid realized this so quickly? How did she know there wasn't an inch of this world that would allow them the freedom they wanted?

Perhaps because she, herself, was a little more human than the rest of them. She knew how they thought, where their minds wandered, and she always made certain to know how they thought.

Know your enemy, she used to say. Even if it means becoming them.

Camilla pulled out of Hallmar's arms, dashing her eyes so he wouldn't see how badly she was crying. He didn't need to have any added pressure. Not now when so much was happening and so many people were...

A thought shattered through her mind like a stone thrown through stained glass. "What did the Bymerian Sultan say?"

Hallmar shook his head. "It's not good, Camilla."

"That's... that's why you came," she whispered. "You were coming here to ask for help weren't you?"

"He has no interest in ending this war. He wants to continue it, simply because there's no way to stop the tsunami he's created." Hallmar paused and swore under his breath. "I thought if I could speak with Sigrid that she might... might protect the land she came from in the off chance that something like this will affect your people as well."

"But she's not here." The words scraped through her throat like a knife she'd swallowed down. The truth wanted to claw its way out of her body. To scream that Sigrid could still be found, maybe, that she could come back and end all this when they needed her most.

"I thought he would see reason," Hallmar continued, his voice hoarse with anger and rage. "I thought the boy could see reason. That perhaps after all this time he had grown."

"He does see reason," Camilla replied. "If there was one thing I learned while being there, it's that the sultan is a far more intelligent man than any of us give him credit for. He knows what he's doing, and now that he's taken back the kingdom as his own... he's unpredictable. At best."

"Unpredictable doesn't mean unreasonable."

"Well, he's that too. But for reasons that neither of us could likely understand. He wants to see his kingdom prosper, and he's willing to do anything to ensure that." she cleared her throat, crossing her arms tightly over her chest. "Even letting go of someone who is very dear to him."

Hallmar frowned. "Sigrid?"

"They grew... close. Probably closer than either you or I could have imagined. Yet, when it came down to it, they both chose their own people and countries over each other."

"The battle."

"More. Their story is not a good one, Hallmar. I don't know what to tell you. She's still broken, far worse than I've ever seen her with anyone else. Leaving him was like leaving a part of herself in that desolate place."

His eyes narrowed and she realized what she'd said at the same time he did. "Still?"

Camilla scrambled, knowing that she'd already been caught in the lie but not able to say anything other than what Sigrid had begged of her. "My apologies, Highness. I still forget sometimes that she's gone."

"Hmm." His grunt was little more than a realization.

She'd seen that look on his face many times. Hallmar was a highly intelligent person. He knew how to play the political game better than anyone she'd ever met. Likely why he was king of the Earthen folk and no one else had taken his throne yet. They used to be a warring people before he'd come into power. Now, no one had a chance to even think past his suspicions.

Finally, Hallmar cleared his throat and shifted his weight onto the opposite foot. "If Sigrid were still alive—"

"She's not."

"But if she were." He held up a hand so she couldn't interrupt him again. "Then I would tell you to find her as soon as possible. This war is going to destroy Wildewyn. Not the humans, not just the peasants and royals, but everyone. The Beastkin here will be drawn into the fight, they won't have a choice. But if someone were to intervene, perhaps speak with the sultan so he might see some kind of reason... we would have the time we need to prepare."

Camilla licked her lips. "She's gone, Hallmar. There's no way anyone can speak with the dead." In her mind, she prayed he'd understand the words underneath the ones she had said. There was so much she wished she could tell him.

Sigrid was gone, far beyond her reach. No one could find the ancients unless they wanted to be found. Even Sigrid could be dead on a mountain somewhere, failed in her quest to find the help they all needed.

He shrugged. "There's always a way. I'm certain the Beastkin know a ceremony which can find someone dear to them. Or perhaps, that someone might be able to fly ahead and scout for the person we're all seeking."

"It's impossible."

"Nothing is impossible. That's a word we all made up so we wouldn't feel guilty stopping ourselves from reaching greatness." He stepped forward and wrapped an arm around her shoulders one more time. Pressing a kiss to her hairline, he whispered, "Go and find her, Camilla. For all our sakes."

As Hallmar faded into the darkness, making his way back to whatever army waited for him or group of assassins, Camilla realized she really didn't have a choice.

Sigrid needed to return, whether she was ready to or not. She waited heartbeats until she was certain Hallmar wouldn't see her. Then, she burst into the change and flew on silent wings toward the mountains beyond.

SIGRID

SHE SLID DOWN THE STEEP SLOPE OF THE MOUNTAIN, BOW IN HAND.
Eyes trained on the stag straight ahead of her, she made certain her movements were quiet. The beast could hear even the slightest twig snap. Thankfully, the leaves underneath her were still wet and heavy with snow. They didn't crunch as she shifted her grip on the wrapped helve.

Sigrid let out a quiet, long breath as she drew back the bowstring. Each heartbeat was counted as she watched the animal move. It lifted its head for a moment, eyes seemingly finding her in the brush, but then it dropped back down to eat the acorns it had found.

I'm sorry, she thought, as she always did while hunting. The fletching stroked her fingertips as she released the arrow. It sang through the air, striking straight and true through the heart of the stag.

The beast stumbled only once, then fell to the ground.

Her heart clenched at the life taken. Though she knew it

was necessary so the other Beastkin in this clan could eat, it still somehow felt wrong. Animals felt too close to killing her own people. Was it cannibalism for a deer shifter to eat deer?

She'd never had thoughts like this before coming here. Sigrid had simply eaten what was put in front of her, knowing that it was well prepared and safe to eat.

Now, she wondered where it came from. Why it was there, and heaven forbid who had killed it.

One of the male Beastkin from the enclave slid down into the brush beside her. "Nice shot," he muttered, clapping a hand hard on her shoulder and then racing toward the meat. There were other things in these mountains that needed the meat as well. They would gather the stag as quickly as possible, making quick work of the gutting process and keeping every bit of the beast for themselves.

The ancients made use of every part of every kill. It didn't matter what it was. The bones were used for carved runes that they were certain helped keep them safe or speak with the dead. The meat, organs, even intestines were either taken or used in healing.

Sigrid hadn't ever seen anything like it. She watched the male pull a knife from his pocket then turned away. The gutting of an animal always felt a little too personal for her to take part in. There was something that made her stomach turn about that pop of flesh in the initial jolt.

However, it certainly made her dragon pleased. The creature inside her practically slobbered at the mere thought of fresh, bloody meat.

She looked up at the mountain beyond where the brave trials began. Aslaug had explained that many of their young people endured hardships and tests before they were allowed to join a certain sector of the ancients. Braves were those who hunted, protected the tribes when necessary, and most of the people who were considered warriors.

Sigrid had insisted she should train with these people. She'd fought her entire life. She might even be able to train them in new styles of battle they hadn't been exposed to before.

Aslaug had chuckled and said a dragon had no need to learn how to fight. The creature would take care of her far more than a blade or sword. What Sigrid needed was to learn a little patience.

She didn't want to learn any more patience. She wanted to *do* something other than help these people out and feel increasingly more like she was being taken advantage of.

The first part of the brave trails were handholds hammered into the side of the ice cliff. They were precarious at best. They didn't look exactly like anyone who had placed them knew what they were doing. But perhaps that was the point.

Sigrid remembered her own training with her mother, and then Camilla's mother. A warrior was supposed to know how to get out of any situation, even ones that they caused themselves. They needed to be prepared for the surprises of life and battle, reacting accordingly, in a way that would get them out alive.

"Sigrid!" the Beastkin behind her called out. "Come hold the heart for me. I don't want to spoil the meat with a wrong slice."

Just like that, she made her decision. She could stay here, with this man she didn't know, gutting a beast that she hadn't wanted to kill. Or she could explore this land that the people were so sure they needed to hide from her.

Sigrid looped the bow over her shoulder, hooked the strap of her arrow pack so none of them would fall out, then raced toward the handholds.

"Sigrid?"

She launched herself over a fallen tree and the gap in the ice where she might have gotten trapped. Catching hold of the first one, she thumped hard against the ice wall. The breath might have knocked out of her lungs if she hadn't been prepared for the impact. Instead, she'd tightened her stomach muscles and prepared her body.

The next handhold wasn't too far from her reach. She dug her boots into the side of the ice, slipping for a moment before she could swing herself up and grab onto the wooden spike. This one wiggled in her hand, but it was enough that she could continue to hold. Perhaps it would hold her weight, perhaps it wouldn't.

That was part of the fun.

A grin spread across her face as she scaled the mountain. Her arms burned, her legs ached, her back began to strain. Her body might hurt, but it was a good kind of hurt. She hadn't used her muscles like this in so long she'd feared she might forget how. This was what she wanted to do.

Sigrid didn't like feeling trapped. She didn't want to be in the forest providing for others when there were adventures to be had. Wasn't that why she had run from the responsibilities of matriarch? She was a young woman, by the gods! She should be able to explore, to enjoy herself, to find out what she wanted out of life without the weight of a hundred people's lives on her shoulders.

Nearly at the top of the ice mountain, a handhold snapped in half. Crying out, her body rotated until she was facing away from the mountain, holding on by one hand and praying her fingers weren't so tired that they couldn't hold her weight.

She gasped, fear racing through her body and making her palm slick with sweat. But that fear quickly bled away when her eyes feasted on the sight before her.

The valley of the ancients laid out like a painting before her. Everything covered in a fine layer of snow except the very center where there were still green things growing. They'd hollowed out a home for themselves, not just in the mountain but within a crater that allowed them to grow food and everything else that kept them alive.

She could see the tiny dots of people moving through their daily lives. No one knew she was climbing the mountain other than the single Beastkin man who had work to do. He might be finished with the deer by now, but he wouldn't be able to run and tell the others braves what she'd done. Not yet.

For now, she was the only person in the world.

The wind ruffled her hair, cold and biting but still welcome in this moment when she felt a little more than lost. Why had she come here? So far away from her family and friends. She was nothing more than a single speck on the horizon.

Turning back to the ice mountain, she hauled herself up and over the lip of ice. Rolling a few times, she finally laid on her back and stared up at the clouds in the sky. There might be a storm tonight by the looks of it. And she could remain up here, screaming with rage back at the sky which seemed to understand her mood.

Aslaug had said remaining here would help her find who

she was. That she would understand her purpose if she remained with the ancients who knew what the Beastkin were first created for.

But they didn't feel like all-knowing people. They lived in harmony, together with themselves and the land. They were a perfect people, certainly, but that didn't explain where she'd come from or what her purpose was.

All she'd done was help them. And Sigrid liked helping people. It made her feel as though she was giving them back something for hosting her when they hadn't expected another mouth to feed in this never-ending winter.

They'd given her clothing, the same she wore now. Furs that covered her from head to toe. Some of them sheep, the ones closer to more sensitive skin were clearly rabbit. She didn't know who had given up their clothing for her to wear, or if they had more to share with themselves and their families.

She appreciated it all. Gods, she did. The ancient civilization here was more kind than any other she'd ever met. They wanted to keep giving and have her give in return.

It felt like a utopia. But nothing was perfect, especially in this time.

Every corner she turned was as if she were waiting for something to go wrong. Like someone was going to suddenly turn on her, shifting into a bear or lion and attacking her just for disturbing their peace.

Of course, it hadn't happened yet. Likely wouldn't. Aslaug and her people knew how to be generous with their hosting.

And yet, she still didn't know why she was here. What she was learning, or why she was spending so much time with them when her own people needed her back at home.

A cloud drifted past in the shape of a bird. Her heart clenched hard. She *missed* her sisters, and Camilla most of all. What would her sister say if she were here?

Probably that Sigrid wasn't listening. She was going through the motions of being a good guest, but she wasn't trying to learn what the ancients were teaching her.

Taking advantage of the situation was one thing, but actually taking the time to listen? Sigrid had never been very good at that. She was a woman of action. She made snap decisions, remained silent so she could hear what other people were saying. But had she ever actually let it soak in? Hallmar always said there was meaning underneath the words people said. Actions were stronger, that she could draw judgements based off of what people did, not what they said they wanted to do.

She was thinking herself in circles now. How was she supposed to stay here and learn when her own brain wouldn't shut up?

A shadow crossed above her face, far too close for comfort. Flinching, Sigrid blinked up at the wooden mask that stared blankly back at her.

"Eivor?" she asked.

"I said we'd meet again, didn't I?"

When the strange medicine woman stepped back, Sigrid rolled onto her hands and knees, pushing herself to standing. "What are you doing here?"

"I could ask the same of you."

"I wanted to see what the brave trails really were. Aslaug said I have no need to train how to fight when I have a dragon in me." Sigrid brushed snow off her furs. "I disagree."

"As do I. But one doesn't question matriarch when she's teaching a lesson." Eivor danced back, her feet barely leaving impressions on the snow. "So. What is the lesson?"

"I haven't the faintest idea."

"Sounds like Aslaug. She doesn't particularly like having to tell someone what they need to know. It's better for them to learn it the hard way. Lessons like that stick." Eivor tapped her mask with a finger. "Sometimes the mind needs to be punished for bad thinking."

"Is that how she trained you?"

"No one trained me. Medicine women aren't allowed to be touched, remember? We have to find our own way in the world. That's where the magic comes from after all."

What a lonely existence this woman had. Sigrid felt a small surge of pity for the creature who danced back and forth from foot to foot. She'd been alone her entire life, so it seemed. Except for circumstances like this when she was meant to bring someone back to the matriarch.

No wonder Eivor was a strange creature. She'd made her way in the world with no one to guide her, no one to hold her at night.

Sigrid didn't know what to say.

It seemed, neither did Eivor until she jerked her arm up, then lifted the rat's head from her waist. "What is it, Grim? No. No I don't want to ask her that. You can ask her yourself if that's what you want, but there's no reason... Fine." Eivor cleared her throat, and the mask turned back to Sigrid's gaze. "He'd like to know if your soul is still intact."

"I don't see why it wouldn't be."

"Well you—" Eivor hesitated then gesture between them.

"You touched me, you see. The soul is bound to be a little uncomfortable after that. It hasn't affected you? A pulling sensation, perhaps, in your naval?"

"No."

"Now, strange dreams at night or wandering about the plains as soon as you drift off?"

"Not at all." Sigrid smiled. "Really, I'm fine."

"Strange." She lifted the skull to her ear again. "Yes, well I suppose we could, considering."

She was talking to the rat again. Sigrid had her concerns that the "soul" inside that skull wasn't real at all. It made far more sense that this was a woman who had suffered greatly, and whose mind reached out for whatever companionship she could find. Unfortunately, that seemed to be housed in the skulls of dead animals jangling at her waist.

Eivor turned around and began to walk away, talking to the beast inside the skull. "Yes, Grim. I know we're not supposed to show anyone but she isn't really *anyone*, now is she? I agree. It's important that she sees it. Maybe this will explain more than the matriarch is doing. After all, it is part of our history."

"Our history?" Sigrid called out. "What are you talking about?"

"Come with me, dragoness. There's something I want to show you."

"What? Eivor, slow down!"

The Medicine woman sped up. Sigrid was forced to race after her, chasing her through the snow and running across the barren wasteland at the top of the mountain. The flat shelf was made of snow and ice. No footprints marred the pure white. It was as if she had died. Perhaps she had. Maybe she'd fallen off the ice and couldn't remember at all that she had slipped from the cliff and fell to her demise.

Sigrid ran until her thighs burned, eyes locked on the small figure in the distance. And then, as if she'd never existed at all, the medicine woman disappeared.

Slowing, Sigrid tried to catch her breath and spun in a slow circle. "Eivor?"

The woman was well and truly gone. How did she do that? She'd done the same thing in the cave system, disappearing into the landscape.

Magic?

No, that wasn't possible. Sigrid was a logical woman. She knew there was no such thing as magic, other than people turning to beasts at will and dragons coming back to life after so many centuries of...

She shook her head. "Stop thinking that," she muttered. "There's no such thing as magic. Eivor is not capable of something like that. Get your head on straight, Sigrid, and find her."

There, on the horizon, a small slice in the ice shelf created a crevice. The medicine woman must have slipped down the hole, or perhaps leapt directly into it, seemingly disappearing from the horizon.

A smile split Sigrid's face. "You're crafty. I'll give you that, medicine woman. Whoever taught you how to hide did a damned good job."

She eyed the crevice, wondering if she could even fit down it. Her square shoulders didn't make it all that easy, but she'd managed in the cave system well enough. The memory flickered to life, fear seeping into her pores. She didn't want to be crushed between two halves of a mountain, but she also didn't want to remain up here.

Eivor had said there was something here. Something that Sigrid should see, because it was her history. There was so much she wanted to learn and so much that was being withheld from her.

Taking a deep breath, she hovered one foot over the open space, eyed it one last time, and then leapt into the shadows between the ice.

The cold wall behind her pressed against her back, guiding her into what she quickly realized was some kind of tunnel, or perhaps mine shaft created to transport people. Sigrid crossed her arms over her chest and held her breath.

The last thing she needed was to break an arm, because she flailed them in an attempt for balance. Space around her grew progressively smaller and tighter. The front wall of the ice pressed against her chest, freezing her lungs and stealing her breath.

She'd be okay, she told herself. Other people must have come this way before. The ice hadn't shifted, otherwise she was going to hit Eivor rather soon, and they'd both be stuck here.

Not particularly a comforting thought. Of all the people she'd thought to die with, she hadn't imagined it would be a crazed medicine woman with a rat she talked to on regular occasions. A dead rat, she reminded herself. Or whatever Grim was. She honestly wasn't certain that Eivor thought Grim was a human. Maybe it was just something else she'd stolen the soul of.

The ice behind her shifted, curving slightly until her

movements slowed. Gently, she slid to a stop at the end of the tunnel. Wiggling, she pulled herself out of the ice and into a cavern where heat blasted from the ground.

The ground was warm here. She set her feet on the mossy ground, staring around in awe.

Giant blue flowers grew up in bell shapes. Their petals opened as she passed, as if the sound of her footsteps were all they were waiting for. Green, toothed flowers opened as well. The interior of their petals pink as a blush.

Water bubbled up from the ground, creating meandering paths that looked almost like stone. The water was charcoal in color. Steam rose from the snaking rivers. Large trees grew in the distance, their leaves like the fan of a peacock's feathers. Brightly colored, so vivid they shouldn't have been able to exist in a frozen wasteland.

Standing stones dotted between the streams of steaming water. Perhaps that's why the rivers led there. Each stone was carved through the center, one circle and a line straight through the center to the ground.

Standing, Sigrid stooped and pulled off her boots. She left them at the mouth of the tunnel, stepped into the hot water, and waded into the stream.

Eivor was nowhere to be found.

Did it matter? Sigrid realized she didn't really want to see the medicine woman when the trickling music of waterfalls filled her ears. Eddies swirled around her ankles up to her shins. Moss grew on all the stones, lush and emerald in color. An archway of stone, ancient and crumbling, curved above her head.

What was this place? Some kind of ceremonial tomb? Or

perhaps a home of a long forgotten race.

She stepped hesitantly, trying not to tread on watery plants that kicked away from her movements and tumbled down the stream back toward the original hot spring which had given such life to this place.

Letting the furs around her shoulders fall to her elbows, she saw ahead of her a ring of standing stones. Similar to the one where she had first seen Aslaug, it too had an altar in the center of it.

She stepped out of the stream and up the stairs where water poured down the steps. Eivor stood in the center, staring down at what looked like tiles carefully placed in the pattern of gold flowers on the stone steps.

Water bubbled out of the center of the altar. Bubbling and sending more steam in the air as it was released.

"What is this place?" she asked, her voice suddenly quiet and deadened in the strange air.

"An old, forgotten place. We used to come here often." Eivor pointed up at one of the stone pillars. It had the semblance of a carving left. Had they been snakes? She couldn't quite tell, although the one next to it was scaled as well, with the hint of a...wing.

Sigrid sucked in a deep breath. "Dragons?"

"The home of so many people like you. They all hid here when the world was falling apart after they'd created it."

"Created it?" Sigrid shook her head. "Aslaug told me a few of the things that had happened. It was a group of Beastkin."

"And it was the dragons who carved the land into two pieces. They were the ones who dug out Wildewyn, fist by fist, creating a mountaintop for Bymere to remain on for all time.

They were the ones who destroyed the world just to ensure that they were safe." Eivor reached out and touched a hand to the stone. "They were capable of more things than the Beastkin give them credit for."

"How do you know this?"

"When I was little, I used to come here to rest. There was another Beastkin who lived here. A dragon, like you. She was very old, and very tired. Locked in her beast form, she couldn't really talk much other than a few grumbles. Before she died, she turned back into a woman and told me all she knew because she had seen it happen before."

Sigrid swallowed. "Seen what happen?"

"A war between Beastkin. A war between men and Beastkin. It's nothing new. Time doesn't heal itself, and people don't learn from past mistakes. It's easier to forget the things we did wrong." Eivor turned to her then, pointing to the water bubbling out of the altar. "The dragons didn't want to fight. They knew they were too powerful and that the war would end in their favor no matter who they fought for.

"They discovered choosing that side was too hard. They had to decide between their people, those who loved them and had given them life, and those who were their chosen families. The humans, the other Beastkin who wanted to live with the humans. It's not fair to make a person a god."

The words rang far too true. The Bymerian Beastkin wanted to call her a god. They said she was the most powerful thing to ever exist in their lifetime, and that because of that, she was more than just a woman. More than just Sigrid.

"I don't want to be a god," she whispered.

"That's what Aslaug wants. It's what your ancestor was.

All the dragons become gods in their lifetime. They're so much more than a person. They're the last of their kind. Saying you don't want to become a god is like… saying you don't want to breathe anymore."

Was that the solution? Had Eivor brought her all this way to explain there was only one path out of this journey?

Sigrid didn't want to see everything end. This had been a struggle to even get here. But if the fight wasn't worth the end goal then… why would she remain? If all she was going to do was see her people fall steadily into ruin and distrust…

Eivor must have seen the way her thoughts had turned, because the medicine woman let out a sound of sadness. "No. No, little dragoness, you misunderstand me."

"Do I? This has happened before. Every step of my journey has been walked by another person, perhaps many. Those who have seen the writings on the wall of how the Beastkin will steadily decline into nothing. That's why the ancients are *here*. Do you think Aslaug doesn't see what I do? Do you think she isn't understanding that she's chosen to lead her people into oblivion?"

The wooden mask tilted to the side. "I see that Aslaug assumes we will all die off someday. That she won't fight for a world where Beastkin can grow and prosper."

"And why is that?"

"She believes the same as you. That Beastkin were not made to be controlled. That they will eventually destroy themselves and she is comfortable allowing them to live out their lives here. Where at least the few generations left will be accepted by their own people."

Sigrid blew out a breath. Who was she to question the

knowledge of someone like Aslaug? A woman who knew her history so thoroughly that she didn't have to wonder who she was or where she came from.

She shook her head. "Then we've already lost this battle, Eivor. Those who know more than us must be respected. The elders walk this path for a reason."

"The elders look directly ahead of them and follow the footsteps of thousands." Eivor stepped forward, wringing her hands nervously and her voice pitched low. "I'm asking you to turn your head and look for prints elsewhere."

"I don't know where else to look."

"Then you're looking for the wrong prints. Stop putting your feet in shoe prints. Start looking for animals."

Sigrid didn't understand why Eivor was so vehemently arguing this. The medicine woman seemed to be happy in her life. She'd lived here for... well, forever. There wasn't any reason why she would argue it unless she wasn't happy. Unless there was something else going on that Sigrid didn't know.

Hesitantly, Sigrid lifted her hands to the sides of Eivor's mask. "In my homeland, masks are not worn in front of family."

"You are not my family. I don't have family." But Eivor's words were shaking with an emotion Sigrid recognized all too well.

"Family is who we choose, not our blood." And with that, Sigrid slowly took off the mask which had hidden Eivor's face from so many. Likely since she was a child.

She barely held in the gasp, although she might have winced. Someone had ruined Eivor's face with a butcher knife. There were still scales on it from where her beast had tried to stop the harm. Patches of fur and feathers added to the grotesque features the mask had covered.

"This is why they hide you," she whispered. "Isn't it?"

"Medicine women and men are not supposed to exist. We're an abomination and a disgrace to our clan. So we are sent into the mountains to learn how to make ourselves useful to the tribe," Eivor replied. "There is no shame in my features. Only a life that was created by myself and the animals inside me."

"You don't keep souls, do you?"

Eivor shook her head. "Not in the way people think. I learn how to change my shape, but it confuses my beast. Sometimes there's more than one animal in people. Rarely. It happens though, and I have so many inside me I cannot even count."

"They're afraid of you because of how you look."

"They're afraid of what they don't understand." Eivor reached for her mask. "Please."

"No," Sigrid said, taking a step back and taking the mask with her. "You shouldn't have to hide who you are."

"I want to."

Hadn't Sigrid said the same words to herself? Hadn't she tried to justify the mask she'd worn her entire life as something which was comfortable? Now she saw it was a crutch. It was a way to make herself feel more comfortable without other people staring at her.

Hesitantly, she held the mask out to Eivor. "I wore a mask my entire life as well. I can tell you there is nothing more terrifying than revealing your face to others. But there is nothing more freeing, either."

Eivor held the mask in her hands, staring down at the wooden face with her mismatched features. Her eyes roamed over the worn pieces and painted colors. "I don't take it off much," she said. "Sometimes, even when I'm alone, I just leave it on. It's easier that way."

"Just because their culture is ancient doesn't mean they are. Sometimes, the old ways need to be broken so that something else can grow in its place."

Eivor gently set the mask down onto the altar in the center of the room. "That's why I brought you here, you know. I wanted you to see that something else can happen. You don't have to listen to Aslaug or the others. You don't have to listen to anyone other than yourself."

"I don't know what my soul wants."

"What about your heart?"

Warmth bloomed in Sigrid's chest. It wasn't her own heart or a belief in herself, but the dragon that lifted its head and saw something it wanted to protect. A dragoness who had seen a youngling that needed it.

She knew without a doubt that she would protect Eivor until the woman died. This creature was now part of her family, claimed as so few people had been claimed. It didn't matter that she was ugly. It didn't matter that she'd been forgotten by time itself. The medicine woman would stay with her until the kingdoms fell.

"My heart wants war," she replied. "My heart wants to devour and destroy, and that is not something I can allow it."

"Why not?" Eivor gestured to the dragon statues around them. "The age of dragons passed long ago. Who says they cannot wander the earth again? Whether by peace or war, we both know the time of dragons will come again."

Deep in her chest, the dragon unfurled its wings, lifted its head, and roared.

NADIR

HE SHOULDN'T FEEL SO COMFORTABLE HERE, AND YET, THE HIDDEN city of Falldell had quickly become a second home to him. The people here weren't hiding behind the masks of royalty or nobility. They didn't care who he was, what he was, or why he was there. All they cared about was that he would work and that he would work hard.

When was the last time he'd used his muscles like this? He couldn't remember other than his childhood when he'd been training to take over the army from his uncle.

Hakim's voice whispered in his mind, memories of when his older brother had laughed at him, pointing out muscles on his small frame that weren't on the other boys.

"You were made to work, weren't you, little brother?" Hakim *had shouted one day when Nadir had returned from training. "Those muscles cannot lie. You'll make the most impressive general yet."*

He'd ruffled Hakim's hair and chuckled. "Not a sword will touch you while I'm alive, brother."

A sword hadn't touched his brother at all. Poison was the one thing that Nadir couldn't protect Hakim from. No one could have thought a hair comb, a tiny knife, could have brought about so much pain and agony.

If he could have turned back the time of the world, he would have. He would have gone back to that moment when he was but a child and sliced the person's hand from their arm. He would have destroyed them in the only way he knew.

Feed them to the dragon, destroy them with fire, and devour their bones until the anger inside him was finally sated. The beast inside him wanted to feast on the bones of thousands just because its brother was taken away from it. He'd been so lonely, for such a long time. All because someone had thought the royals of Bymere weren't worthy of the lives they had.

Blowing out a breath, Nadir straightened from the home he was helping to rebuild. White clay stained his hands and streaked across his bare chest.

These people weren't like the ones who had wanted to hurt him. Of that, he was certain. They didn't care that he was the Sultan of Bymere. In fact, most of them ignored him because of that. They wanted nothing to do with a noble who led a privileged life.

It had been a personal pleasure knowing that he'd changed their minds. The first time he'd offered to help, they had laughed at him. The second time, they had taken him up on the offer. They put him to work in the most grueling pace he'd ever seen set. But he'd taken it all in stride. If they wanted to test him, then so be it. He would perform better than they could ever imagine.

The other men around him straightened as well, their backs

slick with sweat and their hair sticking up at odd angles. Did he look like them now? The sun had certainly burnished his skin even darker. A beard now scratched his chin, slowly softening in texture until he almost liked the new addition. It was different. And different was what he was looking for.

A woman strode toward them, back straight and the linen cloth blowing at her waist. Tahira was always the messenger for his mother. Likely, the old woman had another thing she wanted him to do. There was no shortage of need in this place.

Tahira paused near the half-built house, looking him up and down. "Seems they've put you to work."

"Better than idle hands."

She scoffed. "Somehow, it's hard to imagine that's what you really believe, Sultan."

"If there's one thing about me to learn, Tahira, it's that I don't lie." Nadir wiped his hands across his chest and arched a brow. "I take it she's interested in seeing me again?"

"She misses her son."

He didn't reply, knowing the tone of sarcasm in her voice. Tahira thought this was all an elaborate plan to get him to do what the Alqatara wanted. And maybe she was right. He wouldn't put it past them to see the use in having a sultan in their pocket.

Yet, there was something more in Nahla's gaze than the intent to use him as her pawn. The leader of the Alqatara was perhaps softening in her old age. She looked at him as though she hadn't seen her son in many ages, looked at him with longing.

The truth was, she still thought of him as her son. She looked at him as the boy she didn't have a chance to raise, but a man who could now still learn from her in the shadow of her great life.

He didn't know what she was dying of. Something important, something likely that could have been fixed in the capital, but she didn't want to be fixed. She'd already told him time and time again, life had a way of taking important things away at the very last second. He needed to learn to use that pain.

Nadir nodded and followed Tahira as she spun on her heel. He already knew where she was going to bring him. Nahla had taken the day in her private gardens, the only place she allowed herself outside the safety of her walls.

The gardens were beyond the mountain range that protected the Alqatara. To make the journey a little safer, they had blasted a hole through the mountain. The dark tunnel was lined with torches, casting the entire journey in a red light that flickered with their movements.

He strode through the darkened place, reminding himself that they didn't want to kill him. There wasn't a reason for him to be here so long only to have death find him. Nahla wanted something from him.

Tahira's voice echoed in the tomb-like chamber. "You know, she's only going to get what she wants in the end."

"A son?"

"A sultan." The woman in front of him shook her head slightly, the long black curtain of her hair shuddering with her movement. "Nahla is not some feeble old woman. She sees the future in ways other people couldn't understand if they tried. Testing her will only end in your own madness."

"I'm not testing her."

"Then why are you still here?"

He thought about the question, wondering if there was a right answer to it. All he settled on was the truth. "I want to find out who I am, where I came from. I think that she can at least tell me part of that. Bymere is my kingdom, and Falldell is a part of that. If I cannot understand your people, then I cannot understand the empire which relies upon me to prosper."

Tahira snorted. "I think you're falling back into your old ways, Sultan. This is just one more person to tell you what to do and how to live. Think for yourself, dragon, before someone else does it for you."

The words stung like salt in an open wound. He winced. Was he falling back into the same habit he'd done his entire life?

Nadir didn't want to entertain the thought at all. He didn't want to think that something was so wrong with him that he couldn't think for himself. What kind of man couldn't do that? What kind of *ruler* would he be if he didn't have the power to even think for himself?

They left the tunnel system and entered the garden beyond. An oasis had formed in the center. Stone wrapped around them on all sides, stretching up toward the sky in the mountain range beyond. No one would have been able to even find this oasis if they didn't have wings.

It was, for all intents and purposes, a way to entrap men. Water bubbled from a death defying plummet high on the mountain peak. If they had traversed the desert and found this place, the only thing they could do was look at the lifesaving water so far from their reach.

Palm trees outlined the pool of water in the center. Their trunks were peeling great strips of vibrantly colored bark.

Fronds bent from their tops, nearly touching the water in a few places.

The Alqatara weren't usually a ritualistic folk. They believed in magic only as a last resort, and the Beastkin among them were only used in dire circumstances. At least, that's what Nahla had told him.

Thus, he found it strange to see the Beastkin Qatal standing in a circle around the oasis with their arms outstretched. Their fingertips didn't quite touch each other. They all stood with heads back, eyes closed, allowing the sun to play across their faces.

"What is this?" he asked Tahira who moved to stand among her brethren.

"Your mother is waiting in her usual spot. Go and see her before you ask any more questions, Sultan of Bymere."

He frowned. What were they up to? He didn't want to take part in any kind of ritual. He wasn't joining the Alqatara. The last thing he needed was for others to say he was an assassin.

But his feet still moved in the direction of his mother. She sat on a small bench, wrapped up in blankets even though it was plenty warm outside.

She was more fragile like this. Her entire body seemed... weak. He had thought she would be a monstrous woman to house a dragon inside her. She wasn't.

Nahla was as fragile as a spring breeze. Cautiously making her way through life while she tried to figure out what would and wouldn't hurt her. He could see why his father had been captivated by her immediately. Everything about her screamed that she needed to be taken care of. Someone had to stop and hold her just for a few moments so she didn't fly apart at the seams.

Perhaps that was her greatest ability in life. She was a woman with a spine of steel who had trained armies of legendary assassins and still managed to look like a delicate creature herself.

At his approach, his mother opened her eyes and smiled. "Come, my boy. Sit with me for a few moments."

"What is it?"

She patted the bench. "You know how long I've waited for you, Nadir?"

The words were the same she said every time she saw him. And every time he replied with, "My whole life."

"Indeed. And now that you're here, it's hard for me to think of anything else than my boy has finally returned."

Somehow, he didn't quite trust those words. Her eyes were too calculating, her mind too quick, and he didn't think she was the type of woman to be distracted by anything that she didn't want to be distracted by.

He settled onto the bench hesitantly. "What is it, Nahla?"

"You could call me mother, you know." She tilted her head back and closed her eyes. "It would make an old woman very happy to finally hear those words from your lips."

He hesitated before replying, "I believe you've already heard them before."

Nadir hadn't wanted to bring up the man who now sat on his throne. Somehow, it felt like something taboo that he wasn't supposed to mention. He didn't know who the man was. Solomon had made it clear he wasn't going to tell Nadir either. But the suspicion was still there.

Solomon looked far too much like him to be anything other

than what Nadir suspected.

"I've been called it by many people," she replied. "Least of all the man whom you think of. That doesn't mean the words coming from your lips would be any less important."

He didn't want to call her mother. The woman who had raised him was his mother. She had held him close at night, wiped away the tears of nightmares. She had been the one who after all this time still appeared in his dreams. The sultana had been far more than just a woman in his life who had taken him in. She had been the woman who raised him, then the woman he knew welcomed him into her heart knowing that he wasn't her child.

Nahla opened her eyes and focused on him. Suddenly, those yellow eyes which looked so much like his own were harder. Chips of gold stuck in a face that had aged but was no less powerful. "Do you not believe in me, Sultan of Bymere? After all these years keeping the kingdom safe, I would have thought you would understand the importance of the Alqatara."

"I do."

"Then why are you questioning me? Why are you looking at me as though I am lying to you?"

He cleared his throat and rubbed a hand at the back of his neck. "I'm not doing that."

"Then call me mother."

The words stuck in his throat. "I cannot."

"Why is that, I wonder?" she asked. "Is it because you still have some lingering loyalty to the family who nearly destroyed the creature inside you? The ones who claimed you were a monster they needed to hide?"

"My family was good to me," he corrected, anger bubbling in his chest like an old friend. "They didn't make me think I was a monster."

"They told you no one could know who or what you were. They made you hide in the shadows your entire life and you say they were good to you? Do you know what that does to a Beastkin? You need to change, to allow the creatures inside you to grow or all you foster is an animal that will stop at nothing to break free from the bonds you've placed on it." Nahla shook her head and growled, "You cannot chain a dragon."

And yet, he had. His entire life he'd done so, and it didn't seem that the dragon was any worse for wear.

At the thought, the beast inside him lifted its head. The colors around him flattened into little more than black and white. Perhaps his eyes had shifted as the dragon peered out, or perhaps his mind had simply snapped at the idea the beast could take over entirely.

It didn't matter in the end. Nahla's pupils elongated in her eyes, and he knew he was no longer looking at the leader of the Alqatara. He was looking at the legendary creature who had birthed him.

A low growl erupted from her lips, the sound grating and far too deep for her to be able to make. "I birthed you," the beast inside her said. "I brought you into this world to maim and destroy. By denying who and what you are, you have forsaken all that I have given you."

"I haven't," he said, his words thick as he battled the dragon inside him. "I would never."

"Then prove your worth to me."

He wanted to. Gods, he wanted to be something more than

just the sultan whose strings were pulled constantly as if he were nothing more than a marionette in a play. But he was afraid of what he would become.

Would he descend into madness as all the books within his palace said? Would he become nothing more than an animal looking for its next meal?

The fear which lived inside him since he was nothing more than a child was a monster he hadn't named. It wanted him to understand that he was nothing. To know that no matter how hard he tried, he would always be a disappointment to his family and to his friends.

Even now, with the woman who had given him life, he was disappointing her by hesitating.

For the first time in a very long time, he tried to think with reason and not with the fear in his heart. What was she asking him to do? That was the most important part of this journey. He needed to know what Nahla wanted before he made any decisions.

"What would you have me do?" he asked. "Tell me."

"Become one with the dragon." Nahla's eyes shifted back to her own and softened immediately. "Learn how to be the man and the beast, together as one being."

"That's not possible."

"It's how you would have been trained long ago. My dragon can speak, because she is me and I am her. And though my age has prevented me from taking her form ever again, I know she is still with me. I will never wonder whether she will shoulder me out of the way and take control forever. Our choices are made as one."

It sounded like heaven. Like he wouldn't have to

constantly fear what he would, or could, do.

Nadir wanted that more than anything. He wanted to feel like he was in control of his life and decisions. Was that really too much to ask?

The feeling of silken hair sliding over his shoulder was little more than the touch of a ghost. She was with him always, it seemed. More than he wanted to admit.

Sigrid's voice whispered in his ear, *"There is always another way."*

But he didn't know what she meant this time. Did she mean trust the Alqatara? Trust the woman who had birthed him to not do something that would forever harm his kingdom?

Gods, he couldn't think. He couldn't do anything other than stare into the eyes that looked so much like his own and were so soft. He missed his own mother so much. She had been taken from him far too early and all he wanted...

Even Nadir's thoughts caught. He wanted someone to love him. Because no one, not a single person in his entire life, did.

"How?" he asked.

Something like triumph flashed in Nahla's eyes. She gestured to the Beastkin surrounding the oasis pool. "Go to them, Sultan of Bymere. They will take you where you need to go."

As if in a trance, he stood and turned toward the men and women who were just like him. They had been discarded by their families. Destroyed so many times he couldn't even count them all. Humans had tried to wipe them out of existence, and yet they were still here.

They dropped their faces from the sky and all watched as he walked toward them. There was something of acceptance in their eyes as he approached. Something that looked like friendship, if he squinted his eyes just a little bit. It couldn't be that they were taking advantage of him. They wouldn't do that to the man who ruled them.

Would they?

Tahira was the one who stepped forward with her hands outstretched. "Welcome, Sultan of Bymere. The Beastkin Qatal of Falldell will bring your second soul forward."

"My what?"

"The beast inside you needs to come out. He needs to see the world as he never has before. This will not be an easy process, and I beg of you to remain calm."

Remain calm? What was she talking about?

She pulled him forward toward the oasis. Perhaps she saw the panic in his eyes, because she licked her lips and flicked her eyes to the others. He could tell she wasn't supposed to talk. Rituals like this were meant to be taken seriously. He could see that much of the truth in her eyes. Still, Tahira surprised him.

She leaned closer and whispered, "This isn't an easy process, Sultan. You need to be prepared for what's going to happen."

"What are we doing?"

"This is a ritual to bring out the dragon. You've kept him caged for so long, he doesn't know when he's allowed to come out. The Alqatara believe that beasts protect us from situations we wouldn't know how to handle, or want to handle. They are a guiding spirit that saves us from ourselves. To bring him out, we have to make him feel threatened."

"Which is why you weren't supposed to tell me that," he muttered. "Now it's going to be harder to draw him out, because he knows what's happening."

"Precisely. But I argued this isn't the safest way to teach you how to merge with the dragon. The reality is that you aren't an owl or a hawk that is easily tamed. A dragon is a massive creature capable of destroying the entire camp. You have to be stronger than it is. Do you hear me, Sultan? Be stronger than the beast or we're all going to die."

"Die?"

He didn't have time to think what she meant by that. Nahla's voice lifted above the others and shouted, "Hold him down!"

The flint and steel words startled him so much that he didn't move even when the other Qatal lunged forward. Each grabbed one of his limbs, two on his legs. They forced him to kneel in the waters of the oasis that lapped at his thighs. The water was barely knee-high. Somehow, it had looked deeper.

Tahira kept her hands on his head. "I'm sorry for this, Sultan."

"Sorry for —"

Nahla whistled, and her warriors were at her beck and call. They all forced him forward, holding his head under the water. He struggled at first, wondering whether they were actually trying to kill him. But then he settled under their hands.

This is part of the process. They wanted to put him in stressful situations so that the dragon would try and protect him. That, he could understand.

Damn, he thought, they were really trying to kill him. They pulled his head out of the water and he gasped in a deep breath.

"Don't make this harder than it has to be, Sultan," Tahira growled. "Just give in."

He didn't know how. Nadir wasn't exactly the kind of person who knew how to let go. He was tightly wound as a bow string ready to snap.

They plunged his head back under the water.

His lungs burned with the need to breathe, but he trusted them not to kill him. They didn't want to destroy the kingdom. They didn't want his half-brother to remain on the throne. They wanted a dragon.

Why wasn't his brother a dragon as well? He wanted to know the answer to that before he died.

His own beast didn't even lift a finger to protect him, even when his mouth gaped open in an attempt to breathe. Water filled his nostrils and mouth. The Qatal again pulled him out and allowed a single gasping breath.

A growl echoes from behind him. Tahira's fingers shifted into the claws of an eagle. "That's enough. Pin him down."

He was stretched out by their hands until they laid him out on the ground. She held his head just enough so that he could still breathe. Nadir stared up at her angry eyes and wondered who had hurt her so much that she could bear to drown a man like this.

She leaned down and her eyes shifted as well as her hands. Was she partially changing? He hadn't thought that was possible.

"Listen to me, Nadir. There is a man who looks exactly like you seated on your throne. We wanted a dragon, but there are always other plans. If you don't let go, if you don't allow the dragon to take over your body, I will drown you. Don't look at me like you don't believe me. I've done it before, and I'll do it again."

With that, she plunged him back under the water. He looked up at her through the murkiness of the oasis, watched her eyes shift back to human and the suddenly sad gaze in them.

He waited heartbeats. His lungs burned, his mouth gaped open. He needed to breathe, but didn't struggle because of course they would pull him up again. This tactic would eventually work, he would grow tired of the torment, but not quite yet.

Again his mouth gaped open, his chest shifting as his body tried to breathe in air it would not find. He widened his gaze. Tahira looked back at him, her arms shifting and muscles bulging.

And they did not pull him up.

He flexed his biceps, trying to pull up and out of the water toward the air which was two inches above his face. He could reach it, if he had to. They couldn't hold him under the water forever. He tightened the muscles in his legs, but the Beastkin all around him were partially shifting. They were holding him down, forcing him to remain until he realized something with crystal clarity.

They were going to kill him. If he didn't fight, if he didn't do what they wanted, they would kill him and he would lose...

Everything.

He struggled further. Contorting his body in ways he hadn't thought possible to try to slip out of their grasp. But they held him further, not allowing him to move at all until a ripple of scales unfurled down his body.

He had to breathe soon. His lungs were screaming, his chest tightening over and over as it tried to force him to inhale.

Water splashed over his vision. It churned in the wake of his frustration, and yet, through it all he could see her eyes. Tahira's eagle eyes that stared him down.

The dragon took notice then. It wondered why he wasn't fighting harder, why he would let these creatures hold him down when he could devour them in a single bite.

Still, he fought against his own urges. Nadir didn't want to hurt them. They were holding him so tightly.I If he changed, they would be sent flying away from his body. But his heart was beating in his ears and the dragon was roaring in his mind and *he couldn't think.*

A blast of echoing pain rocked through his form. He arched in the hands of the Beastkin who suddenly released him and ran. Why was he still underwater? Why wasn't the dragon taking over as it had before?

Blistering heat seared his flesh from his bones. Fire sizzled along his hair and he vaguely realized the water around him was boiling. Why couldn't he take control over his body?

Sit up, he told himself. *It's two inches of water, just sit up.*

He opened his mouth and inhaled. Water rushed past his lips, filling his lungs and leaving a leaden touch upon his very soul.

The last sultan of his line, the greatest in all history of Bymere, dying in two inches of water. His last thoughts echoed before the dragon inside him let out a primal scream of rage and blasted forward to take control.

SIGRID

"THE AGE OF DRAGONS?" SIGRID REPEATED, THE WORDS ECHOING IN her mind like a long forgotten prophecy. "There's no such thing."

"Look into the waters of ancestors long past. See for yourself, dragoness. That time has a way of healing all things."

Something whispered in the back of her mind. A voice she hadn't heard in ages, a motherly voice that wanted her to go forward. To see where she had come from, where they had all come from.

Stepping toward the altar, she stared down into the water which bubbled up from deep inside. A small hole had been bored through the center by the spring. Staring through it, a beam of light highlighted the small dragon carved deep below.

"What—"

Excruciating pain hit her in the back of the head like a hammer. She dropped to her knees, holding her head between her hands and screaming through the agony.

What was happening? What was that sound of roaring echoing through her head?

She vaguely heard the medicine woman cry out and race away through the streams. Sigrid could hardly stay on her knees. She wanted to curl into a ball, because the sound wouldn't stop. It was someone, or something, screaming so loud she couldn't think of anything but their pain.

Their anguish.

Tilting her head back, she let out a scream that matched the rage in the roaring of her mind. Whatever had caused such pain would find she had little pity for those who harmed the weak. The dragon inside her roared its anger and vowed to find whomever had caused the sound of anguish.

NADIR

THE DRAGON WAS SO ANGRY. NADIR COULD HARDLY THINK, HE JUST LET the beast take over and disappeared into the darkness of their shared mind. The beast raged and slammed upon the bars of Nadir's own mind.

Why hadn't he let the dragon help them? Why couldn't he let the beast do what it was meant to do?

It screamed again, and he swore he felt his ears start to bleed.

"Stop it," he told it, his voice weak and reedy. "I cannot let you free."

But the beast didn't want to hear his excuses. It wanted to fly out into the world and destroy whomever thought they could tame it. The beast wanted to claw and bite, to break stone and mountain beneath its claws.

The scream grew louder and louder until it shook the bars of its cage.

"Please," Nadir tried again. Too late.

The beast was free.

SIGRID

"WHAT IS THIS MADNESS?" SHE CRIED OUT. "STOP IT!"

The echoing call grew louder and louder. Liquid dripped between her fingers where her ears had started to bleed. Another stream leaked from her nose and fell onto the stones before her. She couldn't hear the drops striking the water or granite. All she could hear was the beast in her mind.

The dragon inside her whispered, "I can fix this."

Sigrid didn't question how or why. She simply let the dragon take over everything. They didn't change forms, but suddenly she wasn't in control as much as she had been before. Their minds tangled together like a woven tapestry, and she knew what the dragon knew.

The creature rumbled low in their mind, sending out the call across the vast expanse of the kingdoms. The guttural sound was like the purr of a cat and the settling of ice in winter.

Again and again, the dragon made the sound until the echoing cry of pain slowed. Quieter and quieter until it was nothing more than a moan.

Only then did the dragon inside her ease its control, and then Sigrid swore she heard it whisper, "Call out to him."

So she did.

NADIR

THE SOUND OF FLUTES AND THE WIND IN CHIMES CALMED THE DRAGON.
It raged and slammed against the cages, bursting free and
forcing a painful change upon their body. Scales rippled in the
boiling waters. Its tail lashed back and forth, catching a body
and slamming it against the mountain around them.

Again, the sound whispered through his mind, and Nadir
caught upon it with desperation. He focused on the voice. The
sound of singing and the calling of an ancient animal that
played for his soul.

The dragon slowed its movements, huffing out an angry
breath and settling.

Then, he heard the voice.

"Be at peace," she whispered. "I am here."

Scales melted to flesh, horns flattened on his skull, and
Nadir knelt in the pool of the oasis breathing hard.

Gooseflesh raised upon his arms and down his back. His
hands shook in the water as the dragon purred in his mind.

"It's you," he said out loud. "It's really you."

How was it possible? She wasn't here. He would know if she were here. But she was still in his mind, speaking to him as if she wasn't more than just a mirage he dreamed of.

"Sigrid."

SIGRID

THE SOUND OF HER OWN NAME, GRUNTED IN THAT VOICE OF A DRAGON and the ancient call of a mountain falling in the distance, made her hands shake.

She slumped against the altar, pressing her back against the spine, and ignored the water that sank through the furs she wore.

Ragged breaths escaped her lips. It wasn't possible. He wasn't here. She would *know* if he was here. And yet she could still hear him, clear as day and as haunting as a spirit. She tilted her head back, let it rest against the rock.

"Nadir," she said, and the words felt like a prayer. "Hello, husband."

RAHEEM

RAHEEM AWOKE TO THE SOUND OF ARMOR CLANGING. ROLLING OVER on his small cot in the army chambers, he watched as a few of the men in his regiment prepared themselves.

He rubbed the back of his head and slowly sat up. "Soldier," he barked. "Report."

"The sultan is calling for war, general."

What? That couldn't possibly be right. Solomon had made it very clear that war was not on the horizon. He was here to prevent Bymere from making any foolish moves before Nadir returned. That was his role and nothing else.

Why was the man going against his word?

Raheem pulled himself from bed and yanked on the shirt which lay across the foot of his cot. He would have words with the strange new sultan, who appeared to be little more intelligent than the last one.

"War?" he muttered, shaking his head and jerking the fabric so hard the seams at the shoulders protested. "Just what has gotten into the boy? The last battle didn't work out so well for this kingdom."

A passing soldier snorted. "That's why he's bringing this one to Wildewyn's doorstep."

If Raheem was a swearing man, he would have started right then and there. He almost let loose an ancient god's name who would likely have struck him down where he stood. There was no reason to attack Wildewyn on their own land. The last time Bymere had tried... a bloodbath unlike any other had occurred.

Bymere was suited for fighting in the desert. They knew how to find water when there was none. They knew how to hit an enemy from hundreds of yards away with a single arrow. But they didn't know how to fight in close quarters with trees between them and their enemies.

They were marching into a slaughter.

He raced through the halls, clapping shoulders as he went and advising men to return to their quarters. There was no reason for this. Some misunderstanding must have caused this, but he couldn't imagine it was the sultan himself who had ordered this.

Solomon knew what this would do to the kingdom. He'd be breaking more than just a promise. He would be taking over the kingdom once and for all.

He'd kill the man himself if he thought to step into Nadir's shoes permanently.

Sliding across the hall where the sultan's quarters were, Raheem skidded to a halt when he saw who stood in the center of the sultan's bedroom.

"Saafiya," he growled. "I thought they'd locked you up

somewhere nice and dark."

"No, my dear." She turned and smiled. The crimson gown she wore poured over her body, shifting with her movements and the embroidered gold thread caught in the light. "I thought you were dead."

"Apparently, I'm a hard man to kill."

She shrugged a delicate shoulder. "No one is invincible, General. I hear congratulations are in order. You've managed to win yourself a place back in the great chess game."

"This isn't a game. This is people's lives."

A shadow crossed over her expression and he realized she knew that. She knew this was her people's lives that she played with, and *it didn't matter to her.*

He lunged forward, only to be caught at the shoulder by strong hands.

"Peace, General." Solomon's voice was pitched low. "There is much for us to talk about."

"I'd kill you myself if I thought I could get away with it," he snarled.

Saafiya chuckled and clapped her hands. "Ah, Raheem. I wondered how long it would take you to hate him as we all do. Foolish man, you had so much hopes for the boy king who would always fall back into my hands."

Solomon's spine stiffened. Raheem didn't miss that, but the man still remained silent with his back turned to the first wife.

He'd take care of it then. This viper didn't need to be out of her cage for too long. It only meant the rest of them were in danger.

Raheem hooked his chin toward the door. "Back to your cage, woman. I'll rattle the bars if I need you again."

She sauntered by him, waggling her fingers. "Sultan, my love. If you have need of me again, you know where to find me."

Gods, he hoped Solomon hadn't slept with her. That woman must have been dipped in gold the way she captured the attention of so many men. He didn't understand the allure. Raheem would sooner cut off an arm than touch that one. Saafiya was the kind of woman to poison herself if it meant getting what she wanted in the end.

When the door closed behind her, Solomon let out a breath. "I suddenly understand why my brother had such a difficult time ruling this place."

"She's not even the worst of them."

"I'm well aware of that."

The false sultan stepped away and headed toward the desk. He lifted a bottle of fine whiskey out of it, then saluted Raheem. "I apologize, to both you and to the Sultan of Bymere. I thought this would be a much easier mission than it was."

"Was?" Raheem repeated.

"The advisors have made it very clear to me that if I do not support their movements to attack Wildewyn, then they will have me removed from the throne."

Raheem shook his head when offered a glass of whiskey. "They cannot do that. You are the one with royal blood."

"Apparently they can." Solomon drained the first glass and placed it on the table. He braced his arms on the worn wood. "They have some false proof that Nadir is not the sultan's son."

"Ridiculous," Raheem barked with laughter. "It's not possible. He looks more like his father than Hakim did, and that boy was a full-blooded royal."

"Papers can be forged. People can be paid to agree with their statements and then where would we be? Everything we've done, all the things we've worked for, will be wiped off this world immediately. I cannot let that happen."

All the anger simmering in Raheem's chest disappeared. His knees grew weak, and he sank into a chair beside the desk quietly. "Then what now?"

Solomon mirrored his actions and took off the wrap on his face. Every loop revealed more and more of the man's exhaustion. "War."

Gods, it sounded terrible. They were taking the lives of so many men and women in their hands and sending them to their death. For what? The hopes that Nadir would return some kind of changed man? That he would be able to come home and...

Raheem moved forward and placed his head in his hands. "We're all doomed, aren't we?"

"There's still a chance the true sultan can change this."

"How?" The Qatal warrior would have to explain, because Raheem saw nothing more than danger in this place. Death and blood already scented the air. The Earthen folk would destroy the army and then they would move forward with their march.

Bymere would disappear under the weight of a world which no longer saw fit for the people who floundered under the rule of misguided fools.

Solomon cleared his throat. "I haven't been entirely truthful with you. The leader of the Alqatara, she's more interested in Nadir because he's a dragon than anything else."

"What does she want with that beast?"

"In the old legends, dragons could fly into battle and end it immediately. But... that's not what she wants."

Raheem watched as the man's eyes darted to the side. He was clearly uncomfortable with the conversation. But why?

Narrowing his eyes, he watched as Solomon continued to fidget. Finally, Raheem pressed him. "What does she want with Nadir?"

His halting words sent a chill down Raheem's spine.

"In the ancient legends, humans worshipped dragons as gods. It is her belief that if we bring back all the old ways, that the humans will stop fighting and look to the Beastkin for all their needs."

"She wants to make him... what? A legend? A myth?" he asked, the words falling from his lips like stones. They dropped into his lap and weighed him down into the floor.

"She wants to make him divine."

They'd all lost their minds. That was the only thing Raheem could think. Completely mad. There was no way to make a man a god. Nadir was nothing more than a boy, a child who had yet to learn who or what he wanted to be.

"I was too late," he muttered. "I should have been here only a week sooner, and I might have stopped you all from this madness."

"It's not madness. This would work." Solomon leaned forward, his eyes gleaming brightly. "I know it seems insane and that you might not believe me when I say this, but the leader of the Alqatara has weighed all the possibilities. She *knows* this is the only way to save the kingdom from itself."

"You've all turned into zealots. You want more than just the kingdom, more than the empire itself. A god?" He shook his head. "He's just a boy."

"He's more than a boy, now. Dragons shouldn't exist

anymore, but they do. Haven't you ever wondered why they've never died out? And now there are two people out there capable of so much power, you and I can't even fathom what they can do."

"No," Raheem said, swallowing hard. "I never wondered what he could do. I always just looked at him as a child, a lonely child who wanted a family. You were supposed to give him a family, a mother and a brother who could show him what good there is in the world. All you've done is make him a monster."

The sadness in Solomon's gaze was all Raheem needed to see. It didn't matter that Nadir was a person. It hardly mattered that he existed at all. The Alqatara meant to see him become something far more than the Sultan of Bymere.

This would end poorly.

He waited until the other man cleared his throat and pushed a tumbler of whiskey toward him.

"Drink up, General," Solomon said. "As little as we both wish to see it happen, war is coming. And I need you with our men."

Raheem drank deeply of the amber liquid and stared up at the ceiling for a moment. If there were gods, he sent a prayer that they assist him. He would need all the help he could get to stay alive in this one.

THEY'D MOVED THE ARMY WITH REMARKABLE SPEED, BUT HE supposed that was understandable when it was a group of men who wanted nothing more than bloodshed. Raheem sat on his horse at the End of the World. The giant cliff dropped off into open air below them.

Green spread out in front of him. Hadn't he just been here? He'd swear only moments ago he'd been climbing up this mountain in secret, hoping to find the boy king who he'd come to care very much about.

Now, they were lowering the army down into the lush greenery beyond. An elephant beside him trumpeted its distress. They'd have to tie the beast down to the lift just to make sure it didn't tumble off the side of the mountain.

He'd argued not to bring them. They wouldn't do well in the forests. He knew what was beyond this swamp. The underbrush grew so dense even a child had a hard time slipping through it.

Abdul had disagreed. He'd argued that Raheem couldn't be trusted since he'd run away with the one person who had destroyed the city. That they couldn't take his word for more than a grain of salt because, of course, he could still be working with Sigrid. What if he lied? What if he brought them to certain death?

If he could have, Raheem would have strangled the man once and for all. Let the vipers nest burn for all he cared. The advisors were finished in this kingdom the moment Nadir returned.

Raheem would rot in the cells of the palace for the rest of his life if the boy would just let him slit their throats. He could do it in their sleep and no one would be the wiser.

Another horse joined his. The red coat shuddered with the beast's anticipation of a fight. Everyone knew the moment they

311

touched the ground, the Earthen folk would be prepared for them.

"General," Solomon said, his eyes staring down at the land beyond. "What awaits us?"

"Death."

"Surely our soldiers have been trained better than that. What can we expect as we descend? Will the Earthen folk's armies be prepared for us? Give me more information than your distrust for how we have chosen to go about this, General."

Raheem blew out a breath. The man wanted him to reassure him? Now? There weren't any reassurances to be had.

He pointed at the trees beyond. "Wildewyn always has defenses watching the walls. Considering how long it takes us to get down into their kingdom, there will already be people waiting for us. They favor bows and they favor hiding. We won't be able to see them. Likely won't even hear the arrows as they fly through the trees for our throats."

"Shields then."

"They'll find a way through them. There's a reason we haven't attacked Wildewyn on their own soil in centuries. They know how to use their kingdom to their advantage."

At least Solomon looked discomforted. Raheem had been convinced the man didn't know the difference between battle tactics and throwing themselves off a cliff.

The false sultan tightened his grip on the reins in his hand. "I've trained my entire life as one of the Qatal. I know how to fight better than any man here, likely better than most. But this?" He shook his head. "I don't know how to prepare for this."

"There isn't a way to prepare to fight on soil you've never

stepped foot on before. We can only hope our men survive the first battle."

"I didn't give any of you enough credit," once again, the sultan said the words. "These people... there's something dark in the shadows. As if people are constantly listening to everything you do and are trying to twist the words in a way that suits them better."

"Welcome to life in the palace." Raheem clapped him on the shoulder and yanked his horse toward the first lift. "It won't get any better. All you commoners think the royals are languishing in their beds of roses waiting for the next time they can make you angry. The truth is, they've got it just as bad. Only in other ways."

He didn't wait for the other man to reply. Truthfully, he didn't care what the assassin had to say. There was too much happening now in his own home to care what the Alqatara thought. They were a band of assassins who had their heads buried so deep in the sand they wouldn't see war coming for them if they tried.

And Raheem? He was the general of this army. He'd trained most of these men himself, and he intended to ensure as many of them lived as possible. If that meant taking arrows for them, then he would.

"Hold!" he shouted at one of the lifts. The men paused, eyeing him with equal parts awe and anger as he guided his own horse onto the rickety wood.

"General?" one of the soldiers asked. He was little more than a boy really. Just barely growing hair on his chin and with wide, frightened eyes. "Should you be coming with us?"

"I don't believe in a first wave that's only meant to feed the ground with blood. We'll fight boys, but we're going to do it the smart way."

The reins in his hands creaked. The horse beneath him shuddered, knowing what was going to happen and afraid of what would come. Raheem had ridden this horse into many a battle. He knew it wouldn't shy away at the last second. But he feared he might lose it either way.

He leaned down and patted a hand to the beast's neck. "Easy," he murmured. "Soon, my friend."

The touch of war laid upon his shoulders as if an old friend had leaned down and grasped him. He knew what this felt like. The aching wait for the moment when the battle would begin. He saw it in the faces of the other men.

Some men felt the fear more than the anticipation. Those who hadn't been in battle before would wonder what was going to happen to them. Would they die? Would they be wounded and forced to live a life where there was nothing for them left other than a bed and a cane?

Others, mostly those who had lived this before, knew what to expect. They understood the blood and the pain were only part of the thrill. War had a way of sinking into a man's bones. Forced to find ways to keep themselves alive, they would do anything it took to see their families the next days. These were the soldiers he wanted with him.

The young man who had spoken to him stood at the very edge of the lift. His knee bounced as he held onto the rope and watched the ground approach.

"First time?" Raheem asked, his eyes still on the forests beyond.

"Aye, sir."

"How old are you, boy?"

"Eighteen summers. I've been training my whole life though."

Raheem didn't care if he'd been training. A farmer could step onto a war zone and be just as prepared as the young man who didn't know what the slaughter would be like. He almost pitied the boy, knowing there was only sadness here for him.

A rustling in the trees beyond wasn't simply the wind. There were men there, he was certain of it. He could almost feel their eyes and the hardened tips of their arrows. This wouldn't be an easy fight. In fact, he'd say it would be the most difficult battle the army had to face. There were only so many of them.

"Keep your eyes on the trees," he muttered to the men. "That's where they're hiding, and that's where the attack will come from."

"How do we stop their arrows?" the boy next to him asked.

"You don't. If you're hit, take your sword and snap the end off. It's something the others can grab onto and you don't want that. Let the arrow stay inside you for the battle. We'll take them out at the end."

The boy gulped, and his face reflected a fear Raheem hadn't felt in a very long time.

The lift hit the ground and the very first whistle of an arrow flew through the air. He watched it come, old soldier's eyes knowing exactly where it was going. He was the only man on a horse. Of course they would know he was more important than the others.

Raheem didn't flinch away from the pain. He let the arrow strike him in the shoulder.

Not a muscle on him reacted to the pain. Instead, he

reached up, snapped the shaft as he'd told the others to do, and dropped the arrow onto the ground.

"Soldiers of Bymere!" he shouted, lifting his scimitar above his head. "Attack!"

CAMILLA

HER WINGS SHOOK. HER VISION HAD ALREADY SKEWED TO THE SIDE A few hours ago, but she couldn't stop flying. She'd circled the mountain where they'd thought the ancients were a few times. Nothing is there to suggest there was a hidden place where Beastkin lived.

She didn't know what to do until she saw the pillar of smoke. There shouldn't have been a fire this time of year. Winter was already covering the mountain peaks with snow. The runoff should have been enough to keep the wetlands so wet a fire wouldn't start.

Then it dawned on her. Hallmar had said the Bymerians were coming. Surely, he didn't mean *this* soon, had he?

She'd taken a detour that exact moment. Sigrid could wait a little longer. The rest of them could wait for her when there was clearly something happening in the middle of Wildewyn. They needed her.

Unfortunately, the moment she reached the fires, she didn't

know what to do.

Great swaths of land had fallen under the hungry flame. Bonfires were piled as far as the eye could see over the swampland. They dotted nearly every patch of land that wasn't swallowed by the floods of winter. Bodies burned upon them.

Bymerian soldiers were gathering their own men and those of the Earthen folk, stripping them down for whatever they could use, and then tossing them atop the pyre. A few of the Earthen folk were still alive. She could hear them groaning and then the angered shouts as the flames consumed them.

Even in the form of an owl, she gagged. How could they do this to people? It didn't matter that they were enemies. They were still *human,* and they could so easily throw them into the flames. Alive or dead?

She eyed all the moving pieces of the army, surprised that the number was so small. Then, she realized the lift was still moving. They were still delivering more and more men into her homeland. This would be a war to end all wars. The dual kingdoms of this empire would end, and soon it would be under one ruler.

Unless she could stop it.

Though her wings were aching, she lifted into the air and took flight. Making her way across the battlefield on silent wings.

Nadir must be here. Maybe he would listen to her, or see reason when she explained what was happening. Sigrid wouldn't have wanted this. Didn't he love her enough not to attack her own home? Let her have her peace for a little while longer.

But she didn't see the Sultan of Bymere at all. No one here

looked like Nadir that she could see. A fact that made her heart ache. Why wasn't he here? Would he attack his enemies without even coming himself?

A familiar man stumbled away from a burning pyre, his arm covering his face. Even so, she knew the large man at once. Camilla followed Raheem to a tent which had been set up near the base of the mountain, surrounded by soldiers with flint-and-steel eyes.

She waited until he was hidden in the tent before landing behind it. As she had so many months ago, she wiggled underneath the flaps between stakes driven into the ground.

Raheem was alone, a rarity she was sure if they were truly at war. How had he managed to get his own tent? Had Nadir made him general once again? Camilla found it hard to believe when he'd sided with the Beastkin. The Bymerians couldn't possibly be so forgiving of that kind of transgression.

Yet, here he was. Standing alone in a tent guarded by a handful of soldiers armed to the teeth.

She waited until he'd settled down. He reached for the hem of his shirt to pull it over his head, then she changed while the fabric covered his eyes.

Let him be frightened of what she could do. Camilla might be an owl, but that didn't make her any less weak than a dragon.

"Hello, Raheem," she said quietly.

He froze in his movements, then slowly continued to pull off his shirt. She'd always thought he was a younger man, but his body revealed a story of years. Hardship decorated his flesh in the shape of scars. Small, deep, long, all manner of injuries dotted his body across nearly every surface. He was a network of fighting and battle.

No wonder they'd made him general again.

Slowly, he turned toward her and placed a hand on his bleeding shoulder. "Camilla. I thought I might find you here."

"Here, of all places? Did you think I would run to you the moment you attacked my homeland?"

"No," he said, sinking down onto a small cot in the corner. "I thought you would wonder what was happening though. I didn't expect the Beastkin to fight for the kingdom which has forsaken them time and time again."

A shadow passed in front of the tent flap. "General? Do you need something?"

"You're dismissed, soldier."

"With all due respect, the advisors have stated we're to remain by your side." The soldier's voice was hesitant, as though he didn't want to follow the orders of the people who led his country.

"I think I've earned the right after today's battle. Go, be with the others and see what you can help with. I don't need good soldiers wasting away outside my tent."

They both waited for the sound of footsteps. Camilla counted them as they left. She'd thought they would leave at least one soldier with them. Bymerians were ever so fond of eavesdropping.

"There," Raheem said. He grunted and leaned back on the cot, pulling sticky fingers away from the wound on his shoulder. "We've at least some privacy now."

"What have you done to yourself?"

"I think you should ask the Earthen folk who are likely in the trees somewhere nursing their own wounded."

She wanted to be angry with him. She wanted to shout at

him for his foolishness and explain that this attack wasn't going to end well for anyone. He'd started something he couldn't end. Or, well, the sultan had.

Camilla had to remind herself that Raheem was a man of the crown. He didn't have a say in what the sultan did.

Sighing, she strode to his side and pulled his hand away from the wound. "What has Nadir done now?"

"Not Nadir."

Her hand froze just a hair's breadth away from his wound. Camilla looked up and met his dark gaze. "Then who?"

"The Alqatara. They're a… insane group of people in Bymere who have always been the last effort for war. They trained their children as warriors, raise them with no fear of death or repercussions. I have my suspicions they also are partly involved with the Beastkin as well." He winced, shifting until he could prop his back against one of the wooden posts holding the tent up. "They want to turn Nadir into a god, apparently."

Camilla smiled, then went about prodding at his wound. She needed to take the arrow out, and then it would need to be packed with whatever healing herbs the Bymerians had brought. "They're more alike than they know."

"Who?"

"Sigrid left to see the ancients. With their knowledge, and potentially their power, she too would become something like a god."

"Two new gods?" he asked with a coughing laugh. "Whatever will the world do with them?"

"I don't care what the rest of the world thinks. I only care what we think of them. And they are, without a doubt, still the same people. They need us now more than ever, Raheem." Her fingers found purchase on the end of the arrow shaft. It had almost gone all the way through him, which made her job a little easier. "Ready?"

He met her gaze, set his jaw, and nodded.

With a single quick movement, she shoved hard at the muscles of his shoulders. The arrow went through his back just enough for her to grab the metal head. She yanked it out, perhaps a little too aggressively.

Raheem let out a groan, then shook his head. "I guess I deserved that."

"You did just kill many of my countrymen and are out there burning them as if their families don't want to know what happened to them."

"I'm sure they know by now. War isn't something people tend to keep quiet." He grabbed the wadded up fabric of his shirt and pressed it hard against the bleeding wound. "You have to know, I didn't want to do this."

"I know."

"There is no possible way for me to stop them. I have to fight with them if I want to be there when Nadir returns. And I have to be there." He looked at her with a gaze so earnest it brought tears to her eyes. "He cannot be left to fend for himself when all these advisors want to destroy him."

"I know." She did. She truly did. And still, her heart ached for the place they were all in. Fighting each other when all they wanted was...

Peace.

She wanted peace more than she wanted anything else. She wanted to go back to the time when she and Sigrid had lived together in a gilded cage, and Sigrid was going to marry a good man.

Gods. She couldn't even remember his name anymore. He was just a blurry face in the wake of so much pain.

Camilla knelt in front of him, placed her hands on his knees, and stared up at him. "What are we going to do, my dear friend?"

"We need them both back in the same place as they were before. We need to restart everything over in a better way."

"Then I need to find Sigrid."

"Can you?"

She hoped she could. She had all the more reason to now.

SIGRID

SHE LEANED HER HEAD BACK AGAINST THE STONE ALTAR, MOUTH falling open in a silent gasp that made her heart hurt. The sound of his voice… it was a balm on her aching soul.

"Hello, husband," she said.

Tears welled in her eyes even though she shouldn't have allowed them to. He had betrayed her. Betrayed their people and renounced all that he was because of an allegiance to his own people. She couldn't blame him for that. She had done the same.

And yet, her heart still ached. She wanted to hear him speak, to understand where his thoughts were, if he was still okay or if the year they hadn't seen each other had changed *everything*.

"Sigrid." He said her name again, and she couldn't tell if it was because he couldn't hear her anymore or if it was a whispered prayer. "How is this possible?"

"I don't know," she replied. "But I'm glad it is."

How could she tell him that she'd missed him? That leaving him had been the hardest choice she'd ever had to make. She'd do it again, but her heart would shatter a thousand times over. It killed her every time she thought about leaving his kingdom. Of the pain she had caused.

A tear slid down her cheek. Water seeped through the furs around her legs but she didn't care. If she froze to this spot, she would do it with happiness.

"Where are you?" he asked, his voice sounding as though he were standing next to her.

"A cave filled with ice actually," she replied with a laugh. "I'm no longer with the Earthen Beastkin. I have so much to tell you."

"As do I." Was that the sound of rustling? As if he were moving and sitting right next to her? "I made a decision I shouldn't have, Sigrid."

"That's not particularly new."

"I'm afraid I changed everything again," he whispered. "I shouldn't have done it, but it's already over with, and now I don't know what to do."

"What did you do, Nadir?"

"I have to see you," he replied. "There's too much to explain, and too much of it affects us both."

Her stomach turned. "I was about to say the same thing to you."

A crunching sound far from her suggested more people had arrived in this ancient place. She hadn't thought Eivor would go to find the others, but apparently she'd thought too little of the medicine woman. She had been in a lot of pain. Bleeding from her ears and nose probably wasn't what the medicine woman had expected when she had brought Sigrid to this place.

"I have to go," she said, not sure how to turn off this connection they suddenly had between them. "They're coming."

"Who?"

"We call them ancients. The ones who came before all the Beastkin, the legendary ones that still live in the old ways. There's..." She paused to exhale a long breath. "There's so much I need to tell you."

"Good." There was a long hesitation between them, and then Nadir added, "I've missed you."

Gods, she'd missed him as well. More than she could really say to him when the figures of the ancients were striding toward her.

Water splashed around Aslaug's legs in great, diamond waves. Sigrid tilted back her head and stared up at the ceiling made of blue ice above them. This place shouldn't be able to exist, and yet, here it was. *She* shouldn't exist, and yet, a dragon lived inside her.

Eivor raced in behind the matriarch, and a small band of braves slowed behind the two of them.

The medicine woman stopped in front of her, hand on the rat skull at her waist and mask back on her face. "Sigrid? You are well then?"

"I'm better, thank you." Her eyes weren't on the medicine woman though.

Aslaug stepped forward and reached with a shaking finger. She touched a finger beneath Sigrid's ear, staring at the blood that now slicked her fingertip. "He calls for you, doesn't he?"

"Who?"

"Your mate." Aslaug took a step back, her eyes wide as if this was something she hadn't imagined. "There's another dragon."

"There is."

"Why didn't you tell us?"

Something in the words resonated deep in Sigrid's chest. It was almost as though Aslaug was accusing her of something, but she didn't know what the accusation was. She sat up further, bracing her shoulders against the altar. "I wasn't aware you needed to know."

"Of course we need to know!" the matriarch spat. "There are prophecies that are being fulfilled in this moment. If we had *known* this was the prophecy, then I never would have—"

The silence that rang in the room after her angry words were like stones falling from a mountain peak. Sigrid watched as an avalanche of emotion fell among the ancient Beastkin. Even Eivor, trusted and kind, took another step away from Sigrid.

"What is this?" she asked. "What prophecy are you speaking of? How could anything change just because another dragon exists?"

"It's not that he exists," Aslaug corrected. "It's that you're mated. It's too late to change that now. Your dragons have seen something in each other that cannot be broken except by death. I will not see the last dragons fall into ruin for fear."

"You have to explain."

"I cannot. I will not, because there is far more here than you know."

"I want to help, but I can't if you won't—"

Aslaug lifted a hand for her to stop speaking. Sigrid watched lines of exhaustion appear on the matriarch's face. "It is done. There is no going back from the future in which we now find ourselves. We will endure, as we always have. For now, you must go back to your people. Prepare for the war which is coming, and do all that you can to keep the Beastkin armies alive."

"What?"

The matriarch turned and left with the braves. The trickling sound of water was all that remained, other than her own ragged breath and the ticking of Eivor's nails scratching the skull at her waist.

Sigrid shook her head in disbelief. "That's it? That's all they're giving me?"

"I'm sorry," the medicine woman whispered. "I didn't know."

"What didn't you know?" Sigrid stood then, marching to the medicine woman's side and grabbing her shoulders. "Eivor, tell me what is going on."

"I can't."

"Eivor, *now*."

When the woman still didn't respond, Sigrid did the only thing she could think of. She reached up, grasped the edges of the woman's mask, and ripped it off her face. Throwing the hated thing away as far as she could, she listened for the sound of breaking wood.

Eivor whimpered and covered her face. She whined and fell to her knees, scrambling to find something, anything to cover her own ugliness.

"No," Sigrid growled, slapping the woman's hands away from the monstrosity of her own features and following her to the ground. "You will no longer hide your face. I don't care what they say of you or who you think you are. I declare it now, Eivor of the ancient Beastkin, *you are mine.*"

The medicine woman froze. Her shaking hands came up to grasp Sigrid's wrists. "I don't want to hurt anyone."

"You are under the protection of a dragon. I will stand between you and all harm, but you need to pledge your life to me. Everything that you are is now mine. I will take you from this place, and you will return to the Earthen home with me. Together, we will stop whatever it is the ancients think is coming, but *I need you to tell me what it is.*"

Tears welled in Eivor's eyes, slipping down to disappear in fur and feathers. "I can't tell you, Matriarch. I'm sorry to disappoint you, but I cannot go against everything I am to tell you. It's forbidden."

Sigrid released her hold on the woman with a harsh exhale of breath. She wouldn't hurt Eivor. The creature had been thoroughly useful. She would break eventually. For now, she needed to return home.

She straightened her spine, squared her shoulders, and glared down at the creature which huddled at her feet. "Soon, nothing will be forbidden to *me.*"

Eivor looked up at her with wide eyes. "Then you are choosing the path of a god?"

"That is what the ancients wanted, isn't it? To turn me into a god, and then use me in whatever way they wanted? Now they throw away their only tool. I will find out what this prophecy is whether you tell me or not. And I will use it against them all to make this world become what it deserves to be."

She didn't like the choice. It burned in her throat like the words were lacerating her as they left her body. But it was the only way. She couldn't think of anything else that would save her people, her kingdom, and the man she loved all at the same time.

In that moment, Sigrid realized she didn't want to have to choose between any of them.

She wanted them all. And she would have them all.

Eivor slowly stood, her hands twitching at her sides. "There was a woman who arrived in camp. She said she was looking for you."

"What was her name?"

"Camilla."

"Good." Sigrid looked up at the ice again and then all around them at the shattered remains of an empire long forgotten. "She'll help us get home."

"Us?" Again, Eivor looked up at her with so much emotion in her eyes that it almost made Sigrid uncomfortable.

"Yes, us. Did you think I was going to let you stay here? When there are so many who don't see your worth?"

Sigrid felt almost a little guilty at the order. Eivor might want to remain here with her people, regardless of how they treated her. But she refused to leave the medicine woman who had been so kind throughout this entire ordeal. She wanted to make certain Eivor saw the world the way it should be. That she didn't have to hide her face just because she was different.

Although, she wasn't all that certain the other Beastkin would't react the same way the ancients had. She was strange looking even for them. But that didn't mean time couldn't change the way they saw her. Sigrid was certain, given the right chance, her people would see Eivor as something more than just a woman to cast aside and never touch. They would see her as a person. Odd, yes, but a person.

She held out a hand for Eivor to take. "Come home with me, medicine woman. Come and see the world that you have been denied. If you wish to return once you have seen all the world has to offer, then I will carry you back."

Eivor didn't hesitate to take her hand. "I want to see the world beyond the ice."

"Then so be it."

Sigrid took a few steps away from the medicine woman, letting her hand fall and the dragon beneath Sigrid's skin awaken. The creature was becoming more and more like Sigrid every day. She didn't want to deny the dragon anything it wanted, because she wanted the same thing.

Taking a deep breath, she let the change shift through her body. Painless and easy, scales covered her body and a long snout erupted through her skin. Wings unfurled where her arms had been. Suddenly, she felt so much more powerful than she had been before. This was her true form. This was the form she loved and adored above all others.

Huffing out a breath, she stepped forward and lowered herself so Eivor could hop on.

The woman's eyes widened. "No, I couldn't. It wouldn't be right."

Again she shifted until it was clear they weren't going to move without Eivor doing as she asked. Did the woman really think they were going to walk out of this ancient cavern? There were no secrets left here. Just relics of a time Sigrid knew had to end.

The moment Eivor managed to drag herself up onto her back, Sigrid reared back and let out a roar that shook the ceiling.

She stared up at the ice and wondered how long it would take for the ancients to punish her for this. She opened her jaws, then let out a stream of blue fire so hot it burned through the ceiling in a perfect hole.

Cold air rushed down upon them, falling from the air like snow.

With a great flap of her wings, she launched herself out of the cavern and out into the open air. The remains of the ice brushed the tips of her wings. Cold and still streaming water, it coated her wings and froze them solid for a moment before she flexed her muscles. The leathery fabric of her body shook free from the cold with ease.

Sigrid hovered in the air, holding herself still and trying to think where she would go. She didn't want to return to the ancient's stronghold. They had given her nothing but history. A history she refused to repeat.

And yet, Camilla was still there. Waiting for her, expecting that Sigrid would come.

She opened her jaws again and let out another stream of fire that struck the air like thunder. Cold air wrapped around her head, set out a reverberation, and the answering echo shook the ground beneath her.

Eivor shivered on her back. The poor creature had already wrapped her arms so tightly around Sigrid's neck, she almost couldn't breathe. There wasn't time to reassure her passenger. They had very little time.

A small dot appeared on the horizon, darting toward her

faster and faster. She watched as the grey owl rose above her in the air, and then changed into a woman plummeting toward Sigrid's back.

She held herself perfectly still as Camilla landed between her wings. They'd never done this before, but she trusted her sister. The woman could climb trees with the best of them, and had been nicknamed *monkey* as a child.

If anyone could clamber across her in the air, it was Camilla.

Warmth bloomed in her chest at the touch of her sister. It hadn't been that long… had it? A few months at best, and she still felt as though it had been a lifetime.

Camilla hooked a hand on one of Sigrid's spines, slid down her belly, and landed in Sigrid's waiting foot.

Carefully, oh so carefully, Sigrid closed her claws around Camilla. She lifted her up close to her head, winged arms beating at the air to keep them still with the added weight.

Her sister looked as though she'd lost weight. Sigrid tilted her head to the side so her large eye could sweep over Camilla's form for a moment. Was she all right? Too much could have happened in her absence, and Camilla hadn't anticipated having to find her.

Something had happened. Sigrid was certain of that.

Camilla reached up and touched a hand to Sigrid's chest. "Sister."

An answering rumble in Sigrid's chest conveyed what she hoped was happiness. Even if Camilla had something terrible to say, Sigrid was glad to see her.

"You have to return home," Camilla called out. "Although, I suspect you already know that."

Sigrid inclined her head in a nod. It was long past time she come back, even if her people thought she were dead. She would handle that fallout in the only way she knew how. With honesty and integrity. If they wanted nothing to do with her after that... then at least she would still have her dignity.

"Sigrid..." Camilla cleared her throat. "There's a war starting."

Again? She didn't want to fight with the Beastkin again. They needed to enjoy their lives for a little while, not fight and watch more death come to their lands.

A warm hand smoothed down her breast, finger sinking between scales to touch her skin. "It's *him*, Sigrid. Not the Beastkin, not anyone else. Bymere has started a war again, and this time it's against our homeland. The Bymerians are here. They brought war elephants and soldiers unlike any I've seen before.

"We don't know what to do. The Beastkin don't want to help those who they feel have imprisoned them. Hallmar specifically asked for you, and I had to tell him you were dead.

"Raheem returned to Bymere to try and talk sense into Nadir but... no one knows where he is. An imposter sits on the throne, something about a league of assassins who know how to help Bymere in times of crisis. But while they focus on their own kingdom, ours burns."

Camilla stared up at her, dark eyes swirling with tears like starlight in a vast expanse of sky. "I would have left you here. I would have let you find yourself for longer but our home is dying, and I knew you wouldn't want me to just... let it die."

There were too many emotions running through her. She could hardly think past the screaming in her head at the mere thought that Wildewyn was dying. She had fallen in love with the green trees. The ones that were burning under the great empire of Bymere as it marched upon her people.

Upon her king.

She didn't notice she was roaring until her ears began to rang. She'd tilted her head back, dropped open her great jaws, and screamed into the sky until it rumbled with her anger.

The emotion was so strong it sent a current of energy through the tenuous thread that connected her to Nadir. It shimmered in her mind, flaring bright with rage and heartbreak.

The moment she realized they could still speak, that this was what had allowed his anger and pain to reach her, she screamed in her mind. Over and over, she screamed until the draconic beast released its hold and she could shout, "You did this!"

Silence was her response for long heartbeats before she heard his reply.

"What has happened?"

"You know," she growled back. "You knew Bymere was going to attack my home and you *did nothing to stop it.*"

"They did what?"

She couldn't speak anymore. Instead, all she projected were images of Wildewyn trees, ancient as the earth itself, burning to the ground. She sent pictures of blood and warfare. Children dying in the streets and their mothers becoming shields made out of desperation and love.

Maybe that was not the scene in Wildewyn. Though she doubted there was any mercy in their actions. Sigrid knew what war was like. What it did to men who felt more fear than anything else.

She'd never thought to see it destroy the only place she'd felt accepted.

Her blood heated, a projected anger shaking the connection between them when he bellowed, *"What has he done?"*

"You know who did this?"

"A man who replaced me so I might learn from the best assassins in the world, the Alqatara. He was meant to stall the advisors, not lead them into a war."

Her wings shook, and she tossed her head. "Enough. We end this now."

"Come to me," he replied, desperation lacing his tone into something rugged and raw. "Come to me, and we will fix this."

It was not a bad idea. She could fly over the Bymerian army, ignore them entirely, and head toward *their* homeland. Perhaps then she could make them feel the anger and the fear she felt in her heart.

She would be the one destroying their home. Let them shake and quiver when they saw her great form fly overhead.

Without question or response, Sigrid turned her great head toward the Edge of the World and the man she called husband.

NADIR

"SULTAN?" THE VOICE INTERRUPTED HIM AS HE TRIED TO CONNECT with Sigrid again. Anything that would let him know *when* she was coming. Where was she? What had happened? From whom had she heard these terrible things?

"What?" he snapped, turning so quickly water rushed off him in droplets.

He stood in the center of the oasis still. Nothing had changed there. How long had they been standing here, doing nothing? Staring off into space like some kind of dolt?

Tahira stood in front of him, her eyes eagle golden and staring through him. "Are you still with us?" she growled back.

"I'm alive, if that's what you're asking."

"I'm asking if you are the one talking to me, or if I'm speaking to the dragon."

"He cannot speak."

"He can." Tahira stared into his eyes a few more heartbeats before her own eyes turned back into the gold gaze of a human.

"But perhaps you haven't learned how to do that just yet. It's good you survived, Sultan."

"I don't think you would have missed me."

"I wouldn't have. But that doesn't mean I don't have enough of a heart to realize there are some people who would." She tilted her head to the side. "Like that woman you were whispering to while you were out. Sigrid, is it? I knew a tale of a woman with that name. She was the most powerful creature to ever exist, according to the rumors. Somehow, I'm not sure if that's true."

"She might be the most powerful woman to ever exist. But we battled once, and I would have bested her."

"Would have, but didn't. What stopped you?"

He hesitated in his reply, because he didn't want to let this woman know where his weaknesses lay. And yet... Tahira had proved herself loyal to the country. If Sigrid were to become even more essential to this place, then he needed someone else to admire her just as he did.

Taking a deep breath, he shrugged. "The other half of my soul."

"A sultana?"

"In name only. She's never needed a crown or a throne to make her a queen." He believed the words with all his being. Long before she had become the Sultana of Bymere, Sigrid was a woman people remembered. She had changed their lives for the better, and the life of his kingdom into something he could be proud of.

He needed to tell her that. It was important she know he thought so highly of her. That his people would think highly of her when they saw him around her.

She deserved better than a boy king. And so, he'd become a god.

Tahira cleared her throat. "A woman I will look forward to meeting. But for now, Sultan of Bymere, I need you to come with me."

"Where are we going now? Are you going to try and drown me again?"

"Never again, Sultan. That I promise." She pressed a fist against her heart and bowed. "Your mother has summoned you."

His gaze flicked toward the bench where he'd left Nahla. She wasn't there at all. Nothing was left in the garden oasis that would even suggest she'd ever sat there. Not a single mark or a scrap of fabric to remind him.

"Where did she go?"

"Your mother is very sick," Tahira murmured. "She's been fading for a very long time. It was her wish to meet you before she went, but now she's stayed longer than her body wanted to. She wishes one more goodbye before she joins the ancestors."

Should he feel more affected by the knowledge? Nadir was sad, of course. The loss of life was a horrible and frightening thing to most of them. The Beastkin believed they would go to live with their ancestors, but the Bymerians didn't. They didn't even have priests in his kingdom. Let alone an afterlife that would give them something more than just oblivion.

Swallowing hard, he nodded and followed Tahira from the oasis. They traveled through the village, while he schooled his face into the appropriate expression.

Should he be distraught? It didn't feel befitting of a sultan. He'd never seen a person die before. Not up close, nor had he ever really seen a dead body. Perhaps the ones that were on display, but even his brother he been hidden from him in those final moments.

As a child, he'd thought that was odd. Nadir had sat by Hakim's bedside while his brother struggled as poison ate his body from the inside out. He had seen the worst of what could happen to a person's body. Death could be a release from such pain.

This was different. Nahla was still a strong woman. Her hands had felt fragile, certainly, but the grip was true. She had been strong enough to hold a conversation with him and wander into the oasis garden.

Why was now the time she wanted to die? Was she making some kind of point to him?

He couldn't force himself to feel for her as a son should feel. She hadn't raised him. In truth, he didn't even know her. He knew her name and that she had spent most of her life with the people here, training them how to fight. But was that enough to feel some kind of attachment?

He didn't think so. A year ago he might have felt something different. The respect in his chest wasn't the same blind faith he might have felt as a boy who was desperately trying to find someone to love him. Now, all new attuned was the respect of a woman who should have loved him. The honor of knowing he'd done the right thing by her, and that she would go into the darkness with some kind of approval.

The first person to approve of him since his brother had died.

Tahira stopped in front of the small hut he knew so well and gestured at the covered doorway. "She's in there. Waiting for you."

"Thank you," he replied, reaching out a hand and grasping her shoulder. "I know this isn't easy for you."

"She is my leader."

"She's more than that to you, isn't she?" He looked deeply into her gaze and saw the truth flickering in those depths. "It's okay," he said. "She's not going to be in pain much longer."

"That's what everyone says. Like that's going to help when she's not going to be here anymore."

Gods, he wished he could share that sentiment with her. But he couldn't bring himself to reply that he would feel the loss of her as well. He'd miss her spirit; the strength she had shown him.

But this woman wasn't his mother. That was the sultana who had brushed his hair and shown him how to braid the long locks. Not the woman who had left him on the doorstep for his father to pick up later on.

Nadir blew out a breath, brushed aside the red fabric door, and stepped into the quiet hut beyond.

No one else waited with the Matriarch of the Alqatara, a realization that made him angry on her behalf. She shouldn't have to make this journey by herself. What if she had passed while he took his time getting here? No one should have to walk across the bridge of life and death on their own.

Shaking his head, he made his way to the side of the bed where a rattling breath echoed. He sank onto his knees beside her cot and reached for her hand resting on top of the patchwork blanket.

"Matriarch," he said quietly.

Nahla tilted her head to look at him, her eyes unfocused

and dark. "Would you call me mother? At least once in your life?"

He wanted to. Gods, it was the right thing to do for a woman on her deathbed who was asking so little.

But he couldn't. The memory of his real mother kept rising to the forefront of his mind. He remembered the way she had smelled like jasmine from the baths she took with the concubines every morning. How she refused to wear jewelry, because she said her skin was plenty pretty enough without marring it with stones from the earth. He remembered how the henna on her hands had always been flowers because she loved them so much.

With a sad look, he shook his head. "My deepest apologies, Alqatara. We both know why I cannot do that."

Nahla sighed. "I do, but I wish that life had been kinder to both of us."

"There's little we can do to change what has been done."

"And yet, an old woman can dream." Nahla's hand shook in his grasp. She threaded their fingers together and hesitantly lifted them up. "You became a good man, Nadir, without any advice from me at all."

"It's hard not to be when I was raised in a group of men who were kind and honest to a fault."

"They were," she whispered. "You'll find that out soon enough. You've survived in a pit of vipers and somehow, impossibly, you turned out to be a dragon who will devour them all."

They were back here already? He'd thought maybe she would want to have some sentimental words. Not talk to him again about becoming a god, leading the people through fear.

342

What was this woman's end game?

Nahla coughed, forcing his gaze back to her face. "Listen to me, boy. I couldn't be there for you when I should have been a mother. I know that."

"You did what you could."

"Don't interrupt me, Nadir. I'm dying, and I only have a little bit of time to say this. You must promise me you will never again fear your dragon. You and he will rule this land without war, bloodshed, or fire. The people need to trust you to protect them, and that they no longer need to fight."

He didn't want to argue this when she was about to die. She didn't need to hear him say he didn't really believe her, or that he didn't think he could do what she wanted him to do.

Instead, Nadir curled her fingers within his hands gently. He pulled her closer and tucked her hand against his heart. "I will do all that I can to make you proud of me, Nahla. Matriarch of the Alqatara. Your memory and your story will live throughout the ages. I will *never* let anyone forget you."

"That is the duty of the Qatal. We are forgotten as soon as the air leaves our lungs."

"I will not forget you. My children will not forget you. Their grandmother was a warrior who saved the kingdom countless times over. No child of mine will not know this."

Nahla's lungs rattled as a breath wheezed out. "Good. That's good, my son."

He drew her hand closer to his chest. Pressing her fingers against his skin in hopes that she might feel his heart beating strong there. Her legacy wouldn't die with her. Nadir was still here, he was still strong, and he would save the kingdom as she'd wished. Perhaps not for her, but because of her.

He didn't know how long he knelt beside the cot. It didn't matter that his knees ached as they pressed into the sand, nor that shivers danced down his spine as wind funneled through the hole in the top of the hut. Instead, he intently listened to her discomfort and waited for the moment when silence fell heavy around him.

The passing of her soul was as quiet as a blanket of snow. It touched upon his shoulders in the sudden quiet. The last exhale from her body sang like the low tune of a flute before it disappeared from this world forever.

Nadir should feel more of a loss than this. His heart ached for her, for the loss of a soul who had been taken too young. But it wasn't that of a son who had lost his mother. For that, he regretted her actions for her. Perhaps, if they were given more time, he might have loved her as she deserved. As it was, he could only gift her with little more than clearing his throat and a quiet nod.

"Rest easy, warrior," he murmured. Leaning forward, he touched a finger to each of her eyes and gently closed them. "Your fight has ended."

Gods, this was his *mother*. The woman who had brought him into the world and she was gone.

Now he would never know where he'd come from. What he'd looked like as a child... Nadir let out a slow sigh. It didn't matter. None of that mattered, regardless of her capabilities to birth him. She'd given him up. That had to be enough, so his thoughts didn't try to drown him.

The tent flap stirred behind him. He knew it was Tahira.

She let out a soft sound. "So she's gone then?"

"Yes."

"Was it—" she hesitated, then cleared her throat. "Was it painless?"

"As far as I could tell."

"She wouldn't have wanted anyone to know how weak she was," Tahira replied. "It's better if we tell people that she went out without a fight at all. That she was… peaceful. In the end."

He watched her throat bob with deep emotion that he couldn't respond to. How did one let another person know that he wanted to be there? That he wanted to share the same feelings as her but couldn't bring himself to think of this cold, dead woman beside him as anything other than the leader of the Alqatara?

Nadir opened his mouth to reply with something, anything. The words didn't want to come out, and they didn't have to. His mind suddenly shook with the weight of another launching deep through his skull.

The pain spread through the back of his head until he couldn't think of anything else other than the words screaming inside his skull.

"Nadir!"

He'd waited so long to hear that voice. He didn't want to hear it ring with anger or disappointment as it was now, but he'd take whatever he could with her. If she wanted to shout at him, to fight, it was still something. Anything was better than the near year of silence.

"She's here," he muttered, standing swiftly and casting a glance at the woman who had birthed him. "I take it you'll lead the ceremony?"

"She would have wanted her own blood to lead that."

He was already striding toward the front of the hut. He

paused beside Tahira and clapped a hand to her shoulder. "You're more her family than I am. If she wanted someone who cared for her to help guide her into whatever afterlife you believe in, then you would be better at that than I."

The emotion in her gaze nearly sent him to his knees. He didn't want to see the pain in those eyes. She was a strong woman, a warrior who had managed to break free from the Bymerian prisons. She shouldn't have to suffer like this when there were so many more who deserved it.

No words came to mind. Instead, Nadir nodded one more time and left the hut. The Alqatara would take care of each other, he was certain of that. There was no reason for him to be there.

Sand blasted up as he strode through the huts. Sigrid wouldn't land here. She didn't like people to see her in the dragon form. Perhaps a bit of her mind rattled along their connection as well. He knew she was angry, nervous, and so tentative to come here after what she'd done.

He felt the same. The Bymerian people were so close to liking her. They wanted to see something in her like a future that they could understand. Then, she'd taken that all away by destroying their capital city.

He should be angrier about that too. He should hate her for what she had done, and all the things she stood for.

And yet... he couldn't. Nadir still felt as though she was the only person in the empire who could understand him. The only one who could look into his eyes and know what he felt.

Did she feel the same?

Somewhere between the hut where his mother's body lay and the outskirts of the Alqatara village, he began to run. His lungs nearly burst with the effort, his muscles burning as he raced toward her. The pain didn't matter. Physical pain was fleeting.

Some of the assassins stared at him as he raced by. They were merely lucky he didn't change into the dragon and let the beast take over for a few moments. Gods knew it was screaming in his head, begging to be released so that it could race to the side of their mate. It knew she was here. It knew they were mere heartbeats away from seeing her again. After all this time.

The gates to Falldell stood open. They remained so during the day in case any stragglers through the sands needed help. So few did, but the great snake heads stared out into the desert, waiting for someone.

This time, he knew they were waiting for the same person he was. He ran like a dying man toward the everlasting oasis. His soul would find her, he knew it. Anywhere she went, he could feel her.

Sand stirred on the horizon and a massive head lifted from the dunes. Opalescent and shimmering in the sunlight, she stood strong and proud. There were two figures next to her, but he didn't care who they were. They could be here to kill him for all he knew. It didn't matter.

She was so close.

Nadir slowed as he approached, stopping ten paces away from her and watching as the scales melted away. She changed back into the woman he knew, and yet... someone so much more than that.

Her hair was longer, he realized. It had been bleached by the sun into a white gold that hurt his eyes to look at. She no longer wore it braided or twisted back from her face, but free hanging nearly to her waist now.

Icy eyes stared at him with an anger that he felt deep in his soul, but a sadness that he didn't understand. Her face had thinned as well. The square jaw he'd so admired many times was more pronounced. The curved edges of her cheeks, so childlike when he first saw her, had hardened into a more aggressive face.

The mantle on her shoulders was made of fur. Leather armor covered her chest and what looked like a loincloth parted at the sides of her legs to reveal long lines of alabaster skin.

He'd never seen so much of her at once. It was overwhelming.

A smear of dirt marred her cheek, and he couldn't help but look at it with fondness. She'd never cared very much for what she looked like. Even the elaborate gowns she wore were always ruined by the end of the day. He'd tried to get her to dress in the ways of his people, thinking she'd do less harm to silks if they were even more delicate. Now, he could see that was always a losing battle.

Sigrid was a woman made of wild abandon and a desire to hear the wind in her ears. She couldn't be tamed by castle walls. He'd been a fool to even try.

Taking one step forward, he reached out a hand and said a single word. "Wife."

Something snapped between them. He didn't know if he was the first one to move or her. But within a heartbeat she was in his arms, and it felt *so right*.

The earth stopped spinning because he could smell the biting mint of her hair, the chill of her flesh, and the strong grip of her arms around his waist.

She was here and real in his arms. It wasn't something out of a dream but she had come for him.

Nadir curled his body around hers, drawing her closer to his chest. The feeling of her fingers splayed wide over his heart was right. He couldn't think of a moment in his life when he'd felt this complete. So utterly enchanted by another person who he had missed for what felt like his entire life.

He leaned down, breathed in her scent, and then rested his cheek against the top of her head.

He'd let go of her soon. Had to. There was so much they needed to talk about. A war on her homeland, his people rebelling against him, what he'd done with his dragon... his plan to become a god.

It could all wait. For a few more moments while he bathed in the feathered touch of her breath against his neck. The warmth of her fingers where she held his heartbeat close to his skin. The weight of her arms around him.

"Husband," she whispered.

He tightened his hold around her shoulders. "It's good to have you home."

SIGRID

SHE TUCKED HER FACE INTO THE CREVICE WHERE HIS SHOULDER MET his neck and willed her heart to stop beating so fast. He'd hear it. Then he'd know that she'd missed him just as much as he'd missed her, and then where would she be?

They hadn't seen each other in... was it a year now? Already?

Somehow, he'd grown into a man. His shoulders were far broader, and she'd already thought him rather large a year ago. His waist had tapered, his arms stronger and hands capable of handling so much more weight.

It was his face that disturbed her the most. The beard was one thing. She hadn't even thought to enjoy facial hair on a man, but found his quite pleasing. There were fanned wrinkles at the corners of his eyes which hadn't been there before, and a line directly in the center of his forehead that was clearly from stress.

He'd aged. More than that, he'd grown into a man while

she was gone.

Sigrid wondered what he saw when he looked at her. A girl still? A young woman trying to pretend that she could lead a group of animals who didn't want to listen to her? Or did he see a queen in the making, one who could take on both kingdoms if it meant that she could save her family?

She blew out a breath, the chilled touch of her breath raising gooseflesh on his skin. She didn't know what her own answer would be to the question. If she looked into a mirror, would she see the same woman as she wanted to? Or would she see a scared child still looking to find herself?

Nadir pulled away just enough to see her face. He notched a finger beneath her chin and tilted her face up to look at him.

Her stomach burst into butterflies. She couldn't think when he was looking at her like that. Like he'd missed her so much it was difficult to breathe now that she was here.

Because she felt the same way.

This wasn't the same boy she'd known a year ago. And that scared her. Who was he now? Was she going to have to get to know him all over again? Would they even like these new versions of each other?

Perhaps he wasn't worried about it at all, because Nadir grinned so wide she worried his face might crack.

"It's so good to see you," he said, his voice deep and rough. "I hadn't thought to ever see you again."

"I don't think either of us planned on it." But that was a lie. She'd come to his room a year ago, hadn't she? The very first Beastkin that she'd taken away from Bymere had come from *him*, after the battle. He'd been the one to start their secret plan to save their kind, and she had been the one to first reach out.

Her fingers fisted in the fabric of his shirt. She didn't want him to back away. Not yet, just a few more moments where she could touch him—know that he was alive and well—when all she'd done was destroy the things he'd tried so hard to build.

"I'm sorry," she whispered. "I don't think I ever said it. But I am."

"I know."

"I didn't want to hurt anyone."

"Neither did I." His hands curled tighter around her waist, drawing her closer to him and his warmth. Had she ever been this warm before? Sigrid wasn't certain. The heat billowing off him in waves reached deep under her skin and warmed her to the very core. "I'm sorry for all the pain I've caused you. It wasn't right."

"You did what you had to do."

"So did you, and that didn't stop you from apologizing." He pressed his lips against her temple, and gods, if she didn't let her eyes drift shut and enjoy the moment. If only for a few seconds. "I'm still sorry our lives can't be just the two of us somewhere alone. Where we could figure out who each other is without the weight of responsibilities and kingdoms."

His words rang with a bitter pain that rocked her to the core. He was right. They would have gotten along very well if they weren't from two separate worlds who hated each other.

She might have even loved him if she'd been given the time and the space to do so. He was a good man in his core. One that was vain and arrogant, certainly, but there was something more in him no one else had ever encouraged. She'd learned that in her time at the palace.

They couldn't stand in the middle of the desert forever. Too many people relied on them to make a decision and stop what was happening between the two kingdoms. Far too many people's lives rested on their shoulders.

Someday, she vowed they would have the time to explore each other. Time where she could ask him what his favorite meal was. How many stars he thought were in the night sky. Whether or not he thought the sky was truly blue or if it was simply a reflection of all the water they couldn't see.

Still, that time wasn't now. Reluctantly, she pulled away from him and stepped a few feet back.

"I flew over your armies," she muttered, wiping a hand over her brow to mask the mist of tears in her eyes. "They seemed quite interested to know I was still alive and heading straight back for the palace. Hopefully that will cause at least half of them to return here and defend the Red Palace."

"Smart thinking. It will give the Earthen folk a chance."

"They can fight in their own forests, Nadir. I was trying to save the lives of *your* people." Did he really think she worried about Wildewyn? They'd been fighting in those forests their entire lives. Even the children knew how to hide in nooks and crannies the Bymerians wouldn't dream of.

Trees and forests were the domain of the Earthen folk.

Nadir raised a brow. "Do you really think peasants are a match for an army who has trained their entire lives to kill?"

"Your people have never seen a forest. They don't know how to look up into the branches and pick out a person where they might only see leaves. The arrows which will rain down upon them will take lives."

"My men have been hunting in your forests much longer than you realize, Sultana." He gave her a mock bow, the glint in his eyes one she recognized very well. "Or did you think I am so foolish I wouldn't have assassins training in your kingdom? They've always been there."

She should be angry that he'd hidden people in the forests of her home. Instead, she felt a grin spread across her face. A feral look that meant she was proud of him, that she'd come to think he wasn't quite capable of something like that.

It was good to have someone prove her wrong again.

Inclining her head, she stared into his yellow eyes and wondered why she'd ever thought to leave. "I'm glad to hear it, Sultan. But if they try to fight the Earthen folk, they'll still lose."

"Are you willing to wager on that, Sultana?"

A voice interrupted them, slicing through the air like a blade. "I don't know if this is some kind of twisted flirting, or if the two of you are really sick enough to wager on the lives of your own kingdoms."

Nadir's brow lifted again. "You brought Camilla, I see."

"I don't travel without her."

"It might be better next time if you travel on your own." He straightened his shoulders and leaned to the side. "Hello again, Camilla. It's a pleasure as always."

"I wish I could say the same."

"You could, if you tried hard enough."

Her sister shrugged a dark shoulder. "But that would be a lie. I make it a rule to tell the truth, especially to men who think they're so much better than they really are."

A huff of breath expelled a small flicker of flame and curl of smoke from Nadir's nose. "Care to test that theory?"

She'd missed this. The banter between the three of them, the strange way they'd all managed to become a family even though they didn't trust each other. A wry grin spread across her face and she rolled her eyes. "Enough, you two."

Camilla pointed at Nadir, jabbing her finger in the air. "He's the reason we're in this mess. It's his army at our doorstep, and if he's here then that means somehow, he's shirking his duties. Again."

"Camilla."

"What's he doing in the middle of the desert anyways? He's out here playing house while the rest of the world is descending into madness. Why aren't you blaming him for this?"

"Camilla." This time, Sigrid said it with a chuckle.

"No! Don't say my name like I'm the one who's out of line here. There's plenty of reasons to be angry with him and you're just... hugging him! Like he's an old friend."

Sigrid took one step closer to Nadir. The heat radiating from his body felt right, somehow. She couldn't describe the way her dragon felt just being near him. It was like she hadn't realized there was a thunderstorm raging in her head until the moment when silence fell. Just because he existed beside her.

"Shirking his duties?" she asked.

"Yes," her sister snapped.

"Wasn't that what I was doing then?"

Camilla's mouth gaped open for a second, her eyes widening in shock before she shook her head. "No. You were seeking the ancients. Providing your people with an answer to all the questions they've had for centuries."

"But him being here while the armies march, that's not the same thing?"

"Well..." she floundered. "I don't know."

Sigrid had made her point. She didn't have to explain it word by word to her sister. Yet again, Nadir was the same as Sigrid in a way that only fate could have provided them.

The guilt of leaving her people while she searched for an answer to her own soul... it still lingered. She didn't know how else to leave them in a way they would have continued to piece together their lives in a way she approved of. And Sigrid knew she was right. There was a reckoning coming for the Beastkin. They had to learn how to be human, how to share the world in a way that the humans would understand, or they would never stop the war. Everything would continue to fall apart over and over again.

She turned back to Nadir, looked up into his yellow eyes, and felt her stomach turn. "Why *are* you here, Nadir?"

He licked his lips, staring back at her with eyes that gradually saddened until she couldn't see anything but their murky depths. "My mother summoned me."

"I thought your mother was dead."

"So did I." He held out his arm for her to take. "Unfortunately, you won't be able to meet her."

"She's difficult to meet?"

"She's dead."

The words froze Sigrid's blood in her veins. The dragon inside of her groaned at the knowledge that yet another of theirs was dead. For a moment, she had been hopeful that there was a chance for the dragons. There was another who could teach her all the things she'd hoped to learn.

Now, it really was just the two of them.

She blew out a breath. "I'm so sorry for your loss, husband. I hope she led a good life."

"It was a life." His eyes turned toward the walls of the city behind them. "In truth, I really didn't have that much time with her. I don't know anything about the woman who birthed me."

She knew the emotion behind those words. The sense of loss that now he would never understand himself. She'd felt the same in the moment she realized the ancients were a dying breed, and they didn't have the hidden meaning to her life locked away in their hidden halls.

Sigrid reached for his hand and linked their fingers. "The history of our lives doesn't shape who we become. That's a choice you and I both have to make."

"History cannot be forgotten."

"But it can be remade." She looked up at him and hoped he would understand her words. "I need you to believe that, Nadir. There's far too much riding on our decisions in this moment. We cannot give up."

A rustling sound behind them made Sigrid glance over her shoulder. She'd almost forgotten the strange creature she'd brought with her.

Eivor revealed herself, large eyes wider than she'd ever seen them. The medicine woman crouched in the sand and carefully picked her way toward them. She looked like a crab scuttling to the nearest place where she would be safe.

"Matriarch?" she asked quietly. "What is this place?"

"Bymere."

"No, the ground resonates with old war. There's blood hidden deep in the sand, like a river beneath us."

Sigrid looked at Nadir whose brow had furrowed.

"Who's this?" he asked.

"Her name is Eivor. She is…" Sigrid floundered. How did

she describe this creature? She couldn't say this was what they would all likely become. She didn't know if that was the truth. But it certainly seemed this was an option for the Beastkin people if they didn't follow the path she was certain was the only one for them.

"Different," he replied.

"That's the way to say it, yes."

He detached himself from her hold and made his way to Eivor who was still low to the ground. Her eyes watched him, the fur on her face stirred by the wind and the scales flattened against her skull in fear.

Nadir bent next to her, then held out his hand. "My name is Nadir. It's good to meet you, Eivor."

"I don't know if you should say that."

"Why not?"

"I'm a soul stealer. Medicine woman of old, but also one that should never be touched by another person without fear they won't be... the same."

A chuckle bubbled out of his chest. "I lost my soul a long time ago, friend."

"To whom?" Eivor's brows furrowed. She sat up straighter, as if his declaration had wiped away all her fear. "I might be able to get it back. Soul stealers can bargain sometimes. If I was the keeper of your soul, I'd make sure it was safe."

Nadir pointed over his shoulder at Sigrid, and she felt her heart flutter.

He looked back at her with heat in his yellow eyes. There was a declaration there, something she couldn't quite imagine but was certain he wanted her to hear. Was he saying that she was the keeper of his soul? That she was somehow more important to him than anything else?

He confirmed her thoughts with a few soft words. "She stole it the moment I first saw her."

Eivor's eyes flicked between them. "Sigrid? But she's not a medicine woman."

The creature didn't understand it, but that was fine. She didn't want Eivor to understand what this man was saying to her.

Her face heated, cheeks no longer hidden by a mask that would have at least saved her the embarrassment. He saw every bit of her emotions flickering over her face. Nadir's eyes heated even more, and she was certain it was a dragon staring back at her.

He straightened, stalking toward her with a determination that made her stomach flip. Sigrid clenched her fists.

Don't touch him, she told herself. He isn't yours to touch, not anymore. They didn't even know each other anymore.

Apparently, Nadir was not thinking the same thing. He notched his hand at her waist and pulled her closer to him. Again, he tucked her against his body and placed his cheek at her hair. "Come home with me," he whispered.

"Where do you want me to go?"

"The palace."

Gods, she couldn't go back there. The people were already afraid of her. She'd nearly destroyed their city.

Memories played behind her eyelids as she hid her face against his neck once again. The way the towers and parapets had crumbled the moment her wings had touched them. The glass domes atop the city had melted beneath her breath. But it was the screams of the people that still haunted her dreams.

Their fear would never leave her side.

She wasn't a monster. She'd never thought herself to be one, knowing she wanted to protect people far more than she wanted to hurt them.

And yet, the Red Palace had still fallen. All because of her.

Nadir tightened his arms around her. "You cannot be afraid of the past. Isn't that what you just said?"

"I'm not." It was a lie. She was more afraid of what they'd think of her now than anything else in her life.

Before, she wouldn't have cared at all. They were the enemy. A group of people who she could discard in her thoughts as people who were careless and wanted to see her own people die. Now, she's lived there. She'd seen the good in the Bymerians and it still hurt her heart to think that she'd become exactly what they'd always feared she would become.

Nadir pulled back and forced her to look at him again. "Fly home with me."

"Do you really think that's a good idea? The last time I flew over your country—"

He pressed a finger to her lips, forcing her to stop speaking. "I think you'll find many things have changed within the Red Palace. They're used to me now. They've seen me as a dragon more times than I can count, and they haven't been afraid of what I could do. There's no reason for you to be so afraid, Sigrid."

Why were his eyes slitted? That was the man speaking to her, but the dragon that existed within his soul.

She narrowed her gaze on him. "What has changed? You don't seem like yourself."

Nadir shook his head. "I'll tell you everything that

happened soon. First, we have to get back to the palace. We can speak with the remaining advisors, tell them to send messengers to return the army."

"You still think that'll work? After everything that has happened, you think the advisors care at all about our people? Mine or yours?"

He bent down and pressed his forehead against hers. "I still have faith that the people of both our countries have a shred of decency within them. We have to believe in them. Otherwise, why are fighting so hard to keep them safe?"

Gods, why was he always right? He'd changed so much in a year. He wasn't the boy who didn't care about anything. He was a man who wanted to fight, to learn, to discover, and she'd missed every moment of the transformation, because she'd been with her own people. Forgetting what it was like to be with someone whose intellect matched her own.

Sigrid blew out a breath. "Then let's go to the palace."

He released her, striding out into the sand and changing into the giant red dragon she remembered so well in her dreams.

Something inside her winced the moment she saw the claws tipping his back feet. Even the twin claws at the joint of his wings had sliced through her scales so easily. She'd almost forgotten how much they hurt.

He was so powerful in this form, and the dragon inside her was still slightly afraid that he wanted to hurt them.

Camilla stepped to her side, pressed a hand on her shoulder, and shoved her forward. "Go on then."

"What? You're coming with me.

"Not with this one." Camilla pointed at Eivor who had

crumpled back to the ground at the sight of the huge male dragon. "She needs to be taught how to act around people. You can't show up with her at your side when the palace already is afraid of you. I'll take care of it."

"We're in the middle of a desert."

"Right next to a city of people who want to help the future of this world." Camilla grinned. "You know I've always been good at making friends. I'll find my way to the palace soon enough. Just give us some time."

"You know, I rarely say how lucky I am to have you as my sister, but I am."

Sigrid didn't know how else to say it. Sometimes, she was afraid she used the woman at her side too much. That someday Camilla would wake up and realize she was done with all this. That, above all else, was her greatest fear.

"I know you're lucky," Camilla replied, snorting and shoving at Sigrid's shoulder again. "Go on. Go with your man and head back to the city. We'll follow along behind. Besides, I'm sure he's leaving some important people behind just so that he can fly around with his favorite person."

"I'm not his favorite person."

"You're fooling yourself if you think that. Go on with you. I'll do the cleanup."

Sigrid stepped away from her sister, gesturing her gratitude before making her way out into the sands. If there was a hero of this story, of saving Bymere and Wildewyn, she wasn't so certain that hero was her. In fact, she was almost certain the real hero of this story was Camilla.

Nadir lowered his head and chuffed at her. The blast of air pushed her back a little bit, but she grinned. This was what she had been waiting for. The returning feeling of elation when it was just her and the only other person in the entire empire who knew what she felt like. Who could understand the rush of power that came from existing within their scales.

She let her body melt away, becoming something more. Something so strong it frightened her sometimes.

Scales unfurled down her arms, and she grew ten times larger than her human form. The sun reflected off her scales like a precious gem. Horns grew from her skull and leather skin spread from her arms to create wings.

A deep grumble echoed in her mind. It wasn't anything that Nadir had said out loud, but now, they had more of a connection than ever before.

His voice deepened, gruff with emotion she'd never heard while he was human. "You're beautiful," he said.

There was a layer of two voices in the words. One she recognized, and the other which was decidedly new.

The second voice was terrifying and wondrous all at the same time. She couldn't focus when it was speaking with her in rumbling tones that made something inside her shiver. Not in pleasure or any human emotion, but with a desire for freedom and the wind under her wings.

She inclined her head, flexed her wings, and launched into the air. She didn't want to think of all these emotions running through her when she didn't know how to process them.

It shouldn't feel like this. She hadn't seen him in such a long time. There should have been some kind of awkwardness in their meeting.

Instead, she felt very much as though they were old friends who hadn't seen each other in a while. The time between them was nothing more than a small blip. They continued on as if nothing had happened.

But it had.

So much had happened between them that her head was spinning. She'd destroyed his city. He'd marched on her country and renounced everything he was. Everything he loved. How could she ignore that? How could she move past that knowledge?

Clouds parted as she soared through them. Beating her wings, she rose above them until all that was beneath her was a sea of rolling white.

What would it be like if they just continued to fly? Was there more out there in the great ocean surrounding their empire? Were there more countries that might be more accepting of them and their differences? Sadly, she had a feeling they'd only find a vast nothingness. The world was empty other than the judgement and hatred of their own people.

A caress of soft leather touched the tip of her wing. She glanced over to see Nadir flying beside her, his wing barely touching hers, but there nonetheless.

They glided through the air together, silence filling their minds. No, there was more than that, she realized. There was the utter sense of relief pouring off both of them like fine wine at a noble's dinner table.

He was so happy she was there. It radiated off him in waves through their connection and she... Gods, she was so pleased to finally be able to be herself and not worry that someone was afraid of her.

The horns on his head reflected the sunlight. The deep burgundy was far more reflective than she remembered, and his scales were far harder. It would make sense that his dragon had aged with him. Perhaps what they'd seen of each other back then was still the teenage version of themselves.

She wondered how much she had changed.

A deep chuckle echoed in her mind. "You are more beautiful," he said. "Your tail is longer, and the spines along your back are like glass."

"You're harder," she replied. "Where you were once weak, you've grown stronger. Your horns are far more impressive, decidedly more deadly, and you look more like a battering ram than the dragon I remember."

Again, he chuckled. "Good. That will serve us well in the coming battles."

"I don't want to fight, Nadir."

"I don't think we have a choice in that, wife. Our people have already made that decision without us. Now, we can only hope to protect them from themselves."

Maybe that was their reason for living after all. She turned her face toward the Red Palace that appeared on the horizon. Sigrid had spent so much time trying to find the reason for her being here, and maybe it had been hidden right in plain sight.

She curved her wings in, diving lower and lower toward the city with him at her side. He glanced at her once, a smile on his dragon face, then dove straight for the city.

Sigrid waited for the screams. They couldn't react well to a dragon flying straight at them. That would only make them remember all the things she'd done.

But no screams echoed at his approach. Instead, all she heard was a few murmurs of people who pointed up at Nadir, then continued on their day.

She did a lap around the city, flying high enough that anyone who saw her would merely think it was a stirring of the clouds above them. She would blend into the sky like this. Perhaps her fear was nothing to concern herself with. Maybe, he was right. Maybe they had really changed and were more accepting of the Beastkin.

Somehow, she doubted it.

Sigrid was careful to fly as close to the gardens of the palace as possible. Here, she would be hidden from most people's prying eyes. She dropped out of the air mid-change, landing lightly in a crouch behind a rather large bush of roses she didn't remember growing there.

They provided the perfect cover for her to catch her breath. The furs on her shoulders made her stand out even more than just changing from a dragon into a woman. They would see her as something even more otherworldly.

She waited until she heard the tell-tale crunch of feet on gravel before she slowly straightened. She knew that gait anywhere, although it made her uncomfortable to admit she still remembered the way he walked. It had been a year. Shouldn't she have forgotten that dancing pace?

"Sigrid?" he called out.

She blew out a breath. She could do this. They weren't going to be afraid of her. There wasn't a chance he would let them attack her anyways. What was going to happen if they were afraid? They'd flinch away? She'd deal with that her entire life. She could do it again.

Walking toward him was one of the hardest things she'd ever done. Guilt rode her shoulders and pressed down on her lungs. She could do this, no matter how afraid of it she was.

Nadir held his hand out for her to take. "There aren't many people here, wife. They won't see you unless we want them to."

"Do we?"

"That's up to you." The softness in his gaze encouraged her to set her shoulders and jaw. "I can take you through the hidden routes, if that makes you feel better."

"There are hidden routes?"

"It's a palace. Or did you think I didn't notice there were crevices in Greenmire Castle as well?" He quirked a brow. "Every noble home has holes in the walls and passages where others can snoop if they wish."

"Hopefully not in the concubines' rooms, or I'll consider you more a peeping tom than a husband."

He shrugged. "I can't say there aren't. I suspect they're more often used by serving boys than anyone else these days."

"These days?" Sigrid reached out and placed her hand in his.

"My brother and I might have used them when we were younger." He drew her closer, eyes shifting into the dragon. "Can you blame us?"

"For sneaking into the women's quarters so you could watch them undress? Yes. I can blame you for that."

He chuckled, tucked her underneath his arm, and pressed a kiss to her head. "I'll give you that. We were perhaps a little too foolish for our own good."

As they strode toward the palace, she slipped an arm around his waist. "That's the first time I've heard you speak about him without your voice cracking."

"I suppose it was," he replied. "Strange how I think of him now with fondness rather than a sense of guilt."

Sigrid didn't find it strange at all. She knew how death could linger in the back of someone's mind until eventually that guilt dulled into a sense of fond memory. She'd seen it happen time and time again with so many of her friends.

Her only wish was that she could figure out how to do that herself. All the deaths here and around the empire weighed heavily on her shoulders. Perhaps someday she could wake up without having to worry. Perhaps someday she wouldn't let the opinion of others affect her so.

They strode up the crimson steps into the palace halls. Sigrid had forgotten how golden this place was. Every corridor was lined with metallic hues. Swaths of red fabric hung from the ceiling and pooled on the ground, starting so high up it would have taken three men on each other's shoulders to even reach the top.

This place was made for someone who shared divine blood. In her furs and strange outfit, she felt decidedly out of place.

Yet, it was her arm around their sultan. It was she who was married to the man who ruled these lands, not some creature who was covered in silken fabric and knew how to simper at the newest nobles.

He'd found something in her that called out to him. The wildness in her heart that made his sing. That was worth far more than the acknowledgement of the other people here.

They'd almost made it to his private chambers before a servant backed out of a room. Her arms were laden with laundry that dropped to the floor the moment she saw Sigrid.

The maid's eyes widened in fear and then horror. How could she recognize Sigrid when she wasn't wearing her mask?

Was it the simple knowledge that a pale woman, clearly from Wildewyn, was here?

Nadir stiffened, opened his mouth, only to be interrupted by the maid who finally managed to gasp.

"Sultana," the maid croaked. "You're alive."

Sigrid slipped her hand out of Nadir's and stepped forward carefully. "I am."

"We all thought... well, the great battle in the sky with the sultan, we didn't think it was possible you had survived."

She didn't know how to process these words. The maid's fear scented the air with blood and violence.

How could she reassure this woman? How could she when she was the one who had destroyed their city?

Sigrid bowed her head. "The battle did not leave any lasting scars. I appreciate your worry, however, after everything that happened."

"War is war, Sultana. We all do bad things in its grip." The maid gulped. "Have done bad things. We don't blame you for that, you know."

"I suspect many do."

"You were kind to us while you were here. Many of us have family who..." The maid's eyes flicked to Nadir then back. "Family who are like the both of you. It's a start, some kind of acceptance and understanding that the Beastkin aren't dangerous. They shouldn't be killed. And they can protect us or harm us if we discard them."

Sigrid's tongue stilled and her heart stuttered. "I don't know how to thank you for your kindness."

"Please don't." The other woman bent to pick up the laundry, filled her arms, and then smiled. "Just keep changing the world, Sultana. It'll thank you for it eventually."

As the woman walked away, Sigrid looked over her shoulder at Nadir and wondered how they were going to do just that.

NADIR

"THEY REMEMBER YOU AS A MASKED WOMAN. SEEING YOU WITHOUT one will be startling for them." He hated even suggesting that she cover her face. Nadir had grown to enjoy watching the emotions play over her features. She had no idea he could read her like an open book when he could see her lovely face.

A delicate chain headpiece dangled from his fingers. He'd seen some of his own people wear something similar. It wasn't a solid piece of metal like she was used to, but individual strands of gold with diamonds inset in each chain link. People would be able to see her face, but only slightly in comparison to what they were used to.

"Easing them into the change," she said with a smile. "I understand it. I did tell them all if they saw my face, I would kill them."

"Better to not have them worrying about that on top of everything else," he replied dryly.

Not that they would worry. The maid had proven he was

correct. His people were more tolerant of the Beastkin, especially when the army wasn't on the premises.

Sigrid remained still and allowed him to weave the gold braid into her hair so it would stay secure. He didn't tell her that nerves twisted his stomach into knots. That he wasn't all so certain his people would accept her as readily as the maid.

Something else burned in his gut. A deep rage that they would ever try to hurt her. That they would again try to start a war where he couldn't be at her side, where he couldn't protect her because of these humans' chains that bound him so thoroughly he didn't know what to do with himself.

This was new. He hadn't ever been possessive over another person. Nor did this make sense. She'd only returned for a few moments, just a couple days at his side. And he wanted to tear apart the world for her? That wasn't like him.

The fire inside him burned hotter than ever before. It was as if the dragon didn't know what to do with itself. It had melted the bars of the cage Nadir had placed around it, and now there wasn't anything to stop it from raging against the sky.

Afraid of what it could do, the dragon didn't know how to proceed. It knew Sigrid was something important to them both. That she had to be protected at all costs, because he was calm at her side. She made him think like a man. Something like that was precious and rare as the most beautiful of rubies pulled from the mines deep below his palace.

She looked up at him through the waving strands of gold and diamonds, then smiled. "How does it look?"

He stared down at her and lost all the air in his lungs. He wanted to shout that she looked incandescent. That the stars in the sky couldn't rival her beauty for they would never shine bright enough to overpower her.

But he couldn't. Nadir wasn't a man who knew how to speak poetry. He'd been raised to be a general. Now his brother, Hakim, he could have wooed her the right way. He wouldn't have been the spoiled child in her eyes, but the man who had sonnets dripping from his tongue.

Nadir cleared his throat and took a step back. He tucked his shaking hands behind him and nodded. "Good. It suits you."

She gave him a strange look. Perhaps she saw there was something more in his gaze. Something he couldn't control. Were his eyes shifted? The colors in the room had skewed a bit, but he could only focus on the gold covering her face. That hadn't changed at all. In fact, the gold looked... so...

Something clattered onto the balcony outside his room. Angry voices drifted through the curtains, pitched low so no one would hear them but his ears picked up on much more than the average person.

"You could have been more gentle!"

"It's not like I was trying to hit your head."

"I was right behind you. How did you *not* know I was right there?"

He recognized both of those voices, although he hadn't thought to see them quite so soon. He glanced down at Sigrid to see she'd recognized them as well. She rolled her eyes and gestured with an arm for him to go get them.

The smile on Sigrid's face hadn't shifted. "It's your palace."

"They're your friends."

"Only two of them. I believe there's also an assassin with

them who hasn't spoken yet."

He listened intently, but couldn't pick up on the sound of anyone else. "How do you know she's out there with them?"

Before Sigrid could respond, Tahira pushed the red curtain aside. "Because she could see me. Really, how did you not have more assassination attempts? Your guards are foolishly simple."

Nadir gritted his teeth. "Need I remind you they don't know their sultan is here?"

"They don't yet?" Tahira lifted a brow. "Then I'll say it again. Your army is lacking in any kind of training, and I'm shocked you're still alive."

Sigrid stepped forward before he could respond with the growl bubbling in his throat. He wanted to change in front of the assassin once more. His lungs still ached from where she'd tried to drown him, and there were plenty of unsaid words between them.

Just because the death of his mother had stilled those words, didn't mean he wasn't going to say them. Tahira had a lot to own up to, and he would ensure she understood he was the dragon. He could pick her bones from between his teeth if he wanted to.

His wife ushered her two, strange friends into the room then turned toward Tahira. "One of the Qatal, I take it?"

Tahira inclined her head. "I see you've heard of us even in Wildewyn."

"No," Sigrid replied, then pointed at Nadir. "He told me everything. The Earthen folk have never heard of your kind, nor are we intimidated by your people in the slightest. I do appreciate that you're... confident in your abilities."

Leave it to his feral wife to bring even a Qatal to her knees. Nadir hid his laugh behind a cough, turning away from the three women so they wouldn't see the grin spreading across his face.

He'd missed her banter so much more than he'd thought. The women here battled with words as well, but they were hidden behind veiled threats and wishes of well health. Sigrid didn't hold back at all. Instead, she just destroyed them.

His woman didn't go to battle unless she knew she'd win.

Turning back toward the women, he realized they were staring at each other with a little too much aggression for his comfort. He cleared his throat, hoping he wouldn't have to step between them. The last thing he wanted was to get wounded while trying to stop a famed warrior and a dragon from murdering each other.

On second thought... the blast of heat that flowed through his veins suggested his dragon would be very interested in breaking up such a fight.

Tahira glanced at him. "Where is this army of yours?"

"I assume they're still in Wildewyn. I haven't revealed myself to anyone just yet."

Camilla stepped forward, her dark skin glistening in the sunlight. He should really tell her that she'd always looked better here in Bymere. She seemed happier here as well, where the sun could stroke her skin and her eyes could stare across the vastness of the sand dunes. "They've returned," she said, snapping him out of his thoughts. "On the way here, we had to go around them."

"They've returned?" He shook his head. "Then why hasn't the sultan returned to his private quarters?"

"You mean the false sultan?" Tahira asked.

Gods, he couldn't keep this straight. So many people were in the room talking over him and he couldn't pay attention when his mind was screaming that they should have told him.

But they didn't know he was here. They all thought he was with them, but that was the sultan who had sent them a war that would end them all. He'd always hoped his people would follow him so blindly to their deaths, and yet, they had.

Shaking his head, trying to clear the thoughts that thundered in his mind, he stepped back. "If they've returned, then why haven't they come back to the Red Palace?"

"I suggest we find out." The voice was the cool touch of chilled water on his heated skin. The rush of a waterfall that crashed heavy against his thoughts and drowned out all the myriad of screams. Sigrid stepped closer to him and placed a hand against his shoulder. "We can go and ask them ourselves, Sultan. Perhaps it's time to end this ruse, and let them know what you've found."

He hadn't found anything. He'd only realized there was more dangers about himself that he couldn't have dreamt of.

There were wrinkles on her forehead, he realized. Worry that had marred her face permanently, although they were more visible right now because she was staring at him with concern on her face. When was the last time someone had worried about *him*? Not the country, not the way he was running the country, but Nadir. The man who had a kingdom laid in his lap and who had no idea what to do with it.

He blew out a breath and nodded. "We can do that."

"No, you can't," Tahira snapped. "That would mean they'll kill Solomon and you cannot allow them to do that under any circumstances."

Anger flared bright again in his chest. He could almost feel the fire burning in him. His eyes snapped to hers again. "And why can I not allow them to kill him?"

The door to his private quarters slammed open and two men strode through. One he recognized as a second face to his own, the other...

"Raheem?" he gasped, taking one stumbling step toward the other man. "Can it be?"

The strong man, larger than a mountain, so dear to his heart that he was family, stepped toward him as well. They had eyes only for each other. And though that might have been strange to any from Wildewyn, Nadir couldn't explain their attachment.

He'd been the father Nadir had always wanted. The brother who had filled the gaping hole left by Hakim's death. The friend who had never faltered to keep his head out of the cloud and the guard who had never allowed a blade to touch Nadir's flesh.

The betrayal of this man had cut him more than that of his own wife. Raheem had left and Nadir felt as though his entire world had shaken.

They stared at each other, hands curled into fists as they tried to decide whether they wanted to fight or hug.

Raheem cleared his throat. "It's good to see you in one piece, boy."

"No thanks to you."

"I think you'll find it's very much thanks to me." Another step closer, Raheem was tempting fate with that movement. "I kept watch over her when I knew you couldn't. You'd have told me to go with her regardless. You know that."

"I didn't ask you to choose anyone over our friendship. Over your duty to your sultan and to your country."

Raheem shook his head. "I never called this my country. You never believed I was here because of some misguided belief in my homeland. This is a barren wasteland which has never been kind to me. I was here for *you*, Nadir. Because I believed in you. Because I believed you could be the sultan this land needed but only if someone guided you. So many snakes surrounded you. Did you really think I was going to let them poison you?"

"But you did." The words rocked through him, torn from his chest with a violent yank that made spittle fly from his lips. "You let them poison me. You let them twist me into something I didn't want to be."

"How was I supposed to stop that?"

Raheem had a point. Even as a guard to the sultan, he had no power in this kingdom. Still, Nadir wanted to blame someone for all the things which had been done to him.

It all rushed back into his mind just from standing in this room. How Abdul had shouted at him so many times while leaning over that table, his finger jabbing in the air and his words barbed. How Saafiya had taken him time and again in the bed, her touch as poisonous as her whispered sweet nothings.

His advisors hadn't cared for him. He was just a tool to give them more power. Standing in this room, with so many of the people who cared for him and so many of those who were still using him, Nadir realized he didn't know how to breathe.

Had he ever taken a full breath? One where he wasn't

worried that something had been put into his drink, or someone wasn't trying to kill him when no one was looking?

For once in his life, he just wanted to be a normal man. With a normal wife. Without a beast in his chest constantly clawing for freedom and for the right to defend him.

He swallowed hard. "I don't know," he finally replied, voice thick and throat tight. "I don't know how you were supposed to help, but someone needed to. And no one did."

At that, Raheem burst forward. He crossed the room and yanked Nadir into his arms, slapping his back hard enough to cause pain. His guard's voice was thick with emotion too when he replied, "I know, boy. I know someone should have."

Finally, someone else admitted it. Someone else who he thought so highly of admitted that he was taken advantage of. That there was something wrong with the way he'd been raised and that it *wasn't his fault.*

He curled his arms around Raheem and held on as though the touch could still the emotions rumbling through him. Were his arms hotter than they should be? He was almost certain of it. He could feel the smoke in his lungs curling up through his nostrils and sneaking out in long tendrils.

Raheem stiffened in his arms, and Nadir immediately let go. He didn't want to hurt the man who had done so much for him. Gods, what if he had hurt him?

He looked up only to find Raheem wasn't looking at him at all. He was staring at Tahira. His cheeks paled and he reached out a hand to put on Nadir's shoulder once more, this time for balance.

It looked as though he'd seen a ghost.

"Tahira?" Raheem whispered, and his hand started to

shake on Nadir's shoulder. "It's not possible."

In return, the Qatal appeared to be more shaken than he ever thought possible from the strange woman. She was an immovable block of confidence and strength. Yet, her own cheeks were pale and her jaw quaked the moment she set eyes on Raheem.

"Husband?" she whispered. "You're alive?"

Husband? Nadir looked over at his friend and remembered all the stories he'd told of his wife. How she'd changed into the most beautiful of birds in Bymere. Nadir had always thought she was some kind of peacock or perhaps a bird of paradise. He hadn't ever thought Raheem had meant a hunting hawk.

It made so much more sense now. Raheem had claimed she was so strong, capable of more than any other woman in Bymere. Nadir had always thought that was her beauty and her abilities to welcome people into their home. Why hadn't he ever realized Raheem wouldn't have wanted that in a wife?

Of course Raheem would end up with someone how could fight as well as he. Or perhaps, this was the woman who had taught his personal guard how to fight so well.

Raheem released his hold on Nadir's shoulder and stumbled forward. "You're alive?" he repeated. "How is that possible? They told me you were dead."

"They said the same of you."

"I watched you die," he murmured, reaching out a hand for her to take. "I saw it from far away. Watched them shoot you from the air and watched you fall. I couldn't catch you in time. The village... they burned everything. I couldn't find you."

A tear slid down her cheek. "Not me," she whispered. "I

wasn't there that day. I was with the Alqatara... *Raheem*."

Then they were in each other's arms, and he couldn't watch the way the largest man he'd ever known cried the moment he touched his wife. It felt too personal. Too much for him to handle when he was already feeling as though he might shatter.

A hand slid into his and tugged him toward the door. "Come on," Sigrid whispered. "Let's give them a little time. The army is back. We need to speak with the advisors and the man who has replaced you."

He didn't want to go. Though it made him feel thoroughly uncomfortable to be intruding on this soft moment between them, he also wanted to remind himself that there was more to this world than just war. He wanted to see the moment families were reunited, because that meant there was something worth fighting for.

Another hand slid into his. This one as dark as the other was pale. Camilla tugged him as well, then the two women from Wildewyn pulled him away from his own private quarters and back toward his responsibilities.

Camilla whispered, "Come, Sultan. There is work still to be done."

He cast one more glance over his shoulder before forcing himself into the hall. The strange creature remained with the couple, watching with wide eyes from a corner where she'd wedged herself.

"Should we—" he gestured to his wife's new pet.

Sigrid shook her head. "In her own way, Eivor will know how to help them. She's strange, I'll give you that, but she seems to know how to fix people better than I know how to kill them."

He'd have to ask her about the strange woman with skulls

at her waist later on. He wanted to hear this story, to understand how his wife always managed to collect the oddities of this world. But for now, there was work to be done. As Camilla had said, the responsibilities of life called him.

Nadir squared his shoulders and looked at Solomon, the man who was a mirrored reflection of himself. Without thinking, he blurted out, "You're my brother, aren't you?"

The other man nodded. "Half."

He didn't know what to think of that. His entire life was shaped by mourning one brother, and the mere idea that there was another tilted his world on its axis.

Nadir nodded. "Our mother is dead."

"I knew she would die while I was gone." Solomon's eyes turned sad and the scar on his face puckered. "It's a shame I wasn't there to say goodbye, but I assume you took care of that for me."

"Perhaps we're even now."

"Even?" Solomon repeated. "You didn't owe me anything."

"You sat on my throne while I went through a ritual of death and watched our mother die. I think I had the easier half of the bargain." He stared down the golden halls and reminded himself Solomon hadn't been born into this life. His brother didn't know the courtly intrigue, the way the world wanted to kill him, and how his closest advisors were his greatest enemies. "Now, where are my advisors?"

"Meeting in the great hall."

"Why were we not called?"

"We?" Solomon arched a dark brow and strode toward the great hall. "Are we interchangeable now, *brother*?"

"If I need someone to stand in for a blade or an arrow, perhaps."

Nadir threw the mantle of Sultan around himself. His shoulders straightened, his mind cleared, and his hands curled into fists as he prepared himself for a battle of wits. This would not be easy. They didn't want him to be anything more than a puppet but he found himself tired of these games.

If they wanted someone to bow at their feet, they would need to find another sultan. But the royal blood which flowed in his veins was the last of a great line.

They would find it very difficult to replace him.

Sigrid strode beside him, her booted feet striking the stone like drums. She'd refused to take off the clothing of her people, and he had to admit feeling a certain level of appreciation for that.

The first time she'd been here, she hadn't tried to fit in either. She insisted on wearing clothing from her own people, never bowing to Bymerian traditions.

Nadir had always thought it arrogance or a level of homesickness he couldn't understand. Now, he realized she wore her nationality with a badge of pride. It didn't matter where she went, she would not bow to another country trying to change her.

It took bravery to do that when everyone around her said there was something wrong with what she was doing. He wished he had that kind of bravery inside him.

The four of them strode into the great hall. The pools of water on either end were still perfectly still. Cerulean glass with large koi fish splashing sunset colors in smudges as they moved. The red curtains hanging from the ceiling dipped into the water as if nothing had changed. But it had.

The advisors all sat in their respective seats, arguing with each other until they saw the four people enter.

He stared at each face as he strode toward them. Nadir's clothing was understated, still the same garments which had been given to him in Falldell. White shirt, simple brown pants that billowed around his legs, and wrapped boots that stretched up to his ankles.

They wouldn't mistake him for someone else. That would be far too foolish for anyone to do.

Each person was more familiar to him now than his own family's faces. They'd guided him through life in the wrong direction, and perhaps they now knew he was going to seek retribution for what they had done to him.

Abdul sat at the forefront with Saafiya at his side. His first wife was supposed to remain in her prison, the rooms which he'd given her filled with everything she'd ever need and enough lady's maids to keep her busy.

And yet, here she sat. Freed even though he'd never given anyone permission to release her.

He pointed directly at her and calmly asked, "Brother, did you release this woman from her imprisonment?"

"I believe she released herself, Sultan."

"That's a problem then."

"I agree." Solomon crossed his arms over his chest. "But I'm not sure what you're going to do with her."

"What I should have done a long time ago."

Abdul stood from his chair, shaking with rage. "What is the meaning of this? Which one of you is... Explain yourselves!"

"I have no intention of doing so," Nadir replied. "Sit back

down, advisor."

"I will not. It appears as though you have deceived the entire country with your antics, and I for one will not stand by while you play foolish games. Enough with this, Nadir. You are not fit to be sultan and this clearly proves it."

Nadir stepped forward. It didn't escape his notice that he now stood where his own people had stood for years begging him to help them. He had sat in that empty throne, staring down at them and never once tried to see what it looked like through their eyes.

Abdul was so far above him. He looked like an angered god staring down in judgement. This wasn't the way his people should feel when they were asking their sultan for help. They shouldn't fear he was going to smite them, or that he would leap from the throne and tear out their throats.

The empty throne stared back at him. This was his place, and his father's place before him. He should have done something great in his life already. Should have filled the history books with all the things his bloodline was capable of, but he hadn't. Instead, all he'd done was wallow in grandeur while his people begged for help. Staring up at him like he was a god.

And he'd promised to become one.

The thought hardened in his mind. He'd promised the Alqatara he would be a god to end all gods. His people would follow him, because he was a terrifying creature who would defend them or destroy them.

Now was the time to take that step forward. To avenge the soul of his mother and father, of his brother who had died, of the woman who had birthed them.

To give all the souls who had died under his name a reason for their death.

Nadir stared up at Abdul and Saafiya, their eyes casting judgement they had no right to give. He looked at his oldest advisor, the man who had trained him as a child, and quietly asked, "Were you ever going to set me free?"

"Free?" Abdul repeated. "What are you talking about? You were Sultan of Bymere. No one had captured you, or forced you to do anything you didn't want."

They had, but he'd let the words remain. "Were you ever going to release your hold on me?"

"What hold?"

Nadir shook his head. "Enough lies, Abdul. You whispered in my ears all the things you knew would force me to become a weapon of your own making. You used me. Changed me into someone that relied on you and you alone. So I will ask you one more time. Were you ever going to free me from your chains? To allow me to think for myself and become the sultan I should have been?"

Abdul floundered for a few moments. His jaw dropped open in surprise and his eyes widened in fear before he managed to clamp down on the emotions. He strengthened his stance, hands curled into fists at his side, and replied, "No."

"You have nothing else to say?"

"There's nothing else to tell you. You've already figured it out, haven't you? The boy king who needed someone to guide him. I did what any good man would have done for the country. I took you under my wing. I helped you see the world as it truly is. Can you blame me for that?"

"I can."

Again, Abdul's jaw opened. He worked at words, moving his lips until they finally came out. "Then you need to see reason again. This country has become better for our help. You casting us aside will only send Bymere back into the chaos it once was."

"You mean the peace my father built? The kindness my brother instilled in the people?"

"I mean the poverty!" Abdul spat. "The Beastkin who ran wild in the streets and hunted our men and women! The creatures in the night that terrified women and children in their sleep. You don't remember the world the way it was when your father and your brother were making changes that no one else wanted. I am doing what is right for this country."

Nadir put his foot on the first step. "You're doing what you *think* is right. That is not your decision, but mine."

"The council has already decided you are not fit to run this country."

"You all decided that a long time ago," he replied, ascending the stairs further. "You did not ever give me a chance. You put thoughts in my head. You whispered accusations and lies that made me choose to do things I never wanted to do."

"We helped this country."

Nadir stepped in front of the throne he'd sat in so many times. The golden edges gleamed in the sunlight that poured from the open glass ceiling. He touched a hand to the ornate carvings, remembering his father doing the same thing.

This country deserves someone better than him. Perhaps that was why he would make a good sultan in the end. He would never feel worthy of this throne, or the people it symbolized.

Saafiya reached out her hand for him. The nails were perfectly clipped half-moons, so pretty it still made him shake. Those caramel fingertips had touched every part of him. Including his heart, at one point.

"Husband," she whispered, her voice a melody he remembered from his childhood. "Don't do this. Trust us, we want to help."

"Help?" he repeated. "You don't want to help. You want to *control*. There's a difference I don't think you have ever understood."

Abdul pointed at Solomon this time, raising his voice with another accusation. "And who is this? Are you not going to explain the man who looks exactly like you?"

"Would you believe me if I said that was Hakim?"

The startled expression on all his advisors faces gave him the answer he was looking for. They would believe it. They stared back at Solomon with grave eyes and guilt he recognized all too well.

Nadir had worn that expression for years. When he thought it was his fault that his brother had died. If he had just stepped in front of the blade. If he had been a better brother, a better soldier, even though he was only a child at the time.

He sank into the throne and leaned forward, elbows on his knees. "You killed him. Didn't you?"

Abdul choked. "I would never attack one of the royal line."

"You didn't have to attack anyone. You paid someone to take that blade. All they had to do was scratch him. Poison such as that is impossible to survive."

"I did no such thing."

Nadir stared down at Abdul's hands. He didn't have to look at them, he could smell his fear. His eyes heated in anger.

"You killed my brother."

"I say again, boy. I did no such thing."

Nadir's hands turned into claws. The scent of fear, guilt, and anger filled the air around him. It wasn't coming just from Abdul and Saafiya. Everyone in the room was filled with the emotions, so thick it was a curtain around them. Sealing them inside the great hall with the memories of what they had done.

"All of you did," he said. The great hall was so quiet he heard the drops of water as one of the koi fish shifted in the pools. "You ordered him killed for what reason?"

Always the brave one. Always the foolish one, Saafiya replied, "To save our country from an unfit sultan."

An admission of guilt. The only one he needed.

Nadir's shoulders curved in. He sank lower over his knees and looked up, down the hall at Sigrid who stared back at him. She was a pillar of justice, sparkling like a diamond in the darkness.

"Go," he told her. "Take him with you."

"Nadir—"

"I don't want you to see."

Her gaze softened, then she nodded and slipped a hand through Solomon's arm. They strode out of the great hall. True to her nature, he heard Sigrid bar the door behind them.

Nadir finally looked at his advisors then. His forked tongue slipped between his lips and tasted their fear in the air.

"Son," Abdul said, leaving his seat to place it between them. "You don't want to do this."

"But I do," he replied, his words lisping as the dragon took over. "Your reign has ended. So begins the true reign of the God King."

The change rippled through him and the screams echoed in his head. Nadir didn't leave the great hall until the cerulean pools had turned red with their blood.

SIGRID

"WE HAVE TO RETURN," SIGRID SAID. SHE TUCKED HER HANDS FIRMLY under her arms, trying hard to hide their shaking. "There's nothing we can do if we remain here."

Camilla stepped forward from her place outside the library. "That's not true. The army has already returned. The Earthen folk won't follow the Bymerians here. They have no interest in desert fighting."

They'd all remained here—Solomon, Camilla, and herself—waiting for Nadir to exit the great hall while wanting to remain out of his way. The screams had echoed for a while and then... silence.

Sigrid had moved them all down the hall much further the moment she noticed blood leaking beneath the doors. The humans didn't need to see that. It would only make them more afraid, and Nadir wouldn't want that. They were his trusted friends and family. They were in no danger from him.

"I don't understand," Sigrid said with a frustrated growl.

"You want to return home. Why are you fighting me on this?"

"I don't think it's prudent to return when everyone thinks you're dead. How many times have you said you wanted to return here? So stay here, Sigrid. Stay with him and help him make this country better. Keep the armies here, and leave the Beastkin to their own devices."

She wished she could. She wanted to leave all those creatures and let them figure out their lives on their own. It wasn't a bad future for them. They wanted freedom, and if she stayed with them, then she would only try to put them in a cage again.

Was this the right path? Sigrid had always thought she'd feel it in her gut if she was making the right choice. But every option right now felt as though it were going to make her sick. She wanted everyone to be happy and safe.

Perhaps that was too much to ask.

Footsteps echoed down the hallway. Sigrid turned, thinking it was Nadir, only to be disappointed when she saw Raheem striding toward them with his wife.

His wife. She hadn't thought she'd ever see the day when that man glowed with happiness. He'd dedicated his life to her, to Sigrid, but now that would all change. Now he had the woman of his dreams back, and she was the fierce, feral woman Sigrid had always assumed she would be.

Raheem stopped in front of them, crossed his arms over his chest, and glared at everyone. "You have to return. Sigrid is right."

"Why's that?" Camilla asked, mirroring his stance.

"The army didn't really return. The advisors left to see what the army had accomplished and then returned here with a small group of men to deal with Sigrid if she attacked again. This wasn't the entire army. In fact, it's only a small portion. The rest are continuing to march on Greenmire Castle."

So that was the gut feeling Sigrid had felt. It was the sick feeling that something bad was going to happen.

She scratched the back of her neck, tugging on her hair. "Then we return."

"There's more bad news I'm afraid," Raheem continued. "The Beastkin heard tales of the battle and joined in."

Sigrid groaned, "Why would they do that?"

"Rumors are their leader is more bloodthirsty than the boy king." He leveled Camilla and herself with a knowing look. "Jabbar seems to be leading them once more."

"And he's attacking... who?" Sigrid asked.

"Everyone."

Of course he was. The man had gone mad with power. She could only assume what her kingdom was facing. They had to return. She had to try and stop this war, and it didn't matter how difficult that ended up being. Everyone needed her.

Raheem met her gaze. "Sultana, there's so much more to this story than just one woman trying to save the world. We need an army to fight a three-way war that isn't going to end any time soon. I don't think this is something which can be fixed by a dragon falling out of the sky."

Another voice interrupted them. "Then how about two?"

There was something wrong with Nadir's voice. She'd only heard such tones in her head, when both the man and the dragon were speaking with her. Now, both voices were laced over his in a way that made her twitch in concern.

He stood at the end of the hall, hands loose at his side, and a deep scratch on one shoulder. The torn fabric of his shirt gaped over the wound, blood dampening the edges. She tried not to look at the bloody footprints he'd left on the golden floor.

He held out a hand for her, flicking the fingers inward as he beckoned her. "Come, wife."

"Nadir, is everything all right?" she asked.

"Why wouldn't it be?"

Because you're covered in blood, she wanted to say. *Because there's something other than a man looking through your eyes.*

Sigrid remained silent and strode to his side. This wasn't something which could be fixed by their friends or the humans who knew him so well. Sigrid had never seen anything like this before. He was utterly unhinged, and so thoroughly beyond her reach that she feared anything would anger him.

But she did not fear him.

She took his hand, slid her fingers between his, and tugged him away from the friends and family who stared in horror.

"We're going to Wildewyn," she called back at them. "We're going to stop the war."

"You can't do that alone!" Raheem shouted.

"They won't be able to stop us."

She hoped they wouldn't even try. A dragon was a dangerous thing, but dragon mates who took flight and attacked a battle together? Getting between the two of them would only end in bloodshed unlike the world had ever seen before.

Sigrid tugged him toward the servants' quarters where she knew there was a pool where she could wash the blood from his body. It was a lesser known one, where Camilla had always washed herself, and hopefully there wouldn't be anyone there to disturb them.

They'd take one look at their sultan in such a state and run away. Her fear was that someone running from him would only set off the dragon's ire more. The chase was so much fun to their beasts.

She tugged him through the door and looked around the room. The still pool in the center wisped hot curls into the air, undisturbed by another body. The open balcony doors allowed a cool wind to brush past them. Two benches on either side of the heated pool already had towels resting on them.

"Go on," she said, turning to bar the door. "That cut on your shoulder needs tending."

"The dragon will heal it."

She flattened her palm on the wood in front of her, refusing to turn around when she recognized the guttural tones. "It would make me feel better to tend it. As a man, Nadir. It's important to remain a man when you can."

"Why?" he asked. Two voices asked the question, one so much weaker than the other. "When it's so much better to be a dragon?"

At that, she did turn. He stood in the center of the room, watching her with yellow eyes. His pupils were little more than slits, and she swore she saw the ghost of a larger form overlaying his.

He wasn't even trying to control the dragon anymore, she realized. Or perhaps he couldn't. The chains were broken, the beast unleashed. And she didn't know how to control that beast at all.

"Nadir—" she whispered the word but didn't have anything else to say.

He shivered at her voice, then turned away from her and stripped the ruined shirt from his body. "I find I no longer wish to be a man, Sultana."

Such a thing would be a shame, she thought. The rippling muscles on his back shifted as he moved. His body was bronze poured over a stone statue of strength and humility. Not a scar laced over his back, not a single muscle out of place. He flexed, his biceps bunching as he pushed the fabric of his pants down, taking the wrappings of his boots with them.

Naked, he strode into the pool with perhaps a little too much confidence. But then again, he'd always been a confident man. A boy who'd been raised with multiple concubines and a wife from a very young age had good reason for such confidence.

Sigrid was not like that. She didn't even like having her face bared, let alone her entire body.

Steeling herself for the conversation ahead, she reached for one of the towels and strode toward him. "There are many reasons to be a man."

"Name one of them." He leaned against the edge of the pool, stretching his arms along the sides.

"Being able to talk with others and have them understand you."

"Twist my words, you mean. The only people who I've ever spoken to have used whatever words comes out of my mouth to their own advantage. I trust no one, other than you." He leaned his head back when she crouched behind him, eyes searching for hers. "And I don't need words to speak with you, Sultana."

He overlaid the spoken sounds with an echo in her head.

The dragon inside him was far more dangerous than she imagined because it knew how to tempt the beast within.

She shook her head. "You are a sultan. You cannot disappear inside the beast forever."

"A sultan of a land who fears him. Of friends and family who betray him and the kingdom." He shook his head. "Your argument is failing, wife."

Sigrid reached out and dipped the towel into the water by his shoulder. She had hoped she might be able to calm him herself. Now, she questioned whether or not that was possible. The water trickled through her fingers, dripping into the pool like a song.

"Could I ask you to stay human for me?" she inquired, watching the water reflect the sunlight. It was like diamonds dancing across the waves he'd created.

"You could."

"Then I ask it for myself, husband. I've had such little time to know you. To understand your thoughts and dreams as a man, not as a dragon."

She touched the towel to his wounded shoulder. Each dab made her wince inside. She recognized this kind of slash as only a sword could make. Someone had drawn a weapon on him. She couldn't blame them. A dragon had been attacking them with the clear intent to kill. Likely it had been Abdul.

That man had always wanted to kill Nadir. She'd seen it in his eyes more times than she could count. He wanted what Nadir had, and was well aware he'd never get it without the boy. But that only filled him with more fury.

What must it have been like to have the man who raised Nadir lift a blade to the man he called son? She almost wished she had been there to destroy him herself.

Nadir reached up and placed a hand on hers, stilling the movement and pressing the white towel against the wound. Blood soaked through her fingers, leaving a blossom of color against the fabric and her skin.

"What are you doing to me?" he asked.

"I'm cleaning your wound."

"You're doing so much more than that." His voice turned gruff and deepened with the rough edge of a dragon. "You walked in here and everything changed."

"I didn't mean to change everything. I had as much choice as you did in our marriage."

"It can't change," he replied. Nadir remained staring away from her, looking at the wall or perhaps through it to the kingdom beyond. "But it already has."

"What are you saying?"

"I love you." He said the words as though they were a curse, but they blasted through her like a prayer. "I've loved you for a long time, and I wondered if you knew."

Words stuck to her tongue. A flame bloomed in her head, and a golden plume of hope took flight within her. Incandescent, it billowed and grew like a storm on the horizon. "I didn't," she whispered.

"Well, I do. I knew it from the first moment I saw you fighting and realized you were divine absolution come to purge the darkness from my soul. From the first moment I kissed you and you tasted like blood. When I saw your hands were stained red, just like mine. I might have dragon within me, but *you* are my wings."

She let out a tiny sound on a sigh. A small, wicked part of

her desiring to devour him in that moment. To breath in the poetry of his words and the love no one else had dared give her.

He loved her.

He loved her.

She didn't know what to say. How did one respond to that when she was so bad with words? Sigrid struggled to think of anything to say, anything that was more than just *I love you too* because he deserved so much more than that.

"Come here," he said gruffly, pulling her into the water with him.

She went gladly. It didn't matter that the leather clothing she wore would be ruined forever. Sigrid sank into the water, legs on either side of him and arms around his neck. She tucked her face into the hollow of his throat and blew out a long breath.

Nadir held onto her hips. His thumbs stroked her hip bones, delicately tracing circles. "You don't have to say anything," he said.

"I want to."

"Don't. I already know, *habib albi.*"

The words were Bymerian. She didn't recognize them, and didn't think she'd ever heard another Bymerian say them before.

Picking her head up from his shoulders, she quietly asked, "What does that mean?"

He didn't reply. Instead, Nadir reached up, stroking a thumb along her jaw. He moved up and touched a gentle finger to her furrowed brows. The wrinkles eased under his touch as he smoothed the worry and fear away.

"*Ya hayati,*" he whispered, touching a fingertip to her lips. "*Ya amar.*"

"Nadir."

He smoothed his hand along her jaw, tunneling beneath her hair. His other hand at her hip pushed her forward. He pulled her into him and slowly pressed his lips to hers.

She sank into his kiss, remembering a time when they hadn't worried about war or violence. They'd only worried about each other and what they might think. His tongue traced her lips, and she allowed him to delve into her mouth while feeling as though he were sinking into her soul.

Sigrid had always wanted a man who would challenge her as a husband. She hadn't wanted the sweet man who'd died at the altar for her. The one who would have worshiped her steps and whispered sweet nothings in her ear.

She'd searched her entire life for *this man*. A monster who would devour her, body and soul. The one who would choose to tear her apart, only to stitch her back together exactly as she was, because he wouldn't change a thing about her person.

But he was also the one she couldn't have. The forbidden fruit who lived in a kingdom which hated hers. The sultan of a people who wanted to see her own destroyed. The man who hated what they were, but loved her with every fiber of his being.

Her claws dug into his shoulders as she kissed him back with all the emotion in her heart. She loved him. She loved this man so much it hurt sometimes. An ache that never left her chest, no matter how long she was away from his side.

The fires of his soul burned inside her. Perhaps, in the year they'd been apart, that fire had dimmed to an ember, but it had never gone out.

She feared it never would.

They broke apart, and Sigrid took a deep breath. "I fear your love will render me to ashes."

He leaned forward and pressed his lips to hers once more. A chaste kiss, one that tasted like tears. "A dragon cannot burn."

And yet, she feared she could.

The world was not prepared for them. It never had been. And if her time with the ancient's had taught her anything, it was that the world had no place for creatures like them. They were from a time long past...

Sigrid didn't know what the future held, and she wasn't certain she wanted to find out.

She reached up and placed a hand against Nadir's face. "I'm afraid of what we might do," she whispered. "I'm afraid of what will happen if we go back to Wildewyn."

"So am I."

"Then why would you give up being a man? Why would you even think about letting the dragon take control?"

He pulled her forward again, this time pressing their foreheads together. She felt him take a deep breath, his ribs touching hers. "I told my mother, the one who birthed me, the leader of the Alqatara, that I would become a god king. That I would lead my people out of the darkness and into a new time."

She licked her lips. "The ancients said there was a prophecy. Of a dragon coming back and saving everyone."

"Then maybe this is the prophecy. Maybe now is the time when we take our place in this world and becomes gods after all. You've said it before. We have no place here when all other Beastkin are simple beasts. We are immortals who are supposed to be dead and yet, we live."

"I don't want to be a god."

"Neither do I, my love. I just don't think we really have a choice in the matter."

This was the man she knew. The longer he talked the more his voice deepened and the honeyed tones of the man she loved disappeared in the wake of a dragon.

His was the crumbling of mountains. The deep burble of a frozen lake and the thundering call of an oak as it fell. The man she loved, the one she knew in the very bottom of her soul, had disappeared.

Sigrid pulled back to stare into those slitted eyes. "Are you going to give him back to me?"

Nadir, or the dragon that was inside him, shook its head sadly. "I don't know how."

"You should be one and the same."

"We are," the graveling voice responded. "In a way. He is within me, part of me, but he is not the dragon and I am not the man."

She remembered the creatures within the ancient stronghold. Half man, half beast, stuck between the change forever because of... something.

Why hadn't she learned?

Someone scrabbled at the door, working through the lock with a small tool. Nadir tensed between her thighs, but Sigrid held him down as she scented the air. The smell of frozen water made her smooth her hands over his shoulders.

"It's Eivor," she whispered.

"The beast you brought with you?"

"The woman who can help you," she replied. "She's part beast, part human. She speaks with souls, or at least, she thinks she does. We can help bring the two of you back together. It doesn't have to be a fight for control."

"It does," he replied. "And I'm sorry for it."

With a swift movement, Nadir scooped his arms under her bottom and stood. She'd never had a man pick her up so easily. Sigrid held onto his shoulders, only releasing them when he strode out of the pool and set her down.

"What are you going to do?" she asked, her eyes remaining fixed on his face and refusing to traverse his body as water dripped down his muscular form.

"What we both should have done a long time ago."

The change rippled through him so quickly. She blinked, and he was a dragon once more. This time, she wasn't certain how much control he retained. His horned head swung back and forth, tail twitching in agitation and eyes watching her with more than a little aggression.

His back foot caught on one of the benches, crushing it beneath his weight. Nadir lifted his head and a horn struck the ceiling. Plaster and gold plates rained down on them. He huffed out an angry breath, trying to flex his wings but getting stuck in the small space.

"Easy," she called out with both her words and her mind. "Nadir, stop it. You'll bring this part of the palace down on us."

He shifted more, the idea apparently pleasing in the moment. A flare of fear made her pulse spike, and he paused to stare at her.

Could he smell the scent in the air? The way she had instantly been afraid for her own safety?

Sigrid lifted her hands. He leaned forward, stretching his neck and touching his nose gently to her outstretched palms.

"What are you doing?" she asked.

His voice echoed in her head. "*Saving the kingdoms, ya amar. Join me. Together, we can finally be the gods they've prayed to.*"

She didn't want to be a god. But he didn't either.

Sigrid struggled to think of a way to fix this, so they weren't both becoming something they shouldn't be. The door jiggled behind them, Eivor peeking into the room. Waiting for the medicine woman would only enrage the dragon in front of her.

They couldn't fight the way Nadir wanted to. She couldn't fight her own people as a dragon. They'd already thought she was a dead. Would she return as some ghostly figure to haunt them from the grave? It wasn't right.

But setting loose a full-grown male dragon wasn't right either.

Instead, she reached out and hooked a hand around a spine at his shoulder. "I'll come with you," she said. "Not as a dragon, but as a woman. I'll try to reason with them."

"*I have little hope it well help.*"

"Hope is hard to find sometimes," she replied, pulling herself up onto his back. "Perhaps this time, it's little more than a wish. I shall wish for peace. You may wish for an end to this madness."

"*Wishes rarely come true, Sultana.*"

Gods, she knew it. But that didn't deter her from wishing harder than she ever had before as Nadir lunged out of the balcony, bursting through the stone walls, and soaring up into the sky.

NADIR

HE DIDN'T THINK IT WOULD BE LIKE THIS. LETTING THE DRAGON TAKE control completely of his mind and body had seemed so simple. They were the same creature, weren't they? That's what everyone had always told him if they were Beastkin.

The animal and the man were one and the same. Combining them only allowed them both to be entirely free. And yet... that's not what happened to him.

He'd noticed the moment he sat down on his throne. The words whispering in his ears weren't those of his own. The angry thoughts, the pain, the hatred that made claws erupt from his fingertips and made his cheeks burn. These weren't the thoughts of a man. They were the thoughts of a hunted animal who had finally changed from prey to hunter.

Tearing them apart had been the only answer to his pain. He wanted to hear them scream, and he had. Their blood had tasted sweet against his tongue, the hot spurts spreading through his mouth like the finest of liqueurs. When had he enjoyed that? Nadir couldn't remember a time when he'd thought that death was a good thing. When he'd enjoyed such a terrible thing.

Then, the madness had faded. He'd stood in the center of the great hall, watching the blood slip down the walls and the pieces of people he'd left strewn about the room. Abdul's head sat on a spike at the back of the throne. Saafiya had laid across it, missing both her arms while her dead eyes stared up at the ceiling.

The others hadn't escaped similar treatment. He'd seen them as nothing more than puppets to play with. Mice in the hands of a cruel feline.

Nadir had thrown up in the pool. Staring down at the red water, swirling with blood. His own face reflected in the crimson waters, but he didn't recognize the man staring back at him.

She'd soothed him. Sigrid. The one whose voice was a breath of cool air, brushing across his face. She'd smoothed her hands down his shoulders, tugged him away from the people whose hearts he could still hear beating in their chest.

What frightened him most was that he recognized the people standing in the hall. He'd named them all in his head. Raheem, Tahira, Solomon, Camilla, all the people who had stood by him throughout so much. He remembered them, and he'd still wanted to tear them apart with claws and teeth.

What had he become?

She'd managed to ease his mind at least a little. The pool had calmed the dragon within him. It wanted to rest, after all. Its belly was full, and its mind had calmed now that the enemies who wanted to hurt them were dead.

And then he'd remembered she was his mate. She was everything to him, the reason why the wind soared beneath his wings and everything had started to fall apart.

The dragon awakened then. It whispered in his ears that he would never be the man she wanted or deserved. That he needed to relinquish his hold on everything, because he was nothing more than a forgotten king who needed to rest.

Gods, he was tired. He didn't want to be the sultan anymore. He didn't want to kill more people who he was supposed to trust, knowing that everyone betrayed him in the end.

He'd told her that he loved her.

What foolish man was he? Of course she couldn't love him back. She was a reasonable woman and knew how dangerous it was for them to be together. The last time they'd even tried to be together, two kingdoms had started a war.

What other manner of darkness would spread from them?

And that was when the dragon had pushed to the forefront of his mind. Nadir had felt the human part of his mind being shoved aside in the wake of something far stronger.

It wasn't like she thought. The dragon and him *were* the same person. They were far more than just man and beast. Whatever his birth mother had done to him, it had worked.

He was a man and a dragon. The instincts within him could easily override anything that was logical or reasonable by the man inside him. He was running on nothing more than instincts. His gut told him Sigrid was necessary in his life for his own happiness.

Damn the word. Damn everything that would separate them.

And that meant he had to stop this war. That meant they would fly above the kingdoms, and he would rage at the sky if it meant he got to keep her by his side. He'd destroy kingdoms for her, if that's what it took.

Her legs squeezed his neck, tightening as he shifted to the side. They would have traveled faster if she were a dragon as well. He could fly higher, burst through the clouds where it was more difficult to breathe.

She refused to travel as anything but a human. Over and again, she claimed it was important to remember who they really were.

How different she was from the first time she came to his kingdom. Back then, she would have said he was finally accepting himself. That they'd finally come to a point in their lives where they recognized the animals were more important than the human.

Someday, she would tell him what she'd seen far off in those mountains. She would explain what the ancestors had done to her, why she suddenly thought it so important to retain the human part of her soul.

Nadir spread his wings wide and felt the last bit of his humanity slip out of his grip. He was filled with fury.

For the people who had hurt Sigrid. At his advisors who had lied to him, taken his brother away from him.

Gods, his brother.

Memories burst into life. Frayed lungs gurgling in a bed while wild eyes stared at him, refusing to let go. A hand which had been so strong once, reaching out for him. A voice, once thundering, weakly begging for mercy.

Nadir hated them. He hated them all and it had to stop. It didn't matter how it stopped, but he was going to ruin them all.

He wouldn't let anyone live. Their blood would coat his tongue like that of his advisors if they stood between him and happiness any longer.

SIGRID

IT WAS SO QUIET UP HERE. SHE HADN'T EXPECTED THAT. NADIR'S BODY flexed underneath her, scales scraping the insides of her thighs. His wings spread out wide as they glided on the wind. Silent and graceful, they blew over the Edge of the World toward her homeland without a single person realizing they were moving.

For a few moments, she was overtaken by the amount of greenery that was so beautiful it made her eyes hurt. This was her homeland. The place where she'd been born lived deep in her soul like a breathing thing. She could *feel* Wildewyn beneath them.

Ancient trees stretched up from the ground. Their roots spread deep below them, carrying stories into the earth so that they would never be forgotten by the souls who had created them. Birds flew out of the branches, the dull and muted colors ready to hide them from anyone who might have tried to hurt them.

This was a place made for dreamers. For those who wanted

to hide in the shadows or watch the land stretch into great mountains in the distance. She'd never thought to leave this place, or that she'd find someone who filled her soul like the land itself.

And yet, she had.

Sigrid reached down and pressed her palm flat against Nadir's back. The muscles twitched beneath her touch, and she felt the warmth of his affection flooding through her mind.

Their connection was more than a little overwhelming. She couldn't think when it was still his emotions filling her thoughts. He touched her now with more than just words or a passing glance. He'd poured his own mind into hers, and she didn't know how to handle that.

How could any woman? Sigrid had thought he was indifferent to her, or merely interested in her, because she was a fanciful thing like him. A creature that shouldn't exist. Another golden trophy to hang on his wall.

Now, she understood it was so much more than that. He wanted to protect her. He wanted her in his life forever, so he could watch over her. And certainly there was a large portion of possessiveness. The idea of someone else having claim to her made his stomach burn and his dragon roll deep within him. The beast would kill anyone who touched her.

Heat bloomed in her chest, an answering fire at the thought of someone else touching *him*. She'd do the same, and the feeling wasn't human at all. She didn't know how to reconcile the beastly desires in her mind. The dragon inside her knew how to handle this man and the other side of him. The draconic side who wanted to tear people limb from limb.

She'd fought that beast inside her for years now. The

creature that wanted to end the world as she knew it and force Sigrid to see the mountains of Wildewyn through dulled eyes.

Leaning forward, she stroked her hand down his side and said through their minds, *"What do you think?"*

"Of what?"

"My home." She let a bit of her own emotions slip through their connection. He must be able to feel the wonder and awe that always filled her when she saw her homeland again. Couldn't he feel it as well? The hope that lit a fire deep inside her.

He let out a grumble. *"It's very green."*

Leave it to Nadir to say the only thing which was obvious when he was given a gift of emerald lands. She leaned back and huffed out a breath.

"It's more than that," Sigrid replied. *"Isn't it the most beautiful thing you've ever seen?"*

"Bymere is that."

"Bymere lacks color."

His laugh made her ears hurt, which didn't seem possible considering it was in her own mind. *"Sigrid. Bymere is filled with more color than this! Did you not see the rainbows of silk hanging from every street corner? The vibrancy of my palace?"*

She rolled her eyes. *"I'm not talking about man-made things. Bymere is filled with sand and that's the same color no matter where you look."*

"And Wildewyn is filled with green as far as the eyes can see. I don't see the difference."

She wanted to argue with him, but in a way, he was right. She just loved this place so much her eyes couldn't see what he could see. This was her home. More than that, it was a piece of her soul which burned deep inside her.

Nadir tilted his wings, gliding closer to the ground than before.

"What are you doing?" she asked.

"Can't you smell that?"

She couldn't really smell anything when the wind was blasting her face. There were too many scents on the wind for her to pick through them and name exactly what they were.

Sigrid screwed up her face and tried again. Moss, decaying leaves, the scent of a few animals below them who were running away. Nothing that made her worry, and nothing that would have made him change course.

"We're going to Greenmire Castle," she reminded him. *"You're not going toward the castle right now."*

"They're not fighting at the castle."

"That's where Raheem said the armies were heading. We don't have any reason to think they would have changed course."

"They would if they had to," he growled.

Then, she smelled it. The scent of fire on the wind and ashes in the air. A plume of smoke rose in the distance, joined by another and another until she couldn't tell where they originated. A wall of shadows and smoke in the distance.

Destroying her homeland.

Sigrid leaned forward on his neck and urged him forward. *"Nadir."*

"I see it."

"What have they done?" She didn't care who had started the fire. Wildewyn was careful to make sure they didn't start. Dead leaves filled the forest, covering the ground and far more flammable than most would have given them credit for. A

single spark could set the entire forest on fire, and they'd never be able to stop it.

That's what they were looking at. A fire which refused to die down and would destroy so much more than just trees and animals. It would destroy homes, people's livelihoods... the future of Wildewyn.

Nadir beat his wings against the air and shot toward the smoke. They reached it in record time, only to see the destruction had already been done.

An entire village had been reduced to nothing more than smoldering ash and blackened wood homes. A few people stumbled below them. They searched the rubble for their families or anything they might take with them toward Greenmire Castle who would hopefully give them sanctuary.

Sigrid wasn't so sure that was possible. Tears filled her eyes as she realized what this would mean for her kingdom. They were all going to fall apart at the seams, and there was nothing she could do to save them.

She had failed them.

"Sigrid," Nadir said in her mind, his voice gentle.

"Not yet. Don't say anything yet."

They flew over the destruction of Wildewyn in silence. Smoke choked the air, billowing from the ashes of ruin that arrowed toward Greenmire Castle. There were so many dead bodies littering the ground. So many children on their knees next to parents who wouldn't wake up. So many dead animals lying on the ground where they had tried to run from the smoke and the flames.

Tears slid down her cheeks freely. She hadn't thought...

"People are capable of many things, Sigrid," Nadir interrupted.

"Even good men do terrible things when they think it will lead toward their own happiness."

"I brought them," she whispered back to him. "I was the one who told them they would be safe here, and I was the one who destroyed my home."

"You can't know it was the Beastkin."

But she could. No one from Wildewyn would be foolish enough to set a fire like this. They didn't even carry torches on hunting parties for that reason. The Bymerians wouldn't have known that fire would do this. She'd seen campfires start a flame, and they didn't do this. Earthen folk knew how to take care of those mistakes, it wouldn't have spread like this.

That left only one group of people who would have used fire. One group of people who knew how much it would hurt Wildewyn, and how much of a distraction it would cause for those armies.

How could her own people do this? They who had grown up in these leaves and had looked down upon it from the safety of the castle?

Nadir darted through the air until they could hear the sound of battle. The clanging crash of sword against sword. The strike of metal and steel, and the screams of enraged animals.

"Sigrid," he muttered, his eyes seeing farther than hers. *"We may be too late."*

"Don't say that."

"It needs to be said. I don't want you to think we can save everyone when —"

"Please." She couldn't hear these words. Not yet. She couldn't think that her entire homeland was destroyed because she had hesitated to wash a man who didn't need cleansing or

415

healing. Sigrid would blame herself for the rest of her life if she had somehow been the person responsible for the destruction of Wildewyn.

"This is not your fault," Nadir continued. Though brutal, she knew he only wanted to make her feel better. *"Those who started this war. The ones who allowed hatred to rule their decisions and to make them afraid. Those are the people who you can blame, but never yourself."*

"You don't get to say what I feel guilty about."

"I do." He spat the words at her, wings striking the air and flames spurting from his nostrils. *"I get to have a say in what you blame yourself for, because I am your mate."*

"I never agreed to that."

"Neither did I."

Nadir tucked his wings close to his sides, and they shot toward the battlefield. Three armies fought there, each in a different corner of a wide open field.

The Earthen folk wore their silver armor which reflected the dull light of flames all around them. They lifted thin rapiers and lances, striking fast and true at those who tried to overwhelm them. Helms with plumes of blue feathers marked those who had come from Greenmire Castle. Those who protected the king.

Bymerian soldiers swarmed the battlefield from the east. The crimson-dyed leather of their armor was an insult to the sultan who hadn't ordered them to attack anyone at all. Scimitars were a blur as they whirled toward their enemies and slashed through whatever flesh they could find.

The Beastkin congregated in the southern part of the field. Some had already changed into their animals. Others waited in the shadows for the right opportunity to strike. Sigrid watched as a familiar leopard launched himself at an Earthen soldier and tore through his throat.

Why were they fighting? Did any of them even know the reason for their hatred of each other? She had a feeling the answer was no.

"Fly to the center of the battlefield," she said.

"That's a death wish, Sigrid. Three armies against two dragons could easily take us down."

"Your army won't attack you. The Earthen folk won't attack me. That's one army we have to deal with, and I don't think the Beastkin are interested in killing their leader who came back from the dead."

He growled, the sound low and deep. *"You're putting a lot of trust in your people."*

"We have to trust them eventually. We are their leaders, aren't we? Haven't we spent the last year gaining their trust just in case something like this happened?"

He huffed out another breath, but descended.

The soldiers hadn't noticed them. She didn't know how no one had looked up, but could only guess that the Beastkin weren't attacking from the air yet. They were allowing the Earthen armies and the Bymerian ones to destroy each other, then were going to pick off the last lingering soldiers.

It was a smart plan, but one she didn't agree with. Killing everyone in the empire would get them nowhere. And there would be many casualties from every side. What was Jabbar's plan here?

Nadir landed hard. The ground shook beneath him and reverberated with a deep grumble at his weight. Every soldier in the field, the thousands of men and women who were defending or attacking, paused to start at the giant red dragon.

He opened his mouth and hissed at the nearest soldiers. Even the Bymerians stumbled back in fear.

Wings spread wide, he lowered himself enough that Sigrid could slip from his back. She hit the ground in a crouch, staring at the armies surrounding them. Would they attack? There was always the chance she was wrong.

Whispers erupted, carried on the wind as people began to recognize them.

"Is that the sultan?" One of the Bymerians nearby asked. "I thought he'd returned to the Red Palace?"

"Sigrid?" A man shoved others aside, tearing off his helmet and revealing white hair and a trimmed beard.

Even her own people began to whisper then. "The matriarch? Back from the dead?"

Gods, she wished she'd chosen something other than the clothing from the ancients. She had dirt smudged all over her body, likely blood smears from where Nadir had killed his advisors, and gods know what else from flying through the air. Her hair was sticking to her cheeks and she was certain she looked exhausted.

Because she was. She was so tired of fighting and all the anger these people insisted on harboring inside them.

Standing straight and tall, she stared into the eyes of those around her. The leopard who had just killed a man changed back into the Beastkin she recognized. His dark eyes swept up and down her form, then he said, "It's not possible."

"I have returned," she replied. "And now we will all stop this war."

Hallmar stepped forward, his hands shaking where he clutched the helm to his chest. "My daughter, I didn't think I'd ever see you again. And looking so much like your mother."

His daughter? *Of course.* Why hadn't she realized it so many years ago? She even looked like him. That white head had once been an icy blonde, and he'd always treated her like something so much more than just a Beastkin woman he'd had trapped in his castle.

She wanted to ask him a thousand things, and not enough time for a single thing to be asked. Sigrid tried to pour as much emotion into her eyes as she could.

Now was not the time to find out the man she'd always considered to be her surrogate father was *actually* her father. Why had he chosen now? Had the words merely burst from his chest because he couldn't contain them anymore?

The distraction was, unfortunately, the only thing necessary for Jabbar's people to reorganize themselves.

She heard the whistle through the air as if she'd stepped back in time. Her husband stood in front of her, but not the one she'd actually married. Instead, it was a kind-faced man with worry in his gaze, because he thought the wedding might be too much for her.

The air rustled with the sound of violence and anger. It stroked through the feathers of the arrow like fingers who knew how to kill, touching the fletching and whispering dark promises along the shaft.

It struck her right above the place where Camilla had planted her arrow. It felt like years ago when that had happened, and perhaps it was that long ago when she'd feigned her own death in front of hundreds of Beastkin.

This time, the arrow was true. It didn't miss her vital organs. Instead, the stone arrowhead sank deep into her heart.

The pain-filled wheeze couldn't have come from her. Sigrid couldn't have made that sound, even when the blinding ache of death filled her lungs. Warm liquid spurted from between her lips.

She rocked forward, fingers clutching the shaft of the arrow and staring down at it in disbelief. Someone had really tried to kill her?

"Sigrid!" The anguished shout was laced with more than just Nadir's voice, more than just the dragon. It was Hallmar, and Brynhild, and Camilla, and Raheem. All the people who cared so much about her who would despair to see her die.

Nadir roared. Fire billowed from his jaws and his tail lashed out at anyone near them.

She fell to her knees. Holding onto the arrow with shaking hands as her dragon mate crouched above her and screamed at the world that he would kill them all. They couldn't understand him, but they could hear the anger in his rumbling cries. His flames turned blue with heat, then white-hot with rage.

Blood coated her fingertips. She stared down at the thing which had killed her and realized she didn't want to die.

What had the ancients said? She didn't need a throne or a crown to be a queen. She was the woman who her people had prayed for. A dragon queen who would take the world by storm whether they wanted it or not.

Her people were led astray by someone who wanted to see the world on its knees. Not because he wanted to see them in a place of power, but because he wanted to see himself in a place of power.

There was so much she and Nadir could do to fix this world. They could force people to see the goodness in each other. They could destroy armies with a single breath. They would never be given the chance, because she knew he would go mad the moment her breath fled from her lungs.

"*Please talk to me,*" his voice finally broke through the pain. "*Please, Sigrid, don't leave me now. Not like this.*"

She looked up and saw a man on the other side of the battlefield set aside a bow. White hair, white skin, pink eyes staring at her from a distance. She could see the grin on Jabbar's face as he celebrated the victory he thought he had won.

Sigrid would finally die. Raising from the grave in her people's eyes would have taken every scrap of power away from him. She'd become more than just a matriarch. She would have become a god in the eyes of the Beastkin.

Looking up, she reached for Nadir's face even though he was still spewing flames upon the battlefield.

"*My love,*" she said through their connection. "*Look at me.*"

Nadir's jaws instantly snapped shut. He swerved, crouching over her, holding his wings around her like he could keep out the world. "*Anything,* ya amar."

"What does that mean?"

"*My moon,*" he replied. "*My life. The love of my heart.*"

Sigrid touched her blood-smeared fingers to the large scales of his jaw, and smiled. "That's beautiful."

"*I don't want to lose you,*" he replied, broken and so sad it made tears drip down her own cheeks. "*They have taken you from me, as they have taken everything else.*"

"Not yet they haven't."

The dragon inside her burst forth. Flames covering her

421

body and engulfing her in so much pain she wasn't certain she could survive it.

But she did, because a dragon could not burn.

Opal scales unfurled down her body and wings stretched wide as her fingers spread into something so much more powerful than just a human woman. Nadir held her within his leathery wings until she finished her change.

Only then did he open his arms and reveal that she had not died. That yet again, she survived certain death and came back to her people when they needed her.

She lifted her slender neck, then touched her head to his. She bumped the top of her jaw along the bottom of his.

"*You said we were to become gods,*" she whispered in their minds.

"*You didn't want to become a goddess.*"

"*And yet, now I am.*"

Nadir stroked the top of her head, running his jaw along hers, and then nipped at her neck with his fangs. "*Kill him, wife. Before I do.*"

Sigrid shot up into the air faster than she'd ever flown before. Jabbar did the same, his form melting away into feathers as he tried to get away from her.

Perhaps he thought he could flee the scene, take them somewhere he might have the advantage. Sigrid almost laughed at the thought. He had nearly lost the last time they fought, and now he thought he could get away from her?

Lightning crackled along the feathers of his wings as he flew into the air and tried to leave. She caught his tail feathers between her jaws. Pulling hard, she disrupted his flight and spat out the long tendrils in her mouth.

"*Come here,*" she thought, shoving the thought through the air and into his mind like a spike.

His eyes widened in horror as he realized she could speak in this draconic form. Not only could she speak, but she could talk directly to him.

"*It is possible,*" she projected, knowing what he was thinking and laughing at his fear. "*Come here, thunderbird. Let me feast on your flesh.*"

He lashed out with claws that tore at her chest. Long talons scraped down her scales, searching for any small bit of a gap between them so he might pierce through her flesh as he had with his arrow.

She didn't care. Blood dripped from the wounds, but she refused to allow him to kill her. Not now. Not when he had done so much already, and she wanted to taste him on her tongue. The dragon was entirely in control now, and the dragon knew how to fight.

Sigrid pushed with her back feet, forcing him away in the air. He spun slightly, wings getting tangled in his own momentum.

Wings striking the air in thunderous claps, she rose above him and then tucked them firmly into her sides. Arrowing down at him, she pushed out a single thought.

"*You thought you were the only one who could create thunder?*" Sigrid hit him then, holding him against her chest with her wings. "*You thought you were the only one who had lightning inside them? Jabbar, you are nothing more than a weak, frightened little man. I am thunder. I am lightning. I am death.*"

They struck the ground hard. It should have killed them both, but Sigrid landed atop him and shoved hard with her back feet. Her own talons shredded his weak belly, and he stared up at her, gasping for air that had already fled his body.

His own feet tore at her wings and the leather gave way. It didn't matter that he'd rendered her incapable of flight. She didn't need to fly when there was so much of a feast laid out in front of her.

She lunged back just enough to give her room. Teeth flashing in the dim light of the battlefield, she snapped forward and took his throat between her teeth.

The ripping of flesh satisfied something deep inside her soul. Blood poured through her mouth in great spurts, crackling with electricity and so much power.

His wings flapped against the ground, talons scrabbling for purchase and then falling flat as the life faded from the last thunderbird alive.

Only when she smelled the death in his body did she step away. Her wings were awkward, one broken from his struggles. It didn't matter then, but it did now.

She listed to the side, slowly changing back into a person. Sigrid held the broken arm against her chest and whirled to stare as the great beast turned back into Jabbar.

There was nothing left of the traitor but gristle.

Her stomach rolled. Had she really done that? Had she torn a man apart, because he'd tried to kill her? Of course, Sigrid had killed before. She had no quarrels about dueling with sword and battle. Men died every day, and she didn't mind being the one to take that life.

But she'd never killed as a dragon. She'd never torn someone limb from limb and destroyed them entirely. No one would even be able to recognize him if they tried.

"*Sigrid?*" Nadir's voice whispered in her mind. "*You did what you had to do, and you were glorious.*"

Was she? Or had she simply become everything she'd always feared she would become?

Sigrid looked around the battlefield at the frightened expressions on the faces of every man and woman surrounding them. They weren't just afraid of her now. It wasn't fear born of something they didn't understand. Now they knew what the dragons were capable of. They had seen the battle above them, had seen the way a beast could devour flesh and tear life away from the bones of a man they all recognized.

She'd made them afraid, and she'd shown them what monsters could really do.

Swallowing hard, she straightened her shoulders and turned to them. "Go home," she shouted, her voice carrying on the wind. "Be with your families and tuck your children into bed. You've destroyed enough this day."

"Why should we?" A voice shouted. "Who are you to tell us where to go and what to do?"

Nadir reared onto his back legs behind her, straightened his wings, and roared. The guttural cry of a dragon rocked through Wildewyn, flattening trees and sending soldiers onto their knees in fear.

When the echo of his rage died down, Sigrid stood beside him and sadly cast her glance over all the people who would never understand them.

"See before you the Gods of the Empire," she replied. "The dawn comes and brings with it nothing more than cobalt shadows. Go home. Feel no fear in your heart, for you know what gods protect you now."

She'd never wanted to say those words, and yet, she had.

Nadir lifted into the air and grasped her with his back foot. Her broken arm crunched under his hold, but it was the safest way to carry her from the battlefield.

She held onto the scales of his foot, feeling the talons dig into her sensitive skin, and watched as her homeland disappeared beneath them.

NADIR

HE HOVERED ABOVE THE MOUNTAINTOP, HOLDING THEM CAREFULLY above the cliff edge where they could watch the sunrise. They'd flown all night. He'd watched the moon rise on the horizon and felt her shivers against his palm, but knew he couldn't stop even to warm her up. Not yet. Not when the entire empire was hunting them and people were going to try their hardest to ensure their end.

Carefully, oh so carefully, he let her slide out of his palm and onto the stone surface of the outcropping. As always, Sigrid landed gracefully.

She was still clutching her arm to her chest. He'd offered to heat her up, to allow her to change so that she might be able to heal the wound with dragon fire.

She'd refused. He'd never forget the sadness in her voice as she insisted on feeling the pain for at least a little while. She deserved it, or so she claimed. After all they had done to the people of this empire, she could be a little uncomfortable for a while.

Nadir didn't like seeing her in pain. It filtered through their connection, just enough that it was already bothering him. The dragon part of his mind wanted to end her suffering immediately. The feelings were distracting enough that he could hardly think straight.

Hovering above her, he opened his jaws and cast a blanket of flames down upon her person. She no longer wore the clothing the ancients gave her, they'd burned away long ago, and he watched in fascination as her bones realigned themselves beneath the flames.

Almost immediately, the ache of her pain disappeared. She let out a sigh and looked up at him, physically saying, "Thank you, Nadir. That's much better."

This time, the change didn't come as easily as it used to. His body didn't want to shift into the weak form of a human. It wanted to feel the power of wings, the capability of sinewy muscle, and the reassurance of scale armor that protected him from all harm.

Nadir had to focus far more than ever before, so much that he panicked for a moment. His body didn't want to let go of the form. Why didn't it want to let go?

Eventually, it gave way back to flesh. He landed beside her in a crouch, fists pressed against the ground while breathing heavily.

"Husband?" she asked, kneeling beside him and sliding her hands along his jaw. "What are we going to do?"

"About what?"

The pain hadn't disappeared from her eyes. In fact, he would argue it had only gotten stronger. "Everything."

He wanted to tell her not to worry. That the world would wait for them to figure out what was going to happen. Both kingdoms had seen how the dragons were even larger than before. They had watched her kill and knew that the sultan dragon could kill as well.

They wouldn't test gods like them. They wouldn't want to know what else the dragons could do if they were angered even more.

But she didn't want to hear that. She wanted him to reassure her. To take away the worry and the pain for a little while at the very least.

Nadir had never been that person for anyone before. He had always been the one who had the worry taken away. His advisors had guided him through difficult situations. They had hidden so much from him that he feared he didn't know how to be the person she wanted him to be.

Carefully, he reached up and slid his hands into the long locks of her hair. "Let's not be kings and queens right now," he said. "Let's just be you and me. Let the stars look upon mortals tonight."

He tugged her forward by the hair and touched his lips to hers. She softened beneath his touch, letting go of the icy rage that had flooded her being since the first moment they saw the battle in her homeland.

She tasted like the first drop of water after a summer of desert sun. The icy touch of winter as it first laid hands upon the lands. She was the soothing touch to his burning ache. Why hadn't he looked upon her beauty before this? Why hadn't he loved her sooner?

He drew her ever closer, touching his fingers to her skin.

"*Habib albi*," he murmured.

"Your love?"

"My love," he replied, pressing her against his chest and pulling away to swipe her hair off her face. "My moon, my stars, my wings. You make me burn, Sultana."

"Then find me in the ashes of your soul, my love." She touched her fingertips to his lips, and he felt his soul take flight. "I choose you over all others now."

"Over your kingdom?"

She didn't answer him with words. Instead, she wrapped her arms around his neck and drew him back into her kiss.

As the sun rose on the horizon, rays of light stroking the land, they laid together for the first time. He fell in love with the curves of her body, with the sound of her sighs. But more than anything else in the world, he fell in love with the look in her eyes as she met his gaze.

She, who could have torn out his throat with her teeth. Who could tear open his belly with her claws. Who could burn him alive with her breath.

She had chosen instead to kiss him with every part of her soul. To love him with her whole heart. To believe in him when no one else had.

Nadir wrapped himself in her like a warm blanket and in turn, shielded her from the world, from decisions, from guilt. He would be the man she wanted him to be. He would take care of her, build her back into the queen he knew she could be, worship her as the goddess she was.

Gods. He would love her as no man had loved a woman before.

EPILOGUE
CAMILLA

"WHERE DID THEY GO?"

Camilla sighed. "I don't know, Raheem. We've been searching for them for what feels like forever. We cannot find them."

"They're two dragons. We can't simply… lose them."

"We can if they aren't changed right now. Two people can easily slip away. It will take some time."

He slapped his hands down on the table. They'd stationed themselves in the old Beastkin castle. Woodcrest was one of the few places that hadn't been destroyed by the fire, although the Beastkin had all seemingly scattered to the wind.

A few had remained. Those who stood around the table were the original women from Wildewyn, lacking a few of their most key people.

No one knew what to do now that both Sigrid and Nadir

had disappeared. Wildewyn was all searching for the two dragons, some people whispering that the ancient gods of old had finally returned to their homeland. Others, afraid for what that would mean if gods now walked the earth.

According to Raheem, Bymere fared even worse. Without a single person from the advisor council left alive, and a sultan who had disappeared entirely, they were being led by the Alqatara. A group who left little to the imagination and were far more military than what the country was used to.

Raheem ran his fingers through his hair, tugging at the roots. "Tahira can only do so much in Bymere before people start to revolt."

"She has the medicine woman with her, does she not?"

"You mean Eivor? That woman is terrifying people left and right. There's already a religious faction certain she was sent to destroy them."

"Good. Then she's creating enough of a distraction to keep people busy. They'll worry about her and not where their sultan has run off to. That gives us time."

"Don't you understand—"

The doors to their meeting room slammed open. A small Beastkin woman, blonde like a dandelion and nearly as small, burst into the room. Breathing hard, she pressed a hand against her chest. "Matriarch, we found something."

"Tracks?"

"No, ma'am." The woman shook her head. "This looks like it was once an ancient home."

Camilla froze. This was a place where their ancestors had lived? Why hadn't they known that long ago?

Raheem glanced over at her suddenly paling face. "What's

that supposed to mean?"

"The ancients are a group of people who lived before us. The oldest of the Beastkin and the originals. They know more than what the Beastkin now know. They're like..."

The other Beastkin woman answered for her. "Gods, sir."

Camilla didn't want to wait. She couldn't handle more gods in this world when her dearest friend had already claimed to be one.

Striding after the girl, they raced through the halls of the keep and down into the cellars. They hadn't really investigated this place much when they came here. What use did Beastkin have for root cellars?

Now, one of the walls had been knocked down to reveal dulled paint on the other side. The yellow Beastkin pointed through them. "Thought you might want to see that."

Taking a torch from the wall, Camilla brandished it up at the paintings only to gasp in fear.

"What is it?" Raheem asked, out of breath from running after them.

"The end," Camilla replied.

She held the torch up, illuminating the prophecy hidden behind the wall.

Two dragons flew up into the sky. One was white as snow, the other red as blood. The male dragon, for it had to be male, blew fire into the sky with a maddened look in his eye. The female stared back at them, sadness in her gaze.

"What is this meant to mean?" Raheem asked, stepping up to the painting and pointing at a single moment in it. A moment where both dragons stood on piles of bodies with flames surrounding them.

"It's an old Beastkin legend, my mother used to tell it to me." Camilla swallowed hard. "In the old days, there was a sickness. Beastkin wouldn't be able to change back. They descended into madness and had to be killed before they would destroy everything they loved."

"So this is predicting... what? That Sigrid and Nadir will come down with this sickness?"

"The sickness was eradicated years ago. It's just a story told to children to make them behave. The last dragon queen destroyed the sickness," she shook her head and met his gaze. "This is predicting they will bring it back."

AFTERWORD

I hope you enjoyed their story as much as I did! Nadir and Sigrid are quite possibly my most favorite characters I've ever written.

However, this story is not completed just yet! Look out for book three soon.

After all, Gods don't just disappear.

ABOUT THE AUTHOR

Emma Hamm grew up in a small town surrounded by trees and animals. She writes strong, confident, powerful women who aren't afraid to grow and make mistakes. Her books will always be a little bit feminist, and are geared towards empowering both men and women to be comfortable in their own skin.

To stay in touch
www.emmahamm.com
authoremmahamm@gmail.com